P9-CAD-134

**Praise for *New York Times* bestselling author
RaeAnne Thayne**

"RaeAnne Thayne gets better with every book."
—Robyn Carr, #1 *New York Times* bestselling author

"[Thayne] engages the reader's heart and emotions,
inspiring hope and the belief that miracles are possible."
—#1 *New York Times* bestselling author
Debbie Macomber

"Thayne is in peak form in this delightful, multiple-
perspective tale of the entwined lives and loves of three
women in a Northern California seaside community....
Thayne skillfully interweaves these plotlines with just
the right amount of glamour, art, and kindness to make
for a warmly compelling and satisfying work of women's
fiction."
—*Booklist* on *The Cliff House*, starred review

**Praise for *USA TODAY* bestselling author
Michelle Major**

"A dynamic start to a series with a refreshingly original
premise."
—*Kirkus Reviews* on *The Magnolia Sisters*

"A sweet start to a promising series, perfect for fans of
Debbie Macomber."
—*Publishers Weekly* on
The Magnolia Sisters, starred review

A COLD CREEK SECRET

NEW YORK TIMES BESTSELLING AUTHOR

RaeAnne Thayne

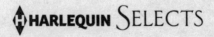

If you purchased this book without a cover you should be aware that this book is stolen property. It was reported as "unsold and destroyed" to the publisher, and neither the author nor the publisher has received any payment for this "stripped book."

ISBN-13: 978-1-335-40988-1

Recycling programs for this product may not exist in your area.

A Cold Creek Secret
First published in 2010. This edition published in 2021.
Copyright © 2010 by RaeAnne Thayne

A Brevia Beginning
First published in 2014. This edition published in 2021.
Copyright © 2014 by Michelle Major

All rights reserved. No part of this book may be used or reproduced in any manner whatsoever without written permission except in the case of brief quotations embodied in critical articles and reviews.

This is a work of fiction. Names, characters, places and incidents are either the product of the author's imagination or are used fictitiously. Any resemblance to actual persons, living or dead, businesses, companies, events or locales is entirely coincidental.

This edition published by arrangement with Harlequin Books S.A.

For questions and comments about the quality of this book, please contact us at CustomerService@Harlequin.com.

Harlequin Enterprises ULC
22 Adelaide St. West, 40th Floor
Toronto, Ontario M5H 4E3, Canada
www.Harlequin.com

Printed in U.S.A.

CONTENTS

New York Times bestselling author **RaeAnne Thayne** finds inspiration in the beautiful northern Utah mountains, where she lives with her family. Her books have won numerous honors, including six RITA® Award nominations from Romance Writers of America and Career Achievement and Romance Pioneer Awards from *RT Book Reviews*. She loves to hear from readers and can be reached through her website at raeannethayne.com.

Books by RaeAnne Thayne

HQN

The Cliff House
The Sea Glass Cottage
Christmas at Holiday House
The Path to Sunshine Cove

Haven Point

Snowfall on Haven Point
Serenity Harbor
Sugar Pine Trail
The Cottages on Silver Beach
Season of Wonder
Coming Home for Christmas
Summer at Lake Haven

Hope's Crossing

Blackberry Summer
Woodrose Mountain
Sweet Laurel Falls
Currant Creek Valley
Willowleaf Lane
Christmas in Snowflake Canyon
Wild Iris Ridge

Visit the Author Profile page
at Harlequin.com for more titles.

A COLD CREEK SECRET

RaeAnne Thayne

To the wonderful writers of Utah RWA
for your support, encouragement and friendship.

Chapter 1

No matter what exotic parts of the world he visited, Brant Western hadn't forgotten how the cold of a February evening in Idaho could clutch at his lungs with icy claws that refused to let go.

In the past hour, the light snow flurries of the afternoon had turned vicious, intense. The active storm front forecasters had been warning about since he arrived for his mid-tour leave two days earlier had finally started its relentless march across this tiny corner of eastern Idaho toward Wyoming.

Icy flakes spit against his unprotected face with all the force of an Al Asad sandstorm. Somehow they found their way to every exposed surface, even sliding beneath the collar of his heavy shearling-lined ranch coat.

This was the sort of Idaho night made for hunkering down by the fire with a good book and a cup of hot cocoa.

The picture had undeniable appeal, one of the many images of home that had sustained him through fierce firefights and long campaigns and endless nights under Afghan and Iraqi stars.

After, he reminded himself. When the few cattle at the Western Sky had been fed and all the horses were safe and snug in the barn, then he could settle in front of the fire with the thriller he'd picked up in the airport.

"Come on, Tag. We're almost done, then we can go home."

His horse, a sturdy buckskin gelding, whinnied as if he completely understood every word and continued plodding along the faint outline of a road still visible under the quickly falling snow.

Brant supposed this was a crazy journey. The hundred head of cows and their calves weren't even his cattle but belonged to a neighbor of the Western Sky who leased the land while Brant was deployed.

Carson McRaven took good care of his stock. Brant wouldn't have agreed to the lease if he didn't. But since the cattle were currently residing on his property, he felt responsibility toward them.

Sometimes that sense of obligation could be a genuine pain in the butt, he acknowledged as he and Tag finished making sure the warmers in the water troughs were functioning and turned back toward the house.

They hadn't gone more than a dozen yards when he saw headlights slicing weakly through the fusillade of snow, heading toward the ranch far too quickly for these wintry conditions.

He squinted in the murky twilight. Who did he know who would be stupid or crazy enough to venture out in this kind of weather?

Easton was the logical choice but he had just talked to her on the phone a half hour earlier, before he had set out on this fool's errand to check the ranch, and she had assured him that after the wedding they had both attended the night before, she was going to bed early with a lingering headache.

He worried about her. He couldn't deny that. Easton hadn't been the same since her aunt, his foster mother, had died of cancer several months earlier. Even longer, really. She hadn't been the sweet, funny girl he'd known and loved most of his life maybe since around the time Guff Winder had died.

Maybe Easton wasn't acting like herself, but he was pretty sure she had the good sense to hunker down at Winder Ranch during a storm like this. If she did venture out, he was pretty sure she was smart enough to slow down when conditions demanded it, especially since he and his foster brothers had drilled that into her head when they taught her to drive.

So if that driver wasn't Easton, who was barreling toward his ranch on the cusp of a ferocious winter storm?

Somebody lost, no doubt. Sometimes these remote canyon roads were difficult to negotiate and the snow could obscure landmarks and address markings. With a sigh, he spurred Tag toward the road to point the wayward traveler in the right direction.

He was just wishing for a decent pair of optics so he could get a better look at who it might be, when the vehicle suddenly went into a slide. He saw it coming as the driver took a curve too fast and he pushed Tag faster, praying he was wrong. But an instant later the driver overcorrected and as Brant held his breath, the vehicle spun out on the icy road.

It was almost like some grisly slow-motion movie, watching it careen over the edge of the road, heading straight for Cold Creek, at the bottom of a maybe five-foot drop.

The vehicle disappeared from view and Brant smacked the reins and dug his heels into the horse's sides, racing as fast as he dared toward the slide-out.

When he reached the creek's edge, he could barely make out in the gathering darkness that the vehicle wasn't quite submerged in the creek but it was a close thing. The SUV had landed on a large granite boulder in the middle of the creek bed, the front end crumpled and the rear wheels still on the bank.

Though he tried not to swear as a habit, he couldn't help hissing out a fierce epithet as he scrambled down from the horse. In February, the creek was only a couple feet deep at most and the current wasn't strong enough to carry off an SUV, but Brant would still have to get wet to get to the vehicle. There was no other way around it.

He heard a faint moan from inside and what sounded, oddly, like a tiny lamb bleating.

"Hang on," he called. "I'll get you out of there in a minute."

Just in the minute or two he had stood surveying the scene and figuring out how to attack the problem, darkness had completely descended and the snow stung at him from every direction. The wind surged around him, taunting and cruel. Even as cold as he was from the storm, he wasn't prepared for the frigid shock of the water through his boots and his lined Wranglers as he waded up to his knees.

He heard that moan again and this time he isolated the sound he had mistaken for a bleating lamb. It was a dog, a tiny one by the sound of it, yipping like crazy.

"Hang on," he called. "Won't take me but a minute and I'll have you out of there, then we can call for help."

When he slogged through the water and finally reached the vehicle, he yanked open the door. The driver was female, in her mid-twenties, maybe. He had a quick impression of wisps of dark curls that looked stark in contrast with her pale, delicate features.

With every passing second, her core temperature would be dropping and he knew he needed to extract her from the SUV and out of the water and the elements before he could completely assess her condition, though it went against every basic tenet of medical training each Army Ranger received, about not moving an injury victim until you knew the extent of injuries.

"Cold," she murmured.

"I know. I'm sorry about that."

He took it as a good sign that she didn't moan or cry out when he scooped her out of the vehicle. If she had broken bones, she wouldn't have been able to hide her discomfort. She didn't say anything at all, just gripped his jacket tightly, her slight body trembling from both the shock and the cold, he guessed.

She wasn't heavy, maybe a hundred and ten pounds, he judged, but carrying her through the ice-crusted water still took every bit of his energy. By the time he reached the bank and headed up the slight slope with her in his arms, he was breathing hard and was pretty sure he couldn't feel his feet anymore.

He'd learned in the early days dealing with combat injuries that the trick to keeping injured men calm was to give as much information as he could about what was going on so they didn't feel completely out of control about what was happening to them. He figured the same technique would work just as well in accident situations. "I'm going to take you back to my place on the horse, okay?"

She nodded and didn't protest when he lifted her onto Tag's back, where she clung tightly to the pommel.

"Hang on now," he said when he was sure she was secure. "I'm going to climb on behind you and then we can get you warm and dry."

When he tried to lift his icy, wet boot into the stirrup, it seemed to weigh as much as the woman had. He had to use all his strength just to raise it that two feet. Just as he shoved it in and prepared to swing the other leg onto the horse, she gasped.

"Simone. My Simone. Please, can you get her?"

He closed his eyes. Simone must be the dog. With the wind howling around them, he couldn't hear the yips anymore and he'd been so focused on the woman that he'd completely forgotten about her dog.

"Are you okay up there for a minute?" he asked, dreading the idea of wading back through that frigid water.

"Yes. Oh, please."

He had survived worse than a little cold water, he reminded himself. Much, much worse.

Returning to the vehicle took him only a moment.

In the backseat, he found at least a half-dozen pieces of luggage and a tiny pink dog carrier. The occupant yipped and growled a big show at him.

"You want to stay here?" Brant growled right back. "Because I'd be just great with that."

The dog immediately subsided and under other circumstances he might have smiled at the instant submission, if he wasn't so concerned about getting them all back to the house in one piece. "Yeah, I didn't think so. Come on, let's get you out of here."

As he considered the logistics of things, he realized there was no way he could carry the bulky dog carrier and keep hold of the woman on horseback at the same time, so he unlatched the door of the carrier. A tiny white mound of fur hurtled into his arms.

Not knowing what else to do, he unzipped his coat halfway and shoved the puffball inside then zipped his coat up again, feeling ridiculously grateful none of the men in his company could see him risking hypothermia for six pounds of fuzzy canine.

The woman was still on Tag's back, he was relieved to see when he made his torturous way back through the water, though she seemed to be slumping a little more.

She was dressed in a woefully inadequate pink parka with a fur-lined hood that looked more suited to some fancy après-ski party in Jackson Hole than braving the bitterness of an Idaho blizzard and Brant knew he needed to get them all back to the ranch house ASAP.

"Is she all right?" the woman asked.

What about him? Brant wondered grumpily. He was the one with frostbitten toes. But in answer, he unzipped his coat, where the furry white head popped out. The woman sighed in relief, her delicate features relaxing slightly, and Brant handed the dog up to her.

He caught a glimpse of the little pooch licking her face that looked oddly familiar as he climbed up behind her, but he didn't take time to analyze it as he dug his heels into the horse's side, grateful Tag was one of the strongest, steadiest horses in the small Western Sky stable.

"We'll get you warmed up. I've got a fire in the woodstove at home. Just hang on a few minutes, okay?"

She nodded, slumping back against him, and he curved his arms around her, worried she would slide off.

"Thank you," she murmured, so low he could hardly hear above the moaning of that bitter wind.

He pulled her as close as he could to block the storm as Tag trudged toward home at a hard walk, as fast as Brant dared push him.

"I'm Brant," he said after a few moments. "What's your name?"

She turned her head slightly and he saw dazed confusion in her eyes. "Where are we?" she asked instead of answering him.

He decided not to push her right now. No doubt she was still bemused from the shock of driving her SUV into a creek. "My ranch in eastern Idaho, the Western Sky. The house is just over that hill there."

She nodded slightly and then he felt her slump bonelessly against him.

"Are you still with me?" he asked with concern. When she didn't answer, his arms tightened around her. Out of pure instinct, he grabbed for the dog seconds before she would have dropped it as she slipped into unconsciousness—surely a fatal fall for the little animal from this height. He managed to snag the dog and shove it back into his coat and his arms tightened around the woman as he nudged Tag even faster.

It was a surreal journey, cold and tense and nerve-racking. He didn't see the lights of the ranch house until they had nearly reached it. When he could finally make out the solid shape of the place, Brant was quite certain it was just about the most welcome sight he had ever beheld.

He led the horse to the bottom of the porch steps and dismounted carefully, keeping a hand on the woman so she didn't teeter to the ground.

"Sorry about this, Tag," he murmured to the horse as he lifted the woman's limp form into his arms. "You've been great but I need you to hang on a few more minutes out here in the cold while I take care of our guest and then I can get you into the warm barn. You deserve some extra oats after tonight."

The horse whinnied in response as Brant rushed up the porch steps and into the house. He quickly carried her inside to the family room where, just as he'd promised, the fire he'd built up in the woodstove before he left still sent out plenty of blissful warmth.

She didn't stir when he laid her on the sofa. As he was bent over to unzip her parka so he could check her injuries, the dog wriggled free of the opening of Brant's own coat and landed on her motionless mistress and began licking her face again, where a thin line of blood trickled from a cut just above her eye.

A raspy dog's tongue was apparently enough to jolt her back to at least semiconsciousness. "Simone?" she murmured and her arms slid around the dog, who settled in the crook of her arms happily.

She was soaked through from the snow's onslaught and Brant knew she wouldn't truly warm up until he could get her out of her wet clothing. Beyond that, he had to examine her more closely for broken bones.

"I'm going to get you some dry clothes, okay? I'll be right back."

She opened her eyes again and nodded and he had the oddest sense again that he knew her. She couldn't be from around here. He was almost positive of that, but then he hadn't spent more than a few weeks at a time in Pine Gulch for fifteen years.

The bedroom he stayed in when he was here was one of the two on the main floor and from his duffel he quickly grabbed a sweatshirt and a pair of cutoff sweats that would likely probably drown her, then he returned to the family room.

"I'm going to take off your parka so I can get a better look and make sure you don't have any broken bones, okay?"

She didn't answer and he wondered if she was asleep or had slipped away again. He debated calling the Pine Gulch paramedics, but he hated to do that on a vicious night like tonight unless it was absolutely necessary. He had some medic training and could deal with most basic first aid needs. If she required more than that, he would drive her into town himself.

But he needed to assess her injuries first.

He would rather disarm a suicide bomber with his teeth than undress a semiconscious woman, but he didn't have much choice. He was only doing what had to be done, he reminded himself. Feeling huge and awkward, he pulled off what seemed pretty useless pink fur boots first, then moved the tiny dog from the woman's side to the floor. The dog easily relinquished her guard dog duties and started sniffing around the room to investigate a whole new world full of smells.

Brant unzipped the woman's parka, doing his best to ignore the soft swell of curves as he pulled the sleeves free, not an easy task since he hadn't been with a woman since before his last deployment. He was only a rescue worker here, he reminded himself. Detached and impersonal.

Her shirt had remained mostly dry under her parka, he was relieved to discover, but her jeans were soaked through and would have to come off.

"Ma'am, you're going to have to get out of your jeans. Do you need my help or can you manage by yourself?"

"Help," she mumbled.

Naturally. He sighed and reached to unfasten the snap and zipper of her jeans. His hands brushed her waist under her soft, blue silk turtleneck. Whether his fingers were cold or whether she was reacting just to the shock of human contact, he didn't know, but she blinked a few times and scrambled away with a little cry.

The tiny dog yipped and abandoned her investigations of the room to trot over and stand protectively over her mistress, teeth bared at him as if a few pounds of fluff would do the trick to deter him.

"You need to get into dry clothes, that's all," he said, using the same calm tone he did with injured soldiers in the field. "I'm not going to hurt you, I swear. You're completely safe here."

She nodded, eyes still not fully open. As he looked at

her in the full light, a memory flashed across his brain of her in some barely-there slinky red dress, tossing her dark curls and giving a sultry bedroom look out of half-closed eyes.

Crazy. He had never met the woman before in his life, he could swear to it.

He pulled her jeans off, despising himself for the little stir of interest when he found her wearing pink lacy high-cut panties.

He swallowed hard. "I'm, uh, going to check for broken bones and then I've got some sweats here we can put on you, okay?"

She nodded and watched him warily from those half-closed eyes as he ran his hands over her legs, trying to pretend she was just another of his teammates. Trouble was, Rangers didn't tend to have silky white skin and luscious curves. Or wear high-cut pink panties.

"Nothing broken that I can tell," he finally said and was relieved when he could pull the faded, voluminous sweats over her legs and hide all that delectable skin.

"Are you a doctor?" she murmured.

"Not even close. I'm in the military, ma'am. Major Brant Western, Company A, 1st Battallion, 75th Ranger Regiment."

She seemed to barely hear him but she still nodded and closed her eyes again when he tucked a blanket from the edge of the sofa around her.

Without his field experience, he might have been alarmed about her state of semiconsciousness, but he'd seen enough soldiers react just this way to a sudden shock—sort of take a little mental vacation—that he wasn't overly concerned. If she was still spacey and out of it when he came back from taking care of Tag, he would get on the horn to Jake Dalton, the only physician in Pine Gulch, and see what he recommended.

He threw a blanket over her. "Ma'am." He spoke loudly and evenly and was rewarded with those eyes opening a little more at him. He was really curious what color they were.

"I need to stable my horse and grab more firewood in case the power goes out. I've got a feeling we're in for a nasty night. Just rest here with your little puffball and work on warming up, okay?"

After a long moment, she nodded and closed her eyes again.

He knew her somehow and it bothered the hell out of him that he couldn't place how, especially since he usually prided himself on his ironclad memory.

He watched the dog circle around and then settle on her feet again like a little fuzzy slipper. Whoever she was, she had about as much sense as that little dog to go out on a night like tonight. Someone was probably worrying about her. After he took care of Tag, he would try to figure out if she needed to call someone with her whereabouts.

Shoving on his Stetson again, he drew in his last breath of warm air for a while and then headed into the teeth of the storm.

He rushed through taking care of Tag and loaded up as much firewood as he could carry in a load toward the house. He had a feeling he would be back and forth to the woodpile several times during the night and he was grateful his tenant/caretaker Gwen Bianca had been conscientious about making sure enough wood was stockpiled for the winter.

What was he going to do without her? He frowned as one more niggling worry pressed in on him.

Ever since she told him she was buying a house closer to Jackson Hole where she frequently showed her pottery, he had been trying to figure out his options. He was a little preoccupied fighting the Taliban to spend much time worrying about whether a woodpile thousands of miles away had been replenished.

When he returned to the house, he checked on his unexpected guest first thing and found her still sleeping. She wasn't shivering anymore and when he touched her forehead, she didn't seem to be running a fever.

The dog barked a little yippy greeting at him but didn't move from her spot at the woman's feet.

He took off his hat and coat and hung them in the mudroom, then returned to the family room. His touching her forehead—or perhaps the dog's bark—must have awakened her. She was sitting up and this time her eyes were finally wide open.

They were a soft and luscious green, the kind of color he dreamed about during the harsh and desolate Afghan winters, of spring grasses covering the mountains, of hope and growth and life.

She gave him a hesitant smile and his jaw sagged as he finally placed how he knew her.

Holy Mother of God.

The woman on his couch, the one he had dressed in his most disreputable sweats, the woman who had crashed her vehicle into Cold Creek just outside his gates and whose little pink panties he had taken such guilty pleasure in glimpsing, was none other than Mimi frigging Van Hoyt.

A man was staring at her.

Not just any man, either. He was tall, perhaps six-one or two, with short dark hair and blue eyes, powerful muscles and a square, determined sort of jaw. He was just the sort of man who made her most nervous, the kind who didn't look as if they could be swayed by a flirty smile and a sidelong look.

He was staring at her as if she had just sprouted horns out of the top of her head. She frowned, uncomfortable with his scrutiny though she couldn't have said exactly why.

Her gaze shifted to her surroundings and she discovered she was on a red plaid sofa in a room she didn't recognize, with rather outdated beige flowered wallpaper and a jumble of mismatched furnishings.

She had no clear memory of arriving here, only a vague sense that something was very wrong in her life, that someone was supposed to help her sort everything out. And then she was driving, driving, with snow flying, and a sharp moment of fear.

She looked at the man again, registering that he was extraordinarily handsome in a clean-cut, all-American sort of way.

Had she been looking for him? She blinked, trying to sort through the jumble of her thoughts.

"How are you feeling?" he finally asked. "I couldn't find any broken bones and I think the air bag probably saved you from a nasty bump on the head when you hit the creek."

Creek. She closed her eyes as a memory returned of her hands gripping a steering wheel and a desperate need to reach someone who could help her.

Baby. The baby.

She clutched her hands over her abdomen and made a low sort of moan.

"Here, take it easy. Do you have a stomachache? That could be from the air bag. It's not unusual to bruise a rib or two when one of those things deploys. Do you want me to take you into the clinic in town to check things out?"

She didn't know. She couldn't think, as if every coherent thought in her head had been squirreled away on a high shelf just out of her reach.

She hugged her arms around herself. She had to trust her instincts, since she didn't know what else to do. "No clinic. I don't want to go to the doctor."

He raised one dark eyebrow at that but then shrugged. "Your call. For now, anyway. If you start babbling and speaking in tongues, I'm calling the doctor in Pine Gulch, no matter what you say."

"Fair enough." The baby was fine, she told herself. She wouldn't accept any other alternative. "Where am I?"

"My ranch. The Western Sky. I told you my name before but I'll do it again. I'm Brant Western."

To her surprise, Simone, who usually distrusted everything with a Y chromosome, jumped down from the sofa to sniff at his boots. He picked the dog up and held her, somehow still managing to look ridiculously masculine with a little powder puff in his arms.

Western Sky. Gwen. *That's* where she had been running. Gwen would fix everything, she knew it.

No. This problem was too big for even Gwen to fix.

"I'm Maura Howard," she answered instinctively, using the alias she preferred when she traveled, for security reasons.

"Are you?" he said. *An odd question,* she thought briefly, but she was more concerned with why she was here and not where she wanted to be.

She had visited Gwen's cabin once before but she didn't remember this room. "This isn't Gwen's house."

At once, a certain understanding flashed in blue eyes that reminded her of the ocean near her beach house in Malibu on her favorite stormy afternoons.

"You know Gwen Bianca?"

She nodded. "I need to call her, to let her know I'm here."

"That's not going to do you much good. Gwen's not around."

That set her back and she frowned. "Do you know where she is?"

"Not at the ranch, I'm afraid. Not even in the country, actually. She's at a gallery opening in Milan."

Oh, no. Mimi closed her eyes. How stupid and short-sighted of her, to assume Gwen would be just waiting here to offer help if Mimi ever needed it.

Egocentric, silly, selfish. That was certainly her.

No wonder she preferred being Maura Howard whenever she had the chance.

"Well, Maura." Was it her imagination, or did he stress her name in an unnatural sort of way? "I'm afraid you're not going anywhere tonight. It's too dangerous for you to drive on these snowy roads even if I could manage to go out in the dark and snow to pull your vehicle out of the creek. I'm afraid you're stuck for now."

Oh, what a mess. She wanted to sink back onto the pillows of this comfortable sofa, just close her eyes and slide back into blissful oblivion. But she couldn't very well do that with her host watching her out of those intense blue eyes.

As tough and dangerous as Brant Western looked, she had the strangest assurance that she was safe with him. On the other hand, her instincts hadn't been all that reliable where men where concerned for the past, oh, twenty-six years.

But Simone liked him and that counted for a great deal in her book.

As if sensing the direction of her gaze, he set the dog down. Simone's white furry face looked crestfallen for just a moment, then she jumped back up to Mimi's lap.

"I'm assuming Gwen didn't know you were coming."

"No. I should have called her." Her voice trembled on the words and she fought down the panic and the fear and the whole tangled mess of emotions she'd been fighting since that stark moment in her ob-gyn's office the day before.

Gwen had been her logical refuge as she faced this latest disaster in her life. Mimi's favorite of her father's ex-wives, Gwen had always offered comfort and support through boarding schools and breakups and scandals.

For twenty-four hours, all she had been able to think about was escaping to Gwen, in desperate need of her calm good sense and her unfailing confidence in Mimi. But Gwen wasn't here. She was in Milan right now, just when Mimi needed her most and she felt, ridiculously, as if all the underpinnings of her world were shaking loose.

First driving her car into a creek and now this. It was all too much. She sniffled and made a valiant effort to fight back the tears, but it was too late. The panic swallowed her whole and she started to cry.

Simone licked at her tears and Mimi held the dog closer, burying her face in her fur.

Through her tears, she thought she saw utter horror in her host's eyes. He was an officer in the military, she remembered Gwen telling her. A major, if Mimi wasn't mistaken, in some Special Forces unit.

She had a vague memory of him telling her that. Major Brant Western, Company A, 1st Battalion, 75th Ranger Regiment.

She would have thought a man would have to be a fairly confident, take-charge sort of guy to reach that rank, but Major Western looked completely panicked by her tears. "Hey, come on. Don't cry, um, Maura. It's okay. You'll see. Things will seem better in the morning, I promise. It's not the end of the world. You're safe and dry now and I've even got a guest room you can stay in tonight. We'll get that cut on your eye cleaned up and bandaged."

She swiped at her tears with her sleeve and a moment later he thrust a tissue in her face, which she seized on gratefully. "I can't stay here," she said after she'd calmed a little. "I don't even know you. I passed a guest ranch a few miles back. Hope Springs or something like that. I'll see if they've got availability."

"How are you going to get there?" he asked.

"What do you mean?"

"Your SUV is toast for now and Pine Gulch isn't exactly flush with cab companies. Beside that, the way that wind is blowing and drifting, it's not safe for anybody to be out on the roads. That storm has already piled up seven inches and forecasters are predicting two or three times that before we're done. I promise, you're completely safe staying here. The guest room's even got a lock on the door."

She had a feeling a locked door wouldn't stop him if he set his mind to breaking in somewhere. No doubt this man, with his serious blue eyes and solid strength, could work his way through just about anything—whether a locked door or a woman's good sense.

"Have you eaten?"

"I'm not hungry."

That was certainly true enough. Just the idea of food made her stomach churn. Ironic that she'd been pregnant for more than ten weeks and hadn't exhibited a single symptom, not the tiniest sign that might have tipped her off. Then the day after she found out she was pregnant, she started with the morning sickness, along with a bone-deep exhaustion. If she had the chance, she thought she could sleep for a week.

"I can't impose on you this way."

He shrugged. "Once you've made a guy wade through a frozen creek twice, what's a little further inconvenience for him? Let me go grab some clean sheets for the bed and we'll get that cut cleaned up and you settled for the night."

She wiped at the tears drying on her features. What choice did she have? She had nowhere else to go. After he left the room, she leaned into the sofa, holding Simone close and soaking in the fire's delicious heat.

Now that she thought of it, this just might be the perfect solution, at least while she tried to wrap her head around the terrifying future.

No one would know where she was. Not her father— as if he'd care. Not Marco, who would care even less. Certainly not the bane of her existence, the paparazzi, who cared only for ratings and circulation numbers.

The world outside that window was a terrifying place. For now she had shelter from that storm out there, and a man who looked more than capable of protecting her from anything that might come along.

She only needed a little breathing space to figure things out and she could find that here as easily as anywhere else.

Only one possible complication occurred to her. She would have to do her best to keep him from calling for a tow when the snow cleared. She knew from experience that people like tow-truck drivers and gas station attendants and restaurant servers were usually the first ones to pick up a phone and call in the tabloids.

She could see the headlines now. Mimi's Ditchscapade with Sexy Rancher.

She couldn't afford that right now. She only needed a few days of quiet and rest. Like that blizzard out there, the media storm that was her life and this latest—and worst—potential scandal would hopefully pass without ever seeing the light of day.

She only needed to figure out a way to stay safe and warm until it did.

Chapter 2

When Brant returned to his living room, he found Maura Howard—aka Mimi Van Hoyt, tabloid princess du jour—gazing into the fire, her features pale and her wide, mobile mouth set into a tense frown.

A few years ago during one of his Iraq deployments, he'd had the misfortune of seeing her one miserable attempt at moviemaking at a showing in the rec hall in Tikrit. He was pretty sure the apparent turmoil she was showing now must be genuine, since her acting skills had been roughly on par with the howler monkey that had enjoyed a bit in the movie.

As long as she didn't cry again, he could handle things. He was ashamed to admit that he could handle a dozen armed insurgents better than a crying woman.

"Everything will seem better in the morning," he promised her. "Once the storm passes over, I can call a tow for your car. I'm sure they can fix it right up in town and send you on your way."

Her hands twisted on her lap and those deep green eyes shifted away from him. In pictures he'd seen of her, he always thought those eyes held a hard, cynical edge, but he could see none of that here.

"I, um, can't really afford a tow right now."

If she hadn't said the words with such a valiant attempt at sincerity in her voice, he would have snorted outright at that blatant whopper. Everybody on the planet who had ever seen a tabloid knew her father was Werner Van Hoyt, real estate mogul, Hollywood producer and megabillionaire. She was a trust fund baby whose sole existence seemed to revolve around attending the hottest parties and being seen with other quasi-celebrities at the hippest clubs until all hours of the day and night.

Did she think he was a complete idiot? The SUV in question was a Mercedes, for heaven's sake.

But if Mimi wanted to pretend to be someone else, who was he to stop her?

"The rental car company should take care of the details. They would probably even send another vehicle for you. Barring that, I'm sure Wylie down at the garage will take a credit card or work out a payment plan with you. But we can cross that bridge once the snow clears. Let's get your face cleaned up so you can get to bed."

She didn't look as if she appreciated any of those options, at least judging by the frustration tightening her features. He had a pretty strong feeling she probably hadn't been thwarted much in her life. It would probably do her a world of good not to get her way once in a while.

He had to bite his lip to keep from smiling. Big shocker there. He hadn't found much of anything amusing since that miserable afternoon three weeks ago in a remote village in Paktika Province.

Longer, come to think of it. His world had felt hollow and dark around the edges since Jo's death in the fall. But somehow Mimi seemed to remind him that life could sometimes be a real kick in the seat.

He had to give her credit for only flinching a little when he cleansed the small cut over her eye and stuck a bandage on it.

"It's a pretty small cut and shouldn't leave a scar."

"Thank you," she said in a subdued voice, then gracefully covered a yawn. "I'm sorry. I've been traveling for several hours and it's been a…stressful day."

"Don't worry about it. Your room is back here. It's nothing fancy but it's comfortable and you've got your own bathroom."

"I hate to ask but, speaking of bathrooms," she said, "Simone could probably use a trip outside."

"Yeah, she has been dancing around for the door for the last few minutes. I'll take her out and try to make sure she doesn't get swallowed by the snow, then bring her in to you."

"Thank you for…everything," she murmured. "Not too many people would take in a complete stranger— and her little dog, too—in the middle of a blizzard."

"Maybe not where you're from. But I would guess just about anybody in Cold Creek Canyon would have done the same."

"Then it must be a lovely place."

"Except in the middle of a February blizzard," he answered. She didn't object when he cupped her elbow to help her down the hall and he tried to store up all the memories. How she smelled of some light citrus-floral, undoubtedly expensive perfume. How her silk turtleneck caressed his fingers. How she was much shorter than he would have guessed, only just reaching his shoulder.

The guys would want to know everything about this surreal interlude and Brant owed it to them to memorize every single detail.

Like the rest of the house, the guest suite was on the shabby side, with aging furniture and peeling wallpaper. But it had a comfortable queen-sized bed, an electric fireplace he'd turned on when he made up the bed and a huge claw-foot tub in the bathroom.

The main house had been mostly empty for the past two years except for his occasional visits between deployments. Since he left Cold Creek a dozen years ago for the military, he had rented the house out sporadically. Gwen Bianca stayed in the small cabin on the property rent-free in exchange for things like keeping the woodpile stocked and the roof from collapsing in.

His last tenants had moved out six months ago and he hadn't bothered to replace them since the rent mostly covered barebones maintenance and county property taxes on the land anyway and was hardly worth the trouble most of the time.

Now that Gwen had announced she was moving away, he didn't know what to do with Western Sky.

"It's not much but you should be warm and comfortable."

"I'll be fine. Thank you again for your hospitality."

"I don't know if this is a warning or an apology in advance, but I'll be checking on you occasionally in the night."

"Do you think I'm going to run off with your plasma TV?"

He fought another smile, wondering where they were all coming from. "You're welcome to it, if you think you can make a clean getaway on foot in this storm. No. There's a chance you had a head injury. I don't think so but you were in and out of consciousness for a while there. I can't take any chance of missing signs of swelling or unusual behavior."

She sat on the edge of the bed with a startled sort of work. "I appreciate your...diligence, but I'm sure I don't have a brain injury. The air bag protected me."

"I guess you forgot to mention you were a neurologist."

She frowned. "I'm not."

"What are you, then?" he asked, curious as to how she would answer. Heiress? Aimless socialite? Lousy actress?

After a long pause, she forced a smile. "I work for a charitable organization in Los Angeles."

Nice save, he thought. It could very well be true, since she had enough money to rescue half the world.

"Well, unless your charitable organization specializes in self-diagnosing traumatic brain injuries, I'm going to have to err on the side of caution here and stick to the plan of checking on you through the night."

"Don't tell me you're the neurologist now."

"Nope. Just an Army Ranger who's been hit over the head a few too many times in my career. I'll check on you about every hour to make sure your mental status hasn't changed."

"How would you even know if my mental status has changed or not? You just met me."

He laughed out loud at that, a rusty sound that surprised the heck out of him.

"True enough. I guess when you stand on your head and start reciting the Declaration of Independence at four in the morning, I'll be sure to ask if that's normal behavior before I call the doctor."

She almost smiled in return but he sensed she was troubled about more than just her car accident.

None of his concern, he reminded himself. Whatever she was doing in this isolated part of Idaho was her own business.

"I put one of my T-shirts on the bed there for you to sleep in. I'll bring your little purse pooch back after I let her out. Let me know if you need anything else or if you get hungry. The Western Sky isn't a four-star resort but I can probably rustle up some tea and toast."

"Right now I only want to rest."

"Can't blame you there," he answered. "It's been a strange evening all the way around. Come on, pup."

The little dog barked, her black eyes glowing with eagerness in her white fur, and followed him into the hallway.

The wind still howled outside but he managed to find a spot of ground somewhat sheltered by the back patio awning for her to delicately take care of business.

To his relief, the dog didn't seem any more inclined to stay out in the howling storm than he did. She hurried back to where he stood on the steps and he scooped her up and carried her inside, where he dried off her paws with an old towel.

He refused to admit to himself that he was trying to spare Mimi four cold, wet paws against her when the dog jumped up on her bed.

When he softly knocked on the guest room door, she didn't answer. After a moment, he took the liberty of pushing it open. She was already asleep, her eyes closed, and he set the dog beside her on the bed, thinking she would need the comfort of the familiar if she awoke in a strange place in the middle of the night.

From the dim light in the hallway, he could just make out her high cheekbones and that lush, kissable mouth.

She was even prettier in person, just about the loveliest thing he had ever seen in real life.

She was beautiful and she made him forget the ghosts that haunted him, even if only for a little while. For a guy who only had a week before he had to report back to a war zone, both of those things seemed pretty darn seductive right about now.

Not the most restful sleep she had ever experienced.

At 6:00 a.m., after a night of being awakened several times by the keening wind outside and by her unwilling host insistent on checking her questionable mental status, she awoke to Simone licking her face.

Mimi groaned as her return to consciousness brought with it assorted aches and pains. The sting of the cut on her forehead and the low throb of a headache at the base of her skull were the worst of them. Her shoulder muscles ached, but she had a feeling that was more from the stress of the past two days than from any obvious injury.

She pushed away her assorted complaints to focus on the tiny bichon frise she adored. "Do you need to go outside, sweetie?" she asked.

Instead of leaping from the bed and scampering to the door as she normally would have done, Simone merely yawned, stretched her four paws out, then closed her eyes again.

"I guess not," Mimi answered with a frown at that bit of unusual behavior. Simone usually jumped to go outside first thing after a full night of holding her bladder. Mimi could only hope she hadn't decided to relieve herself somewhere in this strange house.

She looked around the bedroom in the pale light of predawn but couldn't see any obvious signs of a mishap in any corner. What she *did* find was her entire set of luggage piled up inside the door, all five pieces of it, including Simone's carrier.

The sight of them all stunned her and sent a funny little sparkle jumping through her. Somehow in the middle of the raging blizzard, Major Western had gone to the trouble of retrieving every one of them for her.

In the night, more vague recollections had come together in her head and she vividly remembered he had been forced to wade through the ice-crusted creek to reach her after the accident. In order to retrieve her luggage from the SUV, he would have had to venture into that water yet again. She could hardly believe he had done that for her, yet the proof was right there before her eyes in the corner.

No. There had to be some catch. He just seemed entirely too good to be real. The cynical part of her that had been burned by men a few dozen too many times couldn't quite believe anyone would find her worth that much effort.

She pressed a hand to her stomach, to the tiny secret growing there.

"Are you okay in there, kiddo?" she murmured.

She had bought a half-dozen pregnancy books the moment she left the doctor's office but hadn't dared read any of them on the plane, afraid to risk that someone would see through her disguise and tip off the tabloids about her reading choices. Instead, she'd had to be content with a pregnancy week-by-week app on her cell phone, and she had devoured every single word behind her sunglasses on the plane.

At barely eleven weeks, Mimi knew she wasn't far enough along to actually feel the baby move. Maybe in a few more weeks. But that didn't stop her from imagining the little thing swimming around in there.

Something else that didn't feel quite real to her, that in a few months she was going to be a mother. She had only had two days to absorb the stunning news that her brief but intense affair with Marco Mendez had resulted in an unexpected complication.

In only a few days, the provider of half her baby's DNA was marrying another woman. And not just any woman but Jessalyn St. Claire, Hollywood's current favorite leading lady, sweet and cute and universally adored. Marco and Jessalyn. "Messalyn," as the tabloids dubbed the pair of them. The two beautiful, talented, successful people were apparently enamored of each other.

It was a match made in heaven—or their respective publicists' offices. Mimi wasn't sure which.

She only knew that if word leaked out that she was expecting Marco Mendez's baby, Jessalyn would flip out, especially since the timing of Mimi's pregnancy would clearly reveal that they had carried on their affair several months after Marco had proposed to Jessalyn in such a public venue as the Grammy Awards, where he won Best Male Vocalist of the year.

Mimi probed her heart for the devastation she probably should be feeling right about now. For two months, she had been expecting Marco to break off the sham engagement and publicly declare he loved Mimi, as he had privately assured her over and over was his intention.

The declaration never came. She felt like an idiot for ever imagining it would. Worse, when she had gathered up every bit of her courage and whatever vestiges of pride she had left and finally called him to meet her at their secret place after the stunning discovery of her pregnancy, he hadn't reacted at all like she had stupidly hoped.

Arrogant, egocentric, selfish.

She was all those things and more. She had secretly hoped that when Marco found out she was pregnant, he would pull her into his arms and declare he couldn't go through with the marriage now, that he loved her and wanted to spend the rest of his life with her and the child they had created.

She was pathetically stupid.

Instead, his sleek, sexy features had turned bone-white and he had asked her if she'd made an appointment yet to take care of the problem.

When she hesitantly told him she was thinking about keeping the baby, he had become enraged. She had never believed Marco capable of violence until he had stood with veins popping out in his neck, practically foaming at the mouth in that exclusive, secluded house in Topanga Canyon he kept for these little trysts.

He had called her every vile name in the book and some she'd never heard of. By the time he was done, she felt like all those things he called her. Skank. Whore. Bitch.

And worse.

In the end, she'd somehow found the strength to tell him emphatically that keeping the baby or not would be her own decision. If she kept the baby, it would be hers alone and he would relinquish any claim to it. She wanted nothing more to do with him.

If he touched her or threatened her again in any way, she would tell her father, a man both of them knew had the power to decimate careers before he'd taken a sip of his morning soy latte.

She pressed a hand to her tiny baby bump.

"I'm sorry I picked such a jerk to be your daddy," she whispered.

She loved this baby already. The idea of it, innocent and sweet, seemed to wrap around all the empty places in her heart. The only blessing in the whole mess was that she and Marco had, unbelievably, been able to keep their affair a secret thus far.

Oh, maybe a few rumors had been circulating here

and there. But she figured if she stayed out of the camera glare at least until the wedding was over and then took an extended trip somewhere quiet, she just might muddle through this whole thing. She had no doubt she could find someone willing to claim paternity for enough money.

Or maybe she would just drop out of sight for the rest of her life, relocate to some isolated place in the world where people had never heard of Mimi Van Hoyt or her more ridiculous antics.

Borneo might be nice. Or she could move in with some friendly indigenous tribe along the Amazon.

Staying with Gwen at least until the wedding was over would have solved her short-term problem, if she hadn't been too blasted shortsighted to pick up the phone first.

Why couldn't she still stay here?

The thought was undeniably enticing. Gwen might not be here but, except for her absence, the ranch still offered all the advantages that had led Mimi to fly out on a snowy February afternoon to find her ex-stepmother. It was isolated and remote, as far from the craziness of a celebrity wedding as Mimi could imagine.

She thought of her host wading through a creek in the middle of a blizzard to retrieve her luggage. He seemed a decent sort of man, with perhaps a bit of a hero complex. Maybe Major Western could be convinced to let her stay just for a few days.

She closed her eyes, daunted by the very idea of asking him. Though she had never had much trouble bending the males of the species to her will—her father being the most glaring exception—she had a feeling Brant Western wouldn't be such an easy sell.

Later. She would wait until the sun was at least up before she worried about it, she decided with a yawn.

When she awoke again, a muted kind of daylight streamed through the curtains and an entirely too male figure was standing beside her bed.

"Morning." Her voice came out sultry and low, more a product of sleepiness than any effort to be sexy, but something flared in his eyes for just a moment, then was gone.

Okay, maybe convincing him she should stay wouldn't be as difficult as she had feared, Mimi thought, hiding a secret smile even as she was a little disappointed he wouldn't present more of a challenge.

"Good morning." His voice was a little more tightly wound than she remembered and she thought his eyes looked tired. From monitoring her all night? she wondered. Or from something else?

"Sorry to wake you but I haven't been in to check on you for a couple of hours. I was just seeing if the dog needed to go out again."

"Did you take her out in the night?"

He nodded. "She's not too crazy about snow."

"Oh, I know. Once in Chamonix she got lost in a snow drift. It was terrifying for both of us."

She shouldn't have said that, she realized at once. Maura Howard wasn't the sort to visit exclusive ski resorts in the Swiss Alps, but Brant didn't seem to blink an eye.

"I'm on my way to take care of the horses. I'll put

her out again before I leave and I'll try not to lose her in the snow. How's your head?"

"Better. The rest of me is a little achy but I'll survive. Is it still storming?"

He nodded tersely as she sat up in bed and seemed intent on keeping his gaze fixed on some fixed spot in the distance as if he were standing at attention on parade somewhere. "We've had more than a foot and it's still coming down." He paused. "There's a good chance you might be stuck here another day or two. It's going to take at least that long for the plows to clear us out."

"Oh, no!"

Though secretly relieved, she figured he expected the news to come as a shock, so she tried to employ her glaringly nonexistent acting skills. Then, pouring it on a little thicker, she stretched a little before tucking a wayward curl behind her ear.

She didn't miss the way his pupils flared just a little, even as he pretended not to pay her any attention.

"I'm so sorry to be even more of an inconvenience to you, Major Western."

"Around here I'm plain Brant."

"Brant." It was a strong, masculine name that somehow fit him perfectly.

"Thank you so much for bringing my luggage in. It was so kind of you."

"No big deal. I thought you would feel more comfortable if you had your own things, especially since it looks like you're going to be here another night."

"I feel so foolish. If I'd only called Gwen before showing up on her doorstep like this, you wouldn't be stuck with me now."

"That was a pretty idiotic thing to do," he agreed flatly. "What would have happened to you if you'd slid off in a spot in the canyon that wasn't so close to any houses? You might have been stuck in the storm in your car all night and probably would have frozen to death before anybody found you."

His bluntness grated and she almost glared but at the last minute she remembered she needed his help. Or maybe not. She needed a place to stay, but that didn't necessarily mean she had to stay with *him*.

"I hate imposing on you," she said as another idea suddenly occurred to her, one she couldn't believe she hadn't thought of the night before or this morning when she was mulling over her various options. "What if we called Gwen and asked her if I could stay at her house since she's gone?"

"Great idea," he said, with somewhat humiliating alacrity. "There's only one problem with it. Gwen's furnace went out the day she left. I've got a company coming out to replace it but they can't make it to the ranch until later in the week. With the blizzard, it might even be next week before they come out. Occupied dwellings have precedence in weather like this so I'm afraid you're stuck here until the storm clears."

She tried to look appropriately upset by that news. At least his insistence on that particular point would give her a little breathing room to figure out how she could convince him to let her stay longer.

Four hours later, she was rethinking her entire strategy. If she had to stay here until Marco's wedding was over, she was very much afraid she would die of boredom.

She had never been very good with dead time. She liked to fill it with friends and shopping and trips to her favorite day spa. Okay, she had spent twenty-six years wading in shallow waters. She had no problem admitting it. She liked having fun and wasn't very good at finding ways to entertain herself.

That particular task seemed especially challenging here at Western Sky. Major Western had very few books—most were in storage near his home base in Georgia, he had told her—and the DVD selection was limited. And of course the satellite television wasn't working because too much snow had collected in the dish, blocking the receiver. Or at least that's the explanation her host provided.

The house wasn't wired to the internet, since he was rarely here and didn't use it much anyway.

She probably could have dashed off some texts and even an email or two on her Smartphone, but she had made the conscious decision to turn it off. For now, she was Maura Howard. It might be a little tough selling that particular story if she had too much contact with the outside world.

Her host had made himself scarce most of the day, busy looking over ranch accounts or bringing in firewood or knocking ice out of the water troughs for the livestock.

She had a feeling he was avoiding her, though she wasn't sure why, which left her with Simone for company.

Brant poked his head into the kitchen just after noon to tell her to help herself to whatever she wanted for lunch but that he had a bit of a crisis at Gwen's cabin with frozen pipes since the furnace wasn't working.

Mimi had settled on a solitary lunch of canned tomato soup that was actually quite tasty. After she washed and dried her bowl, marveling that there was a house in America which actually didn't possess a dishwasher, she returned it to the rather dingy cupboard next to the sink and was suddenly hit by a brainstorm.

This was how she could convince Brant to let her stay.

A brilliant idea, if she did say so herself. Not bad for a shallow girl, she thought some time later as she surveyed the contents of every kitchen cupboard, jumbled on all the countertops.

She stood on a stepladder with a bucket of sudsy water in front of her as she scoured years of grease and dust from the top of his knotty pine cabinets.

Here was a little known secret the tabloids had never unearthed about Mimi Van Hoyt. They would probably have a field day if anyone ever discovered she liked to houseclean when she was bored or stressed.

Between boarding school stays, her father's long-term housekeeper Gert used to give her little chores to do. Cleaning out a closet, organizing a drawer, polishing silver. Her father probably never would have allowed it if he'd known, but she and Gert had both been very good at keeping secrets from Werner Van Hoyt.

She had never understood why she enjoyed it so much and always been a little ashamed of what she considered a secret vice until one of her more insightful therapists had pointed out those hours spent with Gert at some mundane task or other were among the most consistent of her life. Perhaps cleaning her surroundings was her mental way of creating order out of the chaos that was her life amid her father's multiple marriages and divorces.

Here in Major Western's house, it was simply something to pass the time, she told herself, digging in a little harder on a particularly tough stain.

"What would you be doing?"

Mimi jerked her head around and found Major Western standing in the kitchen doorway watching her with an expression that seemed a complicated mix—somewhere between astonished and appalled.

Simone—exceptional watchdog that she was—awoke at his voice and jumped up from her spot on a half-circle rug by the sink. She yipped an eager greeting while Mimi flushed to the roots of her hair.

"Sorry. I was…bored."

He gave her a skeptical look. "Bored. And so, out of the blue, you decided to wash out my kitchen cabinets."

"Somebody needed to. You wouldn't believe the grime on them."

She winced as soon as the words escaped. Okay, that might not be the most tactful thing to mention to a man she was hoping would keep her around for a few days.

"You've been busy with your Army career, I'm sure," she quickly amended. "I can only imagine how difficult it is to keep a place like this clean when you're not here all the time."

He looked both rueful and embarrassed as he moved farther into the kitchen and started taking off his winter gear.

"I've been renting it out on and off for the last few

years and tenants don't exactly keep the place in the best shape. I'm planning on having a crew come in after I return to Afghanistan to clean it all out and whip it into shape before I put it on the market."

She paused her scrubbing, struck both that he had been in Afghanistan and that he would put such a wonderful house on the market. "Why would you sell this place? I can't see much out there except snow right now but I would guess it's a beautiful view. At least Gwen always raves about what inspiration she finds here for her work."

He unbuttoned his soaked coat and she tried not to notice the muscles of his chest that moved under his sweater as he worked his arms out of the sleeves.

"It's long past time."

He was quiet for several moments. "The reality is, I'm only here a few weeks of the year, if that, and it's too hard to take care of the place long-distance, even with your friend Gwen keeping an eye on things for me. Anyway, Gwen's leaving, too. She told me she's buying a house outside Jackson Hole and that just seemed the final straw. I can't even contemplate how daunting it would be to find someone to replace her. Not to mention keeping up with general maintenance like painting the barn."

It was entirely too choice an opportunity to pass up. "This is perfect. I'll help you."

Again that eyebrow crept up as he toed off his winter boots. "You want to paint the barn? I'm afraid that might be a little tough, what with the snow and all."

She frowned. "Not the barn. But this." She pointed

with her soapy towel. "The whole place needs a good scrubbing, as I'm sure you're aware."

He stared at her. "Let me get this straight. You're volunteering to clean my house?"

She set the soapy towel back in the bucket and perched on the top rung of the ladder to face him. "Sure, why not?"

"I can think of a few pretty compelling reasons."

She flashed him a quick look, wondering what he meant by that, but she couldn't read anything in his expression.

"The truth is, I need a place to stay for a few days."

"Why?"

"It's a long, boring story."

"Somehow I doubt that," he murmured, looking fascinated.

"Trust me," she said firmly. "I need a place to stay for a few days—let's just leave it at that—and you could use some work done around here to help you ready the place for prospective buyers."

"And you think you can help me do that?"

The skepticism in his voice stung, for reasons she didn't want to examine too carefully. "Believe it or not, I've actually helped a friend stage houses for sale before and I know a little about it. I can help you, I swear. Why shouldn't we both get something we need?"

He leaned against the counter next to the refrigerator and crossed his arms over his chest. As he studied her, she thought she saw doubt, lingering shock and an odd sort of speculation in his eyes.

After a moment he shook his head. "I can't ask you to do that, Ms. Howard."

"You didn't ask. I'm offering."

Five days. That was all she needed to avoid Hollywood's biggest wedding in years. With a little time and distance, she hoped she could figure out what she was going to do with the mess of her life.

"I really do need a place to stay, Major Western."

She thought she saw a softening in the implacable set to his jaw, a tiny waver in his eyes, so she whipped out the big guns. The undefeated, never-fail, invincible option.

She beamed at him, her full-throttle, pour-on-the-charm smile that had made babbling fools out of every male she'd ever wielded it on. "I swear, you'll be so happy with the job I do, you might just decide not to sell."

Though she saw obvious reluctance in his dark eyes, he finally sighed. "A few days. Why not? As long as you don't make any major changes. Just clean things out a little and make the rooms look better. That's all."

Relief coursed through her. Simone, sensing Mimi's excitement, barked happily.

"You won't regret it, I promise."

He shook his head and reached into the refrigerator for a bottled water. In his open, honest expression, she could see he was already sorry. She didn't care, she told herself, ignoring that same little sting under her heart.

Whether he wanted her here or not, somehow she knew that Major Brant Western was too honorable to kick her out after he'd promised she could stay.

Chapter 3

Whateversion kind of game was she playing?

That seemed to be the common refrain echoing through his brain when it came to Mimi Van Hoyt. He still hadn't come any closer to figuring her out several hours after their stunning conversation, as they sat at the worn kitchen table eating a cobbled-together dinner of canned stew and peaches.

First she was pretending to be someone else—as if anyone in the world with access to a computer or a television could somehow have been lucky enough to miss her many well-publicized antics. The woman couldn't pick up her newspaper in the morning without a crop of photographers there to chronicle every move and she must think he was either blind or stupid not to figure out who she was.

But that same tabloid darling who apparently didn't

step outside her door without wearing designer clothes had spent the afternoon cleaning every nook and cranny of his kitchen—and doing a pretty good job of it. Not that he was any great judge of cleanliness, having spent most of his adult life on Army bases or in primitive conditions in the field, but he had grown up with Jo Winder as an example and he knew she would have been happy to see the countertops sparkling and the old wood cabinets gleaming with polish.

He wouldn't have believed it if he hadn't seen it himself—Mimi Van Hoyt, lush and elegant, scrubbing the grime away from a worn-out ranch house with no small degree of relish. She seemed as happy with her hands in a bucket of soapy water as he was out on patrol with his M4 in his hands.

She had even sung a little under her breath, for heaven's sake, and he couldn't help wondering why she had dabbled in acting instead of singing since her contralto voice didn't sound half-bad.

That low, throaty voice seemed to slide down his spine like trailing fingers and a few times he'd had to manufacture some obvious excuse to leave the house just to get away from it. He figured he'd hauled enough wood up to the house to last them all week but he couldn't seem to resist returning to the kitchen to watch her.

The woman completely baffled him. He would have expected her to be whining about the lack of entertainment in the cabin, about the enforced confinement, about the endless snow.

At the very least, he would have thought her fingers would be tapping away at some cell phone as she tweeted or whatever it was called, about being trapped in an isolated Idaho ranch with a taciturn stranger.

Instead, she teased her little dog, she took down his curtains and threw them in the washing machine, she organized every ancient cookbook left in the cupboard.

She seemed relentlessly cheerful while the storm continued to bluster outside.

Somehow he was going to have to figure out a way to snap her picture when she wasn't looking. Otherwise, his men would never believe he'd spent his midtour leave watching Mimi Van Hoyt scrub grease off his stove vent.

But he was pretty sure a photograph wouldn't show them how lovely she looked, with those huge, deep green eyes and her long inky curls and that bright smile that took over her entire face.

Though he knew it was dangerous, Brant couldn't seem to stop watching her. Having Mimi Van Hoyt flitting around his kitchen in all her splendor was a little overwhelming for a man who hadn't been with a woman in longer than he cared to remember—sort of like shoving a starving man in front of one of those all-you-can-eat buffets in Las Vegas and ordering him to dig in.

He'd had an on-again, off-again relationship with a nurse at one of the field support hospitals in Paktika Province, but his constant deployments hadn't left him much time for anything serious.

Not that he was looking. He would leave that sort of thing to the guys who were good at it, like Quinn seemed to be, though he never would have believed it.

Brant treated the women he dated with great respect but he knew he tended to gravitate toward smart, focused career women who weren't looking for anything more than a little fun and companionship once in a while.

Mimi was something else entirely. He didn't know exactly what, but he couldn't believe he had agreed to let her stay at his ranch for a few days. Hour upon hour of trying to ignore the way her hair just begged to be released from the elastic band holding it back or the way those big green eyes caught the light or how her tight little figure danced around the kitchen as she worked.

He shook his head. Which of the two of them was crazier? Right now, he was willing to say it was a toss-up, though he had a suspicion he just might be edging ahead.

"Would you like more stew?" she asked, as if she were hosting some fancy dinner party instead of dishing up canned Dinty Moore.

"I'm good. Thanks."

Though he knew she had to be accustomed to much fancier meals, she did a credible job with her own bowl of stew. He supposed all that scrubbing and dusting must have worked up an appetite.

"Have you had the ranch for long?" she asked, breaking what had been a comfortable silence. "I'm sorry, I can't remember what you told me the name was."

"The Western Sky. And yeah, it's been in my family for generations. My great-great-grandfather bought the land and built the house in the late 1800s."

"So you were raised here?"

He thought of his miserable childhood and the pain and insecurity of it, and then of the Winders, who had rescued him from it and showed him what home could really be.

Explaining all that to her would be entirely too complicated, even if he were willing to discuss it, so he took the easy way out. "For the most part," he answered, hoping she would leave it at that.

Because he was intensely curious to see how far she would take her alternate identity, he turned the conversation back in her direction. "What about you, Maura? Whereabouts do you call home?"

The vibrant green of her eyes seemed to dim a little and she looked away. "Oh, you know. Here and there. California. For now."

"Oh? Which part of the state, if you don't mind me asking?"

"Southern. The L.A. area."

He didn't really follow entertainment gossip but he thought he read or heard something once about her having two homes not far from each other, one her father's Bel Air estate and the other a Malibu beachhouse.

"Is that where your parents live?"

Her mouth tightened a little and she moved the remaining chunks of stew around in her bowl. "My mom died when I was three, just after my parents divorced. My dad sort of raised me but he…we…moved around a lot."

He had to take a quick sip of soda to keep from snorting at that evasive comment—probably Mimi's way of saying her father had residences across the globe.

"And you said you work for a charitable foundation?"

Her wide, mobile mouth pursed into a frown. "Yes. But you probably wouldn't have heard of it."

"And what sort of things do you do there?" He wasn't sure why he enjoyed baiting her so much but it was the most fun he'd had in a long time.

If nothing else, her presence distracted him from the grim events he had left behind in Afghanistan.

"Oh, you know. This and that. I help with fundraising and…and event planning. That sort of thing."

"I don't see a ring, so I'm assuming you're not married."

If he remembered right, she'd been engaged a few years ago to some minor European royalty but he couldn't remember details, other than he thought the breakup had been messy and had, of course, involved some sort of scandal.

"No. Never. You?"

"Nope. Did you ever tell me how you knew Gwen?"

That, at least, was genuine curiosity and not baiting, since his artistic, eclectic, reclusive tenant didn't seem the sort to hobnob with debutantes.

"She was…friends with my father. Years ago. We've always stayed in touch."

Now *that* was interesting. Apparently Gwen Bianca had a few secrets she'd never divulged in the eight or so years she'd been living at the ranch. A past relationship with Werner Van Hoyt? He would never have suspected.

Mimi finally seemed to tire of his subtle interrogation and while he was still digesting the surprising insight into Gwen, she turned the tables on him.

"So how could you possibly want to sell a piece of beautiful land that's been in your family for generations?"

He shrugged. "I don't know if it's fair to say I *want* to sell."

"So don't. The house might be a little worse for wear but it's not falling down around your ears."

"Not yet, anyway."

"A few more years and you'll be retiring from the military, won't you? You'll need a place to settle then, right?"

He had always planned exactly that. But after a half-dozen close calls in his deployment, he'd come to accept that he probably wouldn't live long enough to retire. He didn't have a death wish by any means but he was also a realist.

Since the ambush a month ago, he'd also begun to formulate another motive, one he didn't feel like sharing with a flighty celebrity who spent more on a pair of shoes than some of his men made in a month of hard combat.

"You don't have any other family who might want to do something with the ranch to keep it in the family?" she pressed.

"No. Just me. I…had a younger brother but he died when we were kids."

As soon as he heard his own words, he wanted to take them back. He never spoke about Curtis or his death. Never.

The twenty-year-old guilt might be an integral piece of him, as much a part of the whole as his blue eyes and the crescent-shaped birthmark on his shoulder, but it was private and personal.

"I'm sorry," she murmured, her eyes mossy green with a compassion he didn't want to see. "What happened?"

He wanted to tell her to mind her own business, but

since he had been the one to open that particular doorway into the past, he couldn't very well slam it in her face. "He drowned in the creek when I was eleven and he was nine," he finally said.

"The same creek I crashed into?"

He nodded. "There's not much to it now and it might be a little hard to believe, but it's a far different beast in late spring and early summer during the runoff. You know how your SUV went down a slope about five or six feet? During the runoff, that's all full of fast-moving water. So we were being kids and throwing rocks in the creek, even though we weren't supposed to play around it in the springtime. Curtis got a little too close and the bank gave way. I ran downstream and tried to go in after him but…he slipped past me and I couldn't grab him."

"You could have been killed!"

He should have been. That's what his mother had said once in the middle of a bender. *Better you than my sweet baby,* she had said in that emotionless voice that seemed all the more devastating. He wanted to think she hadn't meant it. Curtis had been the funny, smart, adorable one, while Brant had been big and awkward, far too serious for a kid.

After Curtis's death, what had been a tense home life degenerated to sheer misery. The ranch was falling into chaos, his parents fought all the time and both drank heavily. The fighting and the yelling had been one thing. Then his mother had left them and his father had turned all his anger and grief and bitterness against Brant.

That life might have continued indefinitely until one

of two things happened—either he grew large enough to pound back or until the old man killed him. He didn't know which would have happened first because Guff and Jo Winder had stepped in.

He sipped at his soda pop, remembering the events that had changed his life. He had felt the Winders' scrutiny a few times when he'd been in town with his father and once Guff had even said something to J.D. when his father climbed up his grill about something or other at the farm implement store, but his intervention had only earned Brant a harsher beating when they got home.

Then one day Guff had stopped at the Western Sky to pick up a couple of weaned calves and his visit just happened to coincide with one of J.D.'s bad drunks. Brant had tried to hide the bruises but his T-shirt had ridden up when he'd been helping load one of the calves into the Winder stock trailer.

Guff had taken one look at the welts crisscrossing his back and Brant would never forget the instant fury in his gaze. He had been conditioned over the years to shrink from that kind of anger, but instead of coming after him, Guff had picked up a pitchfork and backed J.D. against the wall.

"You son of a bitch," he had said in a low, terrible voice. "You've lost one son through a terrible accident. How are you going to live with yourself if you lose the other one at your own hand?"

J.D. had blustered and yelled but Guff had kept that pitchfork on him while he turned to Brant. "You know me and my wife, Jo, have taken in a relative, a boy about your age. I think he goes to school with you. Quinn Southerland. We've got plenty of room at Winder

Ranch and I swear on the soul of your brother that no one there will ever lift a hand to you. Would you like to come stay with us for a while?"

He had been as dazed and shocked as his father. Part of him had desperately wanted to leave the Western Sky, to get as far away as he could. But even then, he'd known his duty.

"I'd best stay with my dad, sir. He's got no one else."

Guff had studied him for a long moment, tears in his eyes, then he had dropped the pitchfork. While his dad slid down the wall of the barn to sit in a dazed stupor, Guff had hugged Brant hard and he had realized in that moment that it had been two long years since he'd been touched with anything but malice.

"You're a good boy, son," Guff had said. "I know you love your dad, but right now you have to protect him and yourself. If I promise to see your dad gets the help he needs, will you come?"

In the end, he had agreed, though it had been the toughest choice of his young life, much more difficult than Ranger training or his first combat mission.

He had spent those first few months at Winder Ranch consumed with guilt but certain he would be back with his father at Christmas. True to his word, Guff had paid for his dad's rehab and told J.D. he had to stay sober six months before they would trust him with his son again.

J.D. had lasted only a month before he'd bought a bottle of Jack Daniels, consumed most of it, then wandered into the corral with their meanest bull, where he'd been gored to death.

"I'm sorry."

He jerked his mind from the past to find Mimi

watching him across the table with that sympathy in those big green eyes. It took him a moment to register that she was still talking about his brother's death that had changed everything.

"Thanks. So, yeah. In answer to your question, I'm the only one left in my family. And since I've been here a total of maybe three weeks in the last five years, it seems foolish to hang on to the place."

She looked as if she didn't agree, which he found odd. Still, after a moment, she shrugged. "It should sell easily, especially if you clear out some of the clutter and maybe put a few fresh coats of paint in some of the rooms."

"I don't want to put too much energy into the house," he said, finishing off the peaches. "The only ones who can afford this kind of acreage these days are, uh, Hollywood types who will probably tear down the house and build their own in its place. That's what's happened to several nearby ranches."

As he expected, she ignored the Hollywood jab. How could she do otherwise without revealing her true identity? "You never know. The house has a rustic kind of charm and some people are looking for that. With a little effort, you can show off the lovely old bones of the house. A small investment now could help you set a nice asking price for both the house and the land."

He stared at her. "I thought you said you worked for a charitable organization. For a minute there, you sounded like a real estate agent."

Her cheeks turned pink. "No. I just watch a lot of late-night TV infomercials. You know the ones. How to make a fortune in real estate."

"A dream of yours, is it?" he asked in what he hoped was a bland tone. "To make a fortune?"

"Of course," she said with a tiny smile. "Who wouldn't want to have a fortune?"

Though her words were light, he thought he sensed a ribbon of bitterness twining through them. Maybe being a trust fund baby wasn't all parties and private jets.

"Anyway, right now I don't need a fortune," she said, in what he knew was a vast understatement. "Only a place to stay for a few days and something to do while I'm here. I'm grateful you've been kind enough to give me both."

Yeah, he was going to have a hell of a story when this was all over.

By the next day, Mimi was beginning to think stripping naked and tap-dancing in front of the paparazzi might be easier in the long run than the chore she'd set in front of herself.

She coughed at the cloud of dust that erupted as she yanked down the old-fashioned gingham curtains in the second bedroom upstairs. Simone sneezed, shaking her fuzzy little head. Her formerly pristine little white poochie was now the washed-out, yellow-gray of fading newsprint.

"You are going to need a serious bath," she told the dog ruefully. "Both of us are, I'm afraid."

Simone yipped and continued sniffing around the corners of the room, her tail wagging a mile a minute.

At least her dog was enjoying this little adventure of theirs. Mimi sighed. She wasn't hating it, it was just a bigger task than she had envisioned the day before.

The house wasn't filthy, exactly, just filled with the sort of grime that settled in homes where no one lived. Her father kept full-time staff at each of his residences but even then, dust tended to collect.

After a full day of cleaning and organizing, she was beginning to fear she had taken on a job too big for her to handle. Performing small housekeeping jobs under Gert's supervision in a well-maintained mansion with a large staff was a much different proposition than cleaning out a house that had been largely empty for the past several years.

She felt as grimy as these curtains and she had to wonder what her friends would say if they could see her now, with her hair covered by a particularly ugly Hermès scarf her latest stepmother had given her for Christmas and her skin covered in the same film as the walls.

This had been one of her more harebrained ideas—and that was saying something, since she'd had more than her share.

A few days ago when she flew from L.A. to Jackson Hole, she had expected to find herself being pampered by Gwen, coddled and taken care of by the one person in the world she counted on to care that she was pregnant and frightened and alone.

Instead, here she was dusting out corners and scrubbing baseboards for a man who had hardly said a half-dozen words to her since dinner the night before.

While the storm raged outside after dinner, he had mostly avoided her until she had fallen asleep on the sofa watching a DVD of a romantic comedy she'd seen twice already. He had rather tersely awakened her after nine and suggested she go sleep where she could stretch out.

This morning, he had been awake and out taking care of the horses and checking Gwen's pipes when Mimi awoke, at least according to the brusque note he'd left propped on the kitchen table.

"Help yourself to food," he had instructed, and Mimi had made a face at the note before grabbing a yogurt and a piece of toast.

That was the sum total of her interaction with another human being all day.

She wouldn't feel sorry for herself. That was the old Mimi. The new Mimi was all about finding her own inner strength, taking care of herself. She was twenty-six years old and going to be a mother in six months, responsible for another human being. It was long past time she took that terrifying step into adulthood.

She wadded up the dingy curtains into a bundle in her arms and was just about to carry them downstairs to the washing machine in the mudroom off the kitchen when she heard the front door open.

"Hey, Brant?" a distinctively feminine voice called out. "You know you've got a Mercedes stuck in your creek?"

Oh, crap. Mimi's arms tightened on the curtains. Despite her best efforts at avoiding the outside world, she supposed it was inevitable that Brant might have a visitor.

Her heart pounded as she backed against the wall, out of sight from the foot of the stairs. What should she do? Hide up here and hope whoever it was just went away? Or take her chances that she could bluff her way through and Brant's visitor wouldn't drive away from the Western Sky and immediately call TMZ?

A moment later, Simone took the choice out of her hands. Before Mimi could even think to stop her, the little dog bulleted out of the bedroom and scampered down the stairs, yipping the whole way.

"Well, hello," Mimi heard the woman say in surprise to the dog. "Where did you come from? Brant? What's going on? Whose car and whose dog?"

Mimi drew in a deep breath, dropped the curtains into a heap and walked to the landing at the top of the stairs.

"Mine," she called down. "I slid off the road during the storm the night before last. I haven't had a chance to get a tow out here yet to take care of it. And that little bundle of noise is Simone."

The woman was slim and blonde, dressed in bright red snow pants and a heavy matching parka with navy-blue stripes. She looked at the dog and then looked back at Mimi, her jaw sagging. "You're…"

"A mess," Mimi said quickly. "I know. I was cleaning out one of the rooms upstairs and I'm afraid I tangled with some cobwebs."

She walked down the staircase and held out her hand. "I'm Maura Howard," she said firmly.

The other woman finally closed her mouth, though Mimi could see suspicion still clouding her blue eyes.

"I'm Easton. Easton Springhill. I've got a ranch down the canyon a ways." Her gaze narrowed and she tilted her head. "This is going to sound crazy, but has anyone ever told you that you look remarkably like that silly woman in the tabloids? Mimi something or other? The one with all the boyfriends?"

Mimi forced a smile she was far from feeling. "I

get it all the time. It's a curse, believe me. Ridiculous, isn't she?"

Easton Springhill snickered a little. "I think she's great."

"Really?"

"Sure. She always makes me laugh. No matter what kind of a lousy day I'm having, I can always be glad at least that I'm not as dumb as a box of rocks."

Mimi kept her smile on by sheer force of will. She couldn't really be annoyed. She wasn't stupid, but plenty of her choices certainly had been.

"How did you get here?" she asked instead of snapping at the woman. "Has the snow stopped?"

"It seems to be slowing a little bit. The roads still are a mess but that's not a problem with the snowmobile. I figured I'd better make sure Brant has enough essentials to live on. He doesn't always remember to buy everything he needs for the pantry between visits. I brought over a couple of casseroles from my freezer as well as a few staples I thought he might need. Bread, milk, that sort of thing."

"That's thoughtful of you," Mimi murmured, wondering just what sort of relationship they shared. It must be a close one if the other woman felt comfortable just walking into his house without knocking.

Easton continued gazing at Mimi with that same slightly stunned look in her eyes.

"It's uncanny. The resemblance, I mean."

"Even with the layer of grit I'm wearing from scrubbing the walls upstairs?"

Drawing attention to her less than sleek appearance

seemed to convince Easton that she couldn't possibly be Mimi Van Hoyt.

"It's none of my business," the other woman said, "but were you on your way here to see Brant when you crashed? You must have been, I guess. I can't imagine why else you would be on Western Sky land."

"Actually, I thought I was coming to see Gwen Bianca, his caretaker," Mimi answered. "My visit was sort of a whim and I didn't call ahead of time or I would have found out she was out of the country."

"Yes, Gwen has a gallery showing in Milan. She's been working on it for months and was so excited about it."

Her former stepmother had probably told her in one of their occasional phone conversations and Mimi hadn't registered it, maybe because she was a self-absorbed bitch.

She sighed. Past tense. She was turning over a new leaf, right?

"I'm sure Gwen will be so sorry she missed you," Easton said.

"Not as sorry as I am to have missed her, believe me."

"So Brant gave you a place to stay while you wait for her to come back. Isn't that just like him?" She smiled but after a moment it slid away. "Sorry, I'm a little slow today. Back up a minute. If you're a guest of Brant's, why, again, are you covered in grime from scrubbing the walls?"

"I wanted to thank him for his kindness in giving me a place to stay for a few days so I offered to help him out a little."

Easton snickered. "And I actually thought for a minute you were Mimi Van Hoyt. How funny is that?"

Mimi did her best to force a smile. "Hilarious. Not exactly the housecleaning sort, is she?"

Before Easton could answer, the door opened behind them and Brant came into the entry. The open delight on his features when he saw the other woman erased any question that theirs was a close relationship.

"Hey, East!" he said with as close to a genuine smile as Mimi had seen. "I thought I heard a snowmobile."

"Can't sneak up on an Army Ranger, can I?"

"Not on a 600-horsepower Polaris, anyway."

This time he gave a full-fledged grin and Mimi stared. She had thought him handsome before in a clean-cut, no-nonsense sort of way. But when he smiled, he was the kind of gorgeous that curled a woman's toes.

"Any word from the newlyweds?" he asked.

"Tess called me this morning from Costa Rica to thank me again for hosting the wedding on such short notice. She bubbled, you know? I haven't seen her like that since high school."

"I still can't quite believe it." Brant shook his head. "Quinn and the homecoming queen. It boggles my mind."

"I think she's perfect for him."

Since Mimi had no idea whom they were talking about, she thought about edging back up the stairs and returning to her work and leaving them alone, but Easton seemed to have suddenly remembered she was there.

"Sorry, Maura," the other woman said with a rueful smile. "It's rude of us to talk about people you don't know. A good friend was married two days ago. He was able to coordinate the wedding with Brant's leave so Major Western here could stand up with him."

He was home on leave for a very limited time. Mimi suddenly realized the implications of that fact and she felt every bit the ditzy bimbo everybody believed her to be.

Dumber than a box of rocks, isn't that what Easton said?

She must be or she would have realized that perhaps Brant might have had other plans for his limited leave from a war zone. Instead of enjoying rest and relaxation—and possibly more than that with the very lovely woman who had braved a blizzard for him—he was forced to play host to a stranger. Mimi. A self-absorbed liar who was using him to avoid the unpleasant consequences of her own actions.

She felt small and ashamed and would have been tempted to leave right at that moment if her rental vehicle wasn't still stuck in a creek.

She could at least give them a little privacy now, she thought, even though the idea of the yummy Major Western with this woman made her insides twist unpleasantly.

Just a hint of that blasted morning sickness, she told herself.

"I, um, think I'll just go finish up the bedroom upstairs."

Easton held out an arm. "Wait a minute, Maura. Brant, what are you thinking to make a guest scrub your walls? Gwen or I can hire somebody to do that for you, just like we've always done."

"He's not making me," Mimi protested, disliking the note of censure in the other woman's voice. "I offered to help him prepare the house to sell."

Her words distracted Easton but she didn't look any happier about them than she did the idea of Brant's guest helping him with the cleaning.

"You're really serious about selling, then?"

He looked as if he'd rather be somewhere else. "You know it's for the best, East. The place is falling apart. I can't maintain it when I only come once a year. And as much as I appreciate you and Gwen working so hard to help me, she's moving now and you don't need one more burden now that you're on your own at Winder Ranch."

Easton's mouth clamped into a tight line, as if she were ready to cry. "I hate that everything's changing. If you sell the Western Sky, you won't have any reason to come back."

Feeling excessively like a third wheel, Mimi gave a longing look up the stairs. If she could figure out a way to gracefully escape the two of them without leaving more awkwardness behind, she would.

To her discomfort, Brant folded the woman into his arms, parka and all, and kissed her nose in a tender gesture that had those insides churning again.

"Now you're just being silly," he answered. "You're here. You know I'll always come back for that."

Despite his words, Easton didn't look appeased but she also didn't look as if she wanted to press the issue right now, with "Maura" looking on. "I'd better take off while I still have some daylight. You're going to want to put the food in the fridge."

He tugged the front of her beanie. "Be safe."

"That's my line, Major," she said with a sad sort of smile. "I'll see you again before you ship out."

"Deal."

Her smile widened when she turned to Mimi. "You shouldn't have to work for your room and board. I've got plenty of extra space at my place if you want to bunk there for a few days until Gwen gets back. I'm rattling around out there by myself and wouldn't mind the company at all."

The solution was a logical one, though Mimi was reluctant to take it for reasons she wasn't sure she wanted to examine too closely. "That's very generous of you. But I don't mind the work, really."

Easton looked doubtful. She gave her another long, searching look and she could almost see the other woman thinking how much she looked like, well, herself.

She really hoped Easton didn't say anything to Brant, who just might figure out his houseguest was someone other than she'd claimed.

To her relief, Easton only smiled. "Let me know if you change your mind. It's only a fifteen-minute ride on the Polaris."

"Thank you."

"Call me when you get home so I know you're safe," Brant ordered.

Easton rolled her eyes at him. "I manage by myself three hundred and sixty-five days out of the year, Brant."

"But when I'm here I reserve the right to worry."

"I suppose that's fair since I worry about you every

minute of those other three hundred and sixty-five days when you're not."

There was more than just affection between them, Mimi thought as the other woman left. This was a deep, emotional bond.

The realization left her depressed, for reasons she didn't understand.

Chapter 4

Easton left in a swirl of snow and wind and the roar of her powerful snow machine. As Brant closed the door behind her, he couldn't help thinking about the girl she had been, blond braids and freckles and an eager smile as she followed him and Quinn and Cisco around the ranch.

Their foster mother had called them her Four Winds. Like the Four Winds, they had scattered: Quinn Southerland to Seattle, where he ran a shipping company; Cisco Del Norte to Latin America, where he apparently wandered from cantina to cantina doing heaven knows what; and Brant to the Army and five tours of duty in the Middle East in seven years.

Only Easton had stayed. She had been running Winder Ranch for years, even before Jo's death in October.

As much as he still missed Jo, he knew Easton had

it much harder. Her aunt and uncle had raised Easton after her own parents died in a car accident when she was a teenager. Jo had been more than a mother figure to Easton. She had been her best friend and her confidante and he knew Easton had to be terribly lonely without her.

He wished he could make it right but he didn't think the answer was to hang on to his own ranch simply because he knew Easton would be upset when he sold it.

"She's lovely."

He shifted to find Mimi still standing nearby. What surprised him more, he wondered: that he'd forgotten her presence or that she had actually noticed any other woman existed but herself?

Not fair, he admitted with some chagrin. He was judging her purely on her public persona, which so far seemed to be a very different thing than the way she acted away from the cameras.

"She is. Lovely, I mean. And, as usual, she's right to go after me like she did. You shouldn't have to clean for your supper. You're a guest here and I'm not a very good host for allowing you to scrub my walls and clean my toilets."

"Oh, give it a rest, Major. We've been through this."

"It still doesn't seem right."

"Are you saying you think I should take your friend up on her generous offer and stay with her?"

He should agree. He knew it was the proper thing to do and he certainly didn't want Mimi underfoot if she didn't have to be, did he?

But when he opened his mouth to agree and offer to drive her to Winder Ranch on the Western Sky snowmobile, the words seemed to clog in his throat. Despite his better judgment, he didn't want her to go yet. He wasn't quite ready just yet to give up the guilty pleasure of having her here, of watching her in living color.

"It's your call. Either way, you really don't have to clean the house. You can just be a guest. East is right, I can hire somebody to do all this."

"You did hire somebody," she said emphatically. "Me. We made a deal and I'm not going to let you back out of it. If you're sure you want to sell the ranch, I want to help you ready it for the appraisal."

He shouldn't be so relieved, he told himself. But he couldn't help a little inward smile as he headed for the kitchen, shrugging out of his ranch coat as he went. "Well, thanks to East, it looks like we won't starve, even if the blizzard keeps up for days."

"That won't happen, will it?" she asked with wide eyes, though he thought she looked almost relieved at the idea.

He had to wonder again what kind of trouble she might be running away from that she thought his run-down old ranch offered a safe haven. He could only hope it wasn't anything illegal. One of their decorated officers harboring a fugitive might not go over well with the Army brass.

"It's possible for a series of storms to follow one right after the other if we get on the right weather track," he answered as he began putting away the food items Easton had brought over. "When I was a kid, we had one winter where we missed twenty-one days of school because of snow. Storms just kept coming and coming.

We spent a miserably short summer that year because of all the make-up days."

She looked so astonished that he couldn't resist needling her. "Did it snow much where you grew up, Ms. Howard?"

She looked blank for only a moment, then quickly recovered. "M-Maura," she said. "I told you I moved around a lot when I was a kid. But never anywhere with this kind of snow. It seems…unreal, somehow."

He definitely agreed with that. Since the moment he'd seen that vehicle head for the creek, he'd somehow slipped into *The Twilight Zone*.

"Well, I guess I'd better do something about dinner. I'll see if I can throw one of these casseroles Easton brought over into the oven."

"I'll go finish up the bedroom I was cleaning."

He nodded and tried not to look too obvious as he watched her move back up the stairs, her powder puff of a dog following closely behind. She had some silky-looking scarf thing over her hair, a sunny yellow T-shirt and a pair of what he was quite certain were designer jeans that hugged her figure.

More than anything, he suddenly wished that she really *was* Maura Howard and not Mimi Van Hoyt. Maura Howard seemed like a nice woman, someone he would enjoy getting to know a little better. Someone who might not mind that he was a rough-edged Army officer with a tumbledown ranch full of bad memories.

Wouldn't it be nice if she could be just a regular woman who worked for an obscure charitable organization and who preferred cuddling in bed during a blizzard to walking the red carpet at a movie premiere?

He was fiercely attracted to Maura Howard or Mimi Van Hoyt or whoever she was. He wanted to tell himself it was just a normal, red-blooded reaction to a beautiful woman, but the more time he spent with her, the more he was beginning to fear it was more than that.

He sighed and headed for the kitchen. It didn't matter how attracted he was to her. Maura Howard might be polite enough to him during this surreal experience they were sharing. But he had a feeling that since he wasn't a movie star or a minor European prince or some jetsetting playboy, Mimi Van Hoyt wouldn't give him the time of day.

They shared a pretty good dinner of some chicken-and-broccoli pasta dish. Or at least he thought it was good. Mimi didn't eat much and she seemed subdued.

"I think I'll go start tackling the second bedroom upstairs," she said.

"Forget it." He spoke in the same implacable tone his men knew better than to question, but Mimi didn't take the hint.

"Why not?"

"Because you've been on your feet cleaning all day and you look exhausted."

She frowned. "Didn't anyone ever tell you it's not polite to tell a woman she looks less than her best?"

"Didn't anyone ever tell *you* it's not wise to argue with a man who knows a dozen ways to kill an enemy combatant with a dinner fork?"

"Why, Major Western, is that a threat or a joke?"

"I'll let you choose."

She smiled, apparently deciding on the latter. "If

you're not careful, I might suspect you have a sense of humor."

He shrugged. "I think it's somewhere buried under all that camouflage."

She smiled again and he wanted to soak it in. Given the fierce attraction that coiled through him like concertina wire, spending the evening with her probably wasn't the greatest of ideas. He had found every excuse he could think of all day to avoid spending any great stretch of time with her, but Brant was suddenly in the mood to live dangerously.

"Would you like to watch a movie? Or I can go out and sweep the snow out of the satellite dish. There's a basketball game I wouldn't mind catching tonight."

"Sure. I like basketball," she answered and he suddenly remembered she had once dated one of the Lakers.

When he returned, she was curled up in one corner of the sofa, looking half-asleep with one of his favorite thrillers open on her lap. She seemed subdued and he thought he saw a shadow of sadness in those mossy green eyes. He wondered again what had brought her fleeing to Gwen in Idaho without making arrangements first, then reminded himself it was none of his business.

Though it was always a tricky operation, sweeping the dish out had done the trick to fix the satellite system and he quickly tuned in to the game he had hoped to watch. After a few moments, Mimi set aside her book and seemed to be engrossed in the game, though he still thought there was a hint of melancholy in her gaze.

In her understated clothes and with her hair back in a simple ponytail, she looked a far cry from the sleek and polished socialite. She looked young and fresh and so beautiful it was all he could do to stay on his side of the sofa, to firmly remember they lived in entirely different worlds.

"You know what would make this perfect?" he asked.

She gave him a curious look and he imagined their definition of perfect probably diverged considerably.

"Popcorn. Buttered popcorn, a fire in the woodstove, a knuckle-biter game on TV and a pretty woman to watch it with me. Do you have any idea how many guys in my entire company would volunteer for latrine duty for a year just for the chance to change places with me right now?"

She smiled a little. "You and your company all apparently have simple tastes, Major."

She was far from simple. He was beginning to think there was far more to Mimi Van Hoyt than a big smile and a lot of flash.

Her silly white dog followed him into the kitchen and lapped at her water and the silver dish of food from the supply Mimi had carried in one of her suitcases.

"Not too much of that water. I don't want Mimi to have to take you out all night," he muttered. The dog yipped at him and wagged her tail and he couldn't help but smile.

The Twilight Zone wasn't necessarily a scary place, just different.

When he returned from the kitchen with two bowls of popcorn, he was relieved to see the score was still tied. He came in just in time to catch a car commercial showing a little nuclear family with a father and mother loading a smiling little toddler into a car seat. Just before they drove away into supposedly happily ever after in their dreamy minivan, the father winked at the toddler, who giggled hard.

Almost instantly, another commercial flashed on, this one for peanut butter, a father and a kid of maybe three sitting together at a kitchen table making sandwiches. The little boy had peanut butter smeared across his mouth and a minute later the camera panned back to the dad, who now had the peanut butter on his cheek where the kid had kissed him.

"Do the advertisers really think all the dads watching the game are going to get right up and make PB and J sandwiches with their kids?" he asked conversationally as he handed her a bowl of popcorn. "With a close game like this, most of them have even forgotten they *have* kids right about now."

To his astonishment, she looked stricken at his words.

"What's the matter?" he asked, trying to figure out what he'd said.

She let out a long breath and manufactured what was obviously a false smile. "Nothing. Nothing at all. Thank you for the popcorn."

She ate very little of it, though, he noticed. And she seemed to have lost most of her interest in the game. After only maybe a quarter of an hour of her picking up a kernel here and there, Simone jumped up and scampered to the door in an obvious signal.

"Don't get up," Mimi said. "I'll put her out."

Simone had made it clear she much preferred going out the back kitchen door. The snow was still deep there but the house's bulk had protected the area from the worst of the snowdrifts.

A few moments later, Mimi returned with the dog in her arms, drying her paws with the towel by the back door he'd reserved for that purpose. "I don't think I can make it to the final buzzer," she said. "I'm just going to maybe take a bath and go to bed."

If he lived to be two hundred, he would never understand women, Brant decided. "How can you leave with a tied score and only two minutes left on the clock?"

She shrugged. "It's been a long day and I was thinking about painting the guest room tomorrow. I found some white paint in the utility room that looks fairly new. You'd be amazed what a coat of white paint can do for a room with the right accessories. Do you mind?"

"I think you're crazy. You know that, don't you?"

"I think you're absolutely right. I must be or I would have gone back with Easton earlier." She still looked upset, but for the life of him, he couldn't figure out why.

"Why didn't you?"

"Excellent question." She pushed her face into the dog's fur to avoid meeting his gaze. "I like this place, as crazy as that sounds. Simone does, too. There's a sort of peace here. I can't explain it."

He had to think there was some truth to that. By rights, he should hate it here. His childhood had been a difficult time for him, filled with anger and conflict and insecurities. During the bad years, he had dreaded coming home on the school bus. Once he had even stayed on, hunched down on the seat with some vague idea of camping out there until the next morning so he wouldn't have to face his father. His plan might have worked if their old driver, Jesse Richards, hadn't discovered him when he parked the bus for the night at his own place down the canyon.

Despite the bad memories of the Western Sky when he was a kid, he had plenty of good ones, too. When he was out on a mission, this was the place he dreamed about.

So maybe everybody was right. Maybe he should reconsider his decision to sell.

He pushed away the thoughts for now.

"It's just a broken-down ranch house," he answered Mimi. "Yeah, you do sound a little crazy."

"Not the boil-a-rabbit-on-your-stove kind, I promise."

"And wouldn't that be exactly the thing the boil-a-rabbit sort would say?"

She smiled that little smile again, but it didn't quite reach her green eyes. "I'm sure a big, tough Army Ranger like you can take care of himself. But don't worry. I won't even know if you lock your door."

She headed toward her bedroom on the other side of the kitchen and Brant briefly wondered what she would do if he followed her in there and gave in to the low hum of desire he'd been trying to ignore all day.

No, crazy or not, he wouldn't be visiting Mimi Van Hoyt's room anytime soon, he thought, and forced himself to turn back to the game, though it took a superhuman effort.

He might have been able to stick to his pledge to leave her alone if he hadn't heard her crying.

An hour later, Brant stood outside the guest bedroom listening to the quiet weeping coming from the other side of the door. He hissed out a low curse, though he wasn't quite sure if it was aimed more at her or at himself.

He was a sucker for a crying woman. He always had been—maybe because his mother had so seldom cried.

Paula Western had been a master at containing her emotions. Her reaction after Curtis's death had been to turn into herself and shut him and his father out. Except for that single devastating outburst when she had told him she wished he had been the one to drown instead of his baby brother, she had become an empty husk, void of love or affection or emotions of any kind.

He could vividly remember the first time Easton had cried after he moved to Winder Ranch. He had been twelve and Easton was nine, a little tomboy with blond braids living with her parents on the ranch, where her dad was the foreman.

One of the barn kittens had been run over by a tractor driven by a ranch hand. They had all seen it happen but had been too far away to prevent the accident. Easton had been inconsolable and Brant well remembered his panicked compulsion to do something, to fix the situation somehow, even though he knew that particular tragedy had been far beyond anyone's control.

Nothing had changed. He was still compelled to try to fix things, as much as he wanted to hide out and pretend he didn't hear her.

"Mi—Maura?" He caught himself just in time before he would have used her real name. "Everything okay in there?"

The low whimpering stopped. "Yes. Everything's fine." She didn't say anything else and he sighed, wishing like the devil that he were the sort of guy who could just walk away and leave her to her obvious distress. "Are you sure?"

"Fine."

"Because I could swear I heard someone crying in there."

"I, um, was just humming."

She must think he was the dimmest bulb on the shelf.

"Humming? That's really what you're going with here?"

After another pause, she opened the door a crack and he could see her nose was a little pink, her eyes slightly swollen. He had a feeling Mimi was the sort of woman other females loved to hate for a number of reasons, not least of which was how those subtle signs of distress only made her look impossibly lovely, in a fragile, delicate, take-care-of-me sort of way.

She aimed a glare at him that burst that bubble quickly. "Yes. I was humming. What's it to you?"

He raised his hands in the universal sign of surrender. "You're right. Hum yourself to sleep, for all I care. But here, let me get this teardrop that's not really a teardrop."

He stepped forward and touched his thumb to the skin just at the side of her nose with one finger, where one crystalline bead of moisture pooled.

At his touch, her eyes widened, her gaze caught by his. She was warm and soft, the softest thing he'd ever touched in his life. He wanted nothing more than to slide his hand and cup her chin, to explore the curve of her cheekbone and that delicate shell of an ear.

At that single touch, he wanted to keep touching

and touching until he'd explored every inch of delectable skin.

She stared at him for a long, drawn-out moment and he could swear he saw a spark of answering awareness in her eyes. Her dark pupils expanded, until the black nearly overpowered the green. He leaned forward just a hair and she caught her breath.

The instant before his mouth would have found hers, reality exploded like a shoulder-fired missile in his head. Kissing her would only make this hunger in his gut all the more painfully intense, only make him more cognizant of what he was missing.

He dropped his hand and forced himself to throttle back.

He thought he saw disappointment flicker in her eyes, but she stepped away and lowered her eyes. "I'm sorry if I disturbed you. It won't happen again, I promise."

"Does that mean you're done or just that you'll keep your...humming to yourself from now on?"

She didn't answer, just seemed to grip the door that much harder. "Good night, Brant."

He knew it was corny but hearing her say his name in that throaty voice sent heat rippling through his insides.

For a long, protracted moment, he stared at her standing there in a soft, pale green nightgown that only seemed to make her eyes look more vivid. He still wanted to kiss her, with a heat and urgency that shocked him. But he had learned a long time ago that just because he wanted something didn't make it good for him.

Chapter 5

"Are you sure you're going to be okay now? No more...
humming?"

Mimi gazed at him, so big and commanding and
decent. For one insane moment, she wanted to throw
herself against that powerful chest and sob out everything, all the lousy choices she had made that led her
to this place up to this moment.

She was appalled at herself for breaking down—and
for doing it where she had a potential audience.

It had to be the hormones. She hadn't meant to cry.
When Brant had been making popcorn earlier, a promo
for one of the entertainment news shows had come on,
touting their insider coverage of the fifty-thousand-
dollar Vera Wang dress Jessalyn was going to wear in
only a few days' time.

She probably would have been just fine with that,

but then in rapid succession during halftime had come two sappy commercials showing sweet-as-cotton-candy interactions of fathers and their children, highlighting even more clearly what she knew her child would have to do without.

Even with that, she might have been able to hold back the crying fest. But after her bath, as she had been pulling a nightgown on she had caught sight of her tiny, barely noticeable baby bump in the mirror and out of nowhere she had been overwhelmed with a combination of fierce joy and abject terror.

She was only hormonal, she reminded herself. That's the reason tears seemed to threaten at the oddest moments these days.

She had never been much of a crier, since she had learned early that her tears had absolutely no effect on Werner Van Hoyt. He would look down his aquiline nose in that slightly bored look he'd perfected, glance at his antique Patek Philippe, and then ask her if she was quite finished yet.

But here was Brant Western, a man she barely knew, showing up at her bedroom door with a slightly panicked but determined look on his face at the sound of her tears. Instead of ignoring her and walking by, as most sane men would probably do when confronted with a strange woman's weeping, he stopped and knocked to ask if she was all right.

Sharing her fears with *someone* would be so comforting, but she couldn't tell him, of course.

She barely knew the man. How could she just blurt out that she'd had an affair with an engaged Grammy winner who was getting married in a few days, that she was now pregnant from said affair, and that she planned to keep the child and raise it on her own, despite the father's strident objections?

Framed so bluntly, it all sounded so stark and sordid. And once she put some of it into words, she was afraid she would blurt out everything. Her identity, Marco's, all the stupid choices that had led her to this moment, and then Major Western would despise her, as well he should.

When he touched her cheek with such tenderness to wipe away the tear she claimed didn't exist, she thought she had seen a spark of male interest in his eyes. But of course she couldn't have. He and the so-beautiful Easton had feelings for each other and Mimi had made a personal vow that she would never allow herself to become involved with another woman's man.

Been there, done that. She'd been the "other woman" only once in her life, with Marco—though she knew rumors said otherwise—and she wasn't about to repeat the experience, no matter how tempting the package.

"I'm fine. Good night, Major."

She closed the door firmly behind her, then leaned against it. As tempting as it was, she couldn't spill everything to Brant. She was on her own now. She couldn't count on anybody but herself.

Not her father, not feckless celebrities who cheated on their betrothed with other feckless celebrities, and certainly not soldiers she barely knew who watched her with quiet blue eyes and offered an entirely too appealing shoulder to cry upon.

The snow was still falling when she awoke the next morning. The light outside her window was murky and pale but she could see through a gap in the curtains that soft flakes continued to drift down.

Maybe the snow would continue to fall and fall and fall and she would never have to return to real life.

She couldn't hide out here forever. Eventually she would have to face the consequences of her decision. Her father would have to know. He would no doubt be gravely disappointed in her. Nothing new there.

She didn't care. She would weather that storm like this old ranch weathered all the Idaho winters.

She touched her abdomen. "We'll tough it out together, kiddo," she said out loud, waking up Simone.

The dog stretched and yawned, then jumped off the bed to the floor and skittered to the door, where she stood wagging her tail insistently in a clear indication of her needs.

Mimi sighed and reached for her robe. She cautiously opened her bedroom door and peered out into the hall. She did *not* want to encounter her host yet this morning, not when she was still so mortified about her emotional breakdown the night before.

To her relief, Brant wasn't anywhere in sight, so she quickly let Simone outside. When she opened the door, she saw that the snow had indeed slowed but the drifts had to be higher than her waist in places.

It would take them days to dig out, she thought happily. Real life could wait at least a few days longer.

She showered quickly after letting Simone back inside and spent only twenty minutes on her hair and makeup, definitely some kind of record. Her stylist Giselle would probably blow a gasket if she caught

Mimi with her hair a frizzy mess and wearing only barebones foundation and mascara.

She didn't care. She gazed into the round warped mirror in the bathroom. What did she need with Giselle? She thought she looked good. She had gained a little weight with the baby but for the first time since she hit adolescence, she thought a little extra weight wasn't necessarily a bad thing on her. It filled in some of the hollows of her features, made her almost lush.

Brant still hadn't returned to the house by the time Mimi finished a quick breakfast, so she headed up to the larger upstairs bedroom.

Now that the snow had begun to clear just a little, she had a fantastic view from up here of the west slope of the Tetons, jagged and raw in the distance. It was a breathtaking vista and she thought that if she owned the ranch, she would make this her bedroom and position her bed looking out so that she could always wake to that view.

She caught her breath at the idea. What if *she* bought the Western Sky? It would be a wonderful place to raise a baby, surrounded by dogs and horses and those mountains.

Once planted, the idea refused to die and as she prepped the room for paint, she had great fun imagining what changes she might make if she had full reign here.

A new kitchen would be at the top of her list. And perhaps she would take that wide porch off the back and screen it in so that she could sit out there on summer evenings while the baby played on the floor.

"You weren't lying about the humming."

Mimi gasped and whirled around to find Brant in

the doorway looking tall and gorgeous and completely yummy. How had she missed hearing him come in?

She aimed a glare at Simone for not warning her but the little dog only bared her teeth in her version of an embarrassed smile for slacking on her guard-dog duties.

"I never lie," she lied.

A tiny dimple appeared in the corner of his mouth. "Is that right?"

Just about every word she had said to him since she arrived had either been a half-truth or an outright fib—or had concealed something she hadn't wanted him to know—but she decided to keep that information to herself.

"You must have left the house early. Is everything okay?"

"I was just checking the pipes at Gwen's. So far no breaks in the line. I heard from the furnace company and they're going to try to schedule the job Friday."

"That's good."

"Did you have breakfast?"

"I grabbed a cup of tea and some toast."

"I made fresh coffee."

"I saw it." And she had craved some desperately but she had read in one of those secret pregnancy books that she should avoid caffeine during the pregnancy. She had also read to avoid oil-based paints. To her relief, the cans she found were all water-based.

Funny how there was nothing in the books about avoiding gorgeous soldiers with wide shoulders and elusive smiles. He looked tired, she thought. But then, his eyes had looked tired since she arrived.

"I saw the snow seems to have eased a little bit," she said.

"Some. According to the forecast, it should snow until mid-morning and then we can start the fun of digging out."

"That's a relief, I'm sure."

"I don't know if I'd say that but at least we'll be able to get your car fixed."

She wasn't convinced that was something to stick in the positive column. "When do you have to report back to the Army?"

"Tuesday."

"Less than a week. Oh, Brant, I'm so sorry. You've had to spend your entire free time playing host to a guest you hadn't expected and don't want. It was supremely selfish of me to intrude like this, to just assume I wouldn't be in the way. You have only a few days to call your own and I ruined everything for you."

To her deep mortification, her throat swelled with tears and she again cursed the pregnancy hormones.

He tilted his head, studying her with a puzzled sort of concern. "Please don't start humming again."

She managed a watery laugh and focused on thinking about baby names until she was calmer. "I'm sorry. I'll spare you that, at least."

He was silent for a moment to give her a chance to compose herself, a small courtesy she found touching and thoughtful.

"You've already been busy this morning," he said.

"I think I'm just about ready to start painting."

"Do you need some help?"

She should just tell him now and push him out the

door. But it was his house, after all. If he wanted to spend his limited leave with a paintbrush in his hand, how could she possibly stop him?

"You've lucked out. I've already done the hardest part, the prep work. I'm just about ready to start painting." She held up the angled brush she'd found with the paint supplies in the storage room. "Do you want to roll or cut in the edges?"

"I'm assuming that by the sound of it, cutting in the edges takes some skill with a paintbrush, which is something I'm sorry to say I don't possess. I think I should be able to handle a roller without any major catastrophes."

She smiled and handed him the paint roller she had also found in the utility room. "Just remember that you offered."

He seemed to be wading deeper and deeper into The Twilight Zone.

An hour later, Brant finished rolling paint on the last section of wall and stood back to survey the work.

Mimi stood on a ladder, her arms above her head as she angled the brush carefully to keep the paint away from the ceiling and trim.

Who would have guessed that Mimi Van Hoyt even knew how to hold a paintbrush, forget about how to wield it so expertly. When in her pampered life would she possibly have had the opportunity to paint a room? He would have thought her father hired teams of high-priced designers for projects like this.

The woman was a complete mystery to him. He wanted to ask what she was *really* doing in Cold Creek

Canyon. Who or what was she running from? What was behind that little glimmer of sadness he sometimes caught in her eyes, those tears she hadn't been at all successful in hiding the night before?

At this point, he was going to have to come right out and ask her since all his subtle attempts to extract information had led him to dead end after dead end.

No matter what he asked or how he asked it, she somehow deflected every question, until he had no clearer idea what she might be doing there than he had when she showed up.

He had questioned hardened enemy combatants who weren't as adept at avoiding the truth as Mimi Van Hoyt.

He found her fascinating. Everything about her, from the way she nibbled on her bottom lip while she concentrated on a tricky corner to the way she focused completely on his face when he was talking to the lush curves that gave him entirely inappropriate ideas when she was climbing up and down the ladder.

Nobody would ever believe she was actually here in his ramshackle house, with her curly dark hair tied back in a ponytail and a tiny spray of paint splattering her cheek like white freckles.

He couldn't quite believe it—nor was he particularly thrilled about the way he couldn't seem to stop watching her.

At least for the last hour, she had completely distracted him from the pain and guilt that seemed to follow him everywhere.

"You were right," he said a moment later as he slid the roller back into the tray.

"I was? About what?" She sounded as surprised as if she'd spent her entire existence being told otherwise.

"About the paint. I'm amazed at what a difference a simple whitewash can make. It looks like a whole new room."

"Wait until we put the second coat up. I was thinking I'll move the furniture around a little bit to take advantage of that stellar view. If you angle the bed a little, the first thing your guests will see are those mountains out there. And what do you think about moving that watercolor that's in the hallway where it's too dark to be appreciated? It would fit right there on the south wall."

He gave her a careful look. "You're into this, aren't you?"

She blinked at him from her perch atop the ladder. "What?"

"Giving new life to this old place."

She looked taken aback at first, and then slowly considering as she climbed down the ladder. "I do enjoy it," she said, wiping her hands on a rag. "I told you I've done it before. A friend of mine from school flips houses in L.A. and she sometimes lets me help her stage the place for an open house."

"In between your charity work." He must have missed the paparazzi coverage of her renovating an old house.

"This is just a hobby. You know. For fun."

Before he had become acquainted with her these past few days, he would have thought her whole life was about having fun. After spending a little time in her company, he wasn't so sure. He had a feeling life hadn't been the smooth sail for Mimi that people seemed to think.

"Marisa calls me whenever she needs another set of hands. It gets me out of my routine, you know? A change of pace."

"Have you thought about doing this as a career? Staging houses, I mean?"

"I couldn't!" she exclaimed. "I don't know the first thing about what I'm doing."

"That hasn't stopped you here."

She gazed at him, her eyes a deep, startled green. "You really think I could?"

"Why not?"

"Why not." She looked rather dazed by the idea and he wondered just what he might have unleashed.

"I never thought... I mean, I'm always glad to help Marisa. We always have a good time, but that's just her telling me what to do."

"You don't have anybody telling you what to do here. How to place the furniture or hang the pictures or whatever."

"You're right." She smiled then, that radiant smile he couldn't get enough of, the one the public seemed to adore. "That is a really interesting idea, Major. I'm going to have to give it some thought."

He managed a smile in return, even though his insides were jumping around like sand fleas.

"You've got a little bit of paint on your nose."

"Where?"

"Not so much a smudge as a few tiny splatters. You look like you've got white freckles."

Color rose along her cheekbones, making the spots

stand out in stark relief, much to his astonishment. She took the cloth, found a clean corner, and started dabbing at her face, but in completely the wrong spot.

If the idea of her exploring the possibility of going into the real estate business was a good one, this ranked right up there on the opposite side of the spectrum. It was a phenomenally dangerous impulse but Brant couldn't seem to stop himself from stepping forward and taking the cloth from her hands.

"No. Here. Let me."

He dabbed along the side of her nose and then just along the angled ridge of her cheekbone.

His fingers brushed her skin as they had the night before and he heard her sharp intake of breath, but he was too busy fighting back his own fierce hunger to cup her face in his hands and press his mouth fiercely to hers.

A smart man would turn around and walk out of the room. No, a smart man would just keep on going until he'd put another zip code between himself and a dangerous woman like Mimi Van Hoyt.

But right now he didn't feel very smart. He suddenly ached to taste her, just once. She was a soft, beautiful woman and he was a hardened soldier who had been far too long without much sweetness in his life.

Years from now, when he saw her in the newstands, looking polished and beautiful and worlds away from his life, he could remember how their worlds had once intersected just for a moment.

He stepped forward and lowered his head. One kiss, he told himself. What could possibly be the harm?

She tasted sweet and sensual at the same time, like deep, rich chocolate drizzled over vanilla ice cream.

For a good ten seconds, she stood frozen like a spear of ice as his mouth moved over hers. At first, she didn't exactly respond but she didn't jerk away in outrage, either. As he deepened the kiss, she seemed to give a little shiver, her hands gripping his shirt, and he felt the seductive slide of her tongue against his. And then she was kissing him with as much wild heat as he could have ever dreamed.

He was hard in an instant. How could he not be? She was soft and warm and the most beautiful woman he'd ever seen in his life and she was right here in his arms, kissing him like she never wanted him to stop.

Chapter 6

She was sinking, sinking, sinking.

For long, wondrous moments, Mimi let herself be carried away on the slow, leisurely current of this delicious attraction. His mouth was firm and determined on hers and he was big and solid and muscled and she just wanted to nestle against him and stay here forever.

Gradually, a tiny hint of reason began to flutter cautiously through her, like a tiny moth unfurling its wings for the first time.

She wanted so much to ignore it, to swat at the annoying little thing until it disappeared. In his arms she could be Maura Howard, someone good and decent. Someone much better than she was.

She wanted to stay right here in his arms. For now, the only important thing was the two of them and this delicious heat between them, sliding around and through her like a ribbon of river cutting through a steep canyon.

Brant kissed like a man who put a great deal of thought and energy into it. He seemed to know just how to dance his mouth across hers, just where to slide that tongue.

She wrapped her arms around his back, soaking in the solid strength of his muscles and the scent of him, of laundry soap and some sort of sage and cedar aftershave and the underlying sharpness of paint around them.

More than anything, she wanted to stay in this room kissing him while the snow drifted down in lazy flakes outside. But that annoying moth of a conscience continued to flutter at the edge of her thoughts until she couldn't ignore it any longer.

Easton. Brant had feelings for his beautiful neighbor, with the sleek blond hair and the big blue eyes.

He belonged to someone else and Mimi had no right to kiss him like this. She couldn't do this again. She *wouldn't*. She had just spent three terrible, guilt-ridden months in a furtive relationship with a man who was committed to someone else.

She had believed Marco when he told her his engagement with Jessalyn was just for show, that he didn't love her, that he would figure out a way to break things off before the wedding.

She had known, somewhere deep inside, that he was lying to her, but she had been too caught up in the thrill of the moment and had ignored the voice of reason.

She couldn't ignore it now.

She was going to be someone's mother in six months. Wasn't it past time that she became someone she could like and respect? Tangling tongues with a man whose heart belonged to someone else didn't seem the way to achieve that particular goal.

She closed her eyes, fighting the part of her that just wanted to hang on tight to Brant, to absorb a little of his strength.

No. She needed to stand on her own, to find her own strength.

"Stop."

To her grave chagrin, instead of sounding tough and determined, the word came out a tiny squeak, one she wasn't sure he even heard.

She drew in a breath and tried again.

"Stop!" The second time, the word came out overloud, especially in the quiet bedroom, and Brant froze.

After a long moment, he groaned and wrenched his mouth away and for a long moment they stood bare inches apart, their breathing heavy and their gazes locked.

The raw hunger in his eyes sent an answering throb humming through her. She was so very tempted to smash that little moth of conscience under her shoes and just plunge back into the heat of his arms. But if she couldn't find the strength to do the right thing now, however was she going to stand up against her father and all the others who would have a problem with her pregnancy?

"I don't want this." Her voice wobbled a little but it still held a note of determination. "Not with you."

She saw disbelief and even a little hurt in his eyes before he shuttered his expression. After another moment, he stepped away. "Apparently I misread some kind of sign."

She closed her eyes so she didn't reveal to him that he had misread *nothing*. She had wanted him to kiss her, had craved it desperately.

If she hadn't listened to that blasted fledgling conscience, she would still be wrapped around him. The shame of just how much she still wanted to ignore it turned her voice sharper than she had intended.

"Why would you just jump to the conclusion that I'm the sort of woman who would start tangling tongues with someone she barely knows?"

He gave her a long look. "I don't know. Maybe because that's just what you *did?*"

Her mouth tightened and she opted to go on the offensive. "You took me by surprise and didn't give me a chance to react. I was too stunned to push you away."

"So your hands in my hair and your tongue in my mouth, that was just you being stunned?"

She glared. "I did not come to Idaho to start something with some soldier just trying to hit on anybody warm and willing while he's home on leave."

She immediately regretted the words, especially when his color rose and his jaw tightened. He suddenly looked rough and hardened, every inch a warrior. Not a wise move, taunting a man who lived a dangerous life she couldn't even imagine, especially when she was alone here at his ranch and completely at his mercy.

Easton was the only person who knew for certain where she was, she suddenly realized.

He wouldn't hurt her, she told herself, though the hard anger in his eyes wasn't an encouraging sign.

"Well, you're obviously not willing," he said in a lethally soft voice. "And not particularly warm, either, when it comes to that. My mistake."

She had wounded him, she realized, by implying any woman would do as well as the next one. For a moment, she wanted to apologize, but then she remembered Easton and the obvious affection between the two of them and she glared right back at him.

"Now that we know where we stand, I'm going to go out and check on the horses and see if I can start clearing away some of the snow yet."

The sooner you leave, the better. He didn't say the words but she caught the subtext anyway.

After he stalked out of the room, she eased onto the edge of the bed, to the slick plastic she had found to protect the furnishings in the room from the paint.

She had never been kissed like that, with such fierce concentration, such raw intensity. She touched a finger to her lips and closed her eyes, reliving the heat and wonder of it.

After a long moment, she opened her eyes and slid from the bed with a crackle of plastic. Enough. She had to get back to work and forget the past few moments ever happened, though she had a feeling that was going to be a harder task than scrubbing every inch of his old house.

Brant didn't come inside at all for lunch, something that left her feeling both grateful and guilty—grateful for the space and distance between them right now but guilty over the idea of him going hungry. She could hear the rumble of some sort of heavy machinery outside, and once she had peeked out the window and saw him on a powerful-looking tractor pushing snow with smooth, practiced motions.

Simone jumped up on a chair near the window in the kitchen and watched Brant on the tractor as if she'd never seen anything quite so fascinating.

Mimi knew just how her dog felt. She sighed and dumped the rest of her sandwich into the garbage.

The second coat in the bedroom took her less than an hour since she didn't need to be as precise around the edges. He still hadn't returned to the house by the time she finished cleaning up the brushes and the roller and returning the paint supplies to the utility room. After she finished, she realized she was exhausted, another of those little pregnancy joys.

A small nap was definitely in order, she decided, before she tackled the upstairs bathroom.

When she awoke, she was astonished to see she had slept for two hours and the light outside her bedroom was pale with late-afternoon sun.

Some days back in L.A., she wouldn't even get up until two or three in the afternoon so she could go clubbing all night. She couldn't go back to that world, ever. She didn't want to, even if everything hadn't changed with that simple pregnancy test.

That world, the endless quest for fun and excitement, had all seemed so vital. Now she could clearly see how very empty her life had been.

She was twenty-six years old and didn't know the first thing about responsibility. She had somehow squeaked her way to a degree in public relations and marketing from UCLA, probably because her father had donated a large sum to the university, but she had no idea what to do with her education.

She thought of Brant's suggestion that she consider staging houses. Real estate. Mimi shook her head. Maybe she had inherited more from her father than green eyes and a temper. Still, it was exciting to think about the possibilities.

Her stomach rumbled a bit and she realized the two bites of sandwich she'd eaten at lunch just weren't enough now that she was eating for two and had to consider things like folic acid and calcium intake.

She took a little extra care in the bathroom with her hair and makeup then stood at the mirror for a long moment, wary of walking out into the kitchen and facing Brant again.

Their easy companionship of the morning while they had worked together painting seemed a long time ago and she wasn't looking forward to the tension she feared would tug between them now that they'd kissed.

She couldn't hide out here in the bathroom hugging an old-fashioned bowl sink forever, she reminded herself. She could handle whatever challenges life threw at her, even in the form of a mouthwatering man who gave her entirely inappropriate ideas.

She opened the door to her bedroom and heard him in the kitchen before she saw him. He was talking on the phone and though she didn't intend to eavesdrop, she couldn't help but hear his words.

"I know I told you I would try to make it down for a few days, Abby, but this has been a bear of a storm and there have been…complications at the ranch."

Abby? Yet another woman? She frowned. The man

did get around. But then, he'd been in the Middle East for several months and she imagined dating opportunities weren't exactly thick on the ground there.

Mimi frowned as she suddenly realized *she* was the complication he was talking about at the ranch that made it difficult for him to leave to visit his apparently endless string of honeys.

"Yeah, I understand," Brant was saying. "I'm sorry things haven't worked out like I planned. But I'm still flying out of Salt Lake City and my flight doesn't leave until late Tuesday. What if I come down in the morning and spend the day before I have to be at the airport? A short visit is better than nothing."

He was quiet as Abby, whoever she was, must have responded. "Yeah," he said after a moment. "I know, sweetheart. It's not fair. I hate it, too."

His voice sounded not regretful in the way of a man breaking a date but tight, almost bleak.

"Yeah, I'll call you. Hugs to the girls from me. Love you."

After a long moment of silence from the kitchen, Mimi tried to walk nonchalantly into the room. She didn't know what she expected to see but it wasn't the strong and capable Brant Western sitting at the kitchen table with her dog in his lap, his features tight with pain and a sorrow she couldn't begin to guess at.

She froze in the doorway, not quite sure how to react to the sight of his obvious turmoil. She would have slipped back down the hall to her bedroom before he caught sight of her but Simone barked and scampered off his lap, bounding into her arms.

By the time she had picked up her dog and given the

requisite love, as inconvenient as the distraction was, Brant had schooled his features.

He could tell she had heard, she realized, as he moved away from the table and dumped the dregs of his coffee mug into the sink. She didn't think it was an accident that he avoided her gaze.

He obviously wanted to pretend nothing was wrong but she had never been very good at keeping her mouth shut, even when she knew darn well it was a mistake to speak.

"Having girlfriend trouble?"

He looked baffled. "Girlfriend?"

"On the phone. I heard the tail end of your conversation."

His eyes widened and he stared at his phone and then back at Mimi. "Abby? No! She's not… We're not…"

He looked aghast at the very idea and Mimi shrugged, knowing she shouldn't be so relieved. One girlfriend was enough. "None of my business. You just seemed upset. That was the logical conclusion."

"Well, you were wrong."

"Oh?"

He narrowed his gaze at her and she saw anger there and something deeper, something dark and almost anguished. "Abby is smart and warm and lovely, but she isn't my girlfriend. She's the widow of one of my men."

"Oh." Her small exclamation sounded unusually loud in the sudden hush of the kitchen. "My mistake."

"Right." He paused. "Ty Rigby was a damn good soldier. He was killed three weeks ago in an ambush, along with two other of my most trusted men."

She stood frozen as the words poured out of him

like thick, ugly sludge. "As we were fighting to keep him from bleeding to death, he asked me to watch out for his wife and his two little girls. I'm doing a hell of a job, aren't I?"

"Oh, Brant. I'm so sorry." The words seemed painfully inadequate as she saw the torment in his eyes, the weight of responsibility in him.

She thought of her life, the shopping and the gossip and the parties. While he was risking his life and watching his friends die, she was complaining about eye shadow and the new girl who did her pedicures all wrong and how some restaurant had taken her favorite thing off the menu.

"Bad enough that Abby has lost her husband, but now she's facing financial problems. She's probably going to lose the house. She doesn't have a college degree and even with Ty's death benefits, it's going to be a real struggle for her to make it the next few years while the kids are little."

Mimi sank into a chair, her mind racing as she tried to figure out how she could fix things for the poor woman without revealing that she had more money than she could ever spend in a hundred lifetimes.

"Why doesn't she come here?" she suddenly suggested. "You've got a house that sits empty all the time. She could bring her kids and take care of the house in exchange for rent. It's the perfect solution!"

He looked astonished and rather impressed. "I actually had the same idea," he admitted. "I offered it to her but Abby's a proud woman and she refused. Besides that, her family and Ty's are in Utah and she doesn't want to leave that support cushion right now. She'll probably go live with her parents until she can get back on her feet. She won't be homeless. But she won't have her husband, either."

His voice was grim, desolate, and Mimi chewed her lip, disgusted with herself for the angry thoughts she'd had about him earlier.

"That's the reason I was thinking about selling the ranch. I thought maybe I could, I don't know, maybe set up a trust or something to help. I guess you'd know more about that, since you work for a charitable foundation, right?"

She opened her mouth to respond, wondering why he used such a harsh, goading tone, but he didn't give her a chance.

"It's a crazy idea," he went on. "But I feel really helpless about the whole thing."

"And responsible?" she guessed.

He scraped his chair back from the table and stood quickly. "I need to head back out and see if I can at least finish clearing out the driveway. I don't know if I'll be back inside before it gets dark out there so go ahead and find what you want for dinner. I just ate a late lunch so I won't be hungry for a while."

"Okay." She forced a smile but he was already heading to the mudroom and didn't turn back around.

What had she said that hit such a hot button? she wondered as he stalked from the kitchen.

Why couldn't he have just kept his big mouth shut? Brant stomped outside into the bitterly cold afternoon, shoving on his work gloves as he went.

Mimi didn't give a rat's rear end about a bunch of

soldiers in a world thousands of miles away from her pampered existence. She had more important things to think about, like her next movie premiere.

A woman like her couldn't possibly understand the gritty, hazardous irrevocability of his world. So why had he told her? The words had just bubbled out and he hadn't been able to stop them.

She hadn't reacted quite as he might have guessed. He had seen shock in her eyes, certainly, but also an unexpected empathy. For a moment, he had wanted to spew all of it to her. His pain and his guilt and the grief for his friends.

Somehow it was only too easy to forget who she was when they were alone here at the ranch. He almost couldn't believe the woman who teased him and scrubbed his walls and spent the morning painting his spare bedroom was the same flighty, shallow publicity-hungry ditz the tabloids seemed so enamored with.

She had kissed him with passion and an urgent heat and then she had pushed him away, accusing him of being some sex-starved bastard putting the moves on any woman who breathed at him.

That had stung, he admitted. And absolutely wasn't true. He had kissed her because he hadn't been able to think about anything else all morning long as they worked together painting the room.

He didn't know what to think of her. Which was the mask and which was the real woman?

None of his business, he reminded himself as he started the tractor, which sputtered to life with a low rumble. In a few days, he would be returning to duty and she would be Gwen Bianca's problem. He would never see her again and this strange interlude would simply be a story for him to tell his men on boring transports.

That was what he wanted, right? So why did the thought of never seeing her again leave him feeling as cold and empty as the February sky?

Chapter 7

The room looked fantastic, if she did say so herself.

An hour after Brant left in such a hurry to return to the endless task of shoveling snow, Mimi stood on the second to top rung of the stepladder in the newly painted bedroom, trying to rehang the curtains.

Lucky for her the paint had been fast-drying so she could start the fun process of returning the furnishings and really making a difference in the room.

The new coat of paint had brightened the room considerably, making everything look fresh and cheerful. She had found a lovely deep blue crazy quilt in the linen closet and decided to use that as the focal point of the room.

On the top shelf of the bedroom closet, she had unearthed a goldmine of dusty antique bottles of various sizes and shapes in deep jewel tones, including several in a blue that nearly identically matched the quilt. She washed them out with dish soap and water and set them along the frame of the double-paned windows, where they glowed as they caught the pale afternoon light.

She had hung the same now-clean curtains but decided they needed something extra. A further search of the attic found a length of fabric in a pale blue, long enough to use as a graceful swag above the other drapes.

It would be a small change, maybe, but sometimes tiny changes had the power to rock the world. Just look at her pregnancy.

Okay, it had rocked *her* world. But wasn't that enough for now?

She reached to arrange a fold that wasn't quite even and she wasn't exactly sure what happened next. She must have leaned just a few inches too far, upsetting her balance, or perhaps the ladder tilted on an uneven spot on the carpet at just the moment she was off-kilter.

Whatever happened, one moment she was reaching across the window to adjust the curtain, the next she was tumbling down, taking the fabric and a few of the antique bottles with her.

She hit the ground, her gasp frozen in her throat as her lungs froze at the impact.

Even as she panicked and fought to catch her breath, pain screamed out from her right side and she realized she must have banged against the small square table she had situated beneath the window to be used as a writing desk.

Simone barked and rushed toward her, her little body wriggling and her black eyes wide with concern. She licked at Mimi's face and the action of that tiny wet tongue on her skin seemed to jolt her lungs back to action, for some strange reason.

She lay on the floor, focusing only on inhaling and exhaling for several long moments before she dared move to scoop the anxious dog against her.

She hurt everywhere.

Her head, her side, the wrist that she had instinctively thrown out to catch her fall.

Several shards of broken glass from the bottles were embedded in her palm and blood dropped onto the carpet until she pulled it across her chest so it could drip on her shirt.

At the movement, a heavy cramp suddenly spasmed across her lower stomach and then another, so intense, she had to curl up. For several endless moments, she couldn't think past the sudden raw, consuming panic.

No. Oh, please. Dear God, no.

"You're okay, kiddo," she whispered, her words a ragged whimper. "You're all right. I'm sorry. I'm so sorry. It was an accident."

Her abdomen cramped again, a rippling wave that took what was left of her breath.

Simone whined, snuggling closer, and Mimi clung to her.

She couldn't lose this baby. Not after she had reached the monumental decision that she wanted it so very desperately. She needed help. A doctor. She had to find Brant. He would help her. Oh, why hadn't she asked for his cell phone number?

Through her panic, she heard a steady rumble outside. The tractor. He must be plowing closer to the house.

Though the very magnitude of the task overwhelmed

her, she knew she had to somehow make her way down the stairs and out into the bitter cold to attract Brant's attention so he could help her.

The next few moments were a blur of pain and fear as she made her way slowly through the house, one painful step at a time.

By the time she reached the front door, she was breathing hard and soaked with sweat from the effort. Her abdomen had cramped twice more and she'd had to stop each time as the pain washed over and through her.

Finally she reached the front door. When she staggered to it and yanked it open, Simone raced out and off the porch, barking furiously on the shoveled sidewalk.

The dog's urgent call for attention might have been more effective if she wasn't a tiny white dog standing amid all that snow, but Mimi still appreciated the effort. She moved to the edge of the porch and grabbed the nearest column as the cold sucked at her bones.

The tractor had an enclosed cab and she knew he wouldn't hear her yelling over the machine's noise, so she waved her uninjured arm as much as she could, blood dripping from her other hand to fall in stark contrast to the snow.

After what felt like the longest moments of her life, her efforts finally paid off. Brant caught sight of her and shut off the tractor. Mimi didn't think she had ever heard a sweeter sound than the sudden silence, and she knew she had never felt such relief when Brant leaped from the tractor and raced toward her, faster than she would have believed possible.

"You're bleeding. What happened?"

"I fell...off the ladder." She could barely squeeze

the words out through her fear. "The baby. Oh, please, I...need a doctor."

He stared at her. "Baby? Baby! You're pregnant?"

She gave a tiny nod, all she could manage, and an instant later he scooped her into his arms and carried her back into the house.

"I'm cramping. It started right after I fell. Oh, please. I don't want to lose my baby. Please help me, Brant."

His face looked carved in granite as he carried her to the family room and laid her gently on the sofa. The fire's warmth soaked into her, warming her from the chill of the outside air, but it did nothing for the iciness in her heart.

"Let me call Jake Dalton and see what we should do."

We. Why had she never realized what vast comfort could be contained in the simple word?

He covered her with the throw from the back of the couch and Simone snuggled against her. Mimi closed her eyes, grateful beyond words that he was a strong, determined, take-charge man, since she barely had a coherent thought in her head beyond her terror.

"Maggie," Brant said urgently into the phone, "this is Brant Western. Yes. I was calling for Jake but you can help me out here. I've got someone staying at my ranch who just fell off a stepladder. She's pregnant and she says she's cramping. What should we do?"

He was quiet for a moment, listening to something on the other end, then he turned to Mimi. "How far along are you?" he asked Mimi. Though she could still see the shock in his eyes, she recognized he was no stranger at adjusting to the unexpected.

"Eleven weeks," she answered. "That's what the doctor said anyway."

He relayed the information to this Maggie person, paused a moment, then turned back to Mimi.

"What about, uh, bleeding?"

If she weren't so terrified she might have smiled at this sign of his discomfort at the intimacy of their discussion. Instead, she only shook her head.

"Negative," he answered into the phone, a look of obvious relief on his features.

"I'll get her there," he said after a moment, his words sounding like a solemn vow. "I can't guarantee how long it will take us to get down the canyon, but we'll make it as soon as we can. Yeah. Okay. Thanks, Mag. See you."

He hung up and turned back to Mimi. "Maggie Dalton is the nurse practitioner at the clinic. Her husband is the town doctor. She thinks it's best to have an ultrasound and check everything out. Are you up for a ride to town?"

"Anything, as long as they can help me. Can we make it through the snow?"

"One of the ranch pickups has a plow. I can't promise you the most comfortable ride you've ever had and it might take us some time, but we'll get there."

"Thank you." Her abdomen cramped again and she folded both arms around it and gave a little moan.

His eyes reflected something close to panic. "Hang on," he said. "You're going to have to give me a couple minutes to get the truck out of the garage and drive it up here. Just wait here and I'll come help you outside."

She nodded and hugged Simone to her, praying

fiercely the entire time he was gone. It was probably only five minutes or so but each second seemed endless.

When he returned, he spent another few moments putting a reluctant Simone in her crate and helping Mimi into her coat, and then before she quite realized what he intended, he scooped her into his arms and carried her outside to an aging blue pickup truck with an extended cab.

"I would suggest you lie down on the backseat but, with the snowy conditions, you're going to need to wear your seat belt and you can't do that lying down. I'm sorry."

"It's fine. Just go."

As soon as she was settled, he backed the truck up and headed down the driveway at a rapid clip. She might have been nervous at his speed under the current conditions, but he drove with confident skill, so she decided to just close her eyes and continue praying.

He didn't speak until they had turned off the access road to the Western Sky and onto the main canyon road.

"Why didn't you tell me you were pregnant?"

Despite her fear, she bristled at the accusatory note in his voice. "Maybe because I didn't think it was any of your business."

"You made it my business when you showed up at my ranch, giving me some cock-and-bull story about needing a place to stay for a few days. Dammit, Mimi. If I'd known you were pregnant, I never would have worked you so hard."

She stared at him, her mouth open. Mimi. He'd called her Mimi.

"I thought it was a joke," he said, his voice disgusted.

"Some funny story I could tell my men when I went back to my unit. Mimi Van Hoyt scrubbing my cobwebs and painting my spare bedroom."

"I'm not…"

"Cut the crap. We both know who you are."

A muscle flexed in his jaw and his eyes blazed and she gauged suddenly that he was furious with her.

"You…knew all along?"

"Of course I knew! I'm not an idiot, despite what you apparently think. And yeah, I might have been living in a cave in the desert on and off for the last few years, but you were a little hard to miss whenever I did resurface."

She thought of all her ridiculous efforts to conceal her identity, all the half-truths and the outright prevarications, and her face burned with embarrassment. All for nothing. He had known, probably from the moment she crashed her car.

What must he have thought of her?

That didn't matter, she reminded herself. The important thing right now was doing all she could to save her baby.

"Why all the subterfuge?" he asked. "Why not just call one of your father's people to rescue you the minute you woke up after your accident and found yourself on the ranch? Instead, just about the first words out of your mouth were lies and they just kept coming."

She let out a breath. "You wouldn't understand."

"Not if you don't explain it to me, *Maura*."

She made a face at his deliberate emphasis on the false name she'd given him. "Haven't you ever wanted to be someone else for a while? Maura Howard is safe. Ordinary. Just a nice woman living her nice comfortable life in anonymity. She hasn't made a total disaster of her life."

She hadn't meant to add that last part but it seemed particularly appropriate right now as she fought to save her baby.

"Why here? Why were you running to Gwen?"

"I needed a place away from the limelight for a while and the idea of escaping to Gwen's just felt right. I only found out myself about the baby the day before I arrived and I needed time to…come to terms with everything."

"So you decided to pretend to be someone else and worm your way into me letting you stay at the ranch."

That just about summed it out. "Yes," she admitted. "But whether I'm Mimi or Maura doesn't matter. I don't want to lose my baby."

"I'll do what I can to make sure you don't," he said.

Though he still seemed angry with her, after a long moment, he reached across the cab of the old pickup and folded her hand inside his much larger one.

Despite everything, her embarrassment and her anger that he had let her dig herself into a deeper hole of lies, she felt immensely comforted by the solid, corporeal reassurance of her hand in his.

He couldn't remember a more white-knuckle driving experience, counting the times he'd had to drive a Humvee down a precarious cliffside goat trail in the pitch-black wearing night-vision goggles that cut his peripheral view to nothing.

The road in Cold Creek Canyon had been plowed but was still icy and dangerous around the curves.

He could handle the road conditions. He'd been driving in snow since he was fourteen. But he'd never driven through snow with this abject fear in his gut. Every time Mimi caught her breath beside him at a bump or a sharp turn in the road, he wanted to just pull over and call for heli transport to take her to the nearest level-one trauma center, five hours away in Salt Lake City.

Though he knew he needed to keep both hands on the wheel because of the driving conditions—and he did for the most part—every once in a while he could sense her panic and fear start to break through her tight control and he couldn't resist reaching over and squeezing her fingers.

"Hang in there. We're almost there," he said.

She gave him a grateful look as she clung tight to his fingers.

By the time he reached the small medical clinic in Pine Gulch, his shoulders were knotted and he ached all over as if he had just finished hauling seventy pounds of gear on a fifty-mile march.

The parking lot and sidewalks of the clinic had been plowed already, he was relieved to see. Brant parked the truck near the entrance then hurried around to Mimi's side and scooped her out.

"I can walk," she murmured.

"Shut up and let me do this," he snapped, not at all in the mood to argue with her.

She raised an eyebrow but said nothing as he carefully made his way to the double front doors. Before he could thrust them open, Maggie Cruz Dalton appeared, pushing an empty wheelchair.

"I was watching for you," Maggie said, her features

so calm and serene that a little of his panic naturally ebbed away.

She smiled at them both, though her attention was mostly fixed on Mimi, as he set her into the wheelchair. "I'm Maggie Dalton, Ms. Van Hoyt. My husband, Jake, is the town doctor and he'll be in to look at you as soon as we get you settled in an exam room."

Mimi shot Brant an accusing look as Maggie used her name instead of the whole Maura Howard alias, but he merely shrugged.

He wouldn't let her make him feel guilty for telling the Daltons the truth. He had called Maggie back when he went to get the pickup truck, after it occurred to him it was only fair and right to warn them their impending patient might require somewhat complicated security measures.

"We've cleared the waiting area and we'll get you back into an exam room right away," Maggie said.

"I... Thank you."

Mimi looked a little bit lost and a whole lot overwhelmed and he fought the urge to haul her back into his arms and promise her everything would be okay.

He was way, way out of his depth in this whole situation and felt completely inept and very male. If he had his preference, he would head over to The Bandito for a stiff drink while he waited, but he didn't think mentioning that right about now would earn him points with either Maggie or Mimi.

"I'll, um, just hang out here," Brant said.

He tried to pull his hand free from Mimi's grasp but she wouldn't let go and they tussled a little as Maggie pushed her down the hall toward an exam room.

"Would you feel better if you had someone familiar with you?" Maggie asked.

"Yes," Mimi admitted softly.

No, Brant wanted to say, horrified. *Hell* no.

But how could he just walk away when she apparently was in desperate need of a friendly face. "Do you want me to stay with you?" He voiced the obvious.

"You don't have to," she said in a small voice, and he sighed, giving up the liquor fantasy altogether.

"Sure, if that would make you feel better."

He was uncomfortably aware of the speculative glances Maggie was sending him. He glared at her, dreading the interrogation in store for him after all this.

He'd always had a tender spot in his heart for Magdalena Cruz Dalton, in part because of the courage she had shown when, as a former Army nurse, she had been injured in a bomb blast in the Middle East and lost her leg below the knee.

He had never seen her in action in her capacity as a nurse and he had to admit he was even more impressed when he witnessed her calming demeanor toward Mimi.

At the exam room, she turned to him. "Brant, please wait here in the hall while I help our patient change into a gown and get her settled."

How about the waiting room? Or the parking lot? Or back at the Western Sky?

"Sure," he said instead.

He leaned against the wall and was thinking how surreal this all was, when Maggie came out of the room a few moments later, closing the door behind her.

"You can go back in now."

"Do I have to?" he muttered, and she gave him a long look.

"You don't have to answer because it's none of my business. But I have to ask. Just out of curiosity, how on earth did Mimi Van Hoyt come to be threatening a miscarriage at the Western Sky?"

"It's a long story."

"And a fascinating one, I'm sure."

He sighed. "She's a friend of Gwen's, apparently, and she didn't know Gwen was in Europe. She came out to see her and ended up with me instead."

"So you're not the father."

He glared. "No! I just met the woman three days ago. I only gave her a place to stay while we waited out the storm."

"I'm guessing there's more to the story than that."

"No." *Except I've held her and kissed her until I couldn't see straight.* "Really, I barely know her."

"Be that as it may, it looks like you're her only support right now since Gwen's out of the country. It's good she has someone."

He would rather that someone be any other soul on earth except him, but Brant was determined to do his best to help her. He owed her, especially since it was his fault she was in that exam room right now. If he hadn't gone along with her deception—if he had admitted from the first day that he knew who she was instead of finding unexpected humor in watching her pretend to be someone else—she would not be in this situation. She would have been at one of the high-priced hotels in Jackson Hole sipping lattes in her fluffy pink designer boots instead of hanging curtains and falling off ladders in his spare bedroom.

His fault. He sighed. Just one more thing for which he bore responsibility. He had a feeling that one of these days the weight of all the guilt piled on top of him just might bury him.

Through the next twenty minutes, Mimi didn't let go of his hand. She clung to him while Maggie drew blood and checked her blood pressure. She wouldn't even let him leave when Jake Dalton came in to do an exam, though he was at least allowed to wait behind a little curtain near her head and away from the action, wishing like hell he was somewhere else.

When Jake was finished, he had Maggie hook a band with a monitor on it across Mimi's stomach and a moment later, a steady pulsing sound filled the exam room.

At the sound, the tension seemed to whoosh out of Mimi like a surveillance balloon shot through with mortar fire.

"That's the heartbeat, right?" she said, her famous green eyes bright with excitement and wonder and the echo of her fear.

"That's the heartbeat." Jake Dalton smiled at her, that winsome smile he shared with his two brothers, the one that managed to charm just about any woman in view of it. Mimi didn't seem to be an exception. Since the moment the Pine Gulch physician had come into the exam room, she had visibly relaxed, as if Jake could make everything right again.

Brant supposed that was a good technique for a doctor, to be able to inspire such trust in his patients.

"I'm happy to report that, despite your cramping, the heartbeat sounds strong and healthy," Jake said.

Mimi made a sound of relief mingled with a little sob and tightened her hand on Brant's. He squeezed back, wondering again how the real Mimi could seem so very different from her flighty, ditzy public persona.

"If it's all right with you," Jake went on, "I'd still like to do an ultrasound to get a little better look and check everything out."

"Whatever you think best."

"I can wait outside if you want," Brant offered.

She shook her head. "I'd like you to come," she said. "If you don't mind."

"Sure," he answered. What else could he say?

So he sat beside her while Jake covered her stomach with gel and then moved the ultrasound sensor over her. Brant couldn't seem to move his gaze from the monitor and the various mysterious shapes there, intrigued despite himself by the process and by that little alien-looking shape with a big head and tiny fingers.

Mimi looked enthralled. "Can you tell what it is?" she asked.

"Not yet. A few more weeks," Jake replied. After a few more moments, he set down the wand and handed her a huge pile of paper towels to wipe off all the goop.

"You haven't miscarried, despite the cramping. I can't say it's not still a possibility, but right now your baby is alive and appears to be healthy."

Mimi exhaled a long breath and squeezed Brant's fingers. "Oh, thank you, Dr. Dalton. Thank you so much."

Jake smiled. "I didn't do anything but check things

out. I want you to come back immediately if you have more cramping or spotting."

"Of course."

"And I don't know what your travel plans are, but I would feel better if you stay put for now. In fact, I would recommend limited bed rest for at least a few days. That means you can get up to move from room to room, but not much more than that. Can you swing that?"

She pulled her hand away and didn't look at Brant. "I don't... It's not right for me to impose on Major Western more than I already have. Perhaps I could check into a motel in the area."

Brant frowned. "Stop right there. You're staying at the Western Sky."

He was invested in this now. No way was he going to sit by and let her fight to save her baby without him.

"When do you have to report back?" Maggie asked him.

"My flight leaves Tuesday." He could request an additional few days of emergency leave but he and Maggie both knew he wouldn't get it, not for these circumstances.

"She can stay with me until I have to take off," he said. "If she still needs bed rest after that, she can stay with Easton at Winder Ranch."

For some strange reason, Mimi didn't look exactly thrilled at that idea, which he found odd. Everybody liked Easton.

"Or with us," Maggie said. "We've got plenty of room. Don't worry, we'll find a place for you, Ms. Van Hoyt."

"Thank you," she said, with a fairly good rendition of her usual radiant smile.

She hadn't moved her slim hands from her abdomen since he'd found her standing so frightened and pale on the front porch. By all appearances, it looked as if Mimi was excited about this baby.

Who was the father? he wondered, trying to rack his brain to see if he had remembered seeing her with some special date in the tabloids lately. He hadn't paid enough attention to really care but now he wanted to run over to the grocery store and buy every copy of the gossip rags off the stands.

One kiss, no matter how earthshaking, didn't give him the right to be jealous, he reminded himself.

"Just take it easy, eat healthy foods and drink plenty of fluids," Jake was saying. "I'd like to see you again on Friday. I'll see if I can swing out to the Western Sky."

"Thank you. Both of you," she said to the doctor as he and Maggie headed out of the room. Brant rose to leave with them in order to give her privacy to dress, but he didn't move away from the exam table as a new thought occurred to him.

"Do you need help getting dressed? I can send Maggie back in."

"I think I can handle it. Thank you." She paused and, just before he reached the door, she gripped his fingers again. "Thank you so much for everything, Brant. I don't know what I would have done if you hadn't been here with me."

She wouldn't have been hurt in the first place if not for him.

"You would have been fine. I think you're tougher than you think, Mimi."

"I'm not," she said, but as he left, he thought she looked intrigued at the idea.

Tough or not, Mimi must have been completely exhausted from the stress of the afternoon. By the time he drove the short distance from the clinic to the mouth of Cold Creek Canyon, she was asleep, curled up beside him with her cheek resting against the worn upholstery.

Even though the return trip to the ranch lacked the urgency that had pushed him so hard to drive a little faster than conditions warranted on the way to town, the drive home seemed shorter somehow. Maybe because his stomach wasn't a knot of nerves this time.

At twilight, the canyon seemed spectacularly beautiful, with the mountains looming in the distance and the dark shadows of the Douglas fir a bold contrast to the pure, blinding white of the snow.

When he passed Hope Springs, he saw Nate Cavazos clearing snow from his neighbor's driveway with his tractor, headlights beaming. He lifted a hand in the customary wave and Nate smiled and waved back.

He loved that about Pine Gulch. That sense of community, of being part of something bigger. Shoveling out your neighbor's driveway, casseroles and chicken soup on your doorstep when you were sick, helping anybody in need just because you can.

He remembered when Curtis drowned, the outpouring of support for his parents. Some of the men in town had helped his dad put in his crops that year when he'd been too stunned to do it, then had been there throughout the haying season to help him cut and bale when he was too drunk to bring in his own crop.

It had been that same sense of community, he supposed, that had impelled Guff Winder to keep an eye out for his neighbor's son and then to step in and take care of business when he saw things weren't right.

Maybe that's why he was so conflicted about selling the ranch. He loved it here and found something deeply compelling about being tied to a place, something that wasn't just about geography.

Would he lose that if he sold the ranch?

He would always be connected to Pine Gulch and Cold Creek Canyon through Easton. She and Quinn and Cisco were his family, all he had, and nothing would ever change that. But he had to admit that Easton was right. If he sold the ranch, nothing would be the same.

When he reached the house, he turned off the engine of the big truck and glanced in the fading light at his passenger.

He wasn't crazy about this protective mode that seemed to take over him when he was around her, something that made no rational sense.

Why should he feel any sense of obligation toward the woman? She had more money and resources at her disposal than he could even imagine, enough to probably contract a small private army of her own.

She probably had a dozen houses around the world where she could be recuperating right now. Paris. London. New York. So why was she determined to hide out in Podunk eastern Idaho with him?

Was she escaping her father? The baby's father? The paparazzi? Or all of the above?

Whatever it was, he knew damn well he ought to just let her deal with her own troubles. But at this point, he knew it was far too late for him to step back.

"Mimi, we're home," he said, after allowing himself only a few more moments' indulgence to just look at her.

Her big, long-lashed green eyes blinked sleepily at him as she hovered on the edge of consciousness.

"I'm…sorry," she said with a yawn. "I fell asleep. How rude of me."

"To sleep when your body demanded it? That's not rude. If there's one thing any soldier understands, it's the value of sleeping whenever you can steal the chance."

He moved around the truck and opened the door for her. "Come on, let's get you inside," he said as he scooped her small, curvy weight into his arms.

"You don't have to carry me," she protested. "Dr. Dalton never said I couldn't walk."

He ignored her objection—just as he tried to ignore how warm and feminine and sweet smelling she was in his arms.

"I would hate for you to fall out here. It's still slick."

"What if *you* fall?"

He knew he shouldn't enjoy the way her body slid against his chest when he shrugged. "Then I'll figure out how to hit the ground first so I spare you the brunt of it."

"Could you really do that?"

He smiled a little at the disbelief in her eyes. "I have no idea. But since I'm not going to slip, we won't have to find out, will we?"

For some reason she was staring at his mouth and his smile slid away.

"Don't stop," she murmured.

"I'm only opening the door," he said. "I was planning to set you down on the sofa in the family room by the fire."

"I meant, don't stop smiling. You're far less terrifying when you smile."

Terrifying? She was afraid of him? After he had just spent a deeply uncomfortable afternoon holding her hand in a doctor's office?

His gaze met hers and suddenly he remembered the kiss between them, the softness of her mouth and the way her hands had curled into his hair and the sweet, sexy sounds she made when his mouth found hers.

She was the first to look away. "The sofa would be a good place to set me, but the, um, powder room would actually be better."

He set her down outside the door of the bathroom just off the kitchen. "I imagine Simone's going to need to go out. I'll take care of that and then build up the fire in the woodstove again."

"Thank you." To his discomfort, she reached up and brushed her fingers on his cheek. "Thank you for everything. I'm really sorry I dragged you into this."

"You wouldn't have been hurt if not for me," he said in a low voice.

She dropped her hand and gazed at him in surprise. "What do you mean?"

"If I had admitted from the first that I knew who you were, you never would have been up on that ladder."

"This was *not* your fault, Brant. If anyone's to blame, I am. I lied to you and used you, only because I needed a place to stay for a few days and the Western Sky was convenient for my needs. I selfishly didn't think for one minute about you only having a few days of peace to yourself. I never considered you might have better things to do with your brief free time than entertaining me."

She looked sad suddenly, as bereft as she had on the way to the clinic when she had been in fear for her child.

"That's who I am," she said in a low voice. "Selfish, irresponsible Mimi Van Hoyt, who never thinks of anyone but herself. So now you know."

She closed the door between them firmly before he could reply. A few days ago, he would have agreed. But right now, Brant didn't know what to believe.

Chapter 8

"Oh!" Mimi exclaimed four hours later. "You are nothing but a dirty, rotten cheater!"

The louse in question raised an eyebrow. "Hey, I won that hand fair and square. Is it my fault you're a lousy poker player?"

"Oh!" Mimi grabbed a kernel of popcorn from the bowl beside her and tossed it at him. To her regret, it hit his chest and bounced off again. "Who ever would have guessed that the upright, honorable Major Brant Western cheats at cards?"

"I did *not* cheat." He gave her a long look, that sexy mouth of his tilted slightly at one corner. "I could have, about a dozen times when you weren't paying attention, but I opted to claim higher ground."

She sniffed at this with a dismissive gesture at the pile of toothpicks in front of him. Compared to her very tiny winnings, his stash of toothpicks looked like a beaver dam.

"When you asked me if I wanted to play five-card stud, it might have been fair for you to mention you're as relentless as an Atlantic City card shark."

"You mean I forgot to mention the three years I spent on the pro poker circuit?"

"I believe it. I'm curious, though. How did you fit the poker circuit in between deployments."

"It wasn't easy but I managed."

She shook her head at his teasing, though she had to admit she loved this lighthearted side of him. Except for those few dark moments after they returned from the clinic when he tried to shoulder the blame for her threatened miscarriage, he had seemed like a different man throughout the evening.

Every now and again she had seen a certain brooding look in his eyes but he took pains to keep everything between them light and easy.

"I'm just about down to my last toothpick so I guess that means you've cleaned me out," she said.

"I might be persuaded to stake you a little more if you want to keep going," he said.

"And end up having my kneecaps broken by your little toothpick loan sharks? I don't think so, Major."

He laughed a low, rich laugh she was quickly coming to adore.

He was doing his best to keep her mind off her lingering worry by distraction. So far it had been a remarkably effective strategy. Not perfect, but nearly so.

"Who taught you to play poker so well?" she asked him. "Did you learn from your Army buddies?"

He shook his head with a grin. "That would be Cisco. He never met a game of chance he didn't like. Craps, dice, whatever. Our favorite game was called Bull, er, shoot. Have you played it?"

"Is that where you hold a card faceup on your forehead and no one can see his own card but you can see what everyone else has?"

He smiled. "Nope. That one is called Guts. The game I'm talking about is also called Cheat."

"Oh, that's appropriate. I can see why you liked it."

He gave her a mock glare. "I didn't cheat! Tonight, anyway. But the whole object of Cheat is to lie your way through. You deal the whole deck and then you take turns with every player discarding all their cards by rank in order from aces down. Whether you really have that number of cards or not, you BS your way through. Too bad it doesn't work very well with only two people. Cisco, Quinn, Easton and I would play for hours. Cisco could beat all of us, just about every time."

She adjusted to a more comfortable position on the sofa. "Why's that?"

"Well, Quinn was always too busy trying to count the cards so he could figure out who was lying and Easton had some really obvious tells. She would tug the ends of her hair when she was trying to bull us. To this day, she doesn't realize she does it."

Easton again. She swallowed her frown. She was growing tired of the other woman's name. "You must all have been good friends."

He shuffled the cards with great dexterity. "We were more than friends. I guess you could say we were more like brothers, or the closest thing to it."

"Easton's not a boy." She had to point out the obvious.

He smiled. "No, but she thought she was. She was a real tomboy and loved to follow us around. We didn't mind. She was a cute kid."

"The others—Cisco and Quinn—did they live close by?"

"Sort of." He was quiet for a long moment. "We all lived together at a ranch just down the canyon. Winder Ranch. We were in foster care there."

"Foster care?" She forgot all about the cards and her hands tightened so much on Simone that the dog jumped off her lap in a huff and moved to Brant's lap. "But you told me you grew up here."

"I said I lived here for the most part. That means until I was twelve. Then the neighbors took me in because of…problems here."

"Problems?"

He looked as if he regretted saying anything. "I told you about my brother dying. Nothing was the same after that. My parents both drank afterward and then my mom ran off and things got worse. I guess you could say things around here hit rock bottom and a neighbor couple took me in. They already had one foster son, Quinn Southerland. I was only there a few months before they found Cisco Del Norte living by himself in a stolen tent in the mountains after his dad died. After that, we were inseparable. The Four Winds, Jo called us, because of our names."

"Southerland, Del Norte, Western. Easton's the fourth?"

He smiled, even after Simone did her favorite little lap-hopping thing and jumped onto him. "Right. She was the Winders' niece who lived on the ranch with her parents since her dad was foreman. She was more like a little sister to us. Still is."

Sister. He considered Easton a sister.

"She's not your girlfriend, then?"

"Easton? No way!" He was quiet for a moment. "Truth is, I've always suspected she and Cisco have feelings for each other but neither of them has ever said anything about it and I don't want to go there."

Mimi suddenly decided she liked the other woman much better.

"The four of us got into so much trouble," he went on. "You wouldn't believe it. Sneaking out for midnight fishing trips into the mountains, taking the horses when we weren't supposed to, playing pranks on the home-coming dance committee."

"You hellions."

He flashed her a wry look. "We were. Though I will say, I usually tried to be the voice of reason and man-aged to talk the others out of almost everything im-moral or illegal."

"So you were the boring one," she teased.

"True enough." He paused. "I probably tried a little too hard to be perfect so Jo and Guff wouldn't have any reason to change their minds about giving me a home."

Her heart ached for the boy he must have been. "But you didn't want to be perfect, did you?"

Her guess surprised another laugh out of him. "No. I wanted to be like Cisco. He wasn't afraid of anything. He could talk his way out of just about any kind of trou-ble that came along. Still can, for that matter."

"Does he live around here?"

His eyes clouded a little. "No. He hasn't since he was eighteen. He's in Latin America somewhere."

"What does he do there?"

"He's pretty closemouthed about it. I have a few guesses but I don't know for sure. To be honest, I'm not sure I want to know."

"Something illegal or immoral?"

"Possibly," he said, with wariness in his voice, and she didn't press him.

"And the other one? Southerland?"

"Quinn." He smiled with genuine affection. "Right now he's in Costa Rica on his honeymoon. Remember, we were talking about his wedding the other day with Easton? He married a girl we knew in high school, Tess Jamison. She's actually expecting a baby, too."

He made a face. "Sorry, I didn't mean to run on. I imagine life around here must seem pretty provincial compared to private Swiss boarding school and holidays in Monaco."

She sipped at the hot cocoa he'd brought her earlier, which was now, unfortunately, lukewarm. "The boarding school was outside Paris, actually, and we generally summered in Cannes."

"A far cry from Pine Gulch, Idaho. You must be bored to tears playing five-card stud and listening to my meanderings down memory lane."

"Not at all," she admitted. "If you want to know the truth, I've been thinking how lucky you are."

"Lucky?" He looked astonished. "Because my brother died and my mom ran off and my dad was a drunk who liked to use his fists a little too much on his surviving kid?"

"Not about that. That part is horrible."

She couldn't imagine it, actually. Though her father had been arrogant and distant, she'd never worried he would physically hurt her.

"I just meant this place. Cold Creek. There's a serenity here. I can't explain it. And you had all these people you love to share it with."

"You didn't have anyone?"

She shifted restlessly on the sofa. "Of course. I refuse to play the poor little rich girl card. I had a life of privilege beyond what most people can even imagine. I know that. Yachts. Penthouse apartments. Private jets. I hate to admit this, but I didn't fly a commercial airplane until the first time I snuck out of boarding school when I was nine, after I bought my own plane ticket back to New York out of my allowance."

"You flew by yourself from Paris to New York when you were nine?"

She shrugged. "It was the Christmas holidays and I wanted nothing more than to be home. My father was newly married again. Number four, I think. Jemma, the wife before Gwen—and they were expecting a baby right after Christmas and they didn't want me there in the middle of the happy event. Turns out my half brother Jack was born on Christmas Eve, just a few hours before I showed up at our apartment in the city. My father wasn't pleased to see me. Neither was Jemma, needless to say, but I adored Jack. Still do, for that matter. Of all the half and step-siblings, he's my favorite."

She smiled a little, thinking of her half brother. He had inherited his mother's looks and their father's brain, a formidable combination.

He was going to be a wonderful uncle to her baby, if Jemma let him see Mimi. But then, he was almost eighteen and his mother wouldn't have much of a choice in the matter.

"You said the wife before Gwen. She was your step-mother? Why didn't she ever say anything?" He looked rather dazed at the idea.

"Gwen considered her brief marriage a huge mistake. She was the only one of my father's wives who voluntarily left him. He dumped all the others."

"Nice."

"If Jack is my favorite sibling, Gwen is my favorite ex-stepmother."

"How many do you have?"

She had to think about it. "Four exes and one current, who at least has longevity. Marta has been married to Werner for going on eight years, which is something of a record for him."

"What about your mother?"

"She died when I was three. I barely remember her. I'd like to think she was the love of his life and he married all the others to assuage his broken heart. But then, I'd like to believe strawberry cheesecake isn't really fattening, either."

She was quiet for a moment. The only sounds in the room were Simone's snuffly breathing on his lap and the low crackling of the fire in the stove.

"None of them was horrible, Cinderella-grade step-mother material or anything, but they mostly just tolerated me. Gwen was the best. She never once made me feel like I was in the way."

"In contrast to your father."

She looked away from that perceptive blue-eyed gaze. "I never said that."

"You didn't have to say it. I'm good at picking up on the unspoken. It's a handy skill when you're dealing with military command."

"Well, I'm afraid you missed the target here by a mile, soldier."

"Did I?"

She made a big production of arranging the throw over her feet as she mulled how to answer him. Lying seemed silly, suddenly, when he already knew more about her than anyone else.

She had been raised to be cautious of talking about herself. After several so-called friends had turned out to be tipping off the paparazzi to her every move, Mimi had a tough time trusting people.

But somehow she knew Brant would never sell her out to the tabloids. He was a good man. If she had any doubt about that, he had proved his worth today at the clinic when he had sat by her side the entire time, despite his obvious discomfort.

She didn't know how she would ever repay him for that kindness.

"What do you know about Werner Van Hoyt?" she asked.

"Not much, really. Only that he's a brilliant real estate investor and the force behind most of the movers and shakers in Hollywood."

"He's also abrasive and overbearing and treats everyone in his life from his current wife to his various children to the damn pool boy with that same detached indifference, as if we were all interchangeable cuff links."

"And so you compensate by jumping from scandal to scandal in the hopes that you can ruffle his calm a little and make him notice that one of his cuff links doesn't quite match."

She had a wild urge to pull the blanket over her head to protect her psyche from that steady gaze of his.

"Aren't you the smart one?" she finally said. "It took me three years on a therapist's couch to pick that up."

"I've only known you a few days," he said, "but I think you're smarter than you let the world see."

She flashed him a look under her lashes, wondering if he was being sarcastic, but he only continued watching her steadily.

"About some things," she muttered. "Relationships, not so much. I'm pretty stupid about those."

He leaned back. "Does the little squirt's father fit in that *stupid* category?"

"He's right at the top of the list." She sighed, knowing she was going to have to tell him, if not all the truth, at least some of it. He deserved that much for standing by her all day.

"The baby's father won't be in the picture. He's… unavailable."

"Married?"

"Not yet, but soon. That doesn't make it better, I know."

He continued watching her steadily, and she traced a finger along the fringed edge of the afghan, avoiding his gaze. "When I told him I was pregnant, he automatically assumed I would take care of the *little problem,* as he termed it, so he could continue on with his big plans to live happily ever after with someone else. He was not very happy when I told him I wanted to keep the baby."

He was quiet for a long moment. "He's the stupid son of a bitch, then, not you."

She laughed a little but then saw by the hardness of his jaw that he was completely serious and something warm and sweet fluttered through her.

"He is. And you know what, he doesn't matter."

He didn't, she realized. Somehow, today, amidst her frantic fear for the child, Marco's harsh words, his fury with her, had become completely unimportant. Her priorities had shifted and rearranged themselves and now all she wanted was for her baby to be healthy.

"I want this baby. And I'm going to be a darn good mother."

He smiled. "I don't doubt it for a minute."

His words soaked through her like spring rains on a parched desert. She hadn't realized how desperately she had needed someone to believe in her until Brant spoke but she suddenly felt tears prickle behind her eyes.

"Hey. Don't cry."

"I'm sorry. It's just…been quite a day."

Before she realized what he intended, he moved beside her on the couch and pulled her into his arms. "You've been a trooper, Mimi. You've been strong and courageous and done everything the doc told you to do. You're going to be a wonderful mother."

He kissed her, something she sensed he meant only as a gesture of affection and maybe respect.

But as his mouth touched hers, firm and strong, she was astonished as tenderness surged through her. She felt surrounded by him, safe and warm and comforted, somehow.

She tightened her arms around his neck, eyes closed as she memorized the scent of him, masculine and enticing. She didn't want to move from this place. She wanted to stay right here beside him feeling each breath against her skin, with the heat of him soaking through her and this fragile tenderness taking root in the empty corners of her heart.

Eventually he pulled away, looking slightly dazed. "You need your rest. Come on, I'll help you to your room."

He would have carried her again but she insisted on walking.

"I'll put Simone out one last time and then bring her to you when she's ready to settle down," he said when they reached her door.

"Thank you."

"Good night, Mimi." He pressed his lips to her forehead again and she felt something dangerous shift and slide inside her heart.

After she closed the door, she leaned against it, her thoughts tangled.

She was in serious trouble here. Once on holiday in Sicily she had climbed Mount Etna and had stood teetering on the edge, her nerves jangling and her heart racing.

She felt exactly like that right now, as if she stood peering into the abyss. She was in grave danger of falling for Brant, tumbling headlong into love with a tall, serious Army Ranger with solemn eyes and a deep core of decency. She had thought herself in love before, but all those other emotions paled in comparison to what she feared she could feel for Brant.

She couldn't love him. Whatever it took, she had to protect her heart. Right now her focus had to be her baby. She couldn't afford to waste her energy and time on a man who was unsuitable and unavailable.

No matter how much she might want him.

Chapter 9

He had to get the hell out of here.

Two days after Mimi fell off the ladder, Brant stirred the coals in the woodstove, then tossed another log on the red embers.

Behind him, he could hear another Alfred Hitchcock movie starting on the movie channel they'd been watching all day and he closed his eyes, not sure if he was man enough to endure the temptation of sitting beside Mimi for another two hours, with her sweet, delicate scent teasing his senses and her famous green eyes sparkling brightly and her wide smile clutching at his heart.

For two days, they had played games, had laughed at Simone's antics, had pored through the stack of baby books Mimi had squirreled away in her stacks of luggage.

This morning, one of the movie channels was having a Hitchcock marathon. They had watched *The Birds* and *Psycho* and next up was *Vertigo*. He wasn't sure he was up for that one, since he was entirely too dizzy around her as it was.

He had been very careful not to kiss her again, fearful that once he started he wouldn't be able to stop.

He needed a little distance from her or he was very much afraid he would find himself slipping headfirst down some dangerous slope with her and be unable to clamber back to safe ground.

The trouble was, he didn't want to leave. He loved her company. Mimi was clever and fun and wholeheartedly embraced everything she did, whether that was playing Monopoly or throwing a toy for her dog or curling up, completely engrossed in an old movie.

Before he'd come to know her these past few days, he might have expected the tabloid version of Mimi Van Hoyt to be petulant and resentful at her enforced inactivity. He could easily have envisioned temper tantrums and hysterics.

Instead, she was sweet and funny and showed a surprising gratitude toward everything he did, whether it was handing her another pillow or bringing her a grilled cheese sandwich and bowl of canned soup for lunch or just putting her little furball outside when Simone had to take care of business.

He was entirely too drawn to this Mimi and for the first time he could remember, he wasn't looking forward to returning to duty. If he could have dragged this time out longer, he would have tried to figure out a way, but he knew he only had three days left here before he flew out.

He only needed a little perspective, he thought. He

had spent just about every waking moment of the last two days with Mimi. Once he was away from her, he would be able to shift his priorities where they should be. The Army had been his life since he was eighteen years old, and a few magical days with a beautiful woman couldn't shake that.

Through the glass door of the woodstove, he watched the flames lick at the log and Brant decided this would be a good time to escape, while the opening credits of the next movie had just started to roll.

"Go ahead and watch this one without me. I'm going to go feed the animals and check on Gwen's place, then I'll come back inside and fix some dinner for us."

Mimi didn't answer him and he turned around to find she was asleep, her long dark lashes fanning those high cheekbones and one arm tucked around Simone, who was curled up beside her on the sofa.

The little white bichon frise opened one black eye when she felt Brant's scrutiny and he could swear she grinned at him.

Yeah, he figured he'd be grinning, too, if he were snuggled up against all that warmth and softness.

One of Mimi's dark curls had drifted across her cheek and he reached a hand to push it out of the way, then froze, his hand extended.

He had to get out of here. Now, before he did something inordinately stupid like sit down beside her, pull her against him and wake her by kissing that delectable mouth. He had to go, even if that only meant escaping to the barn for a while.

Leaving the television buzzing softly, he moved with

as much stealth as he could muster to the mudroom off the kitchen, where his winter gear hung.

A few moments later, he was outside in the icy air. The sun was setting in a blaze of orange and purple and the ranch glowed with that particularly beautiful slant of winter light that turned everything rosy and soft.

When he reached the barn, he turned back to look at the ranch house, sprawling and unpretentious in the sunset.

Even in the worst years, when his family life had been in tatters, he had loved the house and the ranch, with the creek running just a short distance away and the mountains a solid, reassuring presence in the background.

He had dreaded coming home during those years when his father had turned cruel and bitter but he had never blamed the ranch for that. Even in the worst of it, he still hadn't wanted to leave. Guff Winder practically had to drag him away and those first few months at Winder Ranch he had cried himself to sleep just about every night after Quinn was asleep in the room they'd shared.

Eventually he had settled into the routine of life with the Winders and having an instant older brother and then Cisco a few months later. The six years he spent at Winder Ranch were the most peaceful of his life.

Peace.

He remembered Mimi saying she felt peace and serenity at the ranch. As he gazed at his home, he realized that was the indefinable emotion that seeped through him when he was with her.

She soothed him, in a way he couldn't explain. He let out a long breath. That made absolutely no sense but here in the pure clarity of dusk, he didn't see how he could deny it.

He had come home for leave with an aching heart, guilty and grieving at his own failures that had cost good men their lives. He knew he would always regret the ambush, that he hadn't trusted his instincts that something was wrong, but these days with Mimi had distracted him from brooding over it. When he was with her, he could release the pain of regret for a little while and focus on the gift of the moment.

He sighed. What good was it to get away from her physically by coming outside if he couldn't shake her from his mind? With renewed determination, he headed into the barn, resolved to focus on the mundane for a while.

An hour later, he had finished the regular chores and was busy at the woodpile, replenishing Gwen's supply of split logs, when he heard the sound of a vehicle approaching the house.

Easton had said she would stop by sometime tonight or tomorrow. Assuming it was her, he set the split log carefully on the stack, then headed around the corner of the house just in time to find Jake Dalton holding open the passenger door of an SUV and reaching inside to help his wife climb out.

The tenderness of Jake's concern for Maggie warmed Brant. She deserved a safe haven after the hell she'd been through and it looked as if she had found it.

He reached them just before they headed up the stairs. "Hey, Doc. Maggie," he said with a smile.

"Hey, you." Maggie smiled back. "How's our patient?"

"She's had a pretty calm time the last few days. No more cramps. She was sleeping when I came outside an hour ago."

"Just what she needs to be doing," Jake said. "I'll go check on her, if you don't mind."

"Go ahead," Brant said.

Before Jake went inside, he sent Maggie a look loaded with meaning that flew right past Brant.

"Come on inside," he said. "Do you need help up the stairs?"

She shook her head. "I get around pretty well these days. Stairs don't bug me nearly as much as they used to."

To prove the truth of her words, she moved up the porch steps with smooth, easy movements.

Inside, he expected her to follow her husband immediately to Mimi, but she grabbed his arm in the entryway.

"So Mimi's doing better. How about you?"

He flashed her a searching look, wondering at the concern in her eyes. "Fine. I'm not the patient here."

"Easton told me you've had a rough time in Afghanistan in the last month. That you lost some friends."

He sighed. He hadn't intended to say anything to anyone about the failed mission, but Easton had cornered him the night before the wedding and wiggled it out of him.

"Easton's got a big mouth."

"You know East. She worries about you. But she's not talking around town about you, I promise. She wouldn't have even mentioned it to me, I think, except we bumped into each other at the grocery store. I think she thought I might have some insight into the situation because of, well, my past. She was worried about you since you seemed more stoic than usual. Which is saying something, by the way."

He didn't want to talk about this right now, but he didn't know how to avoid it. He could understand why Easton would think Maggie had a special perspective on the situation after her own military experience and losing her leg in Afghanistan.

"I'm doing okay. Things have been…better the last few days." That was as close as he would come to admitting that Mimi had helped him, without even knowing it.

"What happened? She didn't know details."

"Ambush in a little village in the Paktika Province. I was supposed to meet a high-level contact who insisted on giving his information only to a high-ranking officer. We had intel that the village where the meet was supposed to take place was safe, so I picked twelve of my best men to come with me. The intel was wrong."

He had a memory flash of shouts and screams, civilians caught in the middle of what turned into an intense fight for their lives. "We drove straight into it. My team fought back but in the firefight, three good men died."

"Did you do anything wrong?" she finally asked.

He sighed. Trust Maggie to hit the heart of the matter. "Strategically and militarily, no. I followed protocol to the letter and we had duplicate intelligence that said the area had been cleared of insurgents and any IEDs. But I should have listened to my gut. My instincts were telling me the situation was off, that the contact wasn't trustworthy, and I ignored them."

Her features were soft with a compassion he didn't

want to see right now. "And of course you're blaming yourself for the deaths of your men."

His throat felt tight but he ruthlessly crammed the emotions down. "Of course. Wouldn't you?"

She was silent for a long moment and then she reached between them and squeezed his hand. "My first month in Kabul, I cried myself to sleep every night, until you and Nate came to visit me. Do you remember that?"

"I do." He somehow managed a smile, though it wasn't easy. He and Nate Cavazos, a fellow Ranger and Pine Gulch native, hadn't been in the same company but both happened to be deployed in Afghanistan at the same time as Maggie and they'd been able to coordinate leave so they could all meet up a few times.

"Do you remember what you said to me? 'Mag, if being here doesn't scare the hell out of you, then something's wrong with your head.' And you told me only an idiot would be too afraid to talk to somebody when they were hurting or scared. I finally confessed to my commanding officer how terrified I was and he was able to say all the right things to help me through it. I never would have gone to him if you hadn't nudged me in that direction. So I'm going to throw your words back at you. Don't be an idiot, okay? I know you only have a few days before you head back, but if you need to talk, you know where I am."

"Right."

"Nate's here, too, you know. You could talk to him if you'd rather."

"Yeah, I drove past him the other day while he was shoveling snow out at the old Hirschi place but it was the day I brought Mimi to the clinic so I didn't have a chance to talk. How's he doing?"

Brant knew Nate's world had changed radically six months earlier when his sister and her husband had died, leaving him guardian of his two nieces. He'd left the military to take up his responsibilities and Brant had been meaning to catch up with him ever since.

"Did you know he's getting married?" Maggie asked.

"Really?"

"Yes, to a woman from Virginia who stayed at his guest ranch over Christmas."

"No kidding? I hadn't heard."

She grinned, looking very much like the girl he remembered from school. "Then you also don't know the truly juicy gossip."

"Do tell," he said dryly.

"Turns out his guest—and now his fiancée—is actually Hank Dalton's illegitimate daughter."

"Poor thing."

Just about everybody in Pine Gulch had hated Hank Dalton, Jake's father—Maggie most of all.

But instead of agreeing with him, she only smacked his shoulder. "Since Hank's been dead for years, Emery gets all the benefits of being a Dalton without having to ever deal with him. Wade, Jake and Seth are over the moon to have a sister after all these years. You should have seen them all yelling and carrying on when she and Nate came over with the girls on New Year's Eve to tell everyone."

"I'm sorry I missed that."

Instead of spending New Year's surrounded by neighbors and the scents of home, he had been in Afghanistan planning a mission that would end up taking his friends' lives.

Unexpectedly, as if sensing his train of thought, Maggie reached to give him a hug and he felt those emotions jumble together inside him all over again. "You'll be okay, Brant. Just give it time."

"Thanks, Mag."

"Anytime, Major." She stepped away. "Enough of that. Let's go see how your patient's doing."

As she walked toward the family room with barely a limp, he thought he would like to have even a small portion of Maggie's courage and strength to face his own battles.

Dr. Dalton removed his stethoscope from her abdomen and pulled Mimi's sweater back down to cover her skin. "A strong and healthy heartbeat. I can't make any promises, but so far everything looks normal. Perfect, even. I have high hopes that you'll have an uneventful pregnancy from here on out."

A weight she hadn't realized had been pressing down on her heart for two days seemed to lift at his words.

"Oh, thank you. Thank you so much," she exclaimed just as the doctor's lovely dark-haired wife walked in with Brant.

Mimi wasn't really aware of doing it but she must have reached for Major Western's hand. He was at her side in an instant.

"Brant, Dr. Dalton says the baby still has a healthy heartbeat," she said. "For now, everything is okay with the pregnancy. Since I've had no more cramping, he thinks we might be past the immediate danger."

Relief washed across his clean-cut, handsome features. "That's wonderful news."

To her surprise, he hugged her and she returned the embrace, giddy joy bursting through her.

As she lifted her head, she caught a raised-eyebrow sort of look pass between Dr. Dalton and his wife. With considerable chagrin, she realized she and Brant were acting more like a happy couple than the casual acquaintances they should have been.

Her heart ached with the knowledge that she didn't want to be only casual acquaintances with him, especially after these magical few days. She wanted so much more from him, even though she knew the dream was impossible.

She eased away from the embrace and forced herself to turn back to the physician. "I can't thank you enough for coming out to check on things. I thought house calls went the way of rotary phones and beehive hairdos."

"We're still a little old-fashioned here in Pine Gulch when necessary," Dr. Dalton said.

"Well, I'm very indebted to you both."

She didn't know how she would repay them but she would figure out a way. Perhaps a generous donation to their clinic so they could continue the practice Brant told her about of providing free or reduced care twice a month to patients without health insurance.

"Thank you," she repeated, though the words seemed woefully inadequate.

"I was just about to heat up some lasagna from the freezer for dinner if you two have time to stick around," Brant said.

"We can't," Maggie said regretfully. "The kids have

been at Caroline and Wade's all afternoon playing with their cousins and we need to get them home. Thank you for the offer, though."

"You're welcome. Thanks for stopping by. I owe you," Brant said.

"Remember what I said," Maggie murmured to Brant, piquing Mimi's curiosity. "Don't be an idiot."

His mouth lifted in a small smile. "More than usual, you mean? I appreciate the advice, Mag."

She hugged him tightly then kissed his cheek. "If we don't see you again before you ship out, take care of yourself over there, Major."

"I'll do my best," he answered, then shook Dr. Dalton's hand before walking them to the door.

Everyone liked Brant, she realized. There was something so reassuring about him and that air of competence and quiet integrity about him. She wanted to just curl up against him and let him take care of all her troubles. Did others sense it, too?

"What was Maggie talking to you about so seriously?" she asked when he returned to the living room. "What did she think you were being an idiot about?"

The muscle worked in his jaw. "She thinks I'm on edge because of what happened to my men."

"Are you?"

"I'm fine," he said abruptly. "I'm going to go heat up the lasagna. I think I've got some rolls in the freezer. I'll grab some of those, too."

She didn't like the shuttered look on his features or the way he seemed so careful about avoiding her gaze, but if he preferred to confide in Maggie Dalton, Mimi couldn't do anything about it.

* * *

Dinner turned out to be an awkward affair, something she wouldn't have expected at all after the easy camaraderie they'd slipped into the past two days.

Brant was mostly silent, though he ate with the single-minded energy she had come to realize was probably characteristic of a battlefield warrior who wasn't certain when he would find his next meal.

After dinner, she played with Simone for a while, running through the little dog's limited bag of tricks. The dog seemed to have picked up on the tension between the two of them. She was restless, sniffing in all the corners of the room and insisting on going out three or four times until Brant finally picked her up and stood by the window, petting her and looking out into the night.

"Want to watch something?" Mimi asked. "Or you could give me a chance to win back my fortune in toothpicks."

He shook his head and returned to his window-gazing. When he finally turned back, his features were tight, his mouth a hard, implacable line.

She thought he was angry at something, until she saw his eyes and she had to catch her breath at the anguish there.

"I told you that a month ago three of my men were killed in a botched operation."

"Yes."

He let out a long breath, as if all the air in his lungs had turned sour. "I didn't tell you it was my fault they were killed."

"Oh, Brant. I'm sure that's not true. You were doing your job."

"I was. But I put them in that village. I ordered them there as my security detail. I should have sensed we were heading straight into an ambush."

She didn't know what to say, how to comfort him. What did she know about warriors and their demons? But she sensed he needed to talk and she could provide that, if nothing else.

"Maggie told me I should talk to someone about what I've been going through. She thinks that will help me work it out in my head. I want to just forget everything but…somehow it seems important that you know."

She held her breath as she heard the emotion behind his words. He was not a man who leaned on others willingly. She sensed it without any real evidence to back it up, yet he wanted to share his grief and sorrow with her.

Why? She was flighty Mimi Van Hoyt, jumping from scandal to scandal and crisis to crisis. What would he possibly think she could offer that might help him?

But he was trusting her with this. She was important enough to him that he wanted her to know the things that were troubling him.

The weight of that trust burned inside her. She mattered to him and she couldn't bear the idea of letting him down.

"I haven't been sleeping well since the ambush. Things have been…rough." He gave her a long look she couldn't quite interpret. "Until you came along."

"What do you mean?"

"I don't know why. There's no logical explanation. But since you've been here, everything seems…easier."

She stared at him, heat fluttering through her. How was she supposed to respond to that? She didn't have the first idea what to say. Acting purely on instinct, she crossed the room to where he stood by the window, looking out at the black winter night. She took Simone from his arms and set the dog on the carpet, where she sniffed her disapproval but trotted to the rug by the fire as Mimi took her place, wrapping her arms around him.

After a surprised moment, Brant yanked her against him and wrapped her tightly in his arms, burying his face in her neck.

"I'm so, so sorry, Brant. For you, for those men, for their families left behind. But take it from someone who has spent her life screwing up in one form or another, you did nothing wrong here. I don't know anything about it. But I know you and I'm certain you were doing your job to the best of your ability. I am also certain not one of those men who died would have acted differently if they had been the one making the decision."

He held on for a long time and she could feel his ragged breathing against her skin.

She didn't know how long they stood that way in a silence broken only by Simone's snuffly breathing and the fire's low crackling.

That tenderness she had first recognized earlier pulsed through her and she pressed her cheek against his chest, listening to his heartbeat while his warm breath stirred her hair.

She thought it the most natural thing in the world some time later when his mouth found hers, as inevitable as the tide and the moonrise and the spring thaw.

Chapter 10

His mouth was firm and strong on hers and she leaned into him, relishing the solid heat of him. He tasted of cinnamon and mocha and Brant, and she couldn't get enough.

The world outside the walls of this modest ranch-house could be a scary place, full of pain and war and betrayals, but right now none of that mattered. In Brant's arms, she was safe.

His hand caressed her cheek with a sweetness and gentleness that nearly had her bursting into tears. In all her twenty-six years, not a single, solitary soul had ever looked at her like Brant was gazing at her, as if she meant the world to him

"You're so lovely," he murmured. "More beautiful than any picture in any magazine. I sometimes look at you and can't believe you're real."

He cared about her. She saw the tenderness in his eyes, sensed it in his kiss. He wasn't simply trying to claim bragging rights that he'd been with Mimi Van Hoyt, as so many other men had tried, for some kind of a notch in his holster or whatever weapon an officer in the Army Rangers would carry.

Brant had feelings for her. A soft, seductive warmth bloomed inside of her, like the ice plants along the shore unfurling at the first morning rays of the sun, and she wanted to stay here all night and bask in it.

"I'm very real," she murmured. It seemed vitally important that he understand. "Everything else, the magazine covers and everything, that's the illusion."

She wrapped her arms around his neck and pulled his mouth to hers. This was real too, his kiss and the emotions swirling around them, the tenderness that engulfed them.

She was vaguely aware of him moving back to the sofa and pulling her across his lap, of his hands warm and sure under her sweater, of the rasp of his evening stubble on her skin, the solid strength of him against her.

They kissed for a long time, until they were both breathing hard and she burned brighter than the flames in the woodstove.

"We have to stop," he finally said, his voice ragged.

"Why?"

He pressed his forehead to hers. "Two days ago you nearly lost a baby. As much as I want you right now, I don't think the timing is the greatest."

"Dr. Dalton gave me the green light to resume normal activities," she reminded him, trying to keep the pleading note from her voice.

His mouth quirked into that sexy smile she adored. "I think we both know that when this happens between us—and it *will* happen between us—it's going to be anything but normal."

Heat scorched her cheeks, even as his words sparked an answering tug of desire.

"You need to rest if you're going to take care of that baby."

His big, square-tipped fingers covered her abdomen and she felt the heat of him through the knit of her sweater as he touched her gently.

Just like that, the blasted pregnancy hormones kicked in and those ever-lurking tears pricked behind her eyelids.

Oh, how she wished she had chosen someone like Brant to be her baby's father. Someone good and strong and honorable. Not someone *like* him, she amended. There was no one like him. She wished she had waited for Brant himself, the kind of man who would treasure her and their child, who would be eager to step up and take responsibility for the life they had created together.

Marco's harsh words echoed in her ears. *"Your problem...take care of it... I won't let you ruin my life because you're too stupid to take a damn pill."*

He acted as if their brief affair had been entirely Mimi's fault, as if she had tied him to the bed and seduced him.

"Let me know when you've taken care of it," he had ordered. "I'm marrying Jess, Mimi. You know that. This little *oops* of yours changes nothing. What we had was thrilling and exciting, sure. You're Mimi Van Hoyt. But we both knew it was only temporary and that I always had Jessalyn waiting."

He wanted her to take care of it and she would, just not the way Marco intended. Mimi would raise her child and love her and never, *ever* make her feel overlooked or unwanted.

And she would always regret that she hadn't waited for a man like Brant, someone who would cherish their child, who would toss her into the air and read bedtime stories and teach her how to ride a bicycle.

But as usual, she had screwed everything up.

"What's wrong?" he murmured.

She couldn't tell him, of course. He would think she was ridiculous, or worse, that she wanted him to rush in and rescue her from her mistakes.

"Just tired, that's all. I feel like I'm always tired."

He kissed her forehead and stood up from the sofa with her still in his arms, a feat of sheer muscle she doubted any other man of her acquaintance could manage.

"You should be sleeping. Come on, then. Let's get you to bed."

She didn't want to leave the shelter of his arms, where she could pretend even for a little while that this was anything but a deliciously sweet dream.

She wrapped her arms around his neck as he carried her down the hall to her bedroom. He set her on the bed, then kissed her again with breathtaking gentleness. "You and I need to have a long talk in the morning, when we've both got clearer heads."

"About what?"

"I've got five months left in Afghanistan. I hope I'm back before the baby's born and then it's looking like there's a chance I'll be stationed at Los Alamitos on a special assignment for a while. That's not so far from L.A. We can figure this out, Mimi. We will."

Unease clutched at her heart but she ignored it and forced herself to smile. Couldn't she let herself be carried along in the dream for a little while longer?

"Good night."

He gave her that rare smile she found so unbearably appealing then closed the door quietly behind him.

Mimi sat on the bed long after he'd left, her emotions a wild tangle and a hundred thoughts chasing themselves around her head.

One of those emotions clamored to the fore, drowning out all the others.

She was in love with Brant.

Completely. Irreversibly.

Of all her ridiculous stunts, the scandals and the gossip and the poor decision-making, falling for an honorable, decent man had to be right near the top.

How could she have been so foolish? She was in the worst possible place in her life to fall in love. She was pregnant and alone and scared, on the brink of the biggest publicity nightmare her father could ever imagine.

The father of her baby was marrying someone else first thing tomorrow morning, for heaven's sake.

And yet in typical Mimi style, somehow she had complicated everything by falling head over heels in love with a solemn special forces officer who had a deep core of honor running through him.

Worse even than her own insanity was the terrifying fact that this decent, honorable man was cracked enough to think he might actually want some kind of future with *her*.

How insane was that? The tabloid princess and the war hero. The paparazzi would be euphoric.

She flopped back onto the bed, palms pressed over her eyes as nausea slicked through her.

The moment her pregnancy started to manifest itself, the entire celebrity press corps would be orgasmic trying to figure out who the father was. If she and Marco had succeeded in squelching any rumors about their liaison—and she had to believe they had, since not even a whisper had come out—attention would then shift to whomever she showed up with next.

Maybe she could hide out here at Western Sky for the next six months and then just tell people she had pulled a Madonna and secretly gone to some third world country to adopt a baby.

Nobody would buy it. Every corner of her life would be scrutinized.

She couldn't allow Brant to be dragged into the ugliness of her world, into that morass of endless cameras and shouting questions and rampant speculation about every minute detail of her personal life.

She'd been in the spotlight since she turned sixteen, when some intrepid photographer with a long lens had first snapped a picture of her sunbathing topless on her father's yacht in the Mediterranean.

She despised the constant attention, though she had to admit she had utilized it on occasion to tweak her father about something or other. She'd been in car chases with the paparazzi, she'd found them digging through her garbage and peeking in her windows.

How could she drag Brant into that world? She would

destroy him, would take all that was good and right about him and ensnarl him in the sordid circus of her world.

She couldn't do that to him.

She loved him too much.

Those damn tears burned behind her eyes again and this time she couldn't stop one from trickling down.

She would have to leave. What other choice did she have? If she didn't break things off with him in a way that left no doubt in his mind that she didn't want to further their relationship, she had a powerful suspicion he would stubbornly continue trying to rush to her rescue. That was the sort of man he was.

But if she extricated herself from his world now, he would soon forget about this little interlude in his life. He would return to his career, to his life, to his dedication in the soldiers who served under him.

No one would ever connect him to Mimi Van Hoyt and her baby with the mysterious paternity.

She hated the very idea of it. But wouldn't it be far better to make a clean break now rather than later, after she had sucked him into her world, exposed him to the paparazzi, tarnished all that goodness?

Something bright and hopeful in her heart seemed to shrivel as she picked up her cell phone.

She turned it on, the first time she had bothered since she arrived at the ranch and she found more than a dozen texts and voicemail messages waiting for her.

Probably the vast majority of them were from Verena, her personal assistant. She was too cynical to hope any of them might be from her father. She could drop off the grid for months and the most intense emotion Werner would allow himself wouldn't be worry for his oldest child's safety but probably relief that Mimi was keeping her wild escapades out of the public eye for a while.

She didn't listen to any of the messages before she went to her favorites list and hit Verena's cell phone number, right at the top, where Verena had programmed it for her since Mimi was apparently too stupid to do even that.

Her assistant answered before Mimi even heard a ring on the other end.

"Where are you?" Verena Dumond sounded as ruffled as Mimi had ever heard the hyperefficient woman. "I've been trying to reach you for days. You were supposed to call me when you reached Ms. Bianca's so that I knew you arrived safely. When I didn't hear from you, I tried calling both your number and Ms. Bianca's but have had no luck."

"It's a long story," Mimi said, a vast understatement if she had ever uttered one. Her life felt fundamentally changed from the person she had been the last time she saw Verena and she was exhausted suddenly just thinking about all that had happened.

"Listen, I've had a change of plans," she said. "I know I intended to stay for another few days but I've changed my mind. I need you to make travel arrangements for me to leave as soon as possible."

"Will you be returning to Malibu?"

Mimi mentally scanned her options. She absolutely didn't want to return to California until long after Marco and Jessalyn enjoyed their oh-so-romantic wedding. She couldn't go to New York, where her father spent most of his time.

She gazed out the window and saw that the snow was

falling again, fluttery soft flakes that didn't look as if they would amount to much before morning.

"Some place warm," she decided. "Is the St. Thomas house available?"

"I'll find out."

"Do you know what, Verena? I don't really care where I go. Just somewhere without snow. And I want to take the Lear this time, if it can be arranged."

She had flown commercial on her way out to Gwen's because none of the private planes had been available and she hadn't wanted to wait. Beyond that, she'd had some silly idea about not letting her father know where she could be found—as if he wouldn't have wormed the information out of Verena if he'd genuinely cared to know.

"I'll see what I can do but it might take me a few hours to route the plane to Idaho," her assistant said.

"In the morning should be fine. Oh, and I'll need a car service. The rental vehicle you arranged had a bit of a mishap."

"Again?" There was only the slightest note of condemnation in Verena's well-trained voice but Mimi bristled. Okay, she was a little tough on rental vehicles. That's why one rented, wasn't it?

"This time I couldn't help it. I was caught in a blizzard and slid off the road into a ditch."

"Good gracious."

"I'm all right."

That wasn't necessarily the truth. Mimi had a feeling she wouldn't be all right for a long time. When she left this place, this man, she would leave behind a huge jagged section of her heart.

"You're still at Gwen's?"

"Um, not exactly. I'm at the ranch but Gwen had a gallery showing in Europe and she's not here. After my accident, her landlord was kind enough to let me stay at the main house. But the address is the same. The Western Sky in Cold Creek Canyon."

Verena was silent for a long moment. "I see," she finally said in a carefully bland voice that didn't fool Mimi for a second.

"It's not what you think," Mimi protested.

"I don't think anything. I'm not paid for that." Verena used her frostiest voice and Mimi frowned.

"V., cut it out. Major Western was kind enough to rescue me from a creek when the SUV slid off the road. He's been…really wonderful."

"Will we be compensating him for his trouble, then?"

She let out a breath. Brant would hate that. He was proud enough that perhaps offering him money in return for helping her just might be enough to turn that soft affection in his eyes into disgust.

"I haven't decided how I'll repay him yet."

"I'm sure you'll figure out a way."

Again, that slight, barely perceptible note of condemnation in Verena's voice scraped her nerves. What really sucked was that Mimi knew she deserved it. Verena reported directly to her father, who paid her salary, so Mimi had done her best over the years to exaggerate her misdeeds to the other woman. If she went on a date with a man, she turned her version of the evening into a three-day orgy.

At this point in her life, Mimi doubted anyone would believe she had only ever been with three men, including her first love when she was eighteen—a rookie pro basketball player who had been sweet and nervous, even after they had dated for several weeks, her one-time fiancé who turned out to be gay, and Marco.

No sense trying to undo an image she'd spent years creating. Not in one phone call, anyway. "I'd like to make an early start in the morning. No later than eight a.m."

"I believe I can make those arrangements."

"I have no doubt." Mimi paused, thinking of her years of resentment for Verena. Her handler, she'd always thought. Verena approved expenses, coordinated her schedule, worked with the rest of the staff at Mimi's Malibu and Bel Air houses, all while reporting every detail to Werner.

She might also have been a friend, if she hadn't been caught in the crossfire of the war between Mimi and her father.

"Verena, um, thank you. I…don't know what I would do without you."

After a long pause, Verena spoke, sounding uncharacteristically disconcerted. "You're welcome."

Mimi cut the connection and sat on the edge of the bed for a moment, her thoughts tangled.

If Verena, who knew Mimi probably better than anyone for the past five years, had such little respect and regard for her, how could she ever think she would be the sort of woman a man like Brant deserved?

She was right to leave, even if some small part of her was afraid she was making the biggest mistake of a life that had been chock-full of them.

Chapter 11

What ever happened to that pregnancy glow she was supposed to be enjoying right about now?

Early the next morning, Mimi frowned at her reflection in the round guest bathroom mirror of the Western Sky. Her eyes were puffy, her skin red and blotchy.

No big deal. She had concealer and foundation and a half-dozen pair of designer sunglasses she could wear to hide away from the world.

She hadn't slept more than a few hours in the night. Mostly she had lay curled up on the bed, cuddling Simone close to her and watching the moon shift past the window.

She had never wished she could be Maura Howard more than she did right now. Oh, how she wanted to be just an ordinary woman who went grocery shopping and bought her clothes at a chain store and filled her car with gas every payday.

Maura Howard was a school teacher or a nurse or a librarian. Someone kind and uncomplicated, with simple tastes and ordinary parents.

Brant deserved someone like that, without baggage like Mimi's, someone he wouldn't be ashamed to introduce around Pine Gulch, someone who would fit in with the other Four Winds as they sat around the kitchen table sharing memories and swapping stories.

But she wasn't Maura and she could never be. She supposed the real challenge ahead of her was to somehow learn how to be happy being Mimi, but right now she didn't know how that could happen.

She finished her makeup and pulled her hair back into a loose twist at the nape of her neck, then quietly packed the rest of her belongings.

Simone planted her little haunches by the suitcases and whined, giving Mimi a mournful sort of look.

"We have to go, baby," she whispered. "Staying longer will only make everything so much harder."

Simone yipped sharply as if she wanted to disagree and Mimi shot a quick, nervous glance toward the door, afraid Brant would knock any moment.

Her dearest wish right now was that they could slip away to avoid a confrontation with Brant. Yes, it was cowardly, but it would be far easier to just sneak out without having to provide explanations or excuses.

She held her breath as she heard steps outside her door and she prayed he wouldn't knock and see her suitcases piled by the door. To her vast relief, he walked away and a moment later she heard the outside door open and close.

No doubt he was heading out to take care of the

horses. Judging by the past few days, she had a narrow window of less than an hour for the car service to come while he was otherwise occupied.

Verena had texted her that the car should be arriving close to eight, which was still ten minutes away, so Mimi let Simone out, keeping a careful eye on the barn while she waited and let the dog take care of her business.

As she stood on the backsteps to the ranchhouse, she soaked in one more view of the exquisite surroundings. She hoped so much that Brant would decide not to sell, despite the work she had put into sprucing up the place.

Whether he wanted to admit it or not, he needed the peace of this place. Even if he could only spend a few weeks here each year, this was his home. She had a powerful feeling that if he sold it, he would regret it for the rest of his life.

Simone finished up quickly and hurried back up the porch steps, as eager as Mimi to get out of the bitter cold.

She returned to the front room, keeping a nervous eye on the clock while she struggled to write some sort of note to Brant. Nothing seemed adequate so she simply wrote, "I had to go. We both know it's for the best. Thank you for everything. I'll never forget my time here."

She was just signing her name when she heard the approach of a vehicle and then the doorbell.

Oh, thank heavens. She propped the note on the kitchen table where he couldn't miss it and hurried to the front door, where her suitcases was already piled up.

"I have to put my dog in her crate but you can carry

the rest of my luggage out—" Her words to what she thought was the car service driver died in her throat at the familiar strobe of cameras flashing, again and again and again.

Paparazzi, only a handful—maybe two still photographers and a couple of videographers. But here in the quiet of an Idaho winter's morning, it felt like a mass invasion.

Like an idiot, she couldn't think past her shock that they had found her, couldn't move as the questions started flying.

"Where you going, Mimi?"

"Is it true you had an ultrasound at a clinic in Pine Gulch? Are you pregnant, Mimi?"

"Who's the father, Mimi? Is it Prince Gregor?"

Panic flared through her, hot and bright. Jake and Maggie must have a leak in their office staff or one of their other patients must have seen her while she was there.

Whoever it was, someone had tipped off the rabid horde and thrown Mimi into the middle of a disaster.

Today was Marco's wedding. Couldn't they have waited one more day? Would some enterprising gossip columnist somehow make the connection she least wanted out?

Simone continued yipping. Mimi knew she needed to do something, say something, but she couldn't seem to make the connection work between her frenzied brain and the rest of her.

Just as she started to edge back into the house, a new unwelcome sound distracted her—the pounding of horse's hooves and harsh male voice rising above all the others.

"What the hell do you vultures think you're doing?"

Brant. She closed her eyes, fighting the urge to sit on the steps and burst into sobs. He rode up like some kind of damned avenging angel, big and hard and dangerous, plowing the horse right through the middle of the small group of photographers, who had to quickly move out of his way before he mowed them all down. Of course, they didn't stop filming for a second, she saw with resigned dismay.

Brant looked furious, more angry than she had ever seen him. And a livid Army Ranger was a dangerous force to behold.

At the porch steps, he slid down from the horse, threw the rains around the top railing of the porch and bounded up the steps to her side.

"Everything past that gate you went through off the main road is private property. Every damn one of you is trespassing."

"Go away," she hissed to him, barely able to breathe past her misery. "You're only going to make everything worse."

He stared at her, confusion on his features, then his gaze narrowed. "No," he answered, his jaw tight and his eyes a deep midnight-blue.

Before she could argue, he threw one powerful arm around her shoulders and yanked her against him, then turned back around to the gawking photographers.

He was a formidable man, with his powerful build and his steely Army commando stare, and though she wanted him anywhere else in the world than right here beside her, she couldn't help appreciating how the paparazzi almost as one took an instinctive step back.

"You have got exactly three minutes to get into your vehicles and slither back to whatever slime spit you out. I'm calling the sheriff, who just happens to be a good friend of mine. He'll have no problem rushing deputies up here to haul every one of your asses into jail for trespassing and harassment. I'm sure he won't mind confiscating all that nice camera equipment, either."

"Who's the cowboy, Mimi?" one intrepid still photographer, she thought was named Harvey, yelled at her.

"Is he the father of your baby?" another shouted.

"Does Werner know he's going to be a grandpa?" another added.

She was hyperventilating. She could feel the panic attack swell at the edges of her subconscious and she did her best to fight it back.

Brant took one look at her and yanked her back into the house, slamming the door behind them.

To her horror, he reached into the coat closet by the door and pulled out a lethal-looking shotgun.

The sight of it managed to shock her back to reality. She would have time to freak out when she was on the way to the airport but right now she had to keep it together, for damage control if nothing else.

She grabbed his arm. "What are you doing? Put that away!"

He flexed his muscle to keep the shotgun out of her reach and she felt as if she were touching one of those giant slabs of granite peeking through the snow near the river.

"I'm not going to use it. But they don't know that, do they?"

She had to stop him. If the man had no sense of self-preservation, she had to do what she could to protect him. "You have no idea what you're dealing with here. You are way out of your league, Major."

He raised an eyebrow. "I've spent five of the last seven years in heavy combat. I think I can take care of myself against a bunch of photographers with lip rings and ponytails."

"You can't!" she exclaimed but he completely ignored her and opened the front door and walked out onto the porch with the shotgun cradled in his arms.

Mimi let out a sob of frustration and covered her face with her hands.

"Two minutes," Brant barked and then he worked the pump action on the shotgun with that distinctive *ch-ch* sound no one could mistake for anything else.

The paparazzi had been milling around by their vehicles, probably wondering just how far he would go to kick them off or hoping they could squeeze in one last picture of her.

At the sight of Brant in warrior mode, aiming a firearm at them, they snapped a few more images and climbed into their vehicles.

Through the window, Mimi watched them head down the road in three SUVs, tires spitting snow and gravel behind them.

As soon as they were out of sight, Brant returned to the house looking as pleased as if he'd just fought back an entire contingent of enemy combatants single-handedly.

"They won't bother you again," he said with such confidence that she couldn't help herself, she curled up her fist and smacked his shoulder as hard as she could.

She hadn't had much force to put behind it but at least shock had been on her side. He stared at her. "What was that that for?"

"How could you be so stupid?"

"You don't really believe I called those bastards, do you?"

She raked a hand through her hair. "Of course not. You would never do that. Anyway, would you have chased them off with a shotgun if you'd been the one to call them in the first place?"

"How do you think they found you?"

She sat on the sofa and covered her face in her hands, wondering how she was going to explain all this to Verena, to her friends, to her father.

"Any number of ways. I'm guessing someone at the clinic saw me, despite Jake and Maggie's best efforts. Or perhaps someone on their staff wasn't as discreet as he should have been."

"I'll find out," he vowed, with enough menace in his voice that Mimi had to swallow a whimper.

"It doesn't really matter how they found me. The important thing is that they have."

She punched him again, furious all over again that he would step up to defend her, even if one tiny corner of her heart glowed at the gesture.

"You have no idea what a mess you just thrust yourself into. A shotgun, for heaven's sake. What were you thinking? You look like you just stepped off a damn wanted poster. They're going to be calling you Mimi's Outlaw or something absurd like that."

"You think I care about that?"

"Maybe not now, right this moment, in the heat of battle, as it were. But what about a few days from now when you can't walk outside without a dozen clicking cameras? Or when you return to duty and all your men start calling you Mimi's Outlaw, too?"

"You think I care about that? It worked, didn't it? They're gone."

She curled her hands into fists. "I don't believe this! Can you really be so completely naive?"

He aimed a measure of that menacing look at her. "Naive? I've been leading troops into combat for almost a decade. Naivete is in short supply on the battlefield."

"What else would you call it? You solved nothing with your little shotgun act. Who do you think is going to be camped out at the end of your driveway on public property until your leave ends?"

"So what?"

She picked up the still-yipping Simone and set her into her cage. "So they're cockroaches. You might stomp on a few and scare off a few more but they're only going to go call their friends. Before you know it, you turn on the lights of your kitchen at night and they'll be everywhere."

How could she have done this to him? Dragged him into the ugliness of her world?

She had to end this, now.

"Brant, you had no right to come charging in like that to my rescue. I didn't ask for your help and I didn't need it."

"My house, my decision." He glared right back at her.

Mimi let out a long breath, despising herself for what she knew she had to do.

She had no choice. The rumors were already flying about her pregnancy. *Is he the father?* one of the paparazzi had yelled. Everyone would be speculating about it and she couldn't allow Brant's name to be dragged through the mud and muck of her world, anymore than it already would be from those pictures.

She curled her hands into fists, digging her nails into her skin. "You had no right," she said again. "Now everybody will know I've been staying here with you. There's no way I can keep it a secret after you pulled such a ridiculous stunt."

As she had half-hoped, half-dreaded, she saw some of his anger at the photographers shift toward her. "I didn't realize keeping your presence here a secret was our priority," he said stiffly.

Of all the silly, foolhardy things she had done, all the mistakes and the scandals, she had never regretted anything as much as what she was about to do.

And she had never despised herself more.

"Of course I wanted it to stay a secret. Do you really think I want these few days to become public?"

"I don't know. You tell me."

She forced herself to give him her famous ditzy smile and spoke in a lighthearted tone, though the words cut her throat like razor blades. "Of course not. I'm Mimi Van Hoyt. As sweet as you've been, Brant, you're… well, not exactly my type."

A muscle flexed in his jaw but other than that, he went completely still. "Your type?"

"You know. Men like Prince Gregor or an A-list actor or one of the Kennedys. That's what I'm used to."

"Yes, I can certainly see why I would present a change of pace."

He was furious now. She could see the embers flaring to life in his eyes.

"I'm only thinking of you, Brant." That, at least, was the truth, but she twisted her tone to make it sound as if it meant the opposite. "You don't want your name linked with mine, either. You have your career to consider. What would your commanding officers think if they found out you spent your leave cavorting with someone like me?"

He crossed his arms over his chest. "Was there cavorting? Somehow I must have missed the cavorting."

She shrugged. "Just like you're completely missing the point. Our lives exist on different planes, Brant. Surely you can see that. What do we possibly have in common?"

"I thought we were coming to care about each other."

His careful words and the intensity behind them stabbed at her and she forced herself not to sway.

"Sure, I kissed you a few times because you were here and, let's face it, you're hot in that cowboy/soldier, macho kind of way. I'm really sorry if you might have gotten the wrong idea and thought those kisses meant more than they did."

She saw hurt and disbelief in his eyes and she had to dig her nails tighter into her palms to keep from reaching for him.

She put on her fake Mimi smile again. "Look, I'm not sure things are finished with my baby's father, despite what I told you before. You've really helped me put things into perspective there."

The second part also wasn't a lie but Mimi had always been good at twisting the truth to suit her purposes. And right now her purpose was to end things with Brant, once and for all, despite the devastation to her heart.

"Until I know for sure it's really over, I just can't complicate everything by becoming entangled with someone else. Especially not someone so…unsuitable."

She heard the sound of a vehicle pulling up out front. Either one of the photographers had a death wish or her car service had just arrived. Since Brant still wasn't looking quite convinced, Mimi decided she had no choice but to play her trump card.

She gave him her hard, polished smile and picked up the note she had begun to write for him. She smoothly pocketed that one—even as terse as it had been, it somehow seemed far too personal. Instead, she picked another piece of paper from the stack and scribbled a phone number on it.

"Look, here's my assistant's cell number. Her name is Verena Dumond and she's a pain in the you-know-what but she's frighteningly efficient. Just let her know how much you think your time and effort is worth for the few days I spent here and she can cut you a check for any expenses I incurred while I was here. Gas, food, whatever. And don't worry, I'll make sure to tell her to throw in a nice bonus for all your trouble."

Brant stared at the slip of paper in her slim hand that jangled with silvery bracelets.

Ah.

Here she was at last—the Mimi frigging Van Hoyt he had expected to encounter when he dragged her out of her SUV in the middle of a blizzard.

She was condescending and abrasive and right now he was pretty sure he despised her.

He didn't know what was truth and what was an act. Though her words sounded convincing enough—snobbish and bitchy though they were—there was something in her eyes, some shadow, that didn't mesh with what she was saying.

He was so busy trying to sort it all out that he almost missed the sound of another vehicle approaching the house.

When he caught it, he picked up the shotgun again and walked out onto the porch, just as a man dressed in a black uniform stepped out of an SUV with tinted windows.

The driver froze when he saw a man on the front porch holding a Remington but Brant had to give the guy credit for not crawling back into the limo and speeding down the driveway.

"I'm here to pick up a Ms. Howard. Do I have the wrong address?"

"No," Mimi answered briskly from behind him before Brant could get any words out. "I'm here. I've got a few more bags inside if you could be so kind."

"Not at all, Miss."

Brant caught the chauffer's quick double take when he recognized Mimi but he concealed it quickly, too well-trained to react more than that first flash of surprise.

"You're leaving," Brant said, flatly stating the obvious. If he hadn't been so angry, he might have perhaps noticed her luggage by the door.

"Yes. There's a plane waiting for me right now at the Jackson Hole airport."

"Were you going to say anything to me or just disappear without a word?"

Something flickered in her eyes for just a moment then she gave him that bright, fake smile again. "I was starting to write a thank-you note when the photographers showed up."

"A note. You planned to leave me a note."

"Well, yes. Along with Verena's phone number, of course."

He had never been so furious. The rage swept over him like an August firestorm and he had to draw in several deep breaths to beat it back.

"You're angry with me." She actually had the gall to sound surprised.

"That's one word for it," he bit out.

"I'm sorry for that. But since Dr. Dalton told me it's safe to travel now, I decided there was no logical reason to delay the inevitable."

"None at all."

Underneath the anger, lurking several layers down like a hidden reservoir under the desert, was a vast, endless pool of pain, aimed mostly at himself.

How could he have been such an idiot? He had actually spent the night dreaming about building a future with her. Raising her child somewhere away from the cameras and the craziness.

The lunacy of it just about took his breath away. How

could he ever have thought Mimi might want that with someone like him?

As sweet as you've been, Brant, you're...well, not exactly my type.

The chauffeur returned just then and quickly picked up the rest of her luggage.

"Will there be anything else, Ms. Howard?"

Mimi handed him Simone's pink crate. For some crazy reason, the sight of that silly little dog gazing at him with big soulful eyes affected Brant more than he would have believed possible.

"That's everything," Mimi said. "Thank you. I'll be just a few moments more."

The man tapped the bill of his cap respectfully and then left the house. When he was gone, Mimi smiled at Brant but it wasn't the winsome smile he had come to adore these past few days.

"Well, thank you again for not turning me out that first night and for helping me through the last few days."

She used exactly the same tone she used with the chauffeur. Impersonal. Polite. Detached.

"So that's it."

"I suppose it is." She paused for a moment. "Be safe, won't you?"

Her voice caught, just a bit, on the words and he gave her a careful look to see if he could find a crack beneath her veneer but she was once more cool and remote.

"Don't forget to send your expenses to Verena. I'll tell her to be expecting your call."

She stepped forward, brushed her cool lips against his cheek, pulled down her sunglasses from atop her head and walked out of the house and out of his life.

Chapter 12

Brant didn't know when he had ever been so tired.

He'd managed to doze a little on the plane from the military hospital at the Ramstein Air Base in Germany, but except for that restive sleep, he had been awake for close to twenty-four hours. Right now, all he wanted was to crawl into his bed, pull the covers over his head and crash for the next twenty-four.

The pain from his arm and side growled at him and gnawed with sharp teeth. He had a bottle of pain pills in his duffel but he was doing his best not to rely on them. He had a feeling that after a full day of travel, he might not have much choice.

He was also painfully aware that his decision to drive from Idaho Falls might not have been the greatest idea he'd ever come up with. He hadn't been behind the wheel since the incident nearly three weeks earlier and he hadn't realized how difficult it was to drive one-handed, especially when he'd injured his dominant right side. He was learning more about ambidexterity than he ever cared to know.

But he had made it this far. Only a few more miles and he would be home. As his eyes scanned the road in Cold Creek Canyon, he was struck once again by the familiar rugged beauty of the place. He could think of nowhere more gorgeous than Cold Creek Canyon in July, with the mountains a deep, soothing green, the creek flashing silver in the sunset, the scattered patches of columbine and yarrow among the towering stands of pine and fir.

This was home and he had never been more grateful to be driving up this canyon road.

Something sweet and calming seemed to wash through him as he turned onto the Western Sky access road. He drove under the ranch's log arch with a little prayer of gratitude in his heart that he had reached the momentous decision to not sell the place.

He didn't know what had changed during his time here with Mimi but after he returned to Afghanistan, he hadn't been able to shake the strange assurance that he couldn't sell the ranch. Not now. No matter where he traveled, the Western Sky would always be his home and he couldn't think about someone else living here.

Some day he might have a family of his own—though that time seemed a lifetime away. If he sold the Western Sky, his children would never know their heritage, never know they belonged to such a place of peace in the world.

Besides, if he had sold the ranch, where would he

recover for the next month? The impersonal base housing in Georgia, where he had nothing to do but sit and watch television all day?

Oh, he probably could have stayed in a room at Winder Ranch with Easton. The house there had eight bedrooms, after all, and she was living all by herself. But Easton would have wanted to fuss over him and he would have been obliged to let her. This way was much better, here where he could be on his own with only his memories.

The heaviest runoff was done this late in the year, he noted as he drove up the access road to the ranchhouse. The creek burbled along beside the road with cheerful abandon. He was definitely going to spend some serious time with a fly rod while he was here if he could get his blasted arm to cooperate.

In front of the ranchhouse, any thoughts of fly fishing flew from his head. He braked the rental vehicle and climbed out, frowning as he looked around.

What on earth?

This was *not* the same place he had seen in February—even discounting the fact that everything wasn't buried in the two feet of snow he'd left behind when he returned to Afghanistan.

The barn and sprawling outbuildings sported a bright new coat of rustic red paint, the fences had been repaired, the sagging spot on the porch roof looked flush and level. Two white rocking chairs graced the long front porch, angled to take in the best view of the mountains and instead of the weedy, barren flower beds lining the front porch, a riot of color exploded.

He climbed out of the rental car and leaned a hip

against the door, trying to absorb all these small changes that combined to make a huge difference.

The Western Sky looked charming and well-kept, something he hadn't seen here in, well, ever.

Easton emailed him she had hired a new caretaker to replace Gwen but she hadn't said much about her, other than it was someone who had a background in renovation. At the time, he had been too busy planning a couple major raids and hadn't paid as much attention to her email as he should have. He completely trusted Easton to do what was best for him and for the ranch and he'd told her so.

She had come through, in spades. Easton had never mentioned his new caretaker was a genius. His home looked clean and cheerful, the kind of place where a man could kick off his boots and all his worries.

Except for the memories.

Brant let out a breath, trying his best not to think about that last miserable scene with Mimi, when the paparazzi had stood just off the porch there, flashing their cameras and shouting their questions and sending his foolish dreams of a happily-ever-after with her drifting away into the bitter February air like the smoke from the chimney.

He should have known she would haunt him here. He had half-expected it, he just didn't know those memories would be waiting to ambush him the moment he drove onto the ranch.

She was everywhere here. Sitting on the sofa inside watching Hitchcock movies, playing poker at the kitchen table, painting the guest room with those adorable little paint freckles dotting her face.

He closed his eyes and once more saw her heading down those very steps as she walked out of his life.

That last scene had played vividly in his head for months. He had pored over the memory again and again, sifting through her words, her expression, her tone of voice.

What was truth and what was lie?

Once he had stopped reeling from the cold finality of their parting, he had begun to think maybe Mimi hadn't been exactly truthful with him in that last ugly scene. There had been something not quite right in the tone of her voice and the overbright smile.

Big surprise there, that she might have been less than honest with him, since she'd spent her entire time at the Western Sky weaving one lie or another. But he had reached the inevitable conclusion that she wanted him out of her life. That much had been abundantly clear.

Oh, he'd had to deal with some questions and some ribbing after those pictures of the two of them together had been printed. A few junior officers had tried to make tasteless, off-color jokes about it, but only once. Brant had cut them off with a steely glare and a few well-placed threats.

Then had come that brief, shocking statement a few weeks after he returned to Afghanistan where she announced to the world she was having a baby from in vitro fertilization and an unknown sperm donor. Even thousands of miles away in the middle of a war zone, he had seen a little of the controversy and doubt that announcement had sparked.

He had been watching for paparazzi coverage of her—pathetic on his part, he knew—but other than a few well-documented shopping trips for baby clothes and maternity things every so often, Mimi seemed to be keeping a low profile.

She would be due in only a few months. Not that he was counting or anything.

He wasn't going to think about her. Because of his injuries, he had nearly a month in Pine Gulch before he needed to report to his new assignment at Los Alamitos.

In that time, he planned to give his body a chance to heal while he rode horses and fished and savored the serenity here.

But first he needed to sleep for the next day or two.

He grabbed his duffel out of the backseat of the rental and started for the house, interested to see if the inside had received the same spruce-up. He had only taken one step up the porch stairs when he saw a big yellow Labrador retriever round the house with something pink and flowery in its mouth.

The dog barreled to a cartoonlike stop when he caught sight of Brant and then he dropped whatever was in his mouth and started barking—a deep, excited hey-we-have-company kind of bark.

Brant barely had seconds to react to that when another little animal rounded the corner of the house and he could do nothing but stare at the fluffy white furball with bright black eyes as it let out an ecstatic yip and headed right for him.

It couldn't be Mimi's silly little dog. He knew it couldn't be. But why would another bichon frise be wandering around the Western Sky?

The question was completely yanked out of his mind

a second later when a figure—this time a human—followed the dogs.

She was pushing a wheelbarrow loaded with flowers and she was laughing, her green eyes bright in the long, stretched-out shadows of an early-July evening. "Hey, come back here with that, you rascal. You think I'm going to want to wear my gardening hat now that it's all slobbery and gross?"

He couldn't think straight and for a moment he wondered if he was having some kind of pain-induced hallucination. He dropped his duffel and curled his good hand into a fist, not quite believing this was real.

Mimi must have seen the car then. He watched her do the same sort of double take as the yellow Lab and then she turned toward him.

She was hugely pregnant and ethereally lovely, with her curly dark hair swept up in a loose style on top of her head and her skin glowing with color and health.

Something tugged at his heart, something fierce and powerful. For one insane moment, he wanted nothing so much as to rush to her, sweep her into his arms and twirl her in the air again and again.

He saw the shock in her eyes, saw her features go a shade paler, and as he stood with one foot on the porch step, the whole wall of denial he had so carefully constructed tumbled down, brick by painful brick.

He was in love with her. Nothing had changed. All those months of trying to tell himself she meant nothing to him, that he could turn his back on what they might have had just as easily as she apparently could, were meaningless.

He let out a breath, furious with himself and with her. "What do you think you're doing here?" he bit out.

"You… You're not supposed to be home for another ten days."

"You're not supposed to be here at all," he snapped, wondering how she had known his travel schedule, the original one from before his injury. "What are you doing here, Mimi?"

She shrugged, still looking stunned and completely breathtaking. And nervous, he suddenly realized. She looked nervous to see him.

"Oh, you know. Just putting in some flowering annuals to help fill in the holes in your beds. The perennials won't really come into their full color until next summer but it will be glorious by this time next year."

"What are you doing *here?* At my ranch?"

She moved closer, the guilty expression on her features fading to one of concern. "Are you all right? You look a little pale."

He would never admit to her or anyone else that his knees were beginning to go weak at the pain screeching from his injuries. "Mimi! Answer me. What are you doing at Western Sky, planting annuals in my flower beds?"

She gnawed her lip. "Um, I live here. At least for another couple of days. I guess I'll be moving quicker than I'd planned. We really didn't think you were coming home until the week after next. What happened? Why did your plans change?"

He didn't want to explain to her that he'd spent the past two weeks in the burn unit at Ramstein. He hadn't told anyone, not even Easton, and it certainly wasn't

Mimi's business that he had been injured while trying to yank two Marines from a burning Humvee hit by an IED while traveling directly in front of his vehicle in a convoy.

Nor did he want to explain that he was becoming light-headed from the pain and needed to sit down before he fell over. Wouldn't that be a kick in the butt?

"Plans change," he said.

"Well, it would have been nice to know your arrangements," she said with a slightly disgruntled tone. "I planned to move out of Gwen's cabin before you arrived. Easton and I both thought it would probably be best."

"Easton knows you're here." She would have had to know, yet she hadn't said a word to him in their frequent email correspondence, the little sneak.

"Yes," she said warily.

The truth hit him in a rush, then. Everything seemed to shift into focus—the flower beds, the fresh paint on the barn, the hundreds of little changes around the ranch.

"You're the caretaker she's been raving about. The one who has poured so much effort into the house."

Guilt again flitted across her features. "Yes."

None of this made sense. He didn't know what to think. "Why do I always feel like I've stepped into some alternate universe when you're around?"

"I'm sorry."

"No, you're not. You like leaving people off balance, making sure they have no idea what to expect next. It's part of the whole Mimi charm."

She looked as if she wanted to disagree but she only moved toward the porch. "I'm sorry," she said again.

"But if you don't mind, I really need to sit down. My feet are a little swollen right now."

Since that matched exactly with his own hidden agenda that he'd rather be tortured than admit, he shrugged and headed up the stairs, dropping his duffel by the door.

"Before I sit down, I'm going to get a drink of water," she said. "I'm parched. Can I grab you one?"

He shrugged, not eager to accept anything from her even though the thought of the pure mountain spring water that came from the tap here was undeniably enticing.

He waited until she went into the house before he sagged into one of the rocking chairs and let out the tight breath that had been holding in all the pain from his injuries.

Simone had apparently missed him, if no one else had. The minute he sat down, she jumped onto his lap with an eager yip and he carefully kept her away from the bandages wrapped around his abdomen.

The Lab, not to be outdone, curled up at his boots, perfectly at home there.

Brant didn't care, he was just grateful to have a moment to absorb the shock of finding Mimi here in real life when he thought he would only be encountering the ghost of her memory.

She bustled out of the house a moment later with a small tray with two tall glasses, a sliced apple and some crackers and cheese. Seeing her so at home in his house gave him an odd feeling, a tangled mix of consternation and contentment.

While he drank, she lowered herself carefully into the rocker next to him and he watched over the top of his glass, fascinated with the cumbersome process. She looked round and lush and beautiful.

Once she sat, she sipped her own water, then set it on the arm of the rocker.

As the silence dragged on, it occurred to Brant that she was watching him as warily as if he were an IED being disarmed by an explosives ordnance disposal team.

He wanted to ask how she had been feeling. How was the baby? Did she know if she was having a boy or a girl and had she picked out names? Was she nervous about becoming a mother?

All those questions rattled through him but he forced himself to focus on the only thing that really mattered.

"Why are you here, Mimi?"

She chewed the corner of her lip again, and he remembered how delicious that mouth had tasted, how perfectly she had fit into his arms, how for one magical night he had allowed himself the most ridiculous dreams.

She finally sighed. "I convinced Easton to hire me. It's not her fault, honestly. Please don't blame her. I can be...persuasive when I set my mind to it."

"Why would you try to be persuasive?"

"I needed a place to stay away from all the craziness and... I like it here. It's peaceful and quiet and the people are so warm and kind to me. Easton and Maggie Dalton threw a baby shower for me last week. Isn't that great? And nearly everyone they invited showed up. I got the most darling clothes and toys you can imagine for the baby and you should see the crib quilt that Emery Cavazos made. It's a work of art that should be in a museum! You wouldn't believe how kind everyone here is to me."

She seemed so shocked and delighted that he didn't have the heart to tell her most of the people in Pine Gulch were kind to just about everyone.

"How long have you been here?"

"Since March, when Gwen moved to her house in Jackson Hole."

He couldn't seem to absorb it, even with the reality of her sitting beside him. How could she have spent five months in virtual seclusion out here, away from the crowds and the stores and the cameras?

"Why didn't the paparazzi mob you here? I haven't seen anything about you living on a ranch in eastern Idaho."

Not that he'd been looking, he assured himself.

"I made sort of a devil's bargain with them. I would show up once a month in California for a long weekend and go to a few parties, do a little shopping, strictly for their benefit, and in return they would leave me alone the rest of the time. Since my life here is pretty tame, there's not much to photograph except the occasional trip to the hardware store for paint and to the Gulch for lunch with Easton and Maggie and the rest of the friends I've made here."

He tried to picture her walking the crowded aisles of the hardware store and ordering greasy food at the café in town and pushing a cart around the grocery store and couldn't seem to make his imagination stretch that far.

"Why did no one in town happen to mention to me in those five months that Mimi Van Hoyt was living in my house?"

"Not in your house, technically. In Gwen's cabin."

He glared at her nitpicky correction and she sighed.

"Easton knew you wouldn't like it so she purposely didn't say anything. Everyone else probably figured you already knew."

"You could have found a quiet place anywhere else on earth to hide out until you have the baby. There are other peaceful spots around the globe. Why did it have to be here."

"I like it here," she said again. "I really can't give you any other explanation than that. When Gwen told me Easton was looking to hire someone to replace her as caretaker and continue the work I started fixing up the place, I called her right away and applied for the job."

He apparently had to have a long talk with Easton about hiding things from him and about keeping her busybody nose out of his affairs. But then Easton couldn't have known the whole story about what had happened between him and Mimi. He supposed he couldn't be too angry at her for allowing the one woman he least wanted to see to take over his ranch.

"I'm sorry it upsets you," Mimi went on carefully. "I honestly planned to finish everything up and be out of here before you returned."

"So you'll be moving out."

"Yes." She hesitated. "But I should probably tell you, in the interest of full disclosure, that I want Dr. Dalton to deliver my baby, so I'll be sticking around Pine Gulch until after the birth. Nate and Emery have offered me the use of one of the guest cabins at Hope Springs. Caroline and Wade Dalton also have been pushing me to stay at their guesthouse at the Cold Creek. I guess I have to choose now, don't I?"

Some petty part of him wanted to tell her she had

to choose right now, tonight. But she was hugely pregnant and he couldn't just toss her out into the cold, as much as he would like to. "No rush," he lied. "Take a few days to make up your mind where you want to go."

The way he felt right now, he figured he wouldn't be crawling out of bed for the next day and a half so he likely wouldn't even run into her again.

Before he could rein it in, his wayward imagination flashed a picture of falling asleep with Mimi next to him in his big bed, all her warmth and softness curled against him, with her dark curls drifting across his skin, with his hands splayed across that fascinating round belly....

He caught the direction of his gaze and frowned, disgusted at himself. Amazing what kind of crazy images could play with a man's head when he was exhausted and sore.

"I appreciate that," she said, and it took him a minute to realize she was referring to his comment that she didn't have to leave immediately.

He wanted to tell her that was still his preference— that she go and take her little dog with her—but he decided to save his energy.

"Are you all right?" she asked after a long moment.

He blinked at her. "Why?"

"You seem...distracted."

Well, he couldn't take a deep breath because of the burns and he'd just endured three weeks of misery in a military hospital and he was pretty close to falling over from exhaustion.

Other than that, he was swell.

"Just surprised," he said, his voice coming out gruff. "I didn't expect to find you here—or anywhere, really, ever again. It's been a shock and I'm still reeling a little."

"Are you angry?"

Angry? That seemed a mild word when he thought of the heaviness in his heart these past four months.

No. *Angry* would imply he cared about her, that he had been hurt by what had happened between them.

"I would have to care to be angry," he answered. "Now if you'll excuse me, I've been traveling for a day and need to find my bed."

"Okay." She smiled but it wasn't the incandescent Mimi smile he remembered. This one was smaller and a little sad. "Welcome home, Major."

He inclined his head to answer her and pushed Simone onto the ground, then gripped the arms of the rocker and marshalled all his strength to rise.

He probably would have been fine and managed to go inside without her being any the wiser, but he misjudged the width of the rocking chair and his injured side brushed the wooden arm as he rose.

Pain clawed at him—fierce, unrelenting—and he couldn't contain one sharp inhale. His knees went weak and he had to sit back down, more carefully this time.

Mimi paled and was at his side in an instant. "What is it? What's wrong?"

"Nothing. I'm fine. Goodbye."

"You're not fine! You've been hurt, haven't you? That's why you're home early. That's why you're so pale and you're sweating, even here on the cool porch."

He didn't want her to know. She would probably rush right over to Winder Ranch and tell Easton, who was apparently her chatty new best friend.

"It's nothing," he repeated.

"Who's the liar now?" she snapped. "What happened? You might as well tell me. I can find out with a few simple phone calls."

She was right. With her father's clout, she could probably worm out any detail of his life she ever wanted to know.

Anyway, the truth was easier. He was pretty sure he didn't have the energy to stand here and make up some elaborate story.

"No big deal. I suffered a little injury in an incident a few weeks ago."

Her face seemed to leach out of what little color she had left. "How little? What kind of incident? Were you shot?"

He thought of the three weeks he'd spent in the burn unit of Ramstein and the surgeries and the skin grafts and the risks of infection he still faced. He almost thought he would have preferred a nice clean gunshot wound.

"No," he said shortly, hoping she would leave it at that. But of course, being Mimi, she didn't.

"What is it? Tell me, Brant." She spoke in a low, urgent voice, her eyes huge in her lovely face.

He was weak to let her affect him so much, but somehow her concern warmed a cold, achy corner of his heart.

"Burned. We were in a convoy traveling behind a Humvee that hit an IED. My arm and side sustained a little heat damage during the rescue effort." A nice way of saying second-and third-degree burns over a good portion of skin.

Chapter 13

Mimi closed her eyes, trying not to picture the scene in her mind, the screams and the flames and the smell of burning flesh. She could clearly envision Brant rushing to the rescue, taking charge of the scene with that sense of command that was so innate.

She fought down tears, wondering why she seemed to spend so much time blubbering around him.

"You need to rest. I'm sorry I've kept you talking out here when you should be sleeping."

He didn't look as if he had the energy even to argue with her, though she still saw a shadow of the anger she fully deserved in his gaze.

"I'll start making arrangements to find another place to stay," she said. She hated the idea of leaving the Western Sky, but she owed him that, at least.

"Fine," he said shortly, and she caught the message

loud and clear. He wanted her gone. Beyond that, he didn't care what she did.

"Do you need any help with anything?"

His short laugh sounded icy cold. "From you? No thank you."

He rose abruptly, picked up his duffel from the porch and stalked into the house.

She deserved that. Mimi curled her fingers, doing her best to ignore the ache in her chest. He had every reason to detest her after the things she said to him. What else could she expect?

He was injured. She pictured again that shock of pain in his eyes when he had brushed against the chair. Foolish man. He was hurt and he hadn't even told his foster sister. Easton would have told Mimi if she'd known.

How could she leave him alone here at the ranch when he was in pain and possibly needing help?

Brant didn't want her here. She had made sure he wouldn't by pretending condescension and disdain. She couldn't complain now when her efforts paid off.

In her mind, those few days she had spent here with him possessed a magical, dreamlike quality, and she had wondered if she might have imagined the intensity of her feelings for him. Seeing him again answered that question. She was still in love with him, perhaps more now than she'd ever been. She had had five months to think about his strength and his honor, to vividly remember the safety and peace she found in his arms.

Because she loved him, she would leave this place she also loved. He deserved to have his home to himself, especially since he was injured and in pain.

She pressed a hand on her abdomen, to the little

life growing there. "We'll be okay, kiddo," she whispered, repeating the mantra that had sustained her for five months.

She had used the same mantra during those first heartbreaking days after she left the ranch, when she told her father the news of her pregnancy, when she and her extensive team of lawyers met with Marco to convince him to formally relinquish any claim of paternity for the child and never speak of it again, which he had been only too eager to do. As far as Mimi was concerned, while the public statement that she had conceived via in vitro wasn't technically true, Marco had only been her baby's sperm donor, nothing more.

Seeing Brant again made her wish once more with all her heart that she had picked someone like him to father her child. But she wouldn't regret the course her life had taken.

She had grown more these past five months than she ever could have imagined. Here at the Western Sky, she discovered she loved fixing up properties and she was good at it. She had learned she could be completely focused on something when she set her mind to it and she had learned to count on herself instead of a team of handlers to take care of her every need.

Most important, she had found inside herself a strength and courage she never would have imagined before she had been forced to rely on them. She had a suspicion she wasn't finished needing those attributes. Now that she had seen him again and realized she still loved him, she knew she was going to have many days and nights of sorrow ahead.

At least she would have her daughter to help her through.

"We'll be okay, kiddo," she said again, then levered herself up from the rocking chair, not an easy task these days.

"Come, Simone. Come, Hector." She spoke to her bichon frise and to the Lab mix Easton had talked her into a month ago. "We've got flowers to plant."

The dogs jumped up and Mimi walked down the steps after them.

Like the complicated process of maneuvering around with her pregnancy bulk, she would eventually learn how to live with this emptiness in her heart.

He awoke disoriented and with his side bellowing in pain.

Brant drew in a deep focused breath and then another and another until he could force the pain to recede enough that he could think.

He hadn't slept round-the-clock, as he might have hoped, only about ten hours. According to the lighted face of his watch, it was 5:00 a.m. At this time of year, just a few weeks after the summer solstice, the sun rose early. Out his window he could see a pale rim of light along the jagged mountain peaks, a clear indication that sunrise was an hour or so away.

He lay in bed for a long moment, catching his breath and his bearings. He was a lousy patient, as any of the nurses at the Ramstein hospital could have attested. He hated the feeling that his body could be vulnerable, that he wasn't at full fighting form.

The doctors told him he could expect a good two or

three months of healing time before he felt like himself. He was ready for it to happen this minute.

He sighed. He would get over it. He was good at learning to live with things he didn't want.

Like his memories of Mimi.

He didn't want to think about her, so he swung his legs over the side of the bed and headed for the bathroom.

She had made big changes here. New light fixtures, new paint to replace the aging wallpaper, even the vanity was new.

Blasted woman. He washed his hands and headed for the kitchen for a drink of water, dressed only in low-slung sweats. He turned on the low light above the kitchen and frowned again at more evidence of Mimi's handiwork. The paint was new here, as well, and it looked to him as if the knotty pine cabinets had a new coat of stain.

He hoped like hell she hadn't paid for everything out of her own pocket, that Easton had taken care of the expenses out of the ranch maintenance account she was named on with him.

When he had his strength back a little bit, he planned to have a long talk with Easton to find out what she possibly could have been thinking to allow Mimi here.

Not that he could blame Easton for this mess. He knew from past experience that Mimi could talk her way into anything.

But why would she want to? Why was she here? None of it made sense. When she walked away that terrible last day, she had left him in no doubt that she wanted nothing to do with him.

As sweet as you've been, Brant, you're...well, not exactly my type.

She couldn't offer much more clarity than that. And yet she'd spent the past five months taking care of his ranch while she grew huge with child.

He shook his head as he turned on the faucet—a new brushed nickel one that looked complicated and expensive. After he filled his glass, he turned around and nearly spilled the water all over the floor when he found her standing in the doorway in a nightgown, with a blanket wrapped around her shoulders.

"Mimi! What the hell?"

So much for being a highly trained commando. Mortification swamped him that she could catch him off guard like this, sore and sleepy and wearing only loose sweats.

He also had an instant of painful awareness that seeing her like this, lush and feminine and lovely in her soft mint-green nightgown, while he was only wearing sweats, would show her quite clearly just how glad at least some of him was to see her.

"Sorry. I saw the light and wanted to make sure you were okay."

"You sure moved fast from Gwen's cabin," he muttered, willing away his response.

A delicate hint of color climbed her ivory skin. "I slept on the sofa," she admitted. "I know, nervy of me. But you seemed so shaky earlier that I thought maybe I better check on you. I stopped in around midnight and... you were moaning a little in your sleep and I didn't feel right about leaving you here by yourself."

Now it was his turn to flush. He hated that the pain

he fought so hard to contain during the day could growl to life when he wasn't conscious of it.

"I don't need a keeper."

He started to say more but then he caught her expression of horror and realized she was staring at his bandages, the eight-inch-wide gauze wrapped around his middle and the corresponding size encasing his arm from mid-forearm to above his elbow.

One hand fluttered to her mouth and her big green eyes filled with tears. "Oh, Brant."

He shifted. "Come on. Cut it out. Don't cry."

She drew in a ragged breath then exhaled a sobbing sort of noise, those eyes swimming with tears now, and he groaned. Though a big section of his brain was calling him any number of synonyms for nutty as a fruitcake, he crossed the distance between them and pulled her against his uninjured side.

"Come on, don't cry. I'm okay."

"You could have been killed."

"But I wasn't." He was suddenly fiercely glad of that, that he had been given one more chance to hold her again, to feel her soft curves and smell that delicious scent of flowers and citrus and her.

"I told myself not to worry, that you could take care of yourself," she whispered. "But I think I've prayed more in five months than I have the rest of my life put together and I've completely devoured all the coverage I could on Afghanistan."

Something in her words tugged at his Mimi-dazed brain, but it still took a moment for the incongruity of it to click.

"Why do you care?"

She lifted her eyes to his and he saw embarrassment flicker there and something else, something deeper, before she shifted her gaze away. "I just do."

She was lying. He knew it. He lifted her chin to face him again and this time he read everything in her eyes and the truth reached out and coldcocked him.

He stared at her for a long time and then shook his head. "You are a big fat liar, Mimi Van Hoyt."

The corners of her mouth trembled a little but she quickly straightened it out. "I know," she said in a deceptively casual tone. "I'm so big I can barely fit through doorways these days."

"You know that's not what I meant. I think you're more beautiful than you've ever been. But you lied to me that last day. You stood here in my house and fibbed through your perfect little teeth."

She stepped away from him, taking all her heat and softness away and leaving him cold in the predawn chill. "I...don't know what you're talking about."

He thought of the five months of misery he had spent, how it had taken every ounce of hard-fought discipline he possessed to focus on the mission and not wallow in self-pity. "It was all an act to push me away, wasn't it? You didn't mean a word."

She wrapped her arms around her chest, which just made her nightgown stretch across her round belly.

"Yes, I did. I didn't—I don't—want you dragged into my world, Brant. You saw how ugly it could be and those photographers showing up here was just a small sampling of what it can be like. I love you too much to put you through that."

He stared at her, her words surging around and

through him. *I love you too much.* Some corner of his mind had begun to suspect it, but hearing her say the words still stunned him like a percussion round.

"What did you say?"

"I can't put you through that. It's not fair. You're a good, honorable man. I'm Mimi Van Hoyt—stupid, rich, silly socialite. I'll ruin your life."

By the time she finished, she was nearly sobbing and he realized two things simultaneously—that she wholly believed her words, and that he had been a frigging idiot.

"It's my life. Don't you think I ought to have a say in whether it's ruined or not?"

"No." She looked as distressed as she was determined. "You don't know what it's like in the spotlight and I do."

"I don't care."

"You say that now. But you haven't had to live with it day in and day out your entire life."

"Poor Mimi." He couldn't help himself, he pulled her into his arms again.

"You don't want that, Brant. Please believe me on this."

"Hate to break it to you, Mimi, but you don't get to decide what I want and don't want."

She opened her mouth to argue, but he gave a long-suffering sigh and shut her up by kissing her. She stood rigid in his arms for a moment and then she melted against him, her arms around his neck and her belly pressing against him.

It was sweet and wonderful, better even than kicking

off his boots after a two-week mission, and he never wanted it to end.

"I just spent four months missing you every single minute of every single day," he murmured against her mouth. "I fell asleep thinking about you and woke up thinking about you. It took all my concentration to do my job."

She made a tiny sound but he couldn't tell what it meant.

"I love you, Mimi. I love your stubborn streak and your funny sense of humor and your big green eyes. I love the way you chew her lip when you're concentrating and the way you pamper that silly little dog and how you shiver when I kiss you. You want to know what I want, with everything inside me? You. That's all. You. Today, tomorrow, forever."

When her eyes met his, they were dazed and a deeper green than he'd ever seen them.

"What about the media circus?"

"What about them? You said yourself they haven't bothered you much when you're living here. So we'll just spent the next fifty years being boring and they'll lose interest."

"I wish it were that easy."

He kissed her again. "Who said life was supposed to be easy? We can make it work, Mimi. I swear to you. Can't you trust me?"

This couldn't be happening. Mimi closed her eyes, wondering if this was another of those dreams where she woke up with a wet pillow and empty arms.

No. He was real. Big and solid and wonderful and claiming he loved her.

She wanted so desperately to believe him, to hold on to the delicious dream that they could actually build a life together.

If any man was strong enough to face off against the paparazzi, it was Brant. And he was right; they had quickly tired of her sedate pace of life here in Pine Gulch. What was the fun in shooting her when she wasn't doing anything outrageous, just living her life like Maura Howard would?

Could she dare believe him?

"I'm having another man's child. Are you okay with that?"

His mouth quirked up in a half smile. "The way I heard, it was in vitro fertilization."

"You know that's not true."

"As far as I'm concerned, it is." He kissed her again, leaving her no doubts that he meant his words.

A fragile hope began to quiver inside her. A life with him here in Pine Gulch or wherever his Army career took him. She wanted it, more than she'd ever wanted anything in her life.

"Are we having a boy or a girl?" Brant asked against her mouth, and just like that she started to cry again. He kissed away every tear.

She didn't deserve to be this happy, did she? As soon as the thought pulsed through her, she pushed it away. Why didn't she deserve a little happiness? Or huge bushels full of it?

"A girl." She gave him a watery smile, a smile that carried all the love in her heart for him. "I was thinking about naming her Abigail Sage. It was my grandmother's name."

"Abigail Western. Has a nice ring to it, don't you think?"

She stared at him for a long moment and finally had to force herself to breathe. A quiet peace seemed to eddy around them like the rivulets of Cold Creek, washing away all the pain, all the doubt, all the hurt. In his arms, she could believe anything was possible.

"Yes," she said softly. "I think Abigail Western sounds perfect."

Brant smiled and kissed her with a tenderness that nearly made her cry again. "If she's anything like her mother, she will be."

Mimi shook her head. She wasn't perfect. Far from it. She was a work in progress—but now she had her own blue-eyed warrior to help her on the journey.

Epilogue

"You make a beautiful bride."

Mimi hugged Easton, thinking how lovely her maid of honor looked. No one seeing this fragile, feminine creature in the pale sage dress with the long blond hair in a graceful updo would ever guess she spent most of her days riding fence line and fixing tractors.

Easton was stunning, even with that hint of sadness in her blue eyes.

"I appreciate you saying that," Mimi answered, "especially since I'm bigger than one of your cows right now."

"You glow, just like a new bride—and mom-to-be— is supposed to. Brant can't take his eyes off you."

That particular feeling was mutual. Every time she happened to see him in his dress uniform with that chest full of medals, looking tall and gorgeous and commanding, she couldn't seem to look away.

Her gaze unerringly found him, speaking with his friend Quinn Southerland and Quinn's wife, Tess. Brant held their newborn son, Joe, only a month old, and he looked completely natural with a tiny bundle in his arms.

She smiled with anticipation, imagining him holding their child, and she suddenly couldn't wait.

"He's something, isn't he?"

"He is," Easton agreed. "Sometimes I want to wring his neck but I wouldn't change him."

Mimi thought of how dear the other woman had become to her in the six months since she showed up at the Western Sky, afraid and alone. Easton had become the true sister Mimi had always wanted and never found with every new step-sibling her father gave her.

When Easton turned to whisper in Mimi's ear over the noise of the music and the crowd, she leaned closer, expecting maybe a tidbit of gossip or words of encouragement.

Instead, Easton smiled for the benefit of the other wedding guests and murmured, "Screw him over, Ms. Van Hoyt, and I'll come looking for you with a cattle prod."

"I wouldn't dare," Mimi promised with a laugh. Though she knew Easton was completely serious in her threat, she also knew her friend was thrilled she and Brant had found each other. "And it's Mrs. Western now."

"Good. As long we understand each other." Easton smiled back, then changed the subject, her duties as loyal foster sister apparently discharged. "I can't believe the vultures haven't descended yet."

"Thanks for the reminder." Mimi winced. Even now, the press corps would be milling at the end of the access road to the Western Sky, where she and Brant had married a half hour ago next to the silvery creek she had driven into that first day.

She had hoped to keep the wedding a secret, but Pine Gulch was a small town. Even though their wedding was intimate, between the caterers and the band and the florist, word had somehow trickled out. The paparazzi had begun arriving the night before and some of them had even started camping out on the public right-of-way along Cold Creek Canyon Road.

"How did you keep them out?" Easton asked.

"Brant threatened them all with a shotgun again," she said.

"He did not!"

"Okay, he didn't threaten them. But he made sure he had his Remington with him and ever so subtly held on to it at his side when we went down to talk to them this morning. We promised if they wouldn't try to crash the actual ceremony, we would come down and pose for the cameras later."

She supposed it had been foolish to hope she and Brant might avoid the tabloids completely, especially since the public had avidly latched on to the story when rumors of her romance with Brant and the impending wedding started to trickle out. The pregnant society heiress and the gorgeous injured war hero made for great copy.

They would probably have to cope with paparazzi

for a while, what with the wedding and her impending birth, but she had high hopes that they'd lose interest soon. Brant didn't seem to be bothered by it. In fact, he seemed to be finding great humor in their interest, for the most part—especially his new nickname, Mimi's Warrior.

She pressed a hand to her abdomen, hoping she could make it on her feet long enough for a photo session. The vague aches in her back had intensified over the past hour, but she was doing her best to ignore them.

"Uh-oh. Werner alert," Easton said. "Want me to distract him?"

Mimi shook her head. "Thanks for the offer, but I think I'll be okay."

To her shock, her father seemed as close as she'd ever seen to being pleased about something she was doing. He was actually happy about her marriage to Brant, something she never would have expected.

They both had such strong personalities, she never would have guessed they'd rub together so well. Brant hadn't tried to ingratiate himself in her father's graces. In fact, he'd been on the abrasive side, making it clear that while Werner might consider his daughter a bubbleheaded socialite, Brant had far different views. Instead of being offended, her father had treated him with respect and even admiration.

"You look just like your mother did on her wedding day," Werner said gruffly now, and she was aware that Easton, the traitor, had melted away into the crowd.

Mimi laughed. "Was she eight and a half months pregnant, too?"

"You know she wasn't. But she was almost as pretty as you are right now."

He looked at Brant, still holding baby Joe. "He's a good man. He's almost good enough for you."

"Thanks, Dad."

He paused for a long moment, and then he smiled—a little sadly, she thought. "I love you, you know. I'm not always great at showing it, but I do."

Tears welled up in her eyes but she refused to let them ruin her mascara. Not on her wedding day.

She kissed his cheek, the first time in her recent memory she had initiated affectionate contact between them. Werner stood stiffly for a long moment and then he gathered her close in a clumsy sort of hug, made even more awkward by her belly.

She closed her eyes, smelling the cologne he had created exclusively for himself at a Paris fragrance house. In this moment, all the pain of the past and the silly power struggles between them seemed far away.

"He's a good man," her father repeated. "He'll take good care of you and the baby."

Once he recovered from his initial shock at her pregnancy, Werner had once more surprised her. He seemed to actually be looking forward to becoming a grandfather.

Marta, his current wife, gestured to him a moment later and Werner gave her another awkward squeeze then went to join her stepmother.

Mimi felt the heat of someone's gaze on her and turned to find Brant watching her. She smiled at him and headed toward him, but she had only taken a few steps when she felt something strange.

She froze and it took her a full minute to figure out what had happened. When she did, she started to laugh and couldn't seem to stop.

Brant met her halfway and pulled her into his warm embrace. "I never realized being married to me would be such a laugh fest."

This set her off again and she had to wipe her eyes with the little lace-trimmed hankie Easton had given her, the something old that had belonged to Brant's foster mother, Jo Winder.

"Um, have you seen Jake?" she asked him between giggles.

He frowned. "I think I saw him and Maggie out on the dance floor a minute ago. Why?"

She wrapped her arms as tightly as she could manage around him with her bulk in the way. He obligingly leaned his head down so she could whisper in his ear.

"My water just broke."

He jerked back as if she'd punched him and she had to laugh again at his stunned expression.

"You're not due for three more weeks!"

"I guess Abigail was a little put out that we didn't wait for her to be the flower girl at her mommy and daddy's wedding. Either that or she's a bit of a prima donna and wants all the attention for herself."

He still wore that stunned expression but after a moment, it shifted to something else, a complex mix of nerves and shock, underscored by a deep joy. He pulled her into his arms again and she felt his lips on her hair for only a moment, then he loosened his hold.

"Okay. We can do this. Where's Jake? We need to get

your bag from inside. It's still packed, right? I'll drive us to Idaho Falls. Or do you want to take the limousine?"

This man who could coordinate complicated troop movements and arrange logistical support to transport an entire company of soldiers across the world within a few hours looked more than a little panicked.

She smiled and squeezed his fingers. "Dr. Dalton. Let's start with him."

"Right. Jake." He stepped away to go after the doctor, then suddenly turned back to her and swept her back into his arms. He kissed her fiercely, eyes blazing with tenderness.

"I love you," he said.

She managed a smile, even as the first contraction hit. "I still don't know why, but I'm so glad you do. I love you, too."

"You're doing this just to get me out of the photo shoot, aren't you?"

More laughter bubbled out of her. "No, but I wish I'd thought of it. You know they're going to go crazy over this. Not every bride leaves her own wedding reception in labor."

"Let them go crazy. It will be a great story we can tell Abby someday." He paused. "You're going to be a fantastic mother."

"If we don't hurry, I'm afraid I'm going to become a fantastic mother in the middle of my own wedding reception."

He grinned, squeezed her hand and rushed away.

Mimi watched him go, her warrior. She thought of the journey that had led her here, the strange twists and turns. It was fate that had led her to run to Gwen that day, fate that had brought her to this ranch she loved so much. And to this man she loved more than she could believe possible.

She pressed a hand to her abdomen as she saw Brant return with Jake Dalton in tow. "We're going to be okay, kiddo," she murmured. "You, me and your wonderful daddy."

* * * * *

Michelle Major grew up in Ohio but dreamed of living in the mountains. Soon after graduating with a degree in journalism, she pointed her car west and settled in Colorado. Her life and house are filled with one great husband, two beautiful kids, a few furry pets and several well-behaved reptiles. She's grateful to have found her passion writing stories with happy endings. Michelle loves to hear from her readers at michellemajor.com.

Visit the Author Profile page
at Harlequin.com for more titles.

A BREVIA BEGINNING

Michelle Major

To my grandmother, Ruth Keller,
for believing in me and my writing
from the time I was a little girl.
I love you, Gram.

Chapter 1

The street was deserted in the early-morning hours. Sunlight slanted over the roofs of the brick buildings as Lexi Preston huddled on the front stoop of a dark storefront. She rested her head in her hands and watched the wind swirl a small pile of autumn leaves. The air held a chill, but it felt good after being stuck in her car for the last day and a half.

Almost six months had passed since she'd set foot in Brevia, North Carolina. She couldn't imagine the reception she'd receive, but was desperate enough not to care. Her eyes drifted shut—just for a minute, she told herself—but she must have fallen asleep. When she blinked them open again it was to the bright sun shining and someone nudging a foot against hers. She scrambled to her feet, embarrassed to be caught so off guard.

"What the hell do you want?" Julia Callahan's voice cut through the quiet.

Lexi backed away a few steps. Yes, she was desperate, but Julia had every reason to hate her. Still, she whispered, "I need your help. I have nowhere else to go."

Julia's delicate eyebrows rose. Lexi wished she had the ability to communicate so much without speaking. She could almost feel the anger radiating from the other woman. But Julia's furrowed brow and pinched lips did nothing to detract from her beauty. She was thin, blonde and several inches taller than Lexi. The epitome of the Southern prom queen grown up. Lexi knew there was more to her than that. After all, she'd spent months researching every detail of Julia Callahan's life.

"You tried to take my son away from me." Julia shook her head. "Why would I have any inclination to help you?"

"I made sure you kept him in the end," Lexi said, adjusting her round glasses. "Don't forget I was the one who gave you the information that made the Johnsons rescind their custody suit."

"I haven't forgotten," Julia answered. "It doesn't explain why you're on the doorstep of my salon. Or what kind of help you need."

Lexi crossed her arms over her chest as her stomach began to roll. She should have stopped for breakfast on the way into town. "They found out it was me," she continued. "Dennis and Maria Johnson fired my father's firm as their corporate attorneys. Several of their friends followed. We lost over half our business."

Her voice faltered as memories of her father's rage

and disappointment assaulted her. She cleared her throat. "In response, my dad made a big show of humiliating me in front of the entire firm. Then he officially fired and practically disowned me."

Lexi had worked for her father's firm since she graduated from law school six years ago. Following in his footsteps, doing whatever he expected, had been her overriding goal in life. She still lived in the apartment he'd paid for since college. Her eviction notice had come two days ago.

She drew a steadying breath. "He said he regretted the day I'd come into his life. That I'm nothing more than…"

"Your father is an ass." Julia's clear assessment almost made Lexi smile.

"True," she agreed, blinking against the sudden moisture in her eyes. "But he's all I have. Or had."

"What about other family?"

"I was adopted when I was six. I was in the foster-care system and barely remember my biological mother. My dad never married. He was an only child and my grandparents died years ago."

"Friends?"

"I have work acquaintances, country-club cliques and clients. I'm not very good at making friends."

"It's probably hard to be a backstabbing, underhanded, slimy lawyer and a good friend at the same time."

Although the words hurt, Lexi couldn't help but hear the truth in them. "I guess."

"Sheesh. That was a joke." Julia stepped past her and turned a key in the front door. "Lighten up, Lex."

Lexi followed her into the empty salon, the emotional roller coaster of the past week finally sending her off the rails. "Are you kidding?" she yelled. "I just told you that my life is destroyed because I saved you and your son. I have nothing. No job. No home. No friends. No family. And you want me to lighten up?"

Julia flipped on a bank of lights and turned. "Actually, I want you to tell me how I'm supposed to help. Other than playing the tiniest violin in the world in your honor. I appreciate what you did for me. But we both know you put me through hell trying to give custody of Charlie to my ex-boyfriend's family. That doesn't exactly make us long-lost besties."

"I want a fresh start."

"So make one."

"It's not that easy. As ridiculous as it sounds, I'm twenty-seven years old and my father has controlled every aspect of my life. Hell, he even handpicked a personal shopper to make sure I always projected the right image. The image he chose for me. Since the moment I came to live with him, I've wanted to make him happy, make him believe I was worthy of his love and the money he spent on me."

She ran her hands through her hair and began to pace between the rows of styling chairs. "I'd never done anything without his approval until I gave you that file. I don't regret it. You're a great mother and I feel awful about my part in the custody suit."

"You should," Julia agreed.

Lexi sighed. "If I could take it all back, I would. I know it was wrong. But helping you cost my father a lot. I thought he'd understand and forgive me."

"He still might."

"I don't know if I want him to. At least not on his terms. I don't want to be the same kind of attorney my dad is. I don't even know if I still want to be a lawyer. I need time to breathe. To figure out my next move. To make a choice in life for me, not because it's what's expected." She paused and took a breath. "I thought maybe you could understand that."

Julia studied her for a few moments. "Maybe I can."

Lexi swallowed her embarrassment and continued, "If I stay in Brevia for a few weeks, I could figure out my options. I don't want my father to find me. I don't think he's going to forgive me, but I do expect him to come looking. He likes the control and he's not going to give that up so easily."

She patted her purse. "I have five hundred dollars in cash. I don't want to use credit cards or anything to help him track me. Not yet."

"You're kind of freaking me out. Is he dangerous?"

Lexi ran her hand along the edge of a shelf of styling products. "Not physically. But I'm not strong enough yet to stand on my own. Who knows if I'll ever be. But I want to try. I liked Brevia when I was here. I admire you, Julia. Your fierceness and determination. I know you have no reason to help me, but I'm asking you to, anyway."

"And you couldn't have called on your way?"

"I'm sorry," Lexi said quickly. "I wasn't thinking. I just got in my car and started driving. This was the only place I could think of to go. But if you—"

Julia held up a hand. "This is probably more of my typical bad judgment, but I'll help you."

Lexi felt her knees go weak with relief. Julia Callahan was her first, last and only hope. She knew her father well enough to know he was punishing her. That when he felt as if she'd been gone long enough to learn her lesson, he'd pull her back. In the past, Lexi would have been scrambling to find a way to return to his good graces. Something had changed in her when she'd chosen her act of rebellion. From the start, she'd known he'd find out, and she'd understood there would be hell to pay. She also believed it couldn't be worse than the hell she called a life.

"Thank you," she whispered with a shaky breath. "I promise I won't be an imposition on your life. I could answer phones or sweep up hair—whatever you need."

"A job?" Julia looked confused. "I thought you needed moral support. You're an attorney, for Pete's sake. Why do you want to sweep the floors of a hair salon?"

"I'm licensed in North Carolina to practice, but if I register with the state's bar association, my father will find me. I told you, I need time."

"I'm going to make coffee. I need the caffeine." The stylist looked over her shoulder at Lexi. "Have you had breakfast? We keep a stash of granola bars in the break room."

Lexi followed her to the back of the building. "A granola bar would be great. And I really will help out with anything you need."

Julia poured grounds into the coffee filter and filled the machine with water. She turned back to Lexi, shaking her head. "We start renovations next week on the salon's expansion. I can't hire anyone right now."

"I get it. I appreciate the moral support. I guess."

"No wonder your father can manipulate you so easily. Your emotions are written all over your face. You need to work on a tough exterior if you want to do okay on your own. Fake it till you make it, right? I thought lawyers were supposed to be excellent bluffers."

Lexi slid into one of the folding chairs at the small table. "I'm not much of a bluffer. That's why I was usually behind the scenes. I'm good at details and digging up dirt."

"Yes, I remember," Julia answered drily.

"Do you know anyone who's hiring in Brevia? Just temporarily."

A slow smile spread across Julia's porcelain features. "Now that you mention it, I do know about an available job. One of the waitresses at the local bar had twins last night. They came about a month early and were practically born in the back of Sam's police cruiser."

"Are you thinking I'd make a good nanny?"

"I wouldn't wish that job even on you. I'm thinking you'd make a perfect cocktail waitress."

"I don't drink," Lexi said quickly.

"You have to serve the drinks. Not guzzle them yourself."

Lexi unwrapped the granola bar Julia handed to her, her empty stomach grumbling in anticipation. "I don't like those types of places."

"I don't like exercise," the other woman countered, "but I still run five days a week."

Lexi closed her eyes for a moment. Julia's quick wit and no-nonsense attitude were what she'd initially found so fascinating. Almost a year ago, Lexi and her father had been hired by their longtime clients Dennis and Maria Johnson to investigate Julia's life so they could try to take custody of her young son away from her. The boy's biological father was the Johnsons' son, Jeff.

Lexi knew if you threw enough money at a problem, it likely went away. But Julia had kept fighting. Sure, she had her problems, but Lexi had never seen someone stand up to people with so much power. Julia might have been faking her confidence some of the time, but it had made Lexi realize she didn't have to be her father's puppet forever.

Even if she owed him everything, didn't she still deserve to make choices in her own life? To live life on her terms? She had to at least try.

"Could the work last six weeks?"

"I think so. Amy is going to have her hands full, but I know she doesn't want to lose her job. She works at night, so she'll be able to manage around the babies once she gets back on her feet."

"It sounds good, although I don't have any experience as a waitress."

"Are you a quick learner?"

Lexi swallowed. "I made it through law school at the head of my class. I'm not sure how that applies to waitressing, but it's all I've got."

Julia watched her for another moment. "Are you sure you want to do this? It would be easier to go groveling to Daddy and beg him to give you back your cushy little life."

Lexi stood. "I want a real life."

"I know how that feels. I've got a place you can stay while you're in town. Let me text my receptionist to come in early, then we can get you settled." Julia took out her phone and began punching the keypad. "No offense, but you could use a shower and change of clothes."

Lexi looked down at her wrinkled pants and the stain of coffee on her collared button-down. "I stayed at a cheap motel off the interstate last night," she admitted. "The bathroom creeped me out too much to use this morning."

"Clearly." Julia finished her text, then grabbed a set of keys from a hook behind the door. "Are you ready?"

"As much as I appreciate your help, I can't possibly impose and stay at your house," Lexi argued.

"No doubt. You can have my apartment. With everything happening so quickly, I'm still on the lease. I've been subletting it to Sam's dad, but Joe and my mom got married a few weeks ago. The place is empty."

"Two family weddings in one year. Congrats, by the way."

Julia smiled. "Thanks. It's been a whirlwind but I'm happy."

"Your relationship with Sam really started as a fake arrangement to help with the custody case?"

"It did, but then it became so much more."

Lexi thought for a moment, then said, "I guess you could say that I'm partially responsible. Without the custody fight, who knows if or when you two would have gotten around to figuring out you're perfect for each other."

Julia laughed out loud. "Don't push your luck. I said I'd help you. I'll make sure you get the job, and sublet my apartment to you. I've got another three months on the lease. But as far as figuring out your life and growing a spine when it comes to your father, that's all you."

Lexi wondered if she'd ever be able to loosen her father's hold. In the past she hadn't realized how bad she wanted that. Now she did, and if this was her only chance to make it happen, she wasn't going to blow it.

She nodded, her throat tight with emotion. "I'm going to give it my best shot."

Scott Callahan heard the crash as he took another deep swallow from his glass of whiskey. He glanced toward the back of the bar as he jiggled the glass, determined to loosen every bit of liquor that clung to the melting ice.

"Sounds like she broke another one," he said to the waitress who brought him a third round. His instructions upon his first order were clear: as soon as his glass was empty, he was ready for another. No questions asked and there'd be a hefty tip at the end of the night. When Scott drank, he did it fast and he did it alone.

In his case, misery did not love company.

"New girl," the waitress answered. "The absolute worst I've ever seen." She put the fresh glass on the table and picked up his empty. "Julia vouched for her, but it's like she's never even held a tray. Luke is desperate for the help. Hell, he's desperate for a lot of things. But I don't know if we have enough glasses in the back to keep her around much longer."

Scott leaned back in his chair. "You said Julia vouched for her." He nodded toward the red-faced pixie who came around the back of the bar. "That little mouse is friends with Julia—uh, Morgan?"

"Julia Callahan now," the waitress corrected. "She married the town's police chief a few months back."

Scott nodded. "I'm happy for her. Do they make a good match?"

"Perfect." The woman's voice turned wistful. "Sam Callahan was the biggest catch this side of the county line. I never really pegged him for a family man. But he dotes on Julia's boy. It's true love."

"Good for them," Scott mumbled, not wanting to reveal his connection to Sam. He wrapped his fingers around the cool glass once more.

"How do you know Julia?"

He schooled his features into an emotionless mask. "Her hair salon."

"I haven't seen you in here before. You new to town?"

"Just passing through," he said and took a sip. "Thanks for the fresh drink."

"Sure." Realizing the conversation was over, the waitress walked away.

Scott had been in enough bars in his time to know that a good waitress could sense when a customer wanted to chat and when to leave him alone. He was glad he'd sat in the section he had. The little mouse waitress, cute as she was, didn't seem like someone who'd take a hint if you hung it around her neck. Not his type for certain.

He didn't know what he expected from Brevia, North Carolina. He looked around the bar's interior, from the neon signs glowing on the walls to the slightly sticky sheen on the wood floor. The bar ran along the back of the far wall although few stools were occupied. Not the most popular place in town, so no wonder there was a for-sale sign in the window. Still, the lack of customers suited him just fine. The watering holes he usually frequented in D.C. may have been classier and more historic. But as far as Scott was concerned, liquor was liquor and it didn't really matter who poured it or where.

He closed his eyes for a moment and wondered what had brought him to Brevia tonight. After the blowout he'd had with his brother, Sam, at their dad's wedding a few weeks ago, he'd vowed never to step foot in this town again. If he admitted the truth, he had no place else to go. No friends, no one who cared whether he showed up or not. His dad and brother might be the exception to that, but they were both too mad at him for it to matter now.

He drained his glass again. He liked the way alcohol eventually numbed him enough so the dark thoughts hovering in the corners of his mind disappeared. Maybe it had led to some stupid decisions, but it also took the edge off a little. And Scott had a lot of edges that needed attention.

As a few more patrons wandered out, Scott's waitress came over to the table. "It's a slow night, honey," she told him. "I'm heading home. I could give you a ride somewhere or you could stop by my place for a nightcap."

She said it so matter-of-factly, Scott almost missed the invitation in her voice. He glanced up. "What's your name?"

"Tina."

He flashed the barest hint of a smile. "Tina, trust me. You can do way better than me on any given night. Even in a town like Brevia."

"I'm willing to take my chances." She surveyed him up and down. "I could wait years for a man who looks like you to walk into this place."

He took her hand in his and ran his finger across the center of her palm. "You deserve more than the likes of me. Go home, Tina." He pressed a soft kiss on her knuckles. "And thank you for the offer. It's a hard one to pass up."

She sighed. "Enjoy your night then."

He watched her walk away, then shifted his gaze as he felt someone watching him. The pixie of a waitress stood next to a table, her mouth literally hanging open as she gaped at him as if he was the big, bad wolf. A rush of heat curled up his spine. Maybe he should have taken Tina up on her offer. He was clearly in need of releasing some kind of pent-up energy.

He straightened from the table where he sat and lifted his glass in mock salute, adding a slow wink for good measure.

The mouse snapped her rosebud lips together and spun around, sending another glass flying from the tray she balanced precariously in one hand.

Scott shook his head as the crash reverberated through the bar. That was her fifth for the night. A clumsy new waitress wouldn't last long.

He moved to a seat at the bar and ordered another round.

To his surprise, the bartender shook his head. "You've had enough, buddy."

"Excuse me?"

"I said I'm cutting you off."

Scott knew for a fact—almost a fact—that he never

appeared drunk even when he was. It had been his downfall too many times to count. People assumed the idiot things he did weren't in direct relation to the amount of alcohol he'd consumed. "What the hell? I'm not making a scene. It's still early."

"It's 1:00 a.m."

"That means I've got an hour left."

"Not in my bar you don't. I own this place and I'm saying you're done here."

"What's the problem, man?"

The bar's owner was in his late forties, a tall, balding man with a lean face. Scott wasn't acting out of the ordinary, so couldn't figure out what was the problem.

"The problem," the bartender said as he leaned closer, "is that I saw you kissing my girlfriend's hand a few minutes ago. Now get the hell out of my bar."

Scott thought about the lovely Tina and cringed. "I had no idea she was your girlfriend. She invited me over for a drink and—"

He didn't get to finish his sentence as the bartender grabbed at the scruff of his collar. Without thinking, Scott slammed the man's hand to the wooden counter, stopping just short of breaking it.

The bartender yelped in pain, then yanked his hand away.

"I told you," Scott repeated quietly, "I didn't know."

"Luke, is everything okay here?"

Scott turned and saw the tiny waitress standing at his side. She was even smaller up close, her big eyes blinking at him from behind round glasses. As far as he could tell, she didn't wear a speck of makeup, her pale skin clear without it other than a dusting of freckles across her nose and cheeks. Her red hair was pulled back into a severe ponytail at the nape of her neck. She bounced on her toes, looking warily from Scott to Luke.

"Everything's fine, Lexi," the bartender said coolly. "This customer has had enough. He's leaving."

"So Lexi's the bouncer?" Scott smiled at the mouse. "Are you going to throw me out?"

"You don't seem drunk," Lexi observed.

He knew the bartender was right even if he'd never own up to it. Scott wasn't much of a gambler, but he'd perfected a poker face. Nothing good ever came from admitting he'd had too much to drink. Especially at a bar. "I'm not," he answered, even though he knew it was a lie. "But I'd like to be." He settled into his chair and gave her a broad smile.

A streak of pink crept up from the neckline of her Riley's Bar T-shirt, coloring her neck and cheeks. A muscle in Scott's abdomen tightened. He imagined her entire petite frame covered in those sweet freckles and flushed pink with desire. For him.

Whoa. Where had that come from? He blinked several times to clear his head.

"Do you have something in your eye?" the mouse asked. "I have eyedrops in my purse if you need them."

So much for his charm with women. He was rusty these days. "No," he answered.

"He don't need anything," Luke interrupted. "He's on his way out."

"No wonder your bar is so run-down." Scott bit out a laugh. "If this is how you treat your customers…"

He saw Luke's eyes narrow a fraction. "My customers don't bad-mouth my bar. This establishment happens to be a local favorite."

Scott made a show of looking around at the nearly empty stools and tables. "I can see how popular you are. Yes, indeed." He glanced at the waitress, who gave a small shake of her head before dropping her gaze to the ground.

Somehow the disappointment he read in her eyes ground its way under his skin, making his irritation at being kicked out swell to full-fledged anger. He didn't know why it mattered, but suddenly Scott was determined not to let the bartender win this argument. Nobody in this one-horse town was going to get the best of him.

"I'm not leaving until I get another drink." He crossed his arms over his chest and dared the other man to deny him.

"Maybe you should just give him one more," Lexi suggested softly.

"No way." Luke reached for the phone hanging next to the liquor bottles. "This loser is finished, one way or another." He pointed the receiver in Scott's direction. "I'll give the police a call. Tell them I've got a live one making a disturbance down here, and let them haul you away."

The last thing Scott needed was his brother finding him in a town bar tonight unannounced, let alone making trouble. Scott wanted to talk to Sam, but on his terms and in his own time frame.

Sam had moved to North Carolina several years ago and was definitely protective of his new hometown. Scott told himself he'd stopped caring about his brother's opinion years ago, but that didn't mean he wanted to go toe-to-toe with him tonight. He knew it would be easier to cut his losses and walk out now, but he couldn't do it. Not with Lexi and Luke staring at him. Backing down wasn't Scott's style, even when it was in his best interest.

His gaze flicked to the front door, then back to the bartender. "I noticed a for-sale sign in the window," he said casually.

Luke's eyes narrowed. "You in the market for a bar?"

"Someone could do a lot with this space. Make it more than some two-bit townie hangout."

"Is that so?" Luke crossed his arms over his chest. "Why don't you make me an offer, city boy?"

"Why don't you get me a drink and maybe I will."

A slow smile curved the corner of the bar owner's lips. He turned and grabbed a bottle off the shelf.

Lexi tugged on Scott's sleeve. "It's none of my business, but I don't think it's a good idea for you to discuss a possible business transaction now. You might want to wait until the morning."

"I think this is the perfect time," Scott said and leaned closer to her, picking up the faint scent of vanilla. How appropriate for a woman who looked so innocent. "And you're right, it's none of your business."

The bartender placed a drink in front of Scott and clinked his own glass against it.

"Be that as it may," Lexi said, tugging again, "in order for a deal to hold up, there is the matter of due consideration. That won't apply if one or the other party is proved to be under the influence of drugs or alcohol."

Scott shrugged out of her grasp. "Honey, are you

a waitress or a lawyer? Because you handle those big words a lot better than you do a tray of glasses."

"That's right." Luke's eyes lit up. "Julia said you were an attorney when she got me to hire you. Said you worked your way through law school waiting tables."

"She did?" Lexi had worked her way through law school clerking at her father's firm. She hadn't waited on anything other than an airplane before tonight. Still, she nodded. "I did. I am. An attorney, that is. I'm currently taking a break."

Scott eyed her. "As a cocktail waitress?"

Her lips thinned, which was a shame because he'd noticed they were full and bow-shaped. "For now."

Scott couldn't resist leaning closer again. "You might be the walking definition of the term 'don't quit your day job.'"

"You're a jerk," she whispered.

"Yes, I am."

Luke clapped his hands together. "This is perfect." He took a step back and flipped on and off the light switch next to the bar. "We're closing early, y'all," he shouted to the lone couple in a booth toward the back. "Clear out now."

Ignoring the groans of protest, he pointed to Lexi. "You can write up an offer for the pretty boy. Better yet, there's an old typewriter on my desk in the back. Grab it and you can make the contract."

She shook her head. "I don't think—"

"I'm not asking you to think," Luke barked. "You've broken a half-dozen glasses tonight. If you want to keep this job, get the damn typewriter."

She threw a pointed glance at Scott. "Are you sure this is what you want?"

Looking into her bright eyes, the only thing he could think of was that he wanted to kiss her senseless. But he sure as hell had a longer list of things he didn't want.

He didn't want the botched arrest at the U.S. Marshals Service that had taken his partner's life and put Scott on forced administrative leave. He didn't want the resignation letter burning a hole in his back pocket. He didn't want to go back to his empty condo in D.C. and stare at the yellow walls for days on end. He didn't want to feel so helpless and alone.

"Don't tell me you're all talk?" Luke slapped a wet towel onto the bar as he spoke. "I should have guessed you'd be willing to spout out big words but not follow up with any action. If you aren't serious, get the hell out of my bar. I've got better things to do than waste my time with this."

Scott spoke to the bar owner without taking his eyes from Lexi. "I'm all about action." He picked up his glass and drained it again. "Lexi, would you please get Luke's typewriter? We need to talk dollars for a few minutes. See how badly your good old boy really wants to sell."

Chapter 2

Scott felt someone poking at him, but couldn't force his eyes to open. "Go away," he mumbled.

A shower of ice-cold water hit his face. He sat up, sputtering and rubbing his hands across his eyes. Water dripped from his hair and chin.

"Rise and shine, Sleeping Beauty."

"I'm going to kill you," he said with a hiss of angry air, then looked around. He was on a worn leather couch in a small office, the shelves surrounding him dusty and lined with kitchen equipment. "Where am I?"

Sam handed him a towel. "You passed out. Luke Trujillo called me at three in the morning, laughing his butt off. He said he offered you a ride, but you insisted you wanted to spend the night in your bar. When did you get back into town?"

"Last night."

"You didn't call. Does Dad know you're here?"

"Not yet." Scott covered his eyes with the towel, under the guise of drying off his hair. "I didn't call because our last family get-together didn't exactly end on good terms."

Memories of the previous evening came back to him in full force. When he was certain he had his features schooled to a blank mask, he lowered the towel. "But I'm a big boy, Sam. You don't have to worry about me."

"Are you kidding?" His brother paced back and forth across the worn rug between the couch and an oversize oak desk on the far wall. "You didn't know where you were a minute ago."

"I was disoriented. It happens."

"What the hell were you thinking?"

"It was a misunderstanding. The guy was being a jerk about serving me, so I gave him a song and dance about wanting to buy this place."

Sam grabbed a piece of paper from the desk and shoved it toward Scott. "This isn't a song and dance. It's a contract for purchase and sale. You gave him a down-payment check for fifty grand. Luke has wanted to sell for over a year now. To hear him tell it, the place is a money pit. He's got family in Florida. Hell, he's probably already packing his bags."

As Scott read the words on the paper, his head pounded even harder. The contract had his signature on the bottom, along with Luke Trujillo's and one other. In neat, compact writing was the name Lexi Preston scrawled above the word *Witness* on the last line.

The pixie waitress-attorney from last night. Clear green eyes and the shimmer of red hair stole across his mind. Wanting to impress her. Wanting to keep drinking. His two main objectives from late last night. Now, in the harsh light of morning, he realized how stupid and impulsive he'd been.

Again.

Most of the trouble—and there was a lot of it—Scott had in life was a result of being impulsive. He led with his emotions, anger being the top of that list. Normally, he wouldn't let himself slow down enough to care about the consequences. But the botched arrest two months ago, a direct result of his poor judgment, had put him on the sidelines of his own life. It drove him crazy, although he wouldn't have that discussion with Sam.

"I know you're still getting a paycheck and Dad says you've done well on investments, but it's a lot of cash, Scott. What are you going to do when you go back to the Marshal Service? I don't want to see you throw your money away like this."

Sam was the by-the-book brother, the one who'd always done the right thing. The responsible Callahan. At least, that was how it had been after their mother died. But a lot of years had passed since then. Scott was a grown-up now and he wasn't about to admit that he'd messed up yet again.

"I bought a bar. So what?" He threw the towel onto the floor by the couch and combed his hands through his hair. "I can afford it."

"That's not the point," his brother argued.

"Sam, I'm a big boy. I know what I'm doing. Maybe it doesn't make sense to you, but you're going to have to trust me on this." He walked past his brother and down the short hall to the bar's main room. He couldn't let

Sam see how in over his head he felt. He'd done a lot of stupid things in his life, but last night might take the cake. What had felt warm and inviting then now just looked in need of a good scrubbing. The wood floors were scratched and dull and the tables mismatched, several sporting a layer of grime years thick. The place definitely had more charm in the half dark.

"I don't have much of a reason to trust you, and I definitely don't trust Lexi Preston."

Scott spun around, then winced as the abrupt movement made his head hurt more. "What about Lexi?" he asked, not willing to address the issue of trust between him and Sam this early in the morning.

"She represented the family who tried to take away Charlie from Julia."

"I don't understand." Scott had immediately fallen for Julia's toddler son. He didn't know Julia well, but it was clear she was a natural mother. "I thought the ex-boyfriend's family was from Ohio. What's the attorney doing in Brevia? Julia got full custody."

Julia had been embroiled in the custody case when she and Sam were first together. Being with Julia had stopped Sam from taking a job Scott had helped arrange for him with the U.S. Marshals. It had been Scott's big attempt to repair his relationship with his brother, and it had felt like one more rejection when Sam had chosen Julia instead. Scott hadn't quite forgiven her for that, but it hadn't prevented him from forming a quick affection for the boy.

Sam shook his head, frustration evident in the tense line of his shoulders. "I don't understand, either. She got to town yesterday with some sob story about how she needs a fresh start. Julia may talk tough but she's a total softy at heart. She helped Lexi get the job and is renting the woman her old apartment."

"Keep your friends close and your enemies closer?" Scott asked, his mind suddenly on sharp alert. Julia was family now. He protected family, even if his methods were sometimes unorthodox.

Sam shook his head. "I want that woman to stay away from all of us. I don't like the fact that she was involved in this mess with you."

Scott bristled at Sam's condescending tone. "I told you, I can take care of myself. I don't know if she has ulterior motives coming to town, but Lexi Preston didn't influence my decision to buy this bar."

"She let you enter into a contract when you were drunk."

"Who said I was drunk last night? Maybe I bought this place as an investment. It's an historic building and—"

"You're not fooling me. I know the Marshals incident messed with your head. I know you've been drinking more than normal and your normal is pretty damn much." Sam took a step closer. "I think you need help."

Blood roared through Scott's head. He hadn't been back in Brevia twenty-four hours and Sam was already starting another referendum on how messed up he was. He couldn't afford to debate whether it was true. Not yet.

"Get out." He spoke the words slowly, without any of the emotion swirling through his gut.

"Scott, listen—"

"No, Sam, you listen." Scott began straightening

chairs around the various tables, needing something—anything—to do with his hands. Needing to take some action. "The incident didn't mess with my head. It killed a good man. Maybe I use alcohol to dull the memories of that more than I should. But I'm not out of control. I walked away when it was clear that part of the internal investigation meant me smearing my dead partner's reputation. I don't know right now if I'll go back. So I bought this place. It's an investment. Not one that you would make, but it's my money and my life. Back off. Go home to Julia and Charlie. I don't need you here."

The sound of the chairs scraping against the wood floor gave welcome relief to the silence that stretched between the brothers. Finally, Scott stopped and looked over. "I mean it. I'm fine."

Sam gave a curt nod. "I'm here, Scott. When you do need me, I'm here." He turned and walked out of the bar into the bright morning.

As the door swung shut behind him, Scott turned a chair around and sank into it, massaging his forehead with two fingers.

What the hell was he going to do now?

Lexi tried to ignore the pounding on the apartment door. As she stared, arms folded tightly across her chest, the noise grew. Had her father had a change of heart already, prepared to forgive her supposed lapse in judgment if she came home and continued to do his bidding? It was late morning and she'd already unpacked her few belongings and made a run to the local grocery for essential supplies. As silly as it seemed, she'd just gotten a taste of freedom and didn't want to give it up so soon.

She also didn't want her neighbors to worry or, worse, call Julia or Sam. Taking a fortifying gulp of air, she turned the knob and opened the door.

Oh.

Oh, dear.

Scott Callahan loomed in the doorway, irritation and a healthy five-o'clock shadow etched on his handsome face. He was still wearing the same casual sweater and wrinkled jeans from the night before. She looked for the resemblance to Julia's husband, Sam, figuring it was too much of a coincidence to have two Callahans in the same small town.

She'd been shocked when he'd told her his name as she was putting together the contract for sale last night. Although Scott's hair was dark, the two men shared the same brilliant blue eyes, strong jaw and towering height that made them both intimidating and undeniably male.

She took an involuntary step back, hating the blush creeping up her cheeks. Why did this man rattle her so much?

That was easy enough to answer. Just the sight of him made her long-dormant imagination kick into high gear. His hair just grazed his collar, his blue eyes made brighter by the contrast to long lashes that any woman would envy. He was beautiful, the kind of handsome that would attract female attention wherever he went.

Men who looked like Scott Callahan didn't notice Lexi, and last night he'd certainly noticed her. At least it had felt that way. He'd leaned in and his eyes had caught on her mouth as if he wanted to kiss her. She'd imagined what that kiss would feel like as she lay in her bed in the wee morning hours, watching dawn through the curtains in her bedroom. She could almost taste his lips on hers even now.

Now.

She blinked and cleared her throat. "What are you doing here?"

He lifted one long arm to rest on the door frame, muscles bunching under his sweater. A smile played at the corner of his mouth. He seemed a lot less irritated than he had a few moments earlier. "What's your story, Lexi Preston? You look shy and talk like an academic, but you've got a wild side. I can tell."

She hugged her arms more tightly around herself. "You can tell no such thing."

"I can tell you want me to kiss you."

She sputtered, "I do not."

"Liar." He took a lazy step toward her. "But that's not going to happen. Yet."

Lexi was shocked by the ripple of disappointment that rolled through her. "What do you want?" she repeated. "I'm guessing this isn't an official employee meeting."

He pulled a sheet of paper out of his back pocket. "I want to know why you let me sign this damn contract."

"You told me to write it up. I didn't let you do anything. In fact, I advised you not to sign it."

"I was drunk."

She cocked her head to one side and studied him. The rumpled clothes, the hint of bruising under his eyes. "You said you weren't."

"I hide it well."

No wonder he'd been flirting with her. It was the alcohol, not attraction. Of course. A guy as hot as Scott would definitely need beer goggles to flirt with her. "I warned you about due consideration. You assured me you were in full control of your faculties and able to make a rational decision."

"I want out." He came all the way into the apartment, filling it with his large, muscular body and...sheesh, she had a one-track mind.

"The bank has to draw up the final contract. Maybe you won't be approved for the loan."

"I can guarantee I'll be approved, so I want out now."

A whistle sounded from behind her. "It's not that easy." She turned on her heel and padded to the kitchen, pulling two cups from the cabinet. She dropped a tea bag in each and poured the hot water. Turning back, she handed one to Scott. He eyed it suspiciously. "What's this?"

"Green tea. It helps me think." She took a small sip. "Explain to Luke Trujillo that you were inebriated last night. The contract won't hold up if you signed it under the influence. I'm sure Tina will vouch for how many drinks you had over a normal limit."

"That's the problem. No one can know I was drunk."

"Why not?"

He brought the mug to his mouth, sniffed and made a face. "You're kidding with this, right? Where's the coffee?"

"I don't drink coffee. Green tea is full of antioxidants."

"You're an attorney and a health nut? That's some combination."

"My father says... Never mind." She took another drink. "Don't be a baby. It's just tea." She studied him intently. "Why do you want to hide that you were drunk?"

"I'm not a baby," he said and took a huge gulp of tea. "That's disgusting."

"You're avoiding my question."

"You're such a lawyer." He shook his head and reached around her to place the mug on the counter. "My brother's already given me grief about last night. I don't need him on my back for anything else."

"Are the two of you close?"

"Not a bit."

She raised the cup to her lips again, then lowered it as her mind raced. "If you're not close, why do you—"

"It's complicated."

Lexi could just imagine. She'd known him for less than twenty-four hours, but Scott Callahan was already the most intriguing man she'd ever met. At first glance he was all alpha-male bravado, but she sensed something more. His eyes had a haunted look that wasn't related to a hangover, but might have everything to do with a bone-deep loneliness. The kind of lonely people felt if they thought no one in the world truly loved them. As if they had no home.

The kind of lonely Lexi often saw reflected in her own eyes.

She had nothing in common with this man, but she wanted to reach out to him. She yearned to understand what made someone who appeared so sure of himself at the same time give off waves of uncertainty.

She wanted to really know him.

As if he could read her intention, his eyes turned cold. "Never mind. I'll figure something out." His voice cut through her thoughts. "Luke gave me a fair price and I've got the time and money to deal with it. Maybe I'll redo the whole thing and sell it for a hefty profit." His words were sure but his tone still held a hint of uncertainty.

"If you didn't want to own a bar, why did you buy it?"

"I don't know." He ran his hand through his almost-black hair. "I'm known for being impulsive. It's my trademark."

There must be more to the story, but as much as she wanted to know, it wasn't any of her business. Yet. "I never do anything impulsive."

"That's not how I heard it." He glanced over her shoulder at the tray of half-full glasses sitting on the kitchen table. "Here you are, a fancy-pants corporate attorney, renting my sister-in-law's apartment, practicing to be a bar waitress in this sleepy Southern town. Are you telling me this is some sort of master plan?"

She almost smiled. "I guess you're right. I've been pretty impulsive in the last couple of days."

He shook his head. "That wasn't a compliment."

"I'm going to take it as one, anyway." She placed her mug on the counter. When she turned back, Scott had stepped closer. Too close. Close enough that she could smell toothpaste on his breath and the musky scent of last night's cologne on his shirt.

"If you want to get impulsive, I can help." He reached his hand up and trailed the pad of his thumb along her jaw. "I'm an expert at impulsive."

"I'm not that kind of girl," she whispered, hating that he broke straight through to her earlier longing.

"I can't figure out what kind of girl you are." His

mouth turned up at the corner. "But I know you're the worst waitress I've ever seen." He straightened, dropping his hand. "I'm the boss now. So you'd better practice all day with those glasses. Because you helped get me into this mess and I'm not going to let you cost me more money every night. Luke may have owed Julia a favor, but I don't owe anyone anything."

Lexi sucked in a breath. "Are you threatening to fire me?"

"It's no threat," Scott told her. "I'm sure you've got a corner office waiting for you somewhere. I don't care why you're slumming it in a bar. But it's mine now. I don't play favorites. Show up a half hour early for your shift tonight. We're having an employee meeting."

He turned and headed for her door.

"This is because you're mad that I wrote the contract. You want to blame me. It's not fair."

He held up one hand and ticked off several points. "I'm mad that I signed the contract. I blame myself for that, but I don't appreciate you being a part of that moment. And if you haven't realized it before, life isn't ever fair. Deal with it."

Without looking back, he strode from her apartment, slamming the door shut behind him.

Chapter 3

By five o'clock that night, Scott's headache was way beyond a hangover. He'd driven down to Charlotte to pick up some updated electronics the bar needed right away, along with a few extra clothes until he had time to get to his condo in D.C. for his stuff. He'd noticed a bathroom and shower off the office in back, where he'd bunk until he could figure out what to do with his new investment.

Damn. His plan hadn't included staying in Brevia for more than a few days, and definitely not in this run-down bar. He didn't know why he'd come in the first place, other than wandering around D.C. and watching ESPN in his place had been driving him crazy.

He and Sam hadn't been close in years, and he knew his brother still didn't trust him after Scott's part in breaking up Sam's first engagement. He pressed two fingers to the side of his head as the pain of regret mingled with the dull pounding inside his brain.

He'd thought they were going to put the past behind them when Sam was planning to take the job with the Marshals, but the relationship with Julia had ended that. Scott had been mad as hell. He'd stuck his neck out to get Sam the job. Although he didn't want to admit it, he'd craved a second chance at a relationship with his brother.

He knew Sam didn't want him here. Maybe that had been part of the motivation for making this stupid deal. He'd always had a talent for getting under his brother's skin.

Hefting another box of beer bottles into the large refrigerator in the back room of the bar, he spun on his heel as someone cleared his throat behind him.

Scott slammed the refrigerator door and faced a craggy-looking man whose thin blond hair was pulled back into a ponytail at the nape of his neck. He looked to be in his mid-forties and wore faded jeans and an army-green canvas jacket over a white T-shirt.

"You ain't Luke," the man told him.

"Great observation." Scott eyed the stranger, clearly ex-military by the way he held himself. "I'm Scott Callahan, the new owner of this place."

"New owner?" The man's eyes narrowed. "I didn't hear nothing about a new owner."

"It's a recent development." He'd also met earlier with Luke, who'd been thrilled to hand over his keys. He'd offered to stick around for a few weeks to help, but Scott had declined. From what he'd seen this morning going through the bar's accounts and ledgers, Luke hadn't known much about running a business. Scott had certainly spent enough time in bars. He figured he could pick up most of what he needed to know from the staff. As long as he kept the beer cold and the liquor flowing, how hard could it be?

"You can't be any worse than Luke. That guy could barely tap a keg when he got here."

"I've tapped plenty of kegs in my day," Scott assured him. "I didn't catch your name."

The two of them stared at each other for several moments. Finally, the man said, "I'm Jon Riley."

"As in Riley's Bar?" Scott tried not to look surprised.

Joe nodded. "My dad opened this place almost twenty years ago. Luke took over when Dad passed a few years back."

"I'm sorry. You work here?"

"Unfortunately." When Scott didn't reply, Jon continued, "I've worked in restaurants most of my life. Trained as a chef up in New York. But I got hurt over in Iraq and, well…ended up back here."

Scott had noticed the full kitchen, although from the looks of it, nothing had been cooked there for years. "Riley's doesn't serve food."

"Used to when my dad had it." Jon shrugged. "Now I wash glasses, clean up, handyman stuff. Whatever needs doing. You gonna change things around?"

"I've owned the place for less than twenty-four hours. My head is still swimming." And pounding.

"That didn't answer the question."

"You've still got a job if you want one."

"I do." Jon stuck out his bony hand and Scott shook it. "Nice to meet you, boss."

"You, too, Jon."

"I got one more question for you." Jon nodded toward the unused kitchen space. "My apartment's only an efficiency. I can't cook anything worth eating. I clock in here at six-thirty most nights. Would you mind if I brought in some supplies and made myself dinner before I started? I'll keep it clean."

"Is that what you've been doing?"

"Nope." His gaze dropped to the ground. "Luke didn't want to deal with it or have customers smelling my meals, but—"

"I don't care what you do in the kitchen. I'm not using it. We're having a staff meeting in a few minutes. Be great if you could be there."

"Thanks." Jon shrugged out of his coat. "I'm going to get started moving last night's empties."

Scott nodded, feeling overwhelmed by the task in front of him. He liked the fact that he was moving, at least. It gave him less time to think about what he couldn't do. Like his real job.

He heard voices at the front of the building. He glanced out to see four women, including Lexi, come through the entrance. He'd contacted the five waitresses and two male bartenders from the employee records he'd found in the desk. One of the women had just had a baby, which explained Lexi's hire. Both of the guys had come in right after lunch to go over things. Scott had asked the waitresses to meet just before they opened tonight. He had no idea what he was going to say to them. Should he give a football-huddle pep talk or beg for help? He'd never been an employer. Never had to worry about anyone on the job but himself. That was about to change. He had his first employee meeting to run.

"Hello, ladies," he called with more confidence than he felt. "How is everyone doing tonight?"

All four women stopped and stared at him. He recognized Tina from last night, her gaze still an open invitation. Lexi looked wary, making eye contact with everything except him. The other two women he didn't recognize. He'd left messages for both of them earlier, so he didn't know what they thought of the change in ownership.

He stepped forward. "I'm Scott Callahan, the new owner of Riley's Bar."

"I'm Misty," the first woman told him. She was older for a bar waitress—early fifties if he had to guess. Her jet-black hair curled on top and was held back by a shiny clip. She couldn't have been more than five feet tall. It was hard to imagine her hefting a tray of glasses. But that remained to be seen.

"I appreciate all of you coming in."

Tina gave him a slow smile. "I didn't know you were going to buy the place."

Scott returned her smile. "I didn't know Luke was your boyfriend when you invited me for a drink."

She shrugged. "We're on a break."

"I'm single." The fourth waitress piped up. "My name's Erin." The young woman sidled up to him. "I've been here awhile, so I can help you with anything you need." She wrapped her long fingers around his wrist. "Anything."

He heard Lexi snort as he unhooked his wrist and stepped away from Erin. He felt like more of a fraud as he tried to think of what they'd want a new boss to say. "I'm going to do my best to make Riley's Bar the spot for nightlife. I think there are a lot of opportunities for improvement."

"You can say that again," Misty agreed.

"First and foremost, we need to take care of our customers—both current and potential. I'm going to be making some changes that will help with that."

"What kind of changes?"

"Making this place look a little better for one thing. Nightly specials, more events to get locals and visitors in the door. It's your job to keep them happy once they're here. I want good customer service. Be attentive but not overbearing."

"Do we let them hit on us?" All the women but Lexi giggled. She looked horrified.

"Only if you want them to." He smiled. "But I'd prefer you kept your time here professional."

The three experienced waitresses nodded, while Lexi continued to look straight ahead. She seemed as nervous as a deer at a shooting range.

"What about tips?" Tina asked. "Luke used to take part of what we got because he made the drinks."

"He skimmed your tips?" Scott didn't know why this surprised him. He'd checked the liquor on the shelves earlier and found several bottles watered down. Apparently, Luke hadn't been cutting corners only on the alcohol.

"He said it was his fair share," Misty offered.

"What's fair is that you keep the money you make." Scott stepped behind the counter. "Most nights I'm going to be handling the bar. Max and Jasper, the other bartenders, will fill in as needed."

"You know how to mix a decent Tom Collins?" Misty asked.

Scott nodded. "I can mix almost anything." He had spent time as a bartender when he'd been younger and had picked up a thing or two from his favorite haunts in D.C.

They watched him as if they expected more. He'd called them in here, but now had no pearls of wisdom to dispense. Basically, he'd wanted to see what he was working with. Other than Lexi, they all looked competent and at home in the bar.

He pulled shot glasses down from a shelf and grabbed a bottle of Jack Daniel's. He needed something to take the edge off. Just one. He turned to the man standing in the doorway. "We're going to have a round to welcome the new owner. Join us?"

Jon Riley shook his head. "No, boss. I'm five years sober."

Scott's hand paused in pouring. "Sorry. I didn't know."

"It's fine," Jon said quietly and disappeared through the door.

"I don't want one, either," Lexi told him when he pushed four of the small glasses forward.

"You on the wagon, too?" Tina asked.

"I don't think it's a good idea to drink while working."

Scott felt a hot burst of irritation skim along his spine. He didn't need to be judged by his little mouse of a waitress. "It's a special occasion," he told her. "Maybe if you relax, you won't have so much trouble keeping the glasses on the tray instead of the floor."

She narrowed her eyes. "I'll be fine. Thanks." With a huff, she followed Jon.

"Anyone else got a problem?"

In response, the remaining waitresses each picked up a shot glass. They toasted and downed the whiskey. It burned his throat, but after a moment the familiar warmth uncurled in his stomach.

"Thanks, boss," Misty told him and headed toward the back behind Lexi.

The other two women left the glasses on the bar and after a bit of small talk, meandered out the front door. Lexi and Misty were the two working tonight.

When he was alone again, Scott cleaned up the glasses and wiped down the top of the bar. He stared for a moment at the whiskey Lexi hadn't drunk. It seemed a shame to waste perfectly good alcohol, so he quickly downed it before putting the glass in the stack to be washed.

He turned to see Lexi watching him from the side of the bar. "Do you think that's a good idea?" she asked quietly.

"Sweetheart, none of this is a good idea." He returned the bottle of Jack to the shelf. "Luckily, I'm not much one for caring. If it feels right, I go for it."

"And drinking on the job feels right to you?" She took a step closer. "It seems to me that's what got you this bar in the first place." She pulled the apron in her hands over her head and reached behind her back to tie it, causing her breasts to push against the soft material of her light pink T-shirt.

Scott sucked in a breath. Hell, the T-shirt wasn't even formfitting and its conservative crew-neck collar practically covered half her throat. Misty was wearing a low-cut, skintight number that barely held in her ample chest. But it hadn't had any effect on him. Unlike Lexi's buttoned-up outfit.

He walked around the edge of the bar and took her arm, spinning her away from him.

"What are you doing?" she said with a gasp.

"Helping you," he answered and tied her apron strings together. "It seems to me the reason I'm in this mess is because of you and your contract."

"You wanted to buy the bar," she argued.

"I wanted to pick a fight with Luke," he countered, resting his hands on her hips, unable to resist circling his thumbs against the place where her shirt hem met the fabric of her black dress slacks. Attorney clothes, clearly made of expensive material. Not the sort of pants someone wore to serve drinks.

Which reminded him that Lexi wasn't the sort of woman who should be waitressing in a bar. "If it wasn't for your ever-helpful legal skills, we would have exchanged some big talk and called it a night. Now I've got a business I don't want in a town I don't want to live in."

She went perfectly still, whether because of his words or his touch, Scott didn't know. But her voice was breathless when she spoke. "Maybe you should have stopped to think before you agreed to anything. Maybe if your ego wasn't so big you would have left when he told you to go."

Ouch. Scott didn't want to admit how close to home

that hit. The phrase *if you'd stopped to think* could have saved him so many different times in his life.

"I never do," he said quietly. "Stop. Or think."

Because then he might remember how lonely he always felt, how afraid he was of needing someone and being left alone, the way both his parents had done when he was a kid.

"You should try it sometime," she said, her voice just a whisper.

"What's done is done." He pulled her closer to him and whispered against her ear, "It's easier to do what people expected of me—which isn't much."

Lexi felt her heart squeeze tight. It was so quiet in the bar at the moment. She was surrounded by Scott, the warmth of his chest against her back and his spicy, soapy scent mingling with the tangy smell of liquor on his breath.

That was what did it, brought her back to her right mind. The alcohol was the only explanation for why he seemed to want to touch her as much as she wanted to be touched by him.

She drove her elbow back, surprised at how quickly he moved to block the shot. "You're messing with me—"

She stopped when the front door opened and half a dozen men walked through. One called out, "There's an under-new-management sign in the window. What's that about?"

Another gave a long whistle. "Hey, there's a flat screen now. Is that new?"

"I'll be watching you tonight," Scott whispered to her. "Just remember that."

Her mouth went dry as he turned away.

"Put it up today, boys," he answered. "Got cable set up, too. Have a seat and we'll find a game to watch."

A round of cheers went up and the men came over to shake Scott's hand. They moved toward a table, but he pointed to the other side of the room. "You're going to have a better view over there, fellows."

He'd moved them from her section to Misty's, but only smiled as Lexi glared at him.

She spilled one glass the entire night, a huge improvement from her first shift. She didn't have the natural gift of gab that Misty did, flirting and making small talk with the customers. But Lexi did her best to keep up, making sure she got every order right and moving as quickly as her legs could carry her.

She was getting used to the noise and the smell of the bar, the customers who got more boisterous as the night wore on. Lexi didn't have a lot of experience with boisterous. Her father's idea of out of control was playing opera music instead of something mellower during dinner. Even in college, Lexi had stayed away from bars, worried there was something in her, some sort of predisposition for addiction, like her biological mother had had.

Her dad had told her in great detail about how she would have to overcome the deficiencies in her gene pool throughout her life. He'd made her believe that if she got too close to the wild life that had killed her mother, she might end up down that same dark path. She had only a few snippets of memory of her birth mom. The scent of her musky perfume and being left alone in their small apartment for long periods of time.

But she was curious about "the other side of life," as her dad called it.

Being in Riley's Bar, serving customers, was a revelation to Lexi. She didn't really have a desire to drink, but the energy from the people around her made her feel more alive than she ever had.

Scott took a shot with another customer. She didn't know how much he'd had tonight and it wasn't any of her business. He didn't seem wasted, although he hadn't last night, either. She still knew he was trouble. He tempted her to be different than the person she'd worked so hard to become. The way he made her feel could be dangerous to her very soul. She wanted an adventure, but how far was she willing to go to get a real one?

The bar emptied soon after the football game was over, which she figured was normal. She took off her apron and hung it in the back hall, counting the money from the front pocket. She'd made twenty dollars in tips. Not a lot, but the cash meant more to her than any paycheck she'd ever received from her father's firm.

"You did better tonight."

She turned to see Jon Riley in the doorway that led to the unused kitchen. "I practiced carrying drinks around all day," she said with a grin.

"It worked." He returned her smile. "You're not a natural but you'll get there."

"My mom was a waitress her whole life," Lexi said, then wondered why she'd shared that.

"There's worse ways to make a living."

She thought about her father and the underhanded legal deals he'd gotten into the habit of arranging to keep his firm on top. Maybe that was a type of addiction in its own right. She'd never made a connection between her adoptive father and her biological mother, and the thought made her skin crawl the tiniest bit.

"She was an alcoholic," Lexi blurted. "Lost custody of me when I was six. Working in bars killed her."

Jon shook his head. "The booze killed her. You're not like that."

"How do you know?" Lexi asked, suddenly needing reassurance from this virtual stranger.

"I've been down that road," he said simply. "I can recognize a person battling demons. Sometimes it's easier to drown yourself than work on what's really wrong."

She heard Misty's laughter ring out from the front of the bar, followed by the deep tone of Scott's voice.

Jon jerked his head toward the sound. "That boy has a war waging inside him. He's got a good heart but he's going to have to do some digging to find it again."

"Can someone like him be helped?"

The man shrugged. "Maybe. But they've got to want it. And you've got to risk that if they don't, you're gonna be real hurt trying for 'em."

She thought again about her mother, wondered what her demons had been and if anyone had tried to help her.

The door to the front of the bar swung open and Misty's head popped through. "Scott poured an extra glass of wine. Want to join me for a drink?"

Lexi turned her head. "I think…" She paused and glanced back over her shoulder. Jon had disappeared into the kitchen again. "I'm going to head home now."

Misty shrugged. "Your call. Nice work tonight. Scott

thinks you're too slow but I could see you busting your hump the whole time."

Lexi felt color rise to her cheeks. Scott thought she was too slow. She'd been worrying about how to help him, and he'd been talking trash about her. She swallowed against the embarrassment rising in her throat. "Have a good night, Misty," she said. Grabbing her purse from the hook, she headed for the back door.

She wrapped her arms around herself against the cool night air. Fall temperatures were dipping, even here in the South. She hurried to her car, and once back in her apartment, slipped off her shoes. Her feet ached, her shoulders were sore. Most of her body hurt from using muscles she'd never dealt with before. She wore heels as an attorney but never spent hours standing.

Even though it was late, she ran a bath and slipped into the warm water, letting it soak away some of her aches and pains. She liked to be clean. That was one thing she did remember from the time before Robert Preston had adopted her. She'd spent a lot of time dirty.

The bathtub in Julia's apartment might not be large or fancy like the deep soaker she'd left behind, but it did the trick. By the time she put on her soft cotton pajamas, she felt relaxed again.

She'd padded to the kitchen for a glass of water before bed when she heard the soft knock on the door. This time she didn't worry that it might be her father. From the way her stomach dipped, she knew who was waiting on the other side.

Chapter 4

"It's late, Scott." She hated that her voice sounded breathless. "What do you want?"

"I need a place to sleep."

His tone held none of its usual teasing or cocky certainty. But she kept the door open only a crack, not yet willing to let him in. "I thought you were staying at the bar."

"Too damn quiet after everyone leaves. Too empty. And it smells like a bar."

She smiled a little. "You smell like a bar."

"I could use a shower." He lifted a black duffel bag into view. "I brought a change of clothes."

She shook her head. "You should stay with Sam and Julia."

"They're a family. I don't belong there."

"You don't belong here."

He shrugged. "I don't belong anywhere." Lexi knew it was the first wholly honest thing he'd said since they'd met. The smallest bit of vulnerability flashed in his eyes and she was a goner.

Jon Riley's words about being hurt echoed in her head, but she pushed them away as she reached out and took Scott's hand. Pulling him to her, she brushed a wayward lock of hair away from his forehead. Her finger traced the side of his face, much the same way he'd done the last time he touched her. Did it have the same effect? His heated gaze gave her hope that it did.

He looked as if he wanted to devour her, but didn't make a move. He only watched as she explored his skin with her hands, his chest rising and falling with shallow breaths.

"Misty said you think I'm too slow," she told him softly, the words stinging her pride as she repeated them.

"The customers don't seem to mind," he answered. "You made good tips tonight."

"So you're not going to fire me?" She tried to make her voice sound teasing.

"Not yet," he answered.

"I'd threaten you with a sexual-harassment lawsuit but you flirt with everyone at the bar except me. Why is that?"

"You're the one pressed up against me." He shifted, somehow drawing her closer without pulling her to him. "Who's doing the harassing?"

He was right, but she could sense that his need matched her own. In the quiet intimacy of her apartment, it made her bold enough to ask, "Does this feel like harassment, Scott?"

"This feels like heaven," he whispered. "But I didn't come here for this. I'm no good for you."

"That's the point. I'm looking for a wild adventure and developing a new fondness for things that aren't good for me."

He took her arms and lifted them around his neck. Her head tilted and he brushed his lips against hers. Finally. It seemed as if she'd been waiting for this kiss her entire life.

And it was worth it.

His mouth felt delicious, the pressure sending sparks of desire along every inch of her skin. She lost herself in the sensations, reeling from the onslaught of need he aroused in her.

His strong arms wrapped around her, pulling her more tightly against him until she could tell how much he wanted her. She wanted him with the same need, like a drug she couldn't get enough of. She was quickly tipping out of control and the unfamiliarity of that made her push away.

Lexi Preston never lost control. She knew the dark and dangerous path where that might lead.

"You're right," she said around a gulp of air. "I'm slow." She covered her still-tingling lips with her fingers for a moment and stared at the floor. "I'm not one of your usual barflies."

"I never thought you were."

She pulled her shirt hem down where it had bunched around her waist. "You can stay here tonight." She still didn't meet his gaze. "On the couch. There's no furniture in the second bedroom right now. Use the shower, whatever you need. I'm going to bed." She squeezed her eyes shut tight. "Alone."

Before he could answer, she turned and retreated to the bedroom.

Scott watched her go, willing his heart to slow and his body to settle down.

What the hell was he doing in Lexi's apartment?

He'd told her the truth—he'd come here to sleep. After the last stragglers had gone home, he'd sat alone at the empty bar with a glass of Jack Daniel's in his hand, ready to blot out the memories that flooded him when he closed his eyes. But he couldn't lift the drink to his lips.

Sam was right—he'd been doing more self-medicating with alcohol than he should lately. Since his partner had been killed, it was the only thing that numbed the pain and the thoughts that raced around his brain. He'd always enjoyed a good buzz, but he'd never needed it the way he did now.

He'd already lost control in so many areas of his life. How much was he willing to give up? He'd poured out the glass of whiskey and paced the length of the building. There was nothing more depressing than an empty bar after closing, when the lack of body heat and voices made it feel like a sad, lonely shell of broken dreams.

A lot like his life.

He'd gotten in his truck and driven here. Sure, he could have called Tina or even Misty and found a warm welcome and a warmer bed. Instead he'd craved the lightness he felt radiating from Lexi. She was the purest person he'd met in a long time, someone good and innocent and everything he hadn't been in years.

He didn't understand his need for her. He'd never been attracted to the buttoned-up type before. But her strawberry hair, big luminous eyes and creamy skin made him want to fold her into him and not let go.

Except he knew he'd destroy the goodness in her. That was what he did to the people he needed. As much as he might want her, he'd keep his distance. He'd stay on the couch, stay away from her bed. As self-destructive as he could be, he still had a deep need to protect the people around him. Too bad he was the person Lexi needed protection against the most.

Scott slept better on the overstuffed couch than he had in years. He woke, showered and dressed, feeling halfway human again.

By the time eight o'clock rolled around, Lexi still hadn't made an appearance. He knocked softly on her bedroom door. "I know you're awake. I hear you moving around. You can come out—I won't bite."

He heard something bang behind the closed door.

"I bet you have to go to the bathroom pretty bad by now."

The door opened and Lexi appeared, fully dressed in jeans and a shapeless T-shirt that nonetheless gave him a little thrill. She tried hard to hide her petite figure and he couldn't understand why.

"Why are you still here?" she asked warily.

"It's cheery."

"There isn't a lick of decoration in the place," she

said and nudged him out of the way, slamming the bath-room door behind her.

He chuckled and moved back toward the kitchen, calling over his shoulder, "It's a hell of a lot cheerier than the bar."

He opened several cabinet doors. "There's got to be coffee here somewhere," he said as she came into the kitchen behind him.

"I told you I don't drink coffee. Tea is your only choice."

He made a choking sound.

"There's a bakery around the corner." She rolled her eyes. "Have at it."

"I have a better idea," he told her. "Let's grab break-fast. That diner in town is always crowded."

Her eyebrows shot to the top of her head. "I'm not having breakfast with you."

"Why not? All you've got is yogurt and fruit here. That's not going to do it for me."

"What does it for you isn't my concern." She put her hands on her small hips. "I let you stay here."

"Consider it a thank-you, then." He winked. "We'll discuss our future living arrangements. The couch is great but I'm going to need to get a bed."

She shook her head. "This is my apartment."

"Actually," he said slowly, "it's my sister-in-law's apartment. I have more rights to it than you."

Lexi's mouth dropped open and he found himself wanting to kiss it shut. "She's renting it to me."

"I don't like staying at the bar. I'm family." He grabbed her purse from the back of the chair and handed it to her. "My brother doesn't trust you after what you and your father tried to do."

She sucked in a breath.

"Don't make me use the family card."

"I'm ordering everything on the menu," she mumbled and headed out the door.

They drove in silence the few minutes to the restaurant. Scott could feel her frustration. He knew Julia didn't think much of him, and the truth was, his sister-in-law might very well rather rent her apartment to Lexi than him. He wasn't letting on, though.

He didn't want to stay at the bar. Although he would never admit it out loud, he didn't want to be by himself right now. He'd been living alone since he'd left home at eighteen. By nature, he was a loner. Even with girlfriends, he'd never been much of a stay-the-night snuggler. But he'd felt a strange sort of comfort knowing Lexi was sleeping down the hall last night. He had about a decade's worth of decent sleep to catch up on, and he was determined to make it happen.

She didn't order everything on the menu, but did ask for both an omelet and a stack of pancakes, plus granola on the side.

"Where do you put all that food?" he asked after their waitress had filled the table with plates. "You're no bigger than a minute and you've got enough calories on that plate for an NFL quarterback."

Reaching for the syrup, she answered, "It's going to be my dinner, too. I'll get a take-home box."

"So you conned me into buying you two meals?"

"I gave you a place to sleep last night." She took a big bite of pancake.

"Why do you need to hoard food? You don't strike me as someone hard up for money."

"I don't want to use my credit cards while I'm here." She stopped chewing midbite and stared at him, as if realizing she'd shared too much. "I'm trying to save money."

"You're hiding." He took a drink of coffee and studied her, the mystery that was his little pixie mouse falling into place. "From a boyfriend?"

She rolled her eyes. "No. My so-called boyfriend is probably relieved to get a break from me. My father set us up and I'm pretty sure he's only with me to improve his chances at making partner in the firm."

"Then he's an idiot." Scott held up a hand when she would have argued. "Don't change the subject. It must be your father. What happened between you and dear old dad?"

"Nothing," she muttered. "I just want some time on my own."

Scott shook his head. For an attorney, she was a terrible liar. "Tell me," he coaxed, extending his leg so he could brush against hers under the table. "Secrets are better when you share them."

She put down her fork. "It's not really a secret. I gave Julia some information about her ex-boyfriend's family that ensured they'd end the custody suit. They found out and dropped my father's firm. In turn, he dropped me."

"Not for good."

She shrugged. "From the moment I came to live with him, I've done everything he wanted me to. This is new ground for both of us."

"You're adopted?"

"When I was six. I'd been put into the foster system and shortly after, my mother died." Lexi drew in a breath and stared at her plate. "She was an alcoholic. I'd already been in two homes when my father found me. I owe him my life, really." When she looked up, tears shone in her big eyes. "But it's my life and I've never once made a decision just for me. He's mad now, but you're right, it's not forever. He's going to expect me to come back. Before I do, I need a little freedom. I'm going to see what it's like to do what I want to for a change."

"Why go back at all? If you want freedom, take it."

"It's not that simple."

"You're making it complex."

"I owe him."

"He's your father. That's not how it works with parents." Not that Scott had a lot of experience with unconditional love. His mother had died when he was a boy, killed in a car accident when she'd been driving after drinking. Her death had made his father pull away emotionally for years.

"When my father decided he wanted to adopt, he had fifteen kids in the foster system IQ tested. I happened to be the smartest of the bunch. That's how he picked me."

The thought made Scott cringe. "Is that even legal?"

"It doesn't matter. He made it happen." Lexi took a drink of juice, holding the tiny glass in front of her like a shield. "I always understood that I'd been given a great opportunity. And that I'd be a fool to jeopardize it. So I didn't. I was perfect, exactly who he wanted me to be. Up until seven months ago, I was more Stepford daughter than real person. I'm grateful for everything he did for me and I love him." She put down the juice and gestured with her hands. "This is all pretend to me. He made me the person I am and I can't change that. I'm going to take this time and enjoy it."

"Then what?" Scott almost didn't want to hear the answer.

She bit her bottom lip. "Then I go back to regular life. Or I go a different way. I need time to figure that out."

The waitress came to the table. "Could you box all this up for us?" Scott asked, gesturing to the three plates still sitting in front of Lexi.

"Sure thing, sweetie." As she picked up the dishes, she smiled at him. "Aren't you the new owner over at Riley's?" she crooned.

He returned her grin. "Guilty as charged."

"I've always preferred Cowboys," she told him. Scott knew the other bar in town had loud country music, a huge dance floor and a mechanical bull. His version of hell. "But," she continued, leaning closer to him, "it might be worth a change of venue one of these nights."

"We'd love to see you over there."

Lexi cleared her throat and nudged the waitress's arm with one of the plates. "You forgot this."

She turned, as if noticing her for the first time. "Thanks," she muttered before walking away.

"I don't get why you're such a magnet for women." Lexi huffed out a breath. "What's so special about you?"

"Where do I begin?" he asked with a laugh, enjoying how bothered she was by the other woman's attention to him, even if he couldn't quite explain why. "But you're changing the subject again. You think by not using your credit cards, your father won't find you? What about when you use your cell phone?"

"I haven't yet." She fidgeted in her chair. "I don't expect you to understand. I need time, that's all."

He understood better than she knew. After everything he'd seen and done, if he could take a break from his messed-up life for a time, he'd gladly do it. Maybe that was why he'd made the impulsive offer to buy the bar in the first place. It was an expensive way to keep himself busy while he regrouped, but that was what he needed. After the incident, his superiors had wanted him to see a counselor while the internal investigation ran its course. According to his boss, it was standard when a marshal was killed in the line of duty and part of the requirement to have his administrative leave lifted.

Not that it mattered. Scott wasn't sure he'd ever go back. He still had the resignation letter he'd drafted. Any day now he'd get around to sending it.

He grabbed Lexi's hand as she made to stand from the table. "Not so fast. I bought you enough breakfast to feed a fire station. But we haven't talked about our living arrangement."

Lexi stared at him as a shiver ran down her spine. He couldn't be serious. "You can't live with me," she whispered.

"Why not?"

"People will talk about us."

"You think so?" he answered as the waitress came back to the table with a large bag of to-go cartons and the check.

She slid the small piece of paper toward Scott with

a wink. "My phone number's on the back. When you get a night off, give me a call."

"How can she do that?" Lexi said with a hiss as the woman walked away again. "I'm sitting right here. It's like I'm invisible. For all she knows, we're on a date. We could have spent the night together and she's propositioning you while I watch."

"If I was staying at the apartment with you, maybe the flocks of women would back off." He wiggled his eyebrows.

Lexi did a mental eye roll, but at the same time her stomach fluttered. Scott Callahan was exactly the kind of man her father had warned her about for years. A bad boy to the core. Maybe that was part of the reason she found him so appealing.

She knew it was a bad idea, but said, "If I let you stay there, I don't want any more talk about me being fired."

He chuckled. "You're a terrible waitress. You know that, right?"

"*Terrible* is a strong word."

"You break more glasses than drinks you serve."

"I'm getting better," she argued.

"True, but you'll never be a natural."

"Those are my terms." She grabbed the bag of food and made her way toward the door.

Scott caught up to her easily as she rounded the street corner. "How long are you planning on staying here?" He grabbed her elbow and swung her around to face him.

She stared at him, not sure how to respond. "A month. Six weeks? However long it takes."

"I won't fire you for a month. You let me stay at the

apartment for four weeks and I'll let you keep your job. Deal?"

She watched the fall breeze play with the waves of his hair. His hands were shoved in his pockets and he looked as if he didn't have a care in the world. His jeans hugged the strong muscles of his legs and his faded flannel shirt was unbuttoned enough to reveal a small patch of hair on his chest. Every part of him was the essence of cool.

But his eyes told her a different story. A tale of loneliness, loss and a need that called to her own secret, lonely heart.

"Okay," she said quickly, before she changed her mind. "I mean, since you're Julia's brother-in-law, she certainly wouldn't mind you crashing there, too."

He tried to hide the smile that played at the corner of his mouth. "You won't regret it."

"I already do," she muttered. "You need to get your own bed. By tonight."

He nodded. "I can do that."

"Would you really have fired me?"

His grin widened. "You'll never know. I have to be at the bar for some deliveries. I'll give you a lift back to your apartment first."

"I need to do some things in town, so I can walk back later. It's not far. I'll have an extra key made and leave it under the front mat." She lifted the bag. "Thanks for breakfast. And dinner."

She was brushing him off, but Scott didn't want to push the first good luck he'd had in ages. He reached forward and tapped his finger on the tip of her nose. "Have a good day, Lexi."

* * *

She pushed her hair behind her ears and watched him walk away. Her stomach gurgled and she hoped it was from the food rather than her reaction to Scott.

Halfway down the sidewalk, she noticed a light on in Julia's salon. The place was closed until noon, according to the sign in the window. But the front door was unlocked, so she let herself in. Closing the door behind her, she heard the patter of feet, then a dog was in front of her. He was big and gray and barked several times before showing his teeth.

Lexi pressed her back against the wall of windows at the front of the building. "Good doggie," she whispered.

The animal's lip curled back even more and she could have sworn he snarled at her. Lexi felt her recently eaten breakfast threaten to make a repeat appearance. At least that might distract the dog long enough for her to get away. She concentrated on breathing without passing out.

"Casper?"

Lexi heard Julia's voice from the back of the salon. "Julia," she called softly. The dog came a step closer to her. "It's Lexi. I, uh, your dog… Can you come…?"

"He's friendly." Julia walked toward her, hands on her hips.

"Really?" Lexi's voice was a high-pitched squeak. "Why is he snarling at me?"

"He smiles." The woman placed a hand on the dog's broad back. "Casper, sit."

He plopped to the ground.

"Pet him," Julia suggested. "He'll love you."

Lexi swallowed and held out a hand. She ran her

palm along the animal's silky head. He immediately flipped on his back, wriggling in ecstasy as Lexi rubbed him with more enthusiasm. "He's a sweetie."

"Told you so."

"How well do you know Sam's brother?" Lexi asked, keeping her attention focused on the dog.

"Not very," Julia admitted. "He and Sam aren't close. They never have been. Has he been giving you trouble at the bar?"

Lexi shook her head, straightening. "He's been okay. It's just…weird, right? That he bought the bar and is staying in Brevia."

"There's more than one person in Brevia who doesn't belong right now."

Lexi felt herself blush. "I'm sorting things out. This is a little detour, that's all. Does it bother you that I'm here? I put a lot on you and maybe it didn't feel like you had a choice but to help." A thought crossed her mind. "I don't want to make it uncomfortable for you. Scott said Sam doesn't like me."

"Can you blame him?"

"No," Lexi admitted, cringing. She loved her work and the law, but hated some of the things she'd had to do as part of her job. Her father had so many powerful clients and Lexi had spent a lot of her time digging up dirt on their enemies, often people with a lot less money and influence. It made her feel like the stereotypical unethical attorney, and she wished it could be different.

"Actually, I like thinking I'm getting back at your dad in a way." Julia smiled at her. "Not that I'm vindictive or anything, but he and the Johnsons made my life difficult. You know what they say about payback." She absently straightened one of the styling bays. "Don't worry about Sam. He's protective of me. But it's all good."

Lexi noticed Julia's dreamy smile. "You're lucky to have someone who loves you like that."

"Agreed," Julia said. "How is the apartment? Other than the basics, I didn't leave a lot of stuff there."

"It's great. Thank you again. I get paid at the end of this week so I should be able to get you more than the deposit, but…"

"Don't worry about it," Julia told her. "I know you're good for it. It's not too weird in a strange place by yourself?"

Lexi thought about Scott sleeping on her couch and shook her head. "I'm fine." She should tell Julia about their new arrangement, but the words wouldn't form. "I noticed a few dog toys in the closet."

"I found Casper when I was living there." Julia bent forward to scratch between the dog's ears. "Or I should say, he found me."

"So the building is pet friendly?"

The stylist studied her. "You don't seem like a dog person."

"I don't know," Lexi admitted. "My father never let me have pets. Dogs make me nervous." She gave a small laugh. "Almost everything makes me nervous. But this adventure is all about trying new things."

"An animal is a big commitment. It's not just something you try out for a little, then dump when you go back to your real life."

"I know that." Lexi's resolve suddenly got stronger. She'd never experienced unconditional love, but was sure she had it in her to give. She'd always wanted a pet, but had been afraid that even a dog or cat might not think she was good enough. She didn't know anything about caring for an animal. Suddenly, it was very important to prove it to herself. "What time does the animal shelter your mom runs open?"

Julia glanced at her watch. "Not for another hour. But I have an in with the owner, if you know what I mean."

"You don't have to help me with this. You've done more than enough already. I'm not here to take charity from you."

"I've got a good instinct for matching dogs with their forever people." Julia grabbed a leash off the hook on the wall. "But you can return the favor. One of the girls is going through a divorce and she's feeling uneasy about the filing. Frank Davis is her attorney, the same one I used. He's not giving her the time she needs. I'll take you out to the shelter, and in return, you look over the paperwork for her."

Lexi had run away from her life and her job, but she still loved the law. Maybe giving legal advice to someone here could start to make up for all the things she'd done as an attorney that weren't helpful.

She nodded, loving the sound of the word *forever*. She wanted to be a forever person, even if only to an animal. Plus, it would be good to have a distraction in the apartment when Scott was there.

"You've got yourself a deal."

Chapter 5

Scott arrived at the bar in the late afternoon, after spending the day in Charlotte buying more supplies and a mattress set to take to the apartment. At this rate, he was going to run through his savings within the month.

He was tired and, strangely, wanted to return to Lexi's. The two-bedroom apartment was nothing special and not nearly as stylish or comfortable as his condo in D.C., but he felt more at home there than anyplace he'd been in years.

He had work to do at the bar first. As soon as he walked into the building, the smell of spices and roasting…something…hit him. He followed his nose to the kitchen and found Jon Riley at the stove with four men sitting around the small table in the corner.

"Hey, there," he called to the group.

All four men jumped up, turning toward him with

varying degrees of mistrust in their eyes. "He invited us," one of them offered.

"We're allowed to be here," another insisted.

"Who are you, anyway?" a third asked.

Jon turned from the stove. "It's okay, guys." He motioned them to sit back down. "This is Scott Callahan, the bar's new owner. I told you about him. He's cool."

Scott didn't feel particularly cool at the moment. "Uh, Jon? What the hell is going on here?"

"I'm making an early dinner."

"You asked if you could use the kitchen to make yourself food. You forgot to mention company."

Jon turned the heat down on one of the burners and pointed to the hall. With a wary glance at the strangers sitting at the table, Scott turned and followed him there.

"I won't make a habit of it," he said with a shrug. "But these guys are like me. They don't have much and they've given a helluva lot more to this country than they've gotten back."

"They're ex-military?"

Joe nodded. "They need a break and a decent meal. I didn't think you'd be here this early. Thought I could get them fed and out before anyone noticed." He gave Scott a sheepish smile. "Sorry."

Scott scrubbed his hand across his face. His life was so far from the norm, he didn't know which way was up anymore. He was used to action, a mission and constantly moving. He was used to being on his own. Now he'd gotten himself a roommate and had a kitchen full of hungry men waiting for a meal. He shook his head. "Do you have enough for one more?"

Jon's grin looked out of place on his somber face. "You bet."

Scott walked back into the kitchen and sat down with the men, feeling an odd camaraderie with this misfit band of soldiers. They asked him a few questions about his military career, but mainly enjoyed the meal in a companionable silence he could appreciate. Then he took his first bite from the plate Jon placed in front of him and could barely stop himself from moaning out loud. He looked around at the other men, whose faces reflected the same food rapture he felt.

He met Jon's gaze. "This is beyond amazing," he said, then took another large bite. "I'm talking four-star-restaurant good."

"It's only a chicken potpie," Jon said with a shrug. "I like simple food that tastes good."

"It's a little bit of heaven," Scott agreed.

One of the men shook his fork at Jon. "Everything he makes is like this. I look forward to my weekly Jon fix like I used to crave the bottle."

"That's quite a comparison," Scott said with an uncomfortable laugh.

"Denny is in my AA group," Jon explained. "Like I said, I worked as a chef in New York, but the big-city lifestyle didn't exactly agree with me."

"Didn't you say Riley's used to serve food?" Scott asked.

He nodded. "It's where I got my start."

Scott looked around the large kitchen. "What would you think about putting together a menu?"

"Are you serious?"

"Nothing fancy, but a step up from normal bar food.

Like you said, simple food that tastes good. If we could tap into part of the lunch and dinner crowd, it would expand the bar's reach in a great way. Riley's Bar & Grill. What do you think?"

"I think it's the best offer I've had in years," he answered, his voice thick.

A round of applause and several catcalls went up from the men.

Scott felt a smile spread across his face. He stood, shook hands with Jon, then grabbed his plate. "I'm glad you agree. Get something to me by end of day tomorrow. I'd like to get the new menu implemented by early next week."

"Will do, boss."

"I've got to put away some boxes out front, so I'm going to take my dinner to go." He turned to the men. "It was nice meeting you guys." He paused, then added, "If any of you are looking for work, let me know. There's a lot of odd jobs to be done around here, painting and the like."

"There aren't a lot of opportunities for guys like us," Denny answered. A couple of the men nodded in agreement. "Some of us got arrest records, pasts we're not too proud of."

"I know all about that," Scott answered. He pointed to Jon. "If he vouches for you, that's enough for me."

"Thanks, Mr. Callahan." Denny stepped forward and shook his hand. "You're a good man."

Scott smiled. "I don't know about that, but I'm a man in need of good help. Come in tomorrow morning and we'll talk work."

He finished the meal as he unloaded bottles into

the cooler. He walked from the back with more beer and heard the front door open. Annoyance crept up his spine at his hope to see Lexi, who was on the schedule tonight, coming in early. He knew his interest in her would lead nowhere for either of them, but couldn't put a stop to it. Instead, his father and Sam stood inside the entrance.

"To what do I owe the honor?" he asked, setting the box on top of the bar.

"Scotty, it's so good to see you." His dad came forward and wrapped Scott in a tight hug, ignoring the way he stiffened in response. Joe Callahan had been the consummate Boston cop for years, both before and after his wife died. He'd dedicated his life to the force, even when he'd had two young sons at home grieving the loss of their mother. Joe's ability to cut off his feelings had been ingrained early in both his boys, which was just fine by Scott. Recently Joe had rediscovered his "emotional intelligence" as he called it, and was on a mission to make sure Sam and Scott came along for the ride.

Joe had traveled south last spring to reconnect with Sam, and in the process had gotten a second chance at love—with Julia's mother, Vera. Now both Sam and Joe called Brevia, North Carolina, home. Scott was happy for them, but he had no desire to be part of Joe's love-fest. He thought Sam had gone soft, and although he liked Julia and her little boy well enough, the thought of being tied down with a wife and kid felt totally foreign to him.

"Good to see you, old man. Married life is treating

you well so far." He pulled back from Joe's tight hug. "Jeez, Dad, what's up with the tears?"

Joe swiped a hand across his face. "I'm happy to see you, son. Nothing wrong with showing my emotions."

"He's a regular watering pot," Sam added, clapping a hand on their dad's broad back. "How's it going here?"

"Coming along," Scott answered, stepping behind the bar and out of Joe's reach. "Is this a social call or something else?"

"I've got a buddy who's a local Realtor specializing in commercial property," Sam said. "I can make a call and get him over here within fifteen minutes."

"Why do I need a Realtor?"

Sam exchanged a look with their father. "We thought he could help."

Scott pointed a finger at Joe. "You're in on this, too?"

"I want you to be happy, Scotty." He stepped forward. "You've been through a lot. You deserve it."

"It was an impulsive decision to buy this place," Sam said. "We get that. But Mark can help you unload it before things go too far."

"You think you know me so well," Scott muttered, transferring beer bottles into the cooler behind the bar.

"I know you love being a marshal, the action and adrenaline of it," his brother countered. "I know life as a bar owner can't give you that."

"I thought the same thing when you left the force in Boston to take the police chief's job in this Podunk Smoky Mountain town. It's worked out all right for you. Why not me?"

Sam shook his head, but Joe stepped between them. "Is this what you want, Scott? This kind of life change?

Because I'll support whatever you want to do, whether it's going back to D.C. or staying in Brevia. Hell, I'll wipe bar tables for you if it would help."

"Dad, he's not staying in Brevia."

Scott felt his temper flare. Why didn't anyone around him think he could stick? "Is it so hard to believe I could make a life here in your precious town? I get that you don't want me here."

"It's not that, although could you blame me if it was?" Sam let out a breath. "The last time we were living in the same place, you slept with my fiancée. That's a hell of a breach of trust."

"You know why that happened. She'd already cheated on you and you wouldn't believe it. I had to prove it to you."

"By going after her yourself? That's not my definition of brotherly love."

Scott squeezed shut his eyes to ward off the dull pounding inside his head. When he opened them again, he saw Lexi standing just inside the front door. By the look on her face, she'd heard his conversation with Sam and the awful thing he'd done. He'd wanted to protect his brother, but ended up betraying him in the worst way possible. Sam was right—he'd made a huge alcohol-induced mistake when he'd taken Sam's former fiancée, Jenny, to bed.

Buying the bar had also been impulsive and alcohol-induced. Whether it was a mistake remained to be seen. Sam certainly thought it was, and probably their dad, as well. Scott met Lexi's gaze, surprise in her eyes, but not the judgment he'd come to expect from everyone around him. Maybe that would appear later. He couldn't say. But the absence of it bolstered his resolve.

He turned to face his brother and father. "I messed up, Sam. Royally. I'm sorry for what I did, but you have to believe that my intentions were good. Or don't believe it. It doesn't matter anymore. I'm here now and I'm staying in Brevia until I decide it's time to go. I'm not going to make a mess of the bar. I won't embarrass you in front of your wife or your neighbors. You have a life here. I get that."

He expected Sam to argue, but instead his brother gave a curt nod.

Joe put one arm around Sam's stiff shoulders and reached for Scott, hugging both men to his chest. "All three of us together again. I couldn't ask for anything more." He gave a loud sniff and Scott saw Sam roll his eyes. At least they were in agreement in not liking their father's emotional mumbo jumbo. "We should celebrate."

Scott looked over his father's shoulder to Lexi, who was gesturing wildly. He nodded as her meaning became clear. "We should celebrate the fact that both of you bozos were dumb enough to get caught in the marriage net. I'll throw a party here for you—a joint reception with all your friends. As big as you want it to be."

Sam shook his head. "I don't think so."

"It's a great idea." Joe clapped Scott on the back. "When are you thinking?"

"I need a few weeks to get everything running the way I want. How about a month from Saturday?"

"Perfect," Joe answered.

"No way," Sam said. "Julia won't agree to it."

"Nonsense," Joe argued. "Vera will be thrilled and Julia will agree to anything that makes her mother happy."

"I'm sure you want to make your mother-in-law slash new stepmother happy, Sammy-boy."

Joe nodded. "If Vera's happy, we're all happy."

Scott got a good bit of satisfaction in watching his brother's jaw clench. "Why are you doing this?" Sam asked.

How did he answer that? Because his old life held too many reminders of the partner he'd lost. Because he couldn't stand to be alone anymore. Because he had to keep moving, stay busy to keep the demons at bay. His chest tightened but he held Sam's gaze. "I want to make things right between us. At least let me try."

"Fine." Sam looked over his shoulder at Lexi, then back at him. "I thought you were going to fire her."

Scott felt that unfamiliar surge of protectiveness wash over him again. "Leave her alone, Sam. We've come to an understanding."

"She's trouble and I don't trust her."

Scott watched Lexi walk forward until she stood directly behind Sam. Scott had a couple of inches on his brother, but Sam was broader, making Lexi look even tinier so close to him. "I can hear you talking about me," she told Sam.

"I don't particularly care," he said, glancing at her again.

"Do you work here with Scotty?" Joe asked, oblivious to the tension between Sam and Lexi. "I'm Joe Callahan, his proud father."

Proud father? Scott groaned. Next Joe would be

handing out cigars to customers, as if Scott's being in Brevia was cause for a real celebration. It was too bad his dad hadn't been around like this when he was a kid. Joe had been a workaholic cop, leaving the raising of his two young sons mostly to their mother, so he could put his life on the line for the force. And after Scott's mom died, things had gotten even worse, with Joe working extra shifts so he could bury the pain of his loss. Unfortunately, Scott had been stuck with his own pain and loss, but too young to know how to deal with them. Maybe things would have turned out differently if his mom was still around, but he'd never know. All he had was the present moment. "Dad, this is Lexi Preston. She's one of the waitresses here."

"Nice to meet you, Mr. Callahan."

"Call me Joe." He took her hand and brushed his lips across her knuckles. "If all the waitresses are as pretty as you, this place should do a bang-up business."

"Dad, inappropriate." Scott felt his jaw drop as Lexi giggled. He hadn't heard her laugh before. The sweet sound washed over him and made him crave more.

"I don't mind," she said, tipping her chin down as a blush crept up her cheeks.

Scott sucked in a breath as she smoothed her hands across the fabric of her dark miniskirt.

Sam nudged him. "Be careful, little brother. I still don't trust her."

Joe turned to Sam, frowning. "You're being rude, Sammy. I didn't raise you to disrespect a lady like that."

"It's true, Dad."

"Thanks for the compliment, Joe." Lexi met Sam's angry stare and swallowed. "But your son has good reason to mistrust me. I worked on the custody case against Julia Morgan. I put her and Sam through a lot and I'm sorry for that."

Joe crossed his arms over his chest. "Is that so?"

"I also gave Julia the information that helped her get the lawsuit dropped, if that makes a difference." She glanced toward the front of the bar as if she wanted to bolt, then turned back to the three men. "I know I have to earn your trust, and I'm going to do that, Sam. Julia has given me a chance and I'm very grateful to her."

"A chance at what?" Joe asked.

"A chance for a fresh start." Lexi took a deep breath. "I'm going to live by my terms and that means helping people instead of hurting them. I learned a lot in the past couple of months. I've gotten a second chance and I'm going to make the most of it."

Joe studied her with his best hard-nosed cop stare. Scott knew the look well, as he and his trouble-making buddies had caved under it many times growing up. Lexi didn't look away and Scott realized that his little mouse had a lot more backbone than he'd given her credit for. Suddenly, Joe reached out a hand and pulled Lexi into one of his trademark bear hugs.

"You've got to be kidding me," Sam muttered under his breath.

"It takes a lot of guts to admit you've made a mistake. I'm proud of you, Lexi. We'll be here to help you every step of the way."

Joe released Lexi and she stepped back, looking a little dazed, much like Scott felt. "That means a lot, Joe." She quickly swiped at her cheeks and kept her eyes to the ground. "I've got to clock in now. I'll, um... Thank you."

With that, she raced through the door that led to the back of the bar.

Scott wanted to follow her, but turned to his father. "What was that, Dad? You made her cry."

"When are you going to learn there's nothing wrong with tears?"

"Excuse me, but you were the one who told me to man up after Mom died. I was seven, and as I remember, there was a strict no-tears rule."

Joe wiped at his own eyes. "I'm sorry, boys. I know I made big mistakes. But we're all together now and things are going to be back on track with the three of us." He pulled Scott to him and let out a shuddering breath.

"Okay, Dad, sure." Scott looked at Sam. "Is he always like this now?"

"Yep. Welcome to Joe Callahan 2.0." Sam nudged their father. "Come on, old man. Scott has work to do."

"I'll have Vera call you about the details of the reception. She'll be thrilled."

Scott's eyes widened at the thought of dealing with his spirited new stepmother. For the first time today, Sam smiled. "Be careful what you wish for," he cautioned, then turned for the front door.

Joe stopped and looked back at Scott. "Do you have a place yet? You're welcome to stay with Vera and me."

"I'm set. Thanks, though."

Sam's eyes narrowed, but Scott ignored him. "See you, boys," he called, then turned back to his cases of beer.

* * *

Lexi entered another order into the computer and turned away from the bar as a hand clamped down on her wrist.

"You're avoiding me," Scott said, leaning toward her.

"I'm hustling so you don't have a reason to complain about me."

"I wasn't aware I needed a reason."

"Don't you have bottles to open?" She blew a strand of hair out of her eyes, then stilled as he brushed his thumb across her face.

"I'm an excellent multitasker," he said, somehow making the words sound like foreplay.

She shrugged out of his grasp and stepped away from the bar, his quiet laugh flustering her even more. She still hadn't recovered from the emotions that had bubbled to the surface when Joe Callahan said he was proud of her. Never once since she'd been adopted had her own father said anything like that to her, despite the fact that she'd made it her life's mission to make him proud. Instead, the more she'd tried, the more he seemed to expect, until she felt more like a machine than a real person. Now, by her simply admitting she wanted to do better, Scott's dad had given her the validation she craved. How weak and pathetic did that make her?

She was totally off-balance, which may have explained why, when Jon poked his head out of the back of the bar and told her she had an emergency call, she automatically took the cordless phone and held it to her ear.

"Hello," she said into the receiver.

"Lexi." Her father spoke her name like an admonishment. It was a tone she recognized all too well.

She sucked in a breath. "How did you find me?"

"The better question is why are you hiding from me?"

"I'm not hiding," she said softly, holding the phone close to her ear to hear over the background noise in the bar. Although it was a weekday night, a decent crowd had trickled in to watch the evening's game on the big screen. "You fired me. I left. That's how it works."

"No need to be snippy, Lexi," her father said, his voice clipped. "I acted in a moment of anger. I think your leave of absence has gone on long enough. I'll expect to see you at the office Monday morning."

Lexi bit down on her lip until she could swear she tasted blood. She'd known this was going to happen, that her father would reel her back in eventually. She was too valuable a commodity for him to truly let her go. But she'd hoped to have more time. "I'm not ready."

"Excuse me?"

"I want to stay," she said, trying to give her voice a confidence she didn't feel.

"To spend your nights in a bar in that backwoods Southern town? I don't think so. With your biological history, that's a very bad idea. I'll see you Monday and—"

"No!"

Silence greeted her outburst. "I'm taking a month. I have the personal days." She spoke quickly so as not to lose her nerve. "I'll let you know then if and when I'm coming back. Goodbye, Daddy."

With trembling fingers, she clicked off the receiver

and held it tight against her chest, her stomach turning. She'd never disobeyed her father before. Yes, she was twenty-seven years old, but when it came to her relationship with Robert Preston, she felt more like a schoolgirl, afraid of his dissatisfaction, disappointment and ultimately his rejection. Her biggest fear was that the man who'd rescued her from her awful childhood would leave her with nothing and no one in her life. She knew he had the power to do that, at least as far as her career went. Still, she couldn't give up now. She needed to know she could make it on her own if she had hope of going back to her old life with any shred of dignity intact.

She felt someone watching her and looked up to see Scott standing stock-still next to the bar, the waitresses a flurry of activity around him. Lexi tried to throw him a casual smile, but her mouth wouldn't move in that direction so she fled to the back of the bar. With a calming breath, she headed into his small office at the end of the hall and returned the phone to its cradle. Scrubbing her hands across her face, she turned and ran smack into Scott's rock wall of a chest.

"Who was on the phone?" he asked, holding her upper arms to steady her.

"It was personal. None of your business."

"You look like someone called to say they'd shot your puppy."

"That's awful." She tried to step way, but he held her in place, one finger tracing small circles on her skin, as if he was trying to soothe her. She hated to admit that it worked, but felt herself sagging a bit, the conversation with her father draining what little energy she had left from the day.

"I'm guessing you got the call from dear old dad?" Scott asked softly.

She nodded. "I blocked the firm's and his personal numbers from my cell and haven't been picking up callers I don't recognize. It was sneaky of him, phoning the bar."

"He's an attorney—what do you expect?"

"Lawyer jokes. Funny." But she smiled a little. "He wants me in the office on Monday."

Scott's fingers stilled on her arm, which made her glance up into his suddenly unreadable eyes. "Are you going?"

"No. Not yet, anyway. I like it here, the apartment, the small town." She gave a tiny laugh. "Even this crummy job. The boss is a jerk but the customers are great."

"Boss jokes. Funny." One side of his mouth kicked up before drawing into a tight line. "Will your father come looking for you?"

"I don't think so. I told him I needed a month."

"What happens in a month?"

"I'm not sure, but it gives me time to figure it out."

"You can take care of yourself, you know. You had my dad eating out of the palm of your hand minutes after you told him you'd tried to take his grandson away."

"Your dad's a big teddy bear."

Scott grinned. "I've never thought of him that way."

His smile disarmed her, made her breath hitch. She wanted him in a way she couldn't explain and barely understood. Clearly, she wasn't his type, and he was way too much…man for her. But it didn't stop her body's response to him. He met her gaze, and the way his blue eyes darkened made her think he might feel the same. She knew her time in Brevia would eventually come to an end, and she wanted to experience everything she could while she was here. Maybe that was what made her blurt, "Have an affair with me?"

Scott's grip on her arm loosened. His fists clenched and she thought he might walk away. "You can't want that."

"I do." She licked her lip and felt the electricity of desire charge between them. "More than you know."

His hands smoothed up her arms and across her shoulders to her neck, his fingers burning a path along her heated skin. He cradled her head in his hands as one thumb traced the seam of her lips. "You should be gentler with this mouth," he told her, soothing the spot she'd bit down on earlier. "I've grown to like it quite a lot."

She could hardly manage a breath, but whispered, "What if gentle isn't what I want?"

He cupped her face, tilting her chin up and leaning in so they were so close she could smell the peppermint scent of his breath. "You don't know what you're asking, Lexi."

"Show me."

Heaven help her, he did. His mouth covered hers, igniting a fire in her belly that quickly spread out of control. Which was exactly what she wanted: to lose control with this man. Right here, right now. As his lips teased hers, she lifted her arms around his neck, pressing her body against him.

Scott groaned low in his throat and deepened the kiss, his mouth making demands that she tried her best to meet. His hands moved down, just brushing the outline of her breasts, making her gasp. He took the opportunity to tangle his tongue with hers and she lost all coherent thought, so caught up in the physical sensations that were flooding through her.

When he pulled back she thought she might melt into a puddle on the floor, that was how boneless and weightless he'd made her feel. "Don't stop," she said, reaching for him again.

"No."

That one word brought her back to reality like a swift kick to her stomach. She blinked several times to clear her head. "You don't mean that. The way you were just kissing me, you can't mean that."

He shook his head, his hands clenched at his sides. "You're not thinking clearly and you want to get back at your father. I understand that. But I'm not going to take advantage of your weakness."

"I'm not weak."

"I didn't mean—"

"I get to make my own decisions." She adjusted her shirt where it had bunched around her waist, embarrassed that she was still reeling from the kiss, when Scott could clearly pull away with no problem. "Good or bad, the point of me being on my own is to live on my own terms."

"Which involve a relationship with me?"

She crossed her arms over her chest. "Not a relationship. An affair. You know…"

"Sex?" he offered.

"Well...yes. Casual. Fun. Easy. All things that have been missing from my life since...forever, really."

"You don't strike me as the casual-sex type."

"That's the point." She wanted to stomp her foot in frustration. Why was he making this so complicated? Couldn't he just go back to kissing her and see where that led?

"My answer is still no," he said quietly.

Tears of embarrassment clogged her throat. Here she was, all but throwing herself at his feet, only to be rejected. "Because I'm not your type."

"Because of a lot of reasons. I don't—"

"It's fine." She held up a hand. "There's no need to go on. We both need to get back to work."

He shook his head as he watched her. "It's a slow night. Take the rest of it off. You look like you could use it."

Lexi felt a blush burn her cheeks. He was going to reject her, then tell her she looked like hell? Great. Insult to injury, why would she expect anything else?

"What I need," she said, straightening her shoulders and setting her jaw so he wouldn't see how his words stung, "is a drink. It works for you. Why not me? I'm going to have an adventure with or without you, Scott. Just wait and see." Mustering every ounce of dignity she could grasp, she walked past him back toward the bar.

Chapter 6

Scott put his key in the lock, then leaned forward to listen for any sound coming from the apartment. It was late, past 2:00 a.m., and thankfully, things seemed to be quiet here. He wasn't sure if he could keep his temper at Lexi's ridiculous proposition, not to mention his desire for her, in check if she was still awake.

He wasn't sure how things had gone bad so quickly. Not that they'd ever been particularly good between them, but he'd thought they'd reached an understanding. Then he'd seen her take that phone call, shock and misery evident on her face. He'd known it was a mistake to follow her back to his office, but he'd had to make sure she was okay. She wasn't, and after minutes spent kissing her, neither was he. Holding a woman in his arms had never affected him the way being with Lexi had.

When she'd made the offer of an affair, parts of his

body had literally jumped to attention. But he couldn't agree to it. He had a track record of hurting the people he cared about, and although he'd known her only a short time, he felt an undeniable connection to Lexi. Whether it was his mother or Sam or his late partner at the Marshals, Derek, Scott's need and desire to protect them turned to poison.

It had become easier to keep people at arm's length. He'd also become an expert at avoiding the pain of rejection or having someone he cared about not believing him. Lexi was a good person, pure of heart in a way he could never hope to be. For once he was going to do the right thing, even if it killed him.

It just might, he thought as the door opened to reveal Lexi asleep on the couch in nothing but a tank top and boxer shorts. Her legs curled under her, the skin creamy all the way down to her bright red toenail polish. Legs he could well imagine wrapped around him.

A low sound coming from the other side of the couch distracted him. A moment later there was a flash of brown fur accompanied by several high, yippy barks, and a small dog sunk its teeth into the toe of Scott's work boot.

"What the—" He shook his foot but the tiny dog had clamped on tight.

Lexi sat up, rubbing her eyes. "What's going on? What time is it?"

She wiped a hand across her mouth and Scott was momentarily distracted from the dog attack by the fact that Lexi wasn't wearing a bra. Was she trying to kill him?

The small animal holding tight to his boot was certainly intent on the job.

Lexi's sleepy gaze met Scott's, then dropped to his leg. "Oh, no. Freddy, no. Come here, sweetheart." She moved around the side of the sofa, then dropped to her knees on the carpet. "Come, Freddy," she said, and with one last growl, the small pup jumped into her arms.

Scott closed the door behind him and contemplated the picture of Lexi on her knees in front of him. The couch in his office at the bar was suddenly looking more appealing.

"What is that thing?" he asked, dropping his keys on the table next to the door. He went to take a step into the apartment, but the dog turned and barked.

"It's not a thing. It's a dog. He's my dog." She picked him up as she stood, the small animal licking her chin with its pink tongue. "His name is Freddy."

Scott shook his head. "That's not a dog. You could make a case for an overgrown rat, or a football with legs, but it's definitely not a dog."

Lexi cradled the animal close to her chest, covering its ears at the same time. "Don't say things like that. He has a bit of a Napoleon complex. You're going to make it worse."

Scott couldn't imagine this night getting much worse.

"Where did he come from?"

"The Morgans' animal shelter, of course. Julia helped me pick him out. Freddy and I bonded right away. He's a Chihuahua mix."

"Mixed with rodent I'd bet." All Scott wanted was to go to sleep, and now he couldn't get past the apartment's entrance without mini-Cujo gunning for him.

"Scott, please. My father never let me have a pet, not even a goldfish. I love Freddy. He needs me." Lexi's voice was a plea. "He's obviously a good watchdog. That's important when you're a single woman living alone."

"You don't live alone. I live here, too."

She tilted her head. "You never know what I might need protection from."

That was the truth if he'd ever heard it, especially with one thin strap of her tank top sliding down the smooth skin of her upper arm. He refocused his attention on the dog. "He's going to have to get used to me."

"Come sit down on the couch with us."

Areas low in Scott's body tightened. The last thing he needed was to be sitting close to Lexi on the soft couch. "I'm tired. I want to go to sleep."

"In a minute," she argued and reached for his hand, lacing her fingers through his. "I want you to see how sweet Freddy is."

Her smile, both excited and tentative, did Scott in. There was nothing he could do to resist her.

She led him to the sofa, Freddy still nestled in her arms, and they sat side by side, the length of her bare leg pressed against his thigh. Even with his jeans between them, he could sense how soft her skin was. Knew it would feel like silk against his hands, his mouth. With a shake of his head, he looked at her holding the dog. "What do you want me to do?"

"Don't move," she answered. "I'm going to let him go so he can check you out. Don't make eye contact with him."

"Seriously?"

"Julia's mom told me that's how you start when a

dog is nervous." Lexi smiled at Scott again. "Just close your eyes."

"Can I fall asleep?"

"No, but close your eyes."

He sighed and did as she asked, letting his head fall back. Despite how tired he was, there was no chance of him falling asleep sitting this close to Lexi. She smelled like heaven, and as she spoke softly to the dog, Scott imagined her soothing words were for him. That was until she let go of the animal, who promptly stepped into the middle of his lap. Scott let out a grunt of pain and the dog growled.

"Don't move," Lexi commanded, using her hand to push Scott against the cushions once more. "You'll spook him."

"If he bites me, all bets are off."

"He's not going to bite you, but don't open your eyes yet."

Her arm pressed into his shoulder as she spoke to the dog. "Good boy, Freddy. You make friends."

Scott felt a wet dog nose press against his neck. "That tickles," he whispered.

"Don't be a baby," Lexi answered.

"Me or the dog?"

"You, of course. Oh, look at that."

He opened his eyes just as the dog curled into a ball on his lap. Scott's gaze lifted to Lexi, her head tipped forward so close all he had to do was move the tiniest inch to taste her again. He craved her more than he'd ever wanted a drink. More than he could remember wanting anything.

"They say dogs are a good judge of character," she whispered. "Freddy likes you."

"I still think Freddy is more rat than dog."

"Don't be mean. I love him."

"You've had him less than a day."

"It only takes a moment to fall in love."

Scott's mouth went dry. He could say with certainty he'd never been in love. After his mother's death, he hadn't wanted to feel the pain of losing someone he loved again. Sitting here on the couch with Lexi, he could imagine what it would feel like to be in love, to truly let another person in. The crazy part was he'd bet it would feel a lot like the pitch in his heart right now.

Needing to bring the conversation back to a safer subject, he said, "I saw you talking to a few different guys tonight at the bar."

He'd wanted to engage her temper, but she smiled at him instead. "I know. I flirted a ton."

Scott tried not to groan. "Do you think that's a good idea? You don't want to give them the wrong impression."

"I do, though." Her smile grew wider. "Not give the wrong impression," she added quickly. "I want to meet new people, try new things. Flirting is one of them."

"Heaven help the men of Brevia."

She swatted his arm. "One of them asked me out, you know."

The hand Scott was using to pet Freddy clenched into a fist. "Who asked you out?"

"I doubt you know him. His name's Mark. He's a teacher at the high school." Lexi's eyes dropped to

Scott's mouth and awareness traced a long path down his spine. "He seemed nice enough."

Nice. Lexi deserved *nice,* a word that had never been in Scott's vocabulary. He thought of her pressed against him in his office earlier, how open and responsive she'd been and how much it had affected him. Would she melt against Mark the same way?

The thought made Scott crazy. He wanted to pull her to him now, brand her as his so she was ruined for anyone else.

But that wasn't his right, because he had nothing to offer her and they both knew it.

The dog stirred on his lap, a welcome distraction. "Do you have a leash?" Scott asked.

"On the counter."

"Go to bed, Lexi. I'll take the rat out one more time to do his business." He lifted Freddy off his lap, tucking him under one arm. He grabbed the leash from the kitchen.

Lexi stood next to the sofa, arms crossed over her chest. "You're okay with me going on a date?" Her voice was strained.

"It's your life, sweetheart," he answered, not adding how much he wanted to be a part of it. He clipped the dog's collar to the leash and headed out the door.

Lexi walked along the path around the park, Freddy trotting ahead of her. She'd taken to morning walks during the past week to make sure she had as little to do with Scott as possible. Of course, she still saw him every night at the bar, but other than putting in orders, she had almost no contact with him.

She hated to admit how embarrassed she was about her behavior, practically begging him to sleep with her, only to have him reject her. And when she'd told him she was going on a date with another guy, the stupid, girlie part of her had hoped to make Scott jealous. Relieved was more like it, she realized now.

She was so busy wallowing in self-pity she didn't notice someone walk up behind her until she felt a tap on her shoulder.

"You look a million miles away," Julia said, handing Lexi a steaming to-go mug.

"Kind of…. What's this for?" Lexi took the cup, watching as Julia bent down to scratch between Freddy's perky ears.

"I've seen you the past couple of mornings, walking around the park like the hounds of hell are nipping your heels. I thought you could use someone to talk to."

Lexi made a face. "It's supposed to look like I'm out for exercise."

"Sam told me you let Scott move into the apartment."

"It's hard to believe anyone has the power to let that man do anything." Lexi took a sip of the hot tea and sighed. "But, yes, he's there with me. I didn't think you'd mind. It's okay, isn't it?"

"Of course. How's that going?"

"I've been in the park every morning. Do I need to say more?"

"I'll take a lap with you." Julia began walking in the same direction as Lexi. "I also heard you were at Cowboys last night."

"Word travels fast," Lexi muttered.

"Welcome to a small town." Julia sighed.

"It was my night off."

"And you decided to spend it in the only other bar in town? That doesn't seem like you."

"You don't know me very well."

Lexi tried to make her tone sound dismissive, but Julia only laughed. "I also heard you were putting the moves on several different guys."

"What the...? Are you having me followed now? As thankful as I am for your help, it's none of your business what I do with my time, Julia." Lexi looked down at the ground, cursing the blush she felt rising to her cheeks.

"I know. And I know you're here to taste freedom, have a grand adventure, whatever. But I can tell you from personal experience that once you get a reputation, it can stick for a long time."

Lexi stopped to untangle Freddy's leash. The dog nuzzled against her legs and tears sprang to her eyes. "It's a lot of work, being totally on your own." She wiped at her cheek and looked at Julia. "I really admire you for taking care of yourself the way you did."

As part of the custody suit, it had been Lexi's job to delve into Julia's past, trying to dig up dirt that could be used against her. There had been a fair bit of it, mostly stemming from bad decisions Julia had made while trying to hide the learning disability that plagued her most of her life. But Julia was strong and kept fighting. In the process of her investigation, Lexi had come to respect her and understand that there were choices in life beyond doing what people expected of you. Once Julia had started living life on her terms, things had worked out for her. Lexi only hoped she could have an ounce of the woman's personal success.

"You're doing a fine job of taking care of yourself, Lexi." Julia smiled at her. "But you can't hold your alcohol."

Lexi snorted. "I know. But I don't have friends other than the girls at the bar. I didn't want to be alone in the apartment on my night off. That seemed too pathetic."

"There's nothing wrong with being alone if the alternative is hanging out with the wrong people."

They started walking again when Freddy tugged on the leash. "My stylist, Nancy, said you were a big help to her with her divorce case."

"It's not my area of expertise," Lexi said with a shrug, "but her case is pretty cut-and-dried. I'm not sure why Frank Davis couldn't be of more help to her."

"Frank's been Brevia's main attorney for decades now. I think he might be slipping a bit. People are waiting for him to retire or at least bring in a junior associate, but he hasn't done it yet."

"I know from my dad there can be a lot of pride of ownership in having your own practice."

"People still need lawyers. Good ones." Julia pointed her coffee cup toward Lexi. "Like you."

"I'm not practicing law in Brevia."

"But you're certified in North Carolina?"

Lexi hesitated, then said, "I'm taking a break."

"Right. For the grand adventure." They'd done a full turn of the park and Julia stopped at the same place she'd met up with Lexi. "I have another friend who could use some legal counsel. Or at least a second opinion."

Lexi shook her head. "Grand adventure, remember?"

"She's a longtime client and needs help with an estate inheritance."

"Not my area of expertise, either."

"Please. It's a bad situation. She needs someone she can trust. We both know how that feels." Julia raised her eyebrows. "Don't make me beg, Lexi. It's not in my nature."

Lexi threw her cup into a nearby trash can. "Fine. Give her my cell number, but I'd like to go to that attorney's office and give him a piece of my mind."

"I'd like to see that." Julia tipped her cup in Lexi's direction. "By the way, I'm having a girls' night in the salon tomorrow night. Are you off?"

"I can get off." Lexi fiddled with the leash, trying not to show too obviously her excitement at being included. "Are you sure? You don't have to ask me just to be nice."

Julia threw her head back and laughed. "Everyone knows I don't do anything to be nice. Some *nice* girls work at the salon, though. A couple of them are new to town. It would be a better place than a meat-market country bar to make friends."

"Great, then," Lexi said with a grin. "Thank you." She paused, then added, "I have a date."

"With Scott?"

Lexi ignored the wave of disappointment that rushed over her. "No. His name is Mark Childs. He's a teacher at the high school. He moved up from Charlotte last year. He's nice, too." She took a breath. "Sorry, I'm babbling."

"I'm glad for you. That sounds like a good addition to the adventure." To her surprise, Julia leaned forward and gave her a quick hug. "See you tomorrow, then."

"Okay, I'll see you." Lexi turned away quickly, surprised as well that her throat was suddenly a bit scratchy. But she felt better about her life. Funny how one quick conversation could do that. She leaned forward to pet Freddy, who flopped onto his back, always glad to have more attention. After a minute, when she had her emotions in check once more, she headed down the path and toward home.

"Don't even think about taking advantage of that girl."

Scott looked up from the new bar menu at the woman standing, hands on hips, just inside the front door.

Jon Riley stood quickly. "I'll be in the back, boss. Call me when you're through here." In a quieter voice he added, "Or when she's through with you."

"Chicken," Scott muttered as Jon made his escape, clucking over his shoulder.

"To what do I owe the honor, Mrs. Callahan?" Scott stood, rubbing his palms down the front of his jeans. "Or should I call you sis?"

Julia rolled her eyes. "You know who I'm talking about. She's fragile right now."

"You don't give her enough credit."

"She gives you too much."

Scott's jaw tightened because Julia was right. Even though Lexi had avoided him the past week, he'd seen her watching him when she thought he wasn't looking. Sometimes she'd catch him watching her. Either way, instead of the wariness she should have for him, her gaze showed nothing but trust. That was dangerous for both of them. He wasn't someone she could trust, and he didn't trust himself around her. Which made working and living with her a form of torture. But he couldn't walk away.

Not willing to admit any of this to Julia, he shrugged. "In case it matters, your little ray of sunshine propositioned me. I said no."

Julia's eyes narrowed. "Bull."

"It's true, ask her. Despite the fact that you and my big brother think I'm the bad seed of the Callahan clan, I don't want trouble in Brevia."

"You're nothing but trouble."

"From what I understand, you were a bit of the same back in the day."

"I've grown up."

"Who says I can't?"

She studied him, literally looked him up and down. After a moment, she said, "Stay away from her."

"I have every intention of staying away."

"You moved into my apartment."

"You and I are family. I have more right to it."

"I sublet it to her."

"That's right, you rented an apartment and gave a fresh start to the woman who tried to take your son away."

"I'm giving her a second chance."

"Maybe I'd like one, too."

"You betrayed Sam," she said after a minute. "In the worst way possible. He doesn't trust you."

Scott nodded. "I know that. What I did was wrong and I can't apologize any more than I have. That woman was bad news. The way I went about proving it to him was a mistake. But I don't regret breaking them up. She would have hurt him more than I ever did."

Julia's delicate features went soft. "He's a good man."

"And I'm happy he's found you. I'm glad you have each other."

"You were mad he didn't take the job with the Marshals because he wanted to stay in Brevia."

Scott nodded. "I was frustrated. I thought working with him would give us a chance to put the past behind us. But after meeting you and Charlie, I understand why he made the choice he did. I'm not mad anymore." Scott sighed. "I'd still like things to be better."

"He told me you're hosting a reception for us."

"He said you'd be against it."

"I'm not. I hated this town for a long time, but I'm happy here now. Why not celebrate that?" She offered a small smile. "Will you come to dinner this weekend? I'll invite my mom and Joe, too. Vera is thrilled about the party. We can make plans then."

"Sure," Scott said, returning her smile. "I'm not so bad once you get to know me, Julia."

"Maybe," she answered, eyes skimming the bar. "This place looks a lot better."

He followed her gaze to the newly polished floor and the fresh coat of paint on the main wall. He'd put in a lot of hours this week fixing things up where he could. He liked the hard work and couldn't help but feel proud of how much he'd accomplished. "Thanks. We're going to start serving food in a few days. Open for lunch, too."

She nodded. "Anything that brings more people into downtown is good as far as I'm concerned." With a last look around, she turned for the door. "I'll see you later, Scott."

"A pleasure talking to you, sis."

She laughed and walked out into the late-morning sunlight.

Scott glanced at his watch. It was close to noon, which meant he didn't actually have to be here for nearly five more hours. Suddenly, another day of being cooped up in the bar was too much for him.

He poked his head into the back hallway. "Jon?" he called out.

"Yeah, boss." Jon came from the kitchen, wiping his hands on a towel.

"Do you think you can take care of things here for a few hours?"

A smile broke across the man's ruddy face. "I'd be happy to. I used to watch over the place for my dad."

Scott nodded and grabbed his jacket from a hook on the wall. "I'll be back before we open."

Chapter 7

Lexi tossed the book she was reading onto the coffee table. Freddy yawned and stretched next to her. She had a whole day in front of her before she needed to get to work, but couldn't muster the energy to make decent plans.

She heard keys in the apartment's door and turned as Scott walked in. She'd thought he'd already gone to the bar for the day or else she would have been holed up in her room.

"Let's go," he said, pointing a finger at her.

"Go where?" She reached again for her discarded book, ignoring the fact that her heart had picked up its pace. "I'm kind of busy."

He gave her a lopsided smile. "Liar. Come on. We're going to have some fun."

"Can you clarify how you define *fun?*"

"Nope." He leaned over the couch and took her hand to gently pull her to her feet. Freddy stood up, tail wagging. "We'll see you later, buddy."

"Do I need to change clothes?" Lexi asked, smoothing her hands across her T-shirt and jeans. "It would help if I knew what to prepare for."

"We're going on an adventure," Scott replied, his eyes traveling up and down her body like a caress. "You look perfect."

Lexi's mouth went dry but she forced herself to smile. "Somehow that doesn't reassure me."

The truth was she was excited to go with him, wherever they ended up. She knew Scott was bad for her, or at least that was what he kept saying. But she trusted him to keep her safe no matter what. Lexi had never felt that with anyone in her life. It was an oddly freeing sensation.

"Grab a jacket and gym shoes. We don't want to be late."

After gathering her things, Lexi followed him out to his truck and climbed in, both excited and a little bit scared. She wondered if Little Red Riding Hood had felt the same way when she'd gone through the woods to Grandma's house. Scott drove through town and turned onto the highway heading into the mountains.

As the truck climbed the curvy road, Lexi gazed out the window to the forest below. Brevia sat in a valley nestled at the base of the Smoky Mountains. Although mornings were crisp this time of year, by noon the sun was bright in the sky, bathing the tips of trees in a golden light that made the whole area look more alive. She'd grown up in the city, gone to college there, too, so she found herself transfixed by the beauty of nature surrounding them.

Scott didn't say much as they drove, but the silence was companionable. Lexi was used to silence. Other than discussing current cases or other legal matters, her father didn't talk much to her. She often lived in her head and now found her mind wandering along paths of memories that were better left untraveled. Her father's harsh criticism and her fear that she'd never have the courage to truly live life out from under his thumb.

"Don't go there."

She jumped as Scott drew his fingers across her hand where it rested on the seat between them.

"Whatever you're thinking about, let it go today. We're going to have fun, leave the problems for later."

"It's hard not to think about things," she admitted.

"Have you gone on your date yet?"

She was taken aback by his question. "I can't talk about that with you."

"One of the other waitresses mentioned that Mr. High School Science Teacher is considered quite the catch."

Lexi shrugged. "We're supposed to go to a movie next weekend."

"You don't sound too excited."

She glanced at him from under her lashes, but his eyes were fixed on the road. "I'm very excited."

"Do you have a long list of qualifications for a potential suitor?" he asked, and she heard the smile in his voice.

"Actually, being with someone my dad didn't pick out for me is my top priority." She sighed. "My last…

current…whatever boyfriend is a fourth-year at the firm. He wants to make partner in the worst way."

"He thinks making it with the boss's daughter will help his chances?"

"I can't imagine another reason he'd be so serious with me."

"Then he's an idiot." Scott said the words with such conviction that a little ball of emotion began to unwind inside Lexi's chest.

"Do you have a girlfriend?"

"Nope. I don't do relationships." He glanced over at her and winked. "I'm a bad bet, remember?"

"What about your brother's fiancée?" Lexi asked and saw his fingers tense around the steering wheel. "Did you fall in love with her?"

"I fell into bed with her," Scott answered candidly. "Not the same thing."

"Oh."

"I don't believe in love, Lexi. I'm not made that way."

She shook her head. "Everyone is made for love."

"For an attorney, you're kind of an idealist."

"It's not an ideal. It's true. There's somebody for everyone."

"Whatever you say." Scott pulled into a long gravel driveway and slowed to avoid divots on the well-worn track. A sign that read Smoky Mountain Adventures greeted them from the side of the property. They pulled up to a small cabin with several picnic tables in front.

"What are we doing?" she asked again, eyeing the row of shiny Jeeps and ATVs sitting next to an over-size garage. A corral of horses was situated on the side of a long barn, with a few parents and children milling about outside.

"We're going zip-lining."

Lexi clenched the door handle. "You're kidding, right?"

"Have you ever been?" Scott pulled into a parking spot and turned the key, looking at her as the truck went quiet.

"I'm afraid of heights," she whispered.

He squeezed shut his eyes. "I didn't know that."

"If you'd told me our destination back at the apartment, I could have filled you in."

"That's okay," he said after a moment. "Even better, actually." He opened the driver's side door and hopped out.

Lexi would have followed him, but she was paralyzed in her seat. Her stomach churned as a bead of sweat made a slow trail down her back. She concentrated on moving air in and out of her lungs at a normal rate. She might have understated her fear of heights. Petrified was more like it. She could barely walk up an open-air flight of steps.

The door to her side of the truck opened and Scott leaned in. "Ready?"

"No."

"You can do this."

"I'm going to puke," she said, her voice a croak.

He smiled and raised his mirrored sunglasses onto the top of his head. His blue eyes looked into hers, total confidence in her radiating from their depths.

"You left your job, your home and moved to a tiny town hundreds of miles away where the only person you knew was a woman who hated you. You found a job, albeit one you're no good at and totally overqualified for, but it's a job. And for reasons unknown to me, everyone you meet loves you. Customers, the other staff, even the guy who delivers the beer asks about you."

"He does?" Lexi shifted in her seat. "That's so sweet."

"Sweet as pie." Scott reached across her waist and unbuckled the seat belt. "If you can manage all of that in a couple of weeks, sliding down a cable is going to be a cinch."

Lexi dug her fingernails into the seat. "No way."

Scott's fingers found hers, easing them from their death grip on the leather. "You can do this. It's part of the adventure. Once-in-a-lifetime, bucket-list adventure. That's what you want, right?"

"I can't," she whispered miserably.

"Yes, you can." He dropped a soft-as-a-feather kiss on her mouth. "I believe in you, Lexi Preston."

She breathed him in, the crisp, male scent and the taste of mint on his lips. "I believe in you, too, Scott."

He tensed for a moment, then eased back. "Prove it. Let's take our mutual-admiration society to the zip line. I'll make sure you're safe the whole time."

She met his gaze and saw both a challenge and promise there. Sometimes she felt as if she'd spent most of her years avoiding the parts of life that scared her the most, whether it was something physical such as her fear of heights or, more terrifying, feelings and worries. Suddenly, this step represented so much more, and she needed to take it. She wanted to prove that she was worthy of his faith in her.

"Okay," she answered, her voice shaky with nerves.

She let him lead her to the front office, her knees stiff with fear as her insides churned. Scott filled out the paperwork and spoke to the tour operator, a tall man in his early forties with sandy-blond hair and a full beard. Lexi paced back and forth, reviewing legal briefs in her head to stop the panic from consuming her. She could overcome this. Look at how much she'd done in the past few weeks. This was just one more part of her adventure.

"Zach's going to take us out personally," Scott told her as the man disappeared into a room off the side of the main waiting area. "He's the owner, so it will be fine."

Lexi bit down on her lip.

"You can do this," Scott said again and wrapped one arm around her, his fingers tracing circles on her biceps.

"I thought you didn't want to hang out with me," Lexi said softly, grasping on to anything that would distract her from the thought of careening through the forest tied to a metal cable. "Why the change of heart?"

"I never said I didn't want to hang out with you," Scott corrected. "I said having an affair with me was a bad idea."

She looked up at him, searching his pale blue eyes. "So you want to be friends?"

"I don't really have friends, Lexi." He shrugged but kept his eyes on her. "I'm probably as bad at friendship as I am at dating."

"I don't have many friends, either. It would be new territory for both of us." She couldn't help the smile that curved her lips. "I think I'd be pretty good at it, though."

He studied her for several moments. Once again, everything else disappeared as she lost herself in him. "I bet you will." Taking a breath, he added, "We're friends."

Lexi's stomach tightened as she swayed the tiniest bit closer to him. She felt more than friendship for Scott, but she'd been honest about not having many friends. Hearing him say they were seemed like a good step. "You know, friends don't try to kill each other by making them do a zip line."

He took her hand in his and led her toward the front door. "I'm broadening your horizons," he said as they walked outside into the warming air.

Zach, the owner, was waiting in a four-person open-top Jeep. "Y'all ready?" he asked as they came down the steps.

"Sure are," Scott answered.

At the same time Lexi whispered, "Heck, no."

She climbed into the backseat and they headed up a dirt road behind the property. Lexi didn't realize how much Scott's touch had bolstered her confidence until it was gone. She wrapped her arms tight around her middle, trying to quell the panic that rose to the surface once more. Scott looked back several times and gave her a smile or wink. She wanted to climb up between the seats and bury herself in his lap.

After a few minutes, she began to see a web of cables attached to what looked like oversize telephone poles between the trees.

"Scott tells me you're nervous," Zach called back. "We're going to start with one of the shorter lines so you get used to the feeling."

Lexi nodded, but her fingernails dug into her back. When he said *going to start,* she got the distinct impression he expected her to do this more than once. She wondered briefly what would happen if she passed out or literally threw up. There were countless ways she could embarrass herself today, and she figured she had a good chance of hitting them all.

In another moment the Jeep stopped and Zach jumped out and began gathering harnesses and other equipment from the cargo hold. Scott offered her a hand to help her out of the backseat. She snatched hers back when he commented on how cold it was.

"It's going to be fine," he said softly, taking her hand again and warming it between his.

She was a ninny, no doubt about it. She bet the women he knew from his time in the military and the Marshals did stuff that would make this look like a walk in the park. She wanted him to know she was up for the challenge, even one that was so small in the grand scheme of things.

"Let's do this," she said and charged after Zach.

Scott couldn't quite believe the woman careening down the cable, whooping with joy, was the same person he'd practically had to drag out of the car a few hours earlier.

Lexi came to a stop on the landing of the last line and pumped one fist in the air. "That was awesome," she yelled and threw her arms around Zach. "Thank you so much for this," she said, hugging him hard.

As Zach's big hands moved a wee bit lower than was

appropriate, Scott cleared his throat. "It was my idea, if you remember."

She turned to look at him, her smile widening. "Did you see me? I was flying. It felt like I was literally flying."

She came toward him and he grinned, thinking of her launching herself into his arms the same way. Instead, she punched him lightly on the shoulder, then danced in front of him, just out of reach. "I was so scared at the edge of the first zip line, but it was such a rush. That was the best day. Ever."

Scott's best day would actually include her pressed up against him, preferably naked. He inwardly shook his head. "I'm glad you liked it," he told her. "But we should head back."

They gathered the gear and walked toward the Jeep, Lexi and Zach taking the lead as the older man regaled her with stories of other adventures he'd had.

"Maybe I'll try skydiving next," Lexi said with a laugh.

Scott wondered if somehow he'd created an adrenaline junkie, and it made him crazy to think that Zach or any other guy would be with her on subsequent escapades.

His eyes dropped to Lexi's jeans, specifically her hips swaying as she walked. He was a fool, he realized, to think that he could be her friend without his desire for her getting in the way. The more he told himself she wasn't his type, the more drawn to her he became.

He'd wanted to get away from town today, to forget everything from his conversation with Julia to the bar to his family and their expectations of him. The only person he wanted to spend time with was Lexi. She'd been avoiding him and he knew he should have left it at that.

Seeing her face down her fear today and come out on the other side of it more confident and proud had made him want her all the more.

If he could, he'd like to bottle up the light that radiated from her and save it for his darkest moments, like a perfect Scotch he could savor at his own pace.

It had killed him to watch both Zach and the younger man who'd helped them gear up flirt with Lexi, all the while knowing he had no right to stop it. She'd offered herself to him with no strings attached and Scott had been a fool to turn her down. Now the young guide, Matt, jogged up to Lexi. He leaned down to whisper something in her ear. She glanced back at Scott, then shook her head. Matt handed her a small piece of paper, grinning like an idiot until Zach shooed him away.

He watched Lexi tuck the paper into the back pocket of her jeans, looking over her shoulder and giving Scott a thumbs-up before turning away again.

Scott gritted his teeth. This friendship was going to be the death of him.

Lexi knocked on the door of Frank Davis's law office for the third time. She knew someone was in there because she'd seen the blinds move after she'd first knocked.

Finally, the door opened, revealing the older attorney, his button-down shirt wrinkled and a spot of what looked like mustard staining his polka-dot tie. He'd lost weight since she'd last seen him, but not in a good way.

"Hi," she said, holding out her hand. "You may not remember me but—"

"I remember you. You're the little girl who made a fool out of me on the Julia Morgan case."

Lexi stepped forward to prevent him from shutting the door in her face. "I'm sorry about my actions around the custody suit, but I think we can both agree that things worked out for the best in the end."

"I had it under control," he muttered.

"Like you do Nancy Capshaw's divorce and Ida Garvey's latest estate plan? Her will hadn't been updated in almost ten years, Frank. She had no living trust, nothing to protect her family's inheritance of her more recent investments."

His round eyes widened even further. "Listen here, missy, don't you go trying to steal my clients. You have no right. I could report you to the bar association for that."

"I don't want to steal any clients," Lexi said. She glanced over his shoulder. "Could I come in for a few moments?"

"I'm busy right now."

Lexi might not have been the most assertive person in the world, but she pretended she was working for her father once again. Her fear of failing in his eyes always made her more forceful when dealing with people who didn't want to talk to her. Fear was a powerful motivator.

"I'll be quick," she said and easily slipped past him. She looked toward the receptionist's desk in the small lobby, which looked as if it had been deserted for months. A sad houseplant sat on the windowsill behind the desk, leaves brown and shriveled. "Where's your secretary?"

Frank let the door shut and turned to her. "She quit a while back. I don't need her, anyway. Brevia doesn't generate a lot of law business, not like it used to."

"Really?" Lexi found that hard to believe. In the past two days, since her meeting with Ida Garvey, she'd had a half-dozen messages from locals wanting help on a variety of cases. "Is there another law office nearby?"

He scoffed. "Of course not. I've been the main attorney in these parts for over twenty years. I built my life in this town. I've worked on every major case this county has seen." His finger jabbed into the air as if underscoring his importance. He looked around the office and sighed. "It isn't like it used to be. A whippersnapper like you wouldn't understand."

She glanced toward the inner office and sucked in a breath at the stacks of manila files lining the walls. It appeared that Frank hadn't put anything away since his secretary had left. "I understand your clients need an attorney who can keep up with their cases." She stepped forward. "I could help if you want."

His lips pressed into a grim line and she continued quickly, "I don't mean take over. But I'm licensed to practice in North Carolina. I've got time during the day...before my shift starts."

As she said the words, she realized how much she still wanted to work as an attorney. Yes, the bar was a fun diversion, something totally different than what she'd been doing. She was proving that she could take care of herself, and facing some of the demons left over from her childhood and what had happened to her mother.

But despite choosing to become a lawyer to please her father, in her heart she loved working with people and having the opportunity to help fix their problems. She'd lost sight of that in Ohio, when most of her work had been fighting for people who didn't deserve her help. People unlike the ones she'd met here in Brevia.

She realized she felt at home here, and the feeling didn't scare her. Even if it was for only a short time, she wanted to make a difference, pay it forward in her own way. Maybe that would give her some confidence for believing she could do the same thing once she returned to her own life.

"What do you think, Frank?"

"Are you crazy?" He slammed a fist into the wall, making her jump. "I see what you're doing here! You think you're the first young lawyer to walk into this office and pretend you want to help me?"

"I'm sorry, it's just—"

"I don't need your help. You think anyone in this town would ever trust you, with your background?"

"But you do need assistance." She took a calming breath, trying not to let his words hurt her.

"So what if I've slowed down a bit? I can keep up. Maybe I like to play golf a little more than I used to. I get the work done. And I'm my own man. I built this practice from the ground up. I'm not someone's puppet. I never did my daddy's dirty work, digging out every tiny bit of nastiness about the people I was working against."

"I didn't—"

"You're not the only one who can look into some-one's background, Ms. Preston."

Lexi swallowed. "I did things I'm not proud of. I'm trying to make a better life here. I'm trying to start over, to learn from my mistakes."

He walked to the door and held it open. "Then you'd better learn it someplace else. You're not welcome here."

She clenched her fists, both from frustration and embarrassment. Her intentions here had been so good.

"What am I supposed to do when someone comes to me for help? I won't turn them away."

"Run along home to daddy, Ms. Preston. You don't belong here."

"I… You… This isn't…" Frank did nothing but stare at her, arms crossed over his chest.

Blinking back tears, Lexi fled from the office back into the street. She felt as if she were a young girl again, wanting nothing more than her father's approval, but being continually denied no matter how hard she tried to please him. She knew her past wasn't perfect, but wondered if she'd ever get to a point of being able to outrun it.

"What do you think of sweet-potato fries verses reg-ular ones to go with the burger selection?"

Scott finished his inventory of bottles and turned. "Whatever you want, Jon. It's your kitchen."

Jon grinned at him. "We'll be open for lunch on Monday."

"Great. The sign guy is coming tomorrow to change the wording on the marquee to Riley's Bar & Grill." Scott picked up the stack of mail from the bar and began to leaf through it. "We need the bump in revenue to off-set all the cash I'm…" His voice trailed off as his eyes settled on a small white envelope.

"You okay, boss?" Joe took a step closer.

"Yeah, sure. I'm just thinking of when the new bar-stools are going to be delivered."

He picked up the envelope, his fingers holding it so tight that one corner began to crumple. "Can you give a call to the food supplier and confirm we'll need the fresh ingredients Monday morning? I don't want any-thing to go wrong with the rollout."

Jon studied him, but didn't call Scott out on his quick mood change. "Got it. I better get to work." He turned and hustled toward the kitchen.

Scott walked around the bar and sat on one of the high stools. He didn't have to open the letter to know what it contained, but he did, anyway. The short memo indicated that he'd have an official review in D.C. at the end of the month. It was scheduled two days before the reception for Sam and their father. The timing couldn't have been any worse, but Scott knew if he didn't show for it that his career with the Marshals was over.

He wasn't sure what he wanted his future to be, but he didn't want the decision to be made for him. At the same time, he wasn't ready to talk about what had hap-pened.

As if on cue, the front door of the bar banged opened.

"This day stinks," Lexi announced as she stalked through. Scott could almost see the smoke rising from her ears. "I try to help someone and he wants nothing to do with me. Totally ungrateful for my offer. It's ri-diculous."

Scott wasn't sure if she was talking to him or about someone else, but her words hit home. "Not everyone wants to be helped," he muttered.

"That doesn't make sense," she said, her big eyes narrowing as she met his gaze. She took in the letter in his hand and came forward. "What's the matter? What happened?"

It bothered him more than he was willing to admit that she could read him so easily. "Nothing happened for you to worry about." He folded the letter and tucked it into his shirt pocket. Scrubbing his hand across his face, he forced his mouth into a smile. "What's got your cute panties in such a bunch?"

"You have no idea if my panties are cute or not."

"We're roommates." He winked at her. "You left a basket of folded laundry in front of the TV last night. I especially like the little pink ones with bunches of cherries on them."

Her mouth dropped open. "You shouldn't look at my panties, folded or not."

He'd like to do a lot more than look. He'd like to peel them from her hips and...

"I know what you're thinking," she said, pointing a finger at him.

"Honey, if you knew what I was thinking, you'd run out that door right this minute."

He loved the hint of pink that flushed across her cheeks. "Don't distract me. What was that piece of paper you stuffed in your pocket?"

"You're the one who came in here all hot and bothered."

"I had an awful conversation with Frank Davis. He

won't admit he can't keep up with his caseload or why. I offered to help and he was rude."

"Offered to help? You want to practice law in Brevia?"

"Not forever. But I can ease some of his backlog. People are already coming to me. It's strange that there are no other law firms in town. It's like he's hoarded all of the business for himself but can't manage it anymore." She shook her head. "You're getting me off track again. Why are you upset?"

"I'm not upset," Scott said, standing and turning back toward the bar.

She grabbed his arm and pulled him around to face her. "There's a muscle pulsing at the base of your jaw. You're mad as heck about something. Maybe I could help if you told me what it was."

"I doubt it." He glanced at his watch. "Besides, your shift doesn't start for another hour. You shouldn't be here."

"I'm too worked up to go home. I came in to start on the plans for the reception. I need to burn off some energy."

"I know how you can burn off some energy."

She looked straight into his eyes. "I've already asked you for an affair. You said no."

"What if I've changed my mind?" he said, reaching out and pulling her close.

"What's in the letter?"

As fast as he'd drawn her to him, he pushed her away at those words. He walked from the bar to his small office, wishing for a way to burn off some of his own energy. As sunshine-sweet as she appeared, he knew Lexi could be worse than a dog with a bone. She wouldn't give up until he told her something.

As he expected, she followed him back. "You can tell me," she said quietly. "It's okay to let me in."

She was wrong. Scott wouldn't let anyone in, not even Lexi. But he answered truthfully, "It's a summons for a review from the Marshals office in D.C."

"To review what?" She lifted one hip onto the corner of his desk, clearly making herself comfortable. "I thought you were on a leave of absence?"

"An administrative leave," he clarified. "My partner died during a botched arrest. He was one of my few real friends at the agency. We'd gone through the academy at the same time."

"I'm sorry, Scott."

He hated sympathy. "It was my fault. Derek Sanchez was a good officer, a family man with a pretty wife and two small children waiting for him at home. The pressure of the job was bad enough, but trying to balance a normal life would take its toll on anyone."

"What happened?"

"He put himself in the line of fire instead of waiting for backup. It was stupid, a rookie mistake. He knew better but…"

"But?"

"Derek had been drinking the night before. We'd been on a stakeout for days. Sitting around with nothing to do but think can drive you nuts, even in the field."

"He was drinking on the job."

"Technically, we had the night off. But it made him careless the next day."

"How is that your fault?"

Scott shook his head, stopped in front of her. Suddenly, he needed to tell someone…to tell Lexi…the whole story. "I should have stopped him, but he'd been griping for weeks about how his wife was busting his chops, pressuring him to take a desk job with the agency. I knew he needed to blow off some steam, so I didn't stop him."

"He was a grown man," she said softly. "You weren't his babysitter."

"I should have been his friend. I knew Derek had been drinking more than usual in the months before he died, but I wasn't much of a role model. I was trying to protect him, but as usual my methods left a lot to be desired. I fell asleep and left him alone. He drank a lot more than I'd realized. When things went down the next morning, he was in no condition to handle it."

"You think he was still drunk?"

"I sure as hell hope not, but I don't know. I never said anything. If it came out that he was at fault, it could've messed up his life insurance and pension. His wife… she needs that money."

Realization dawned in Lexi's eyes. "So you walked away from your career rather than expose his issues."

"It doesn't matter," Scott said, shaking his head. He balled his fists at his sides, the familiar frustration returning. "I let him down. Like I let everyone down."

She straightened, and Scott expected her to reach for him, felt his whole body stiffen as he both feared and longed for her touch and the way it made him feel. She walked past him instead. He glanced over his shoulder, unable to help himself watch her walk away. Just like his mother had done to a seven-year-old boy who'd needed her more than she could handle.

Chapter 8

But Lexi didn't leave. Her hand reached out and turned the lock on his office door. She returned to him and took his clenched hand in hers, trailing her fingers across his palm the same way he'd done to hers when she'd been frightened of zip-lining. His awareness of her almost overwhelmed him.

"Have you changed your mind, Scott?" she asked softly, her eyes still on their intertwined fingers.

He shook his head, forcing himself to ignore his need for her. "I'm not going to tell them anything about Derek. Even if it means I'll never work for the agency again."

She looked up at him now and her eyes held none of the judgment he expected to see there. "I meant about my offer."

He sucked in a breath and jerked back his hand, but she held tight.

"Do you," she asked, lifting his arm to place a whisper-light kiss on the inside of his wrist, "want to be with me?"

He nearly groaned. "It's not about what I want," he said with a ragged breath. "It's about what's good for you. I'm trying to protect you, Lexi."

"I don't need you to protect me." She stepped closer, taking his other hand in hers, then running her fingers up his arms until they curved around his neck. "I want you, Scott."

He knew he should walk away, but for the life of him, he couldn't move a muscle. "Don't do this," he whispered.

"What?" Her smile belied the innocence in her voice. She reached up and pressed her mouth to his. "Do you mean this?" Her body leaned against his as her scent wound through his mind, filling his head with the most amazing pictures of her moving underneath him. "Or this?" Her tongue traced the seam of his lips like an invitation.

He knew it was wrong, but he couldn't take any more of her sweet torture.

His arms tightened around her and he slanted his mouth over hers, taking control of the kiss. He felt her smile against him and melt into him even more, her desire stoking his until it was difficult to tell where he stopped and she began.

"Don't say I didn't warn you." He ground out the words before lifting her into his arms and carrying her to the couch pushed up against the far wall.

"This is all my fault," she agreed, tugging at the hem of his shirt even as he lay her against the cushions.

He stripped off the shirt and almost smiled at the way her eyes widened. "Having second thoughts?" he asked, sitting up a bit. If she was smart enough to stop this beautiful madness, he had no choice but to let her.

To his surprise, she leaned forward and lifted her own shirt over her head. "Not a single one," she said, watching him from eyes full of need and wonder. "I just hope I don't disappoint you."

Desire unfurled low in his stomach at the sight of her creamy skin under a peach-colored lace bra. "Seriously, how does a woman who dresses like a nun half the time have such great lingerie under her clothes?"

She rewarded him with a saucy smile. "It's my little secret and there's no one to tell me that I can't."

"If anyone tells you to stop, send them to me and I'll break all of their fingers." Scott placed his hand on her neck, feeling her pulse race. "You are so damn beautiful," he whispered.

"You don't have to say that." Some of the light in her eyes dimmed. "I know it isn't true."

When she would have turned her head, he cupped her face between his hands. "Lexi Preston, you are beautiful, desirable, smart and too kind for your own good."

Lexi wanted to believe him. Looking into his eyes, she almost could believe him. The desire she saw there made her bold. With trembling fingers, she eased her bra straps along her arms. Scott sucked in a breath as he reached behind her to unhook the clasp. The small bit of fabric dropped to the floor, suddenly making her self-conscious again. She covered her breasts with her hands until he gently pushed them away.

"I want to look at you," he whispered, his voice filled with something that sounded like reverence.

Lexi groaned softly as his hand covered one sensitive tip, rolling it between his fingers. "So beautiful," he repeated softly and lifted his head to flick his tongue across her heated skin.

She sucked in a breath and at that moment his mouth found hers, melding to her, and he pressed her bare skin along the length of him. He touched her everywhere, running his hands down her back, flipping her over and, in the process, easing her jeans and underpants down her hips. His clever fingers slid up her thigh and she gasped for air, his mouth over hers taking in her tiny moans as he touched her in ways she hadn't imagined.

He continued to kiss her as his fingers stroked her to a frenzy she couldn't control. All her inhibitions seemed to melt away until there was nothing left but sensation and feeling, her entire body throbbing with need.

"Let me hear you," he said against her mouth, speeding the rhythm of his fingers against her.

As if at his command, her body arched and bright pleasure tore through her, shattering her senses. He held her close as her arms and legs trembled, finally coming back to herself and settling under him once more.

He kissed her softly, nuzzling her neck with his mouth and whispering gentling words to her. "You are amazing."

"We didn't…" she began, embarrassed at her body's intense reaction to him. "You didn't…"

"Not here," he told her, raising himself onto his arms

above her. "You deserve more than a roll on my office couch."

She looked toward the ceiling and mumbled, "I like your office couch."

He laughed, dropping a kiss on her forehead. "Then you'll love my bed."

She glanced at him then. "So this isn't over?"

He straightened, his eyes heating once more as his gaze traveled across her body. "We haven't even gotten started."

A knock at the door had Lexi jumping, grabbing for her clothes.

Oh...no.

She was naked in her boss's office. How much more clichéd could she be? "This is bad. What was I thinking?"

Scott picked up her shirt and handed it to her. "You weren't thinking. Neither of us were." He pulled her to him, kissing her once more. "We're going to do more not thinking together later." Then he unlocked the door, slipping out before whoever was on the other side could see that he wasn't alone.

Lexi took a steadying breath as she pulled on her jeans, then smoothed her hair back into a ponytail. She felt terrified and elated at the same time. Good-girl Lexi Preston having a go at it on the job. She put a hand over her mouth to suppress a nervous giggle. Finally, it felt as if her adventure was really beginning.

Lexi took another order from a table of regulars. They were a group of guys from a local construction company who came in for a weekly boys' night out.

She liked the harmless flirting, and when one of them grabbed her hand and loudly kissed it, she laughed before drawing back.

She'd been in Brevia for two weeks and still reveled in how invigorating her new freedom made her feel. A few nights earlier she'd indulged in a dinner of chips, soda and cookie-dough ice cream, savoring the choice to do something her father wouldn't approve of, even it was a tiny stake in the ground of her independence.

She'd been embarrassed when Scott had walked in midfeast, then surprised when he'd grabbed a spoon from the kitchen and helped her polish off the pint while watching some cheesy reality TV show on cable. He hadn't tried to kiss her or made any kind of move, but hanging out with him had been so easy and right that her heart had opened to him even more.

But she'd been avoiding Scott since the encounter in his office, too afraid of her own feelings to pursue anything more with him. Realizing she needed to keep better control on her emotions, she turned away now to collect the table's drink orders, but Misty hauled her off to a corner of the bar.

"What's going on with you and Scott?" the other waitress asked on a hiss of breath.

"I… We… Nothing," Lexi answered quickly. "Why?"

"He just about came over the bar when that guy grabbed you." Misty shook her head. "He looks like he wants to throw you over his shoulder and carry you off."

"A little too caveman for my taste." Lexi laughed as her pulse started to race.

"I wouldn't mind being carried off by that man," Misty said with a knowing smile.

Lexi's gaze tracked to the bar. Scott handed two beers to a couple sitting at the stools in front of him before his eyes met hers. One side of his mouth curved up and the promise in his gaze made Lexi's knees go a tiny bit weak.

"That look isn't nothing," Misty said, whistling softly under her breath. She chucked Lexi on the shoulder. "I don't know how you did it, girl. Most of the waitresses and half of the female customers have been angling for a way to catch Scott Callahan since he got to town."

"And you think I've caught him?"

Misty smiled. "I think you're darn close." She winked at her. "I just hope you know what to do with him once you've got him."

Lexi swallowed hard as Misty walked away. She had no idea what to do with Scott. The things her imagination conjured made her tingle from her toes to the top of her head.

She waited until he was busy at the other end of the bar to retrieve the drinks for a table up front. She'd gotten them balanced on her tray when a familiar voice spoke behind her.

"I can't believe I raised a common barmaid."

She managed to hold the tray steady as she turned to face her father. "What are you doing here, Daddy?" She glanced behind him to see Trevor Montgomery, her onetime boyfriend, standing in the wings. "And you've brought reinforcements. How lovely. Grab a table and I'll get your order after I deliver these drinks."

Her father reached for her. "You'll speak to me now, Lexi, and not to take my order. You're coming home."

"I'm working right now," she said, her spine stiffening. "We're busy tonight and I can't keep the customers waiting." She held her tray in front of her, pushing past her father and Trevor. She brought the drinks to the table, then motioned to Misty. "Could you cover my section for a few minutes?"

Misty looked to where Robert Preston was glowering next to the bar. "Sure thing, sweetheart."

Lexi made her way back to her father, dread making her legs feel as if they were encased in cement. Lord, how she wanted to just run out the front door. She knew her father was serious about her coming home, but she'd never thought he'd actually show up in Brevia to collect her. She'd been stupid and naive to think he'd actually respect her decision. Respect for her wasn't part of Robert Preston's makeup.

"I have return tickets on the late flight out of Charlotte," he told her when she stood in front of him. "We're leaving now."

"You just got here," she answered weakly, pretending not to understand

He shook his head. "Let's go, Lexi. Trevor will drive us to Charlotte, then return to Columbus with your car. You're lucky he's willing to take you back after the way you deserted him. You're lucky we both are."

Trevor's eyes darted to her father before returning to her face. "I've missed you, Lex." He gave her a placating smile.

"Give me a break, Trevor. I doubt you noticed I was gone, besides the fact that you had to find a new way to brownnose my father." She shook her head. "Dad, I'm not going back yet. I told you that on the phone. I want a few more weeks."

"That's ridiculous."

"You're the one who sent me away."

"You ruined the relationship with one of our best clients." He looked around with clear disdain. "What is it about this town that attracts you?"

Lexi forced her gaze to remain on her father. Out of the corner of her eye she could see Scott with a group of men at the far end of the bar. "People are nice here. It feels real. I feel real."

"Nonsense," her father scoffed. "Your life is in Ohio with me. The firm needs you. I didn't pull you out of the gutter only to have you return there."

"This isn't the gutter, Dad, and you didn't pull me out of anywhere."

"Your birth mother was a common bar whore, Lexi. A stereotype of the worst sort. I saw something more in you." He paused, his eyes narrowing. "The adoption agency thought I'd be happier with a boy, but I chose you. I invested in you. Don't make me regret my decision."

"I'm not a piece of property." Her voice caught and she swallowed, trying to get ahold of her emotions. Robert Preston could smell weakness in an adversary and would gladly use it to his advantage. She knew that better than anyone. "I'm your daughter."

"Which is why I can't understand how you could disobey me in this way."

"I'm not trying to disobey you," she argued. "I just need time."

"Time is up and you're coming with me."

She shook her head and backed away. "No."

He reached for her arm, but someone stepped between them.

"She said no." With Scott looming in front of him, her father took a step back, his eyes wide with disbelief.

"This is none of your business," her father said on an angry breath.

"Anything that happens in my bar is my business."

"It's okay, Scott."

He glanced at her. "Are you sure?"

She nodded, wiping at her eyes.

Scott turned to Lexi, his thumb smoothing a tear off her cheek. "You're safe here, you know."

"Safe?" her dad sputtered. "I'm her father, you idiot. I'm the one who keeps her safe."

"I'll take care of this," Scott told her. "You can go in back and get yourself together."

She nodded. "I'll let you know my decision about my future in a few weeks, Dad. Don't contact me again before that."

"Come back with me now or I'll make sure you have no future. Not in the legal community, anyway." He pointed at Trevor. "Do something, you oaf. Ask her to marry you."

Trevor looked visibly shocked, but stepped forward. "Lexi, would you…?"

Her head started to pound. She knew Trevor was her father's henchman, but hadn't realized how far his loyalty went. "You don't have to do that, Trevor. I'm not going to marry you. Now or ever."

He sighed, probably with relief. "I'm sorry, Lexi,"

he whispered, and it might have been the first honest thing he'd said to her the whole time they'd been dating.

She turned away, expecting her father to follow, but found herself alone, leaning on the hallway wall outside the kitchen. She stifled a sob, then jumped when Jon popped his head out of the kitchen. "You look like hell."

"I feel worse," she answered.

He shifted uncomfortably, then offered, "I made an apple pie earlier."

She smiled, grateful for the simple gesture. "A slice of pie is just what I need."

Scott turned to Robert Preston. "Leave her alone."

Preston's eyes narrowed. "I know you, Callahan, and you aren't the Boy Scout your brother turned out to be."

"This isn't about you or me. It's about Lexi."

"I think you're part of the reason she doesn't want to come home."

"I don't give a damn what you think."

"You should." Preston smiled, but it was a mean look on him. "I have contacts in D.C., you know. Some with the U.S. Marshals agency."

Scott felt a muscle clench in his jaw. "So what?"

"I know why you're hiding out here. Based on your history, I'd guess running a bar in Brevia, North Carolina, isn't going to cut it for you. You need action. I can help you."

"You don't know anything about me."

"I know you have a snowball's chance of getting back to active duty without a recommendation from the review board." Preston's smile widened as Scott flinched. "I want my daughter back. I didn't realize how serious she was until tonight. I'm not used to seeing Lexi with a backbone."

"It looks good on her."

"In your opinion. But she belongs with me. Her life is in Ohio, not down here." Preston sighed. "I'll give her the month she wants. I'm not stupid. But at the end of the next few weeks I want her to return home. I want you to make sure she does."

"She can make her own decisions," Scott answered, tension balling low in his gut. This guy was a real piece of work. No wonder Lexi needed to take such drastic measures to gain some sense of independence.

Preston nodded in agreement and reached in his wallet to hand Scott a card. "Let's make sure it's the right one. Call me when you come to your senses."

Scott pocketed the business card. He didn't plan to do anything with it, but Preston didn't need to know that. Right now, he just wanted him out of his bar. "If you knew me at all, you'd know I can't be bought."

Robert Preston only smiled, then turned and walked out of Riley's Bar. Scott hoped it was the last time he'd ever lay eyes on the man.

He looked around the crowded room, surveying the changes he'd made, as well as the groups of people laughing and mingling throughout. In truth, he hadn't missed the action of the field as much as he thought he would. Renovating the bar had taken his time and energy and given him an outlet that was more satisfying than he'd thought it could be. He liked belonging somewhere, getting to know the regulars and making this place part of the community.

The menu was already a success, with local business people coming for lunch and families in the early evening. He'd talked to a couple of local bands and musicians about hosting an open-mic night, and he'd put some events on the calendar to draw people in during the week. Carving out a place in Brevia was good, but he also wondered how long his desire to stay would last. Scott had a long track record of leaving people and places behind. After things were stable, would Brevia still hold his interest? Preston was right that this wasn't the life he'd imagined for himself.

Lexi took another bite of the apple pie, then washed it down with a long drink of milk. "This is fantastic," she told Jon from her seat at the large work island in the middle of the kitchen. "You're a genius."

"Don't plump up his ego too much," Scott said from the doorway. "I've already given him one raise."

Her eyes darted to Scott. "Is my father…?"

"He left, Lexi."

Both disappointment and relief rolled through her. "I guess that's good."

"He's giving you the time you want. He's going to leave you alone for a month."

She nodded. "But he's not interested in me until I come back to Ohio."

Scott didn't answer and his silence told her everything. She took another bite of pie, swallowing back her emotions.

"It's his loss," Scott said quietly.

"Thank you," she answered. She pushed away the half-empty plate and stood. "I need to get back out there. Misty can't cover everyone."

"It's thinned out. People are going home early. She'll be fine."

Lexi took her plate to the sink, then turned to give Jon a small hug. "Thanks for the pie and the company. Your food is going to make this place a huge success. I bet your dad is smiling down on you right now."

A broad grin stretched across the older man's face. "I'm glad you think so. You're a good person, Lexi. I hope your father comes to his senses."

She tried to smile, then swiped at her eyes. "I need to pull it together," she said with a shaky laugh.

Scott took her hand as she came into the hall, tugging her toward the back exit. "Where are we going?"

"Home," he answered, pulling harder when she would have stopped.

"You have a bar to tend and I can't just leave because my dad's a jerk," Lexi argued. "I'm going to pull up my big-girl panties and—"

"Max will finish up the night behind the bar," Scott told her as he opened the door to the alley. "He'll appreciate the extra tips. Misty and Tina can cover the floor. You've had the rug yanked from under you and my day wasn't much better. We're taking the night off. I'm picking up carryout and you can choose the movie."

She dug in her heels as the door shut behind her. Scott turned.

"You don't have to do this."

She squared her shoulders as he studied her. She tried to look brave and tough and unbreakable. All the things she didn't feel.

"I want to," he answered softly. "I want to be with you, Lexi. God help us both, because I know I should

leave you alone. I knew it that first night I banged on
the apartment door. I can't offer you much, but you deserve your adventure or whatever you call it. Especially
if you're going back to make nice with that nasty old
coot you call a father. I'm going to make sure you have
some fun before that happens."

She hated that her lip trembled at his words, that what
he said touched some deep, hollow place inside her. It
didn't matter that Scott couldn't offer her much, because
living with her father had made her believe she wasn't
worth anything. She tried to lighten the mood by asking, "How about a Hugh Jackman movie?"

"As long as he's not singing."

"Let's go for the first *X-Men,* then. It's my favorite."

"You like superheroes?" Scott looked doubtful.

"Only on the big screen," she promised.

He drew her closer, but instead of kissing her he
wrapped his arms around her and buried his face in
her hair.

"I'm sorry your father is a schmuck."

She laughed despite the emotion welling in her chest.
"That about sums it up. But I stood up to him. That's
something, right? I'm still here whether or not he wants
me to be."

"You are," Scott agreed. "Now let's get that food."

Hours later, Lexi glanced up into Scott's sleeping
face. His long lashes rested on the smooth skin of his
cheek, while a shadow of stubble covered his jaw, making his perfect features more human. With his eyes
closed, his face had a sense of vulnerability he made

sure to keep hidden most of the time. He was strong and tough and so alone.

She understood that last part. Despite all her plans and pledges about a big adventure, she was scared to death to be by herself. She didn't know who she was and she wondered if she'd like the person she'd find at the end of her journey.

She was tucked in the crook of his arm, where she'd been through most of the movie. They'd shared Chinese takeout and a couple beers before settling in to watch Professor Xavier and his crew save the world.

If Scott's intention had been to give her some distance from the pain of her father's rejection, it worked. She still felt the hurt, but it wasn't so raw. It was like a prism she could hold out in front of her and study, see the sharp edges and places where feeling unlovable had torn at her soul. But now she could place it on the shelf, add it to her collection of emotional scars.

Maybe that was what someone who'd been physically abandoned by one parent and emotionally rejected by the other did. Lexi was a pro at compartmentalizing her feelings, on tamping them down until she could be in control enough to do what everyone around her expected.

Scott was different. He bulldozed through his emotions, trying to run fast enough that they couldn't touch him with their demanding tendrils. The two of them were so different and yet alike in many ways. That could explain the connection she felt for him. She didn't have to polish herself to a glossy shine for Scott. He'd take her as she was, broken parts and all.

That final thought gave her the courage to lean up

and trace his face with her fingers, then press her mouth to his. After a moment he stirred, moaning softly.

She lost her nerve at the sound of his voice. This was stupid. Women like her weren't meant for seduction. But when she would have scrambled away, his arms came around her, grabbing her tight to him and pulling her across his lap. His hands wound through her hair, his mouth devouring hers. She couldn't get enough of him and she pressed herself along the length of his body, straddling him so she could feel his desire for her. She needed him so badly. He made her feel whole and right. She wanted to capture that feeling and carry it with her all her life.

He gripped her face until she looked into his eyes. "I want you, Lexi. I want this. Now."

"Now," she agreed with a soft intake of breath.

He lifted her easily and she clung to him, ripping at his shirt as he made his way down the hall to her bedroom. He tore away the quilt and lowered her gently onto the bed. She lifted her blouse over her head, then watched as he stripped away his shirt. His jeans and boxers followed a minute later. She felt her mouth drop open at the sight of him. Muscles bunched and rippled across his chest, and her eyes caught on the tattoo banding one firm biceps. His whole body was strong, hard and ready. The breath whooshed out of her lungs as desire pooled low in her belly.

She'd had a couple boyfriends over the years, but nothing had prepared her for the sight of Scott Callahan.

A hint of a smile played around his mouth as he watched her watching him. "You can't leave me standing here all alone like this. Aren't you going to join me?"

She reached for the waistband of her pants, then stilled. "I don't know… I'm not you—"

"Thank the Lord for small favors," he said with a laugh and came toward her. The look in his eyes could only be described as predatory.

Slowly, he moved his hands up her legs to the top of her cotton pants, then bent forward to kiss the tip of one nipple through the lace fabric of her bra as he slid her slacks down her legs. He leaned back as he reached her knees. "Each part of you is perfect," he whispered. "And I plan to become intimately familiar with every inch."

"I hope you're not disappointed," she said, then shut her eyes, embarrassed that he might think she was fishing for a compliment.

"Nothing you do could disappoint me, Lexi. I want to touch you. All of you. But only if you're sure." He bent toward her once more, his kiss soft and exploratory, as if giving her time to change her mind.

"Open your eyes," he said against her mouth.

He sat back and she couldn't help reaching out to run her palm across his taut stomach muscles and up the hard planes of his chest. She could feel his heartbeat, strong and steady under her hand. A small grin curved her lips as she watched his blue eyes darken with desire the longer she touched him.

He swallowed and let out a ragged breath that was almost a groan as she grazed her fingernails along his skin. He was giving her time, she knew, to get her bearings…to take control of this moment between them. His ability to understand her needs, even at a time like this, melted her heart. The knowledge that he wanted her as much as she did him gave her the courage she needed to pull him to her again.

But when the tip of her tongue touched his and her legs wrapped around his body, his mouth turned hot and demanding.

She put out her hand to pull the sheet over them, but Scott ripped it away. "We don't need that."

He trailed his mouth down her neck, along her collarbone and over the swell of her breast. At the same time his hand traced a path up her thigh until his fingers found her core. He teased her until she almost lost control.

"Wait," he whispered into her ear. "Not yet."

He grabbed his jeans from beside the bed and pulled out a condom, ripping it open with his teeth. A moment later he balanced above her once more, and his mouth captured hers at the same time as he entered her. She couldn't tell if the groan of pleasure came from her lips or his.

As if their bodies were made for each other, they moved together. A sensation built low in her stomach as the rhythm intensified. For the moment, they were one, and she reveled in the feel of his body over hers, the sparks of pleasure firing through every part of her. After several minutes, she couldn't hold back any longer and her release echoed through her, followed by Scott's harsh intake of breath. He whispered her name and then his head fell to the pillow next to her, nuzzling against her ear as he said words of endearment.

She'd never known anything like what she and Scott had just experienced together. She knew now what true freedom meant. And that no matter what her future held, she'd hold this night close to her heart for the rest of her life.

Chapter 9

Lexi was able to keep her feelings about her father at bay for the next week. Her feelings for Scott were another story. Things seemed to speed up, both at the bar and between them. They worked to finish renovations, then spent every night together.

As much as she loved being in Scott's arms, her favorite times were the morning. They'd take turns making breakfast, then walk Freddy through the park, talking about everything and nothing. Scott told her about his mother's death, his stint in the army and the work he'd done for the Marshals Service. His life had been an adventure already. He'd seen so much of the world and had to take care of himself in a way she couldn't imagine. Her life up until now had been so structured.

But he seemed just as fascinated with her life as she

was with his. She realized, for all the moving around and excitement, what Scott lacked was a sense of being grounded. She thought maybe the bar did that for him, gave him a sense of purpose. She hoped their time together gave him a sense of home. But if she delved too far into sticky emotions, she could feel him pull away. It didn't matter, she told herself. Her time was ticking, anyway, and she'd have to make a decision about her life.

It was becoming clear that going back to the way things had been wasn't enough for her anymore. She didn't want to give up her law career, but working for her father would suck her down the same black hole she'd finally clawed her way out of. She put together a résumé and began to send it out, using contacts she had from the law community and law school. She applied for positions both in big cities and smaller towns, although nothing in her hometown of Columbus, Ohio. She was too afraid of her father finding out and sabotaging her plans. Several of the openings were in D.C. And Charlotte. She knew it was stupid, but hoped that being in one of those cities might enable her to continue to see Scott after her time in Brevia was done.

She also continued to advise locals, despite Frank Davis's not wanting her to. She couldn't turn away people who needed her help, and she was learning which aspects of the law were most appealing to her. She liked the variety that being a general counsel in a small town afforded her, liked using her skills to help people with their problems.

Scott told her she was being taken advantage of again, since all the work she'd done so far was pro bono.

But she didn't care. It was important for her to believe she was making a difference.

She'd just finished up a meeting with Ida Garvey in one of the back booths at the bar when the front door opened and Julia, her mother and her sister, Lainey, walked in.

It was late afternoon, so other than Lexi, Ida and Scott, the place was almost empty. The reception to celebrate the two weddings was only a couple weeks away, so Lexi expected they'd come in to discuss that. She sank down in her chair a little. Scott had asked her to help with the plans for the reception from a logistical end, and she'd actually enjoyed discussing everything with Julia. But she'd managed not to be around when Vera had come by previously. While Lexi had made amends with Julia, she had a pretty good idea how the rest of the family felt about her, and it sure wasn't friendly.

"Don't let Vera scare you," Ida said with a knowing smile. "She's mostly bluster."

Lexi looked at her client. She'd come to enjoy her weekly meeting with the older woman. Sometimes they discussed her estate, but often Ida filled her in on local gossip. She knew everything that was going on in Brevia. Julia had warned her that Ida was a busybody, but Lexi liked hearing her stories.

She watched Scott greet the three women, then his gaze met hers and he motioned her over.

She groaned softly. "I've got to be a part of this. It was good to see you, Mrs. Garvey. I'll get those motions filed, but you should really talk to Frank. I know he doesn't want me working with his clients."

"He'll deal with it," Ida said with a scoff. "He's gotten plenty of my business and more of my money. If his practice was so important, he'd spend more time on it."

"He's a good attorney," Lexi offered. "I still think you should talk to him."

"Too nice for your own good," Ida mumbled. "Go see to those Morgan women, dear."

Lexi stood and walked toward them. Vera was talking to Scott, pointing to something in a file she'd laid across the bar. Julia smiled, but her sister, Lainey Daniels, narrowed her eyes as Lexi came closer. She'd met Lainey only once, when she and her husband, Ethan, had come in for dinner. Lexi had seen some promotional photos Lainey had taken of the bar for a marketing campaign focusing on the tourist season in Brevia.

"Everything looks good for the reception," Lexi said to Julia. "I confirmed the time with the band yesterday and asked Scott to order the champagne you wanted for the toast."

"Thanks, Lexi." Julia smiled again and turned to her sister. "She's making me look totally on top of things with Mom."

"I still don't understand why she's in charge," Lainey answered, keeping her eyes trained on Lexi. "We all want to trust her but are you sure about this?"

"It's different now." Julia gave Lainey a pointed look. "You should know people can change."

"I agree with your sister," Vera interjected, taking a sip from the glass of water Scott had placed on the bar. "Julia, you've always been too trusting of people. It's gotten you into trouble in the past."

Lexi shook her head. "I'm not here to cause trouble,

Mrs. Callahan. I want everything to be perfect for your celebration."

"Besides," Julia added, "I trust her a lot more than I do Scott."

"He's making changes to this place that are going to help the local economy for years to come." Lexi looked at Julia. "You know bringing more people into downtown is good for all the businesses here, including your salon."

"He's a loose cannon." Julia crossed her arms over her chest. "I don't trust him."

Scott cleared his throat. "I'm standing right here."

"I see you," she said. The look she threw him made Lexi smile. "I'm hoping you'll leave."

He tossed down the towel he'd been holding. "Gladly." His gaze met Lexi's, warming her from her toes up. *Good luck,* he mouthed to her before disappearing into the back.

"If you do anything to hurt my daughter, you'll have to answer to me," Vera said, turning her full attention on Lexi.

Before she could sputter out an answer, Ida Garvey's shrill voice rang out. "Vera Morgan, give the girl a break. It wasn't too long ago that your daughters were practically duking it out in the middle of town. Everyone deserves a second chance."

"Since when did you become anyone's champion, Ida?" Vera asked.

Lexi felt like repeating Scott's comment that she was standing right in front of them. But Julia caught her gaze and shook her head slightly.

"She's been helping me with changes I'm making

to my estate plan. You know Frank Davis hasn't been up to snuff for a while now. That's what makes me her champion," the older woman said with a smirk. "I'm in it for what's best for me."

"Same old Ida," Vera muttered.

"But she's working for you, too," Ida retorted. "You'd see that if you weren't so hardheaded. She's got a whole file with the details of your reception. She's put a lot of thought into it. Half the town is going to be here to celebrate with you. Lexi's the one making sure it will be a night everyone will remember. Give her a chance, Vera."

With a small pat on Lainey's back, Ida shuffled out the front door. Lexi wasn't sure why it meant so much to her to have a woman she'd known for only a few weeks come to her defense, but it did.

Vera's gaze moved to Lexi. "Is this true?"

She nodded. "Yes, ma'am. I hope so."

Julia's mother motioned her forward. "Let's see what you've got then."

Lexi opened up the file where she kept her plans for the Callahan and Callahan reception. She'd never put together a party of this size before, but the organizing and details appealed to her analytical side. Plus, the busier she kept, the less time she had to spend worrying about her future. So when Scott had asked her to handle the celebration, she'd jumped at the chance.

As she pulled out her notes, her excitement overtook her nervousness regarding Vera's reaction. Most of what she was showing her Julia had already approved, so Lexi felt a bit more confident. "Julia told me your favorite color is yellow and hers is blue, so that's what I went for with the color scheme." She took out samples of fabric from the tablecloths and napkins. "Obviously, we're in a bar, and the whole event is a casual, homey family affair, but I still wanted it to be elegant." She glanced at Vera from under her lashes. "Because you seem like a very elegant lady."

"Agreed," she answered.

Julia and Lainey both laughed.

"There will be fresh flowers and candles at every table—understated, but they should look beautiful in the light. I contacted the microbrewery over in Asheville, and they're supplying beer for us. They've agreed to brew a special Amazing Animal Ale for the event and donate a portion of their profits back to your shelter."

Vera nodded. "I like it."

"Congratulations on your wedding, by the way. Joe seems very nice."

"That's why I married him."

"It means a lot to Scott to be here with his dad and Sam." She looked at Julia. "They're all hanging out, you know."

"I know."

"Joe loves his boys," Vera stated. "He'll do anything to make up for how things used to be. He wants it to be right between them."

"Scott wants that, too. He's worked hard on the reception. I think he sees it as a way to prove to both of them that he's changed."

The older woman studied her. "You seem to know Scott pretty well."

"I work with him almost every day," Lexi said

quickly, hoping nothing on her face gave away her true emotions.

"And they're roommates," Julia said.

Lexi saw Lainey choke back a laugh. "You're sharing the apartment with Scott?"

"It's not like..."

"Like what, Lexi?" Julia leaned forward and whispered, "Are you sleeping with him?"

Lexi tried to no avail to stop a blush from creeping up her cheeks.

Lainey shushed Julia, then put a hand on Lexi's shoulder. "Julia doesn't have good personal boundaries."

"And you're one to talk, little sister."

"You've obviously put a lot of work into the reception," Lainey continued, ignoring Julia. "I appreciate your help." She glanced at their mother. "We all do. Right, Mom?"

Lexi blinked back tears as Vera smiled.

"Julia's right that we believe in second chances. We also take care of our own around here. You're included in that now. Scott's family, too. If the two of you make each other happy, we're happy for you."

"I'm not staying in Brevia." Lexi choked on the words, but knew she owed these women the truth. "Scott knows that. What we have...whatever it is, it's temporary."

"You aren't staying?" Lainey looked confused. "But you fit."

"I don't know where I fit. That's what I'm trying to figure out."

Lainey gave her a quick hug. "I know how that feels, so I hope you do." She turned to her mother. "Come on, Mom. I want to show you the dress I picked out for the reception."

"Thank you for everything you've done." Vera pushed away Lexi's outstretched hand and gave her a hug.

"Oh." Lexi breathed out the one syllable, overwhelmed with emotion that these women could forgive her so easily for what she'd put Julia through. That they could accept her with her faults and all.

When Vera and Lainey walked out, Julia turned to her. "That wasn't so hard, was it?"

Lexi swallowed. "You're lucky to have the family you do."

"It took me a while to realize it." She nodded. "But you're right. Speaking of families, have you spoken to dear ole dad lately?"

"He was here a few nights ago. He ordered me to come home with him."

"And yet you're still here." Julia chucked her on the shoulder. "You have more backbone than I gave you credit for."

"You and me both," Lexi agreed. "I'm coming into the salon to see Nancy before my shift starts, by the way."

"She's grateful for all you've done to help with her divorce."

Lexi shrugged. "It wasn't that much. But she offered to give me a complimentary cut and color as a thank-you."

"Hallelujah!" Julia reached out and tugged on Lexi's ponytail. "It's about time you stopped wearing it pulled back."

"It's professional," Lexi argued.

"It's boring." Julia's eyebrows wiggled. "I bet Scott likes it down."

"He says… Never mind." Lexi blushed under the other woman's scrutiny. "I'm a total fool, starting something with him. I know it already so you don't need to tell me."

"You know as well as anyone that I've had my share of romantic missteps. Big ones." Julia glanced toward the back of the bar. "I know Scott has had problems in the past, but maybe he'll surprise us all. Either way, you're a big girl. You get to make your own mistakes."

Lexi nodded. "But it wasn't a mistake coming to Brevia. Thank you, Julia, for giving me a do-over. No matter what happens, I'll always be grateful."

"No mushy stuff. Just buy me a drink if I ever get a night out on the town again." She shrugged at Lexi's questioning look. "My mom and Lainey help with Charlie during the week, but I haven't found an evening sitter he likes."

"What about me?"

"What about you?"

"I could watch him. I'm off tomorrow night. I can come over or you can bring him by the apartment."

"I wouldn't want—"

"Please, Julia. It's the least I can do. I swear you can trust me with him. You and Sam can have a date night."

Julia took a deep breath as Lexi found herself holding hers. Suddenly it was very important to her that Julia trust her enough to babysit Charlie.

"That would be great," Julia said finally. "I'll see if Sam can get off, and text you about the time."

"Perfect." Lexi glanced at her watch. "I need to get to my appointment. Are you walking back to the salon?"

Julia nodded. "Let's hit it."

"I need to…" Her eyes strayed to the back of the bar.

"Oh." Julia rolled her eyes. "Give lover boy a kiss goodbye for me."

"It isn't like that."

"I'm kidding, Lexi." She smiled broadly, then laughed. "Sort of. Either way, I'll wait for you outside."

Lexi walked to Scott's office, but stopped just outside the doorway. Suddenly she felt nervous, wondering if Scott would even care that she was going. Sure, they'd spent every night together for the past week, but it wasn't as if they were dating. More like roommates with benefits, which she supposed should make her feel cheap. But it didn't.

She peeked her head in as Scott looked up from the paperwork on his desk. "Hey there, gorgeous."

Lexi glanced behind her to see if Julia had followed her down the hall.

"I'm talking to you, Lexi." Scott came around the desk and toward her, as if he meant to replay their previous interlude on his couch.

Her breath caught in her chest and she held up her hands, palms out. "I have a hair appointment," she said quickly. "I just wanted to say, um…goodbye, and…"

Her mind went blank for a moment as he reached out and drew her to him, his mouth claiming hers in a deep kiss. After a moment he asked, "How did it go with Vera and Lainey?"

It took a few seconds before Lexi could even remember who Vera and Lainey were. "They're happy with the plans, I think."

Scott cupped her face with his hands. "That's because you've done an amazing job of organizing everything."

"Vera doesn't seem to hate me anymore."

"If she's happy, my father will be over the moon."

"Would you believe Ida Garvey came to my defense?"

"You have the ability to wrap just about anyone around your little finger," Scott said, kissing her again.

"Are you wrapped around my finger?"

"What's it look like?"

She thought about that for a moment. "Like I'm a convenient place to land at night."

He stilled. "You think I'm with you because you're convenient?"

"It's easy for both of us, right?" She didn't like the sparks shooting from his blue eyes. "It's not as if we're dating."

His eyes narrowed. "So it's just sex for you?" His tone was incredulous.

"I didn't say that. But we haven't exactly been out to dinner or a movie or the stuff people do when they're dating. I'm not complaining. We're friends." She smiled to try to lighten the mood. "Like you said, the kind with great benefits."

"Friends," he repeated ominously.

"I need to go," she said, backing out of his arms. "We can talk about this later. Or not."

"Tomorrow night." He crossed his arms over his

chest. "You're off. I'll get someone to fill in for me. We're going out."

"I'm busy tomorrow night." She bit down on her lower lip. "And that wasn't a very nice way to ask me on a date."

He shook his head. "Busy with what? And if you say a date with the high-school teacher, we're going to have a problem."

A little butterfly danced through Lexi's belly. "I canceled my date with Mark. I... It wasn't the right time for me." Was it possible that Scott Callahan was jealous over her? The mere thought made her want to giggle. "I'm babysitting. For Julia and Sam."

"Whoa. Didn't see that coming." Scott looked absolutely stunned and Lexi couldn't blame him.

"I owe Julia a lot." She paused, then added, "And I like kids. You've met Charlie. He's adorable."

Scott nodded. "Another time, then."

She nodded, but wondered if she'd freaked him out so much that there wouldn't be another time. The thought made her heart sink a bit, but she forced a smile. "I'll see you later, then."

He nodded and she turned to go.

"Lexi?"

She glanced over her shoulder.

"Don't do anything crazy with your hair," he said softly. "I like it just the way it is."

More butterflies took flight and she hurried out the door.

Scott knocked on the door to his brother's house, then wiped his damp palms across the front of his jeans.

This was ridiculous. He'd seen combat zones, drug take-downs and everything in between. This night was nothing in comparison.

So why was his heart beating like crazy?

Before he could come up with a reasonable excuse, the door opened to reveal his brother in a pale blue button-down, striped tie and khaki pants.

"A tie?" Scott asked, whistling softly. "That's laying it on a little thick, don't you think?"

Sam huffed out a breath, then pulled at the collar of his shirt. "It's called making an effort, numskull. You should try it sometime."

Scott laughed. "Too bad I won the genetic lottery in our family. With a face like mine, showing up is all the effort I need."

"Is that so?" Sam looked unimpressed. "Then tell me why you're here tonight."

"I thought Lexi could use some help." He kicked his toe at an imaginary rock. "She practically begged me to come with her."

"There are different kinds of effort, Scott." Sam tugged at his collar again. "But I'm glad you're here."

"Because you still don't trust her?" Scott's fists clenched at his sides. "That's not fair if you—"

"Simmer down, bro. I trust her well enough. Lexi Preston is suddenly Julia's new best friend, and from what I've seen, she's making up for lost time, being helpful and kind and all that stuff." Sam stepped back and motioned Scott through the door. "I'm glad you're here because it's about time my son got to know his uncle. Julia's brother-in-law, Ethan, has quite a head start, so you've got some work to do."

Scott felt his nerves sound off like soldiers in a battle line. "I don't do kids, Sam."

"You're here."

"Obviously my first mistake." He shook his head. "Don't get me wrong. I'm happy for you. I'm sure you're a great dad. You were always so damn responsible and honorable and, well, everything I'm not. I think you'd be smart to stick with Ethan to play the doting uncle."

"We'll see. Charlie's pretty irresistible."

"I'm immune to cute." At Sam's raised eyebrows, Scott amended, "Kid cute, that is."

"Lexi's not your usual type."

"She's not."

As if sensing his sudden urge to bolt, Sam backed off. "I like her, Scott. You're obviously happy with her and you deserve some happiness."

"I don't want—"

"You can deny it all you want, but it's written all over your face. It's not a bad thing to care about someone. It took me a long time to realize that. Dad, too. We Callahans are kind of stupid in the face of scary things like love and emotions. But it's not so bad once you get the hang of it."

Scott couldn't help but laugh. "You missed your calling as a poet."

"You'll see," Sam said, giving him a light punch on the shoulder. "Come on in. They're back in the kitchen. Julia and I have a reservation awaiting us."

Scott followed Sam through the Craftsman-style house, wondering if he could be happy with a regular life. He hadn't been there since he'd first come to Brevia. Most of the time he'd spent with Sam or their father had been at the bar, either having lunch or watching a game. He couldn't believe how domestic Sam had become, his home filled with overstuffed furniture and framed photos on the bookshelves. It made Scott's body ache in a way he didn't understand.

This was never what he'd wanted for himself. He liked the thrill of the chase, the adrenaline high he got from putting himself in danger through his work. He would have never guessed that Sam could make a life for himself in a town like Brevia, and he certainly didn't understand the longing he couldn't seem to shake.

That need intensified as he walked into the kitchen to see Lexi seated in front of a high chair, talking softly to Charlie as the boy ate small mouthfuls of macaroni and cheese. She looked so beautiful with the early-evening light reflecting off her strawberry-blond hair. She looked as if she belonged there.

He wanted to belong, too.

"Daddy," Charlie yelled when he noticed Sam. "I got macan for dinner."

"Looks good, buddy." Sam walked over and bent to kiss the top of Charlie's head, a gesture so natural it made Scott's throat burn. "Miss Lexi is going to have help with you tonight. Buddy, do you remember meeting your uncle Scott?"

Charlie gave Scott a toothy smile, then held up a spoonful of macaroni noodles.

Lexi turned, the blush that was now so familiar to Scott creeping up her neck. "What are you doing here?"

"Reinforcements," he answered simply.

"Sam, we need to go if we're going to..." Julia came

in through the back door, but stopped when she saw Scott. "Well, well. What have we here?"

"Be nice, Juls," Sam said quietly.

"One of the bartenders wanted to pick up an extra shift so I… I'm here." Scott crossed his arms over his chest, hating the feeling of being the center of attention in this cozy scene. "If it's a problem I can leave."

Julia flashed a knowing smile. "I don't have a problem. Lexi, do you have a problem?"

Lexi shook her head, but kept her attention focused on Charlie.

"Then let's go, hot husband of mine." Julia crooked a finger in Sam's direction. "I have plans for you." She bent forward and kissed Charlie's cheek. "Be good for Lexi, my little peanut. Mama loves you."

"Bye, bye, Mama. Loves you," Charlie answered and offered her a spoonful of macaroni.

"I love you, too, sweet boy." She looked at Lexi. "We won't be late. Bedtime at seven with a bath first and—"

Sam wrapped one arm around her waist and steered her toward the door again. "You've left a detailed list. They've got our numbers. It's all good."

"Have fun, you three," he called over his shoulder as the door shut behind them.

Charlie raised himself in his high chair to watch them walk out. "All gone," he announced and went back to scooping up his dinner. "Charlie thirsty."

Lexi straightened. "How about some milk, sweetie?"

The boy nodded.

Scott stepped forward, needing to be occupied with something. "I'll get it. Is there a bottle or…?"

"He's almost two," Lexi said with a small laugh.

"There's no bottle." She went to the cabinet and pulled out a plastic cup with a lid. "He uses a sippy cup. They don't spill."

"I have some customers who could benefit from one of those."

Lexi filled the cup with milk, tightened the lid and gave it to Charlie. Then she turned to Scott. "I'm going to run the bath. Bring him upstairs when he's finished with dinner."

Scott grabbed her arm as she went to move past. "You're not leaving me here with him. Alone."

She smiled sweetly. "Reinforcements, remember?"

The way she studied him, Scott knew she was well aware of how uncomfortable he was. What had he been thinking? It was true that one of his bartenders, Max, wanted to make extra money. But there was plenty at the bar to keep Scott busy even when he wasn't serving drinks. Not to mention that several single women came on a regular basis and made no secret of flirting with him. If he'd wanted to occupy himself, there were better ways than babysitting for his brother. In truth, what he wanted more than anything was to be near Lexi. He'd do just about anything to have more time with her.

He had no intention of letting on, though. "Sure. Right. We'll be up in a bit."

With a small shake of her head, she left him alone in the kitchen with Charlie. His nephew. Scott sat on the edge of one of the chairs and watched the toddler as he would have a key witness, not wanting anything to go wrong when he was in charge.

"Relax," Lexi whispered as she peeked into the room once more. "He's a little boy, Scott. He won't bite."

"He might."

"Just have fun with him."

She disappeared again and Scott thought about all the ways he'd had fun in his life. Babysitting had never once been on that list.

Julia's dog, Casper, came to sit next to him, his gray snout almost level with the high-chair tray.

"Good doggie," Charlie said and threw a piece of macaroni in the air. Casper promptly jumped up and caught it, his stubby tail wagging. Charlie exploded into a fit of giggles.

"Um…" Scott said slowly. "I don't think you're supposed to feed the dog your dinner."

Charlie laughed again and threw another noodle, which the dog caught. More laughter erupted and Scott found himself smiling.

He picked up a noodle off the tray. "I once knew a dog who could do a special trick, Charlie. Let's see if Casper knows this one.

"Casper, stay," he commanded, then carefully placed the noodle on the tip of the dog's snout. "Wait," he said slowly, then gave the "Okay" command. Casper flipped the noodle off his nose and caught it.

Charlie squealed with delight. "Again, Unc-le. Do it again."

Scott's heart clenched the tiniest bit at the word *uncle*. As much as he didn't want them to, that word and the boy who spoke it meant something to him. Reconnecting with his dad and Sam meant something. Something more than simply proving he wasn't the schmuck they both assumed him to be. Scott wanted to make it right with his family. He wanted to be the man no one believed he could become.

No one except Lexi. Since that first night in the bar, she'd seen more in him than he'd seen in himself. It made his gut clench to think he had only a couple more weeks with her. For just a moment he entertained the idea that it didn't have to end. What would it be like to make it really work with Lexi? Could he give that much of himself?

He didn't know for sure, but right now he wanted nothing more than the chance to try.

He did the treat-on-nose trick with Casper until there were no more noodles left on the tray.

"Up," Charlie said, raising his arms above his head.

Scott took a breath. Okay, he could do this. He carefully placed his hands under Charlie's arms and lifted, then cradled the small boy against his chest. Charlie immediately wiggled to be let down, and when Scott put him on the floor, he headed for the stairs.

"Baaf-time," the toddler announced as Scott followed on his heels.

"Would you grab a couple of towels from the hall closet?" Lexi called as they got to the second floor.

He did, then made it to the bathroom as she lowered Charlie into the tub. "Have you ever done this before?"

"No," she answered, her eyes never leaving the boy. "But I think I can manage." She handed Charlie an assortment of rubber toys and squeezed excess water out of a duck-shaped sponge.

Scott leaned against the counter and watched Lexi in action. She and Charlie sang several verses of "The Wheels on the Bus" as the little boy sat in the tub.

It was strangely intimate in a heart-tugging way to be a part of such an everyday routine in his nephew's life. Scott thought Lexi had never looked so beautiful. Her hair was pulled back in a loose ponytail, with several tendrils escaping to curl around her face. It was lighter since she'd been at the salon today, highlighting her pale green eyes even more. She laughed as Charlie splashed, leaving the front of her pink T-shirt sprayed with water.

"You'll be a great mother one day," Scott said softly, not realizing he'd said the words out loud until she turned to gape at him.

"I hope so," she said after a moment, her eyes so full of tenderness he wished he could stop time so that she'd always look at him that way.

Still, it scared him. Lexi made him want things he never expected to have and couldn't believe he deserved. He'd always managed to ruin the relationships that meant the most to him, so why did he expect anything would change now?

"I'm going to clean up the kitchen," he said and left the bathroom before she could see how much she meant to him. How much he longed for the stability and caring she represented. How he couldn't bear the thought that he was bound to ruin her, too.

Chapter 10

Lexi finished putting Charlie's dump-truck pajamas on, pulling the bottoms over his diaper. She picked him up and snuggled her face into his neck for a few seconds, reveling in the scent of clean boy. Scott hadn't reappeared since he'd practically run from the bathroom earlier. She knew there wasn't much to clean up in the kitchen, so figured this whole night had freaked him out beyond the point of no return. She half expected that he'd left a note downstairs and already escaped to the bar, where he was much more comfortable.

She bit down hard on her lip to avoid tearing up again when she thought of Scott telling her she'd be a good mother. It surprised her how natural the role felt. She had so little memory of her own mom and found it hard to believe that she had any genetic instincts for parenting. But taking care of Charlie gave her an indescribable joy, while at the same time it left a deep ache in the core of her heart. It was one of many revelations from her time in Brevia. She now knew that, one way or another, becoming a mother someday topped her list of priorities.

She sat down in the rocking chair in the corner and read two books to Charlie, then turned down the lights and slowly swayed around the room with him in her arms, singing softly. When she felt his head grow heavy on her shoulder, she placed him in his toddler bed, dropping a soft kiss on his forehead before turning to go.

Scott stood in the doorway watching her, his eyes cast in shadow so she couldn't read them. He held out his hand and she laced her fingers through his, closing Charlie's door most of the way before following Scott down the stairs.

"I can't believe I'm saying this, but hanging with Charlie is almost fun." He led her to the living room and sat on the couch before pulling her down next to him. His arm wound around her shoulders and he dropped a kiss on her hair, a gesture so unconscious it made her feel they'd been a couple for years instead of weeks.

"He's amazing," Lexi agreed. "You must have quite a knack, too, because I could hear him laughing the whole time I was running the bathwater."

"Kid whisperer. Just one of my many talents."

She laughed and snuggled in closer. After a moment she asked, "Do you remember much about your mom?"

She felt Scott's breath hitch, but he didn't pull away. "I was so young when she died, there's not a lot of details. Mainly random snippets. I can recognize the perfume she wore, and she loved the Beatles, so certain music brings her back to me." He drew his fingers up and down Lexi's arm. "But I try not to remember that it was my fault she died."

Lexi tried to sit up so she could turn around and look at him, but he held her tight.

"My dad doesn't blame me. I think Sam used to. Either way, it's the truth."

"You were seven. She died in a car accident, right? How could it be your fault?"

"My dad worked all the time back then. His whole life was the force. It scared the hell out of my mom. I think she was afraid of being left with two boys to raise alone. She drank every night. My dad either ignored it or didn't want to admit there was a problem. But Sam and I knew, even as young as we were. I could see she wasn't right. Sam compensated by being the perfect kid. He tried to anticipate her every need, make life easier for her, to take away the stress."

"He was just a boy," Lexi said sadly.

"It was his nature." Scott gave a humorless laugh. "Not me. I was mad and I pushed all of her buttons. There was only room for one of us to get the attention from being a good kid, and Sam had that locked up. I went the opposite way. But I still didn't want her drinking. I don't remember my exact thinking, but I knew the bottle wasn't helping her cope with life. She'd hide the liquor and I'd find it and dump it. It would make her so angry, but I couldn't stop. I thought if the alcohol wasn't around then maybe she'd have a chance to get better."

"You were trying to help in your own way."

"The night she died she and my dad had a big fight. She went to get another drink, but I'd poured the rest of the bottle down the sink. That's part of why she drove off that night, to make a liquor-store run to replenish her stock. She wasn't far from the house when the accident happened. If she'd just been at home, she would have been safe."

He said the last words with a ragged intake of breath.

Lexi turned, looking into his eyes, so full of pain and guilt. "You were a kid," she said gently, wanting to reach out and touch him, but too afraid of breaking this moment and scaring him away. "You wanted her to get better."

He looked miserable as he said, "My good intentions didn't save her. If I'd just left her alone, maybe she would have stayed home that night. Maybe she'd never have died."

"It wasn't your fault," Lexi told him. "Children aren't responsible for the actions of their parents. Trust me, I know that better than anyone."

He lifted her hand off his cheek and placed a kiss on the inside of her wrist. "Do you remember your mom?"

"Only a little. An image here and there. But not much more than that. My father—big surprise—sent me to a psychologist when I was younger to 'process' what had happened to me. Basically, I was told not to dwell on the past and to be grateful for my new life and the second chance I'd been given." She sighed. "Which I was. I still am. But there are questions I wish I could have answered about her. I never knew my biological father and sometimes I wonder where I came from, who I'd be if Robert Preston hadn't molded me into his perfect, obedient daughter."

"You're more than the person he tried to make you."

Scott said the words with such conviction, Lexi couldn't help but believe them. "You have a good heart and a kindness that has nothing to do with your father. You're stronger than he knows. If nothing else, you must have learned that since being here."

She swallowed around the lump in her throat. "I never thought of myself as anyone besides Robert Preston's daughter. But now I do. Holding Charlie tonight made me see that I have more to give than I could have imagined."

"But you still plan to go back to Ohio?" Scott asked, as though he'd read her mind.

She stood, the familiar feeling of nervousness coursing through her body. "It's like my time here hasn't been real. I've told myself it was just a break, something temporary, which made it not quite as scary. The thought of really being on my own, that's terrifying." She paced back and forth in front of the couch. "My dad is the only family I have. That's important to me. What would it be like if I had no one?"

"You have me," Scott said quietly.

She stopped and turned to him. "Do I really? What if I told you I was applying for jobs in Charlotte and D.C. so I could stay close to you? Would you stick around if you thought I wanted more than a couple of weeks of fun? You've made it clear you don't have anything more to give."

"You deserve something—someone—better." A muscle ticked in his jaw. "Of course I want time with you. But I've told you before, I mess things up for the people who care about me. Your life is just starting. I'm not going to ruin it for you."

"I don't believe that," she said, feeling her temper rise. "I think that's an easy out you've given yourself because you don't want to do the hard work a real relationship takes."

His eyes went dark. "I can't give you what you want. Isn't it enough—"

He stopped midsentence as the front door opened. Sam and Julia came into the living room, holding hands.

"We're back," Julia called out. She paused, her gaze traveling between Lexi and Scott. "Rough night?"

Lexi shook her head. "Charlie was wonderful. It all went great."

Sam watched the two of them, then threw a pained look at Julia. "She's totally lying."

"I'm not," Lexi protested. "Did you have a good dinner? You're back so early."

Now Sam's expression turned soft as he gazed at his wife. "Dinner was great, but…"

"We're so boring," Julia finished. "We just wanted to come home and watch a movie on the couch."

Scott stifled a yawn. "How old are you two, anyway?"

"That doesn't sound boring," Lexi argued. "It sounds perfect."

"Would you like to join us?" Sam asked after a moment.

Julia elbowed him in the ribs. "Ignore him. He's being polite." She turned and planted a deep, wet kiss on Sam's mouth.

"She's right," he agreed, his arms tightening around Julia. "You should go now."

"Um…right." Lexi grabbed her purse from the side table.

"Get a room," Scott muttered.

"We have a whole house," Julia countered. But she turned and placed a hand on Lexi's arm. "Thank you for watching Charlie tonight. We needed this."

"It was my pleasure," Lexi answered.

"If you stay in Brevia awhile, we'll try a long weekend." Sam laughed when Lexi's eyes widened and Scott groaned. "Think you can handle it?"

"Have a nice time, you two." Scott put his hand on the small of Lexi's back and guided her out onto the porch.

She kept walking down the steps and toward her car, suddenly feeling exhausted. She yearned for the kind of love Sam and Julia shared, but was afraid she'd already given her heart to a man who could never let himself feel the same thing back.

"Hold on," Scott said, tugging on her hand. "Don't leave mad, Lexi."

"I'm not angry." She pulled away and kept moving. "I'm tired. I'll see you back at the apartment."

"Is this our first fight? Should I sleep at the bar tonight?" His tone held a hint of teasing she couldn't return.

"I'm not sure what this is, Scott. I know what I want, but it's up to you to decide whether you can give it to me." She unlocked her car, then looked back at him. "When you figure it out, let me know."

She pulled up to the curb outside her apartment building. Scott had disappeared shortly after they'd left Sam and Julia's street. She wondered if he really planned on sleeping at the bar. There were bound to be several women willing to let him warm their beds if he needed a place to stay. The thought filled her with a hollow feeling of disappointment.

He'd told her he was bound to disappoint her, so who was truly to blame?

She'd hoped for something more even though it was foolish. He hadn't made any promises, but he'd smiled when she told him she was applying for jobs in D.C., answering her unspoken question about their future with a kiss. The way he looked at her, the way he held her close every night made her believe they could have one. He might not say the words out loud, but she knew he cared for her.

Every morning for the past week he'd warmed her towel while she was in the shower, leaving it ready for her on the sink when she got out. It was a small gesture, but to her it represented the essence of Scott. He could be cool and detached on the outside, but he had the softest heart of anyone she'd ever met.

Now her own heart ached at the thought that she wanted things Scott would never be able to give her.

She sat in the car for several minutes before climbing the steps to her apartment. The wind blew cold as darkness fell. A light mist that promised more rain enveloped her, giving the air a heavy weight that matched the pressure in her heart.

This evening had started out with so much promise and now here she was, alone again. Just as she put the keys in the lock, a noise behind her made her turn.

Scott stood at the end of the hallway, a bouquet of fresh flowers held out in front of his chest.

"I thought you'd gone to the bar," she whispered.

"I'm sorry," he said as he walked toward her. "I'm sorry I don't have all the answers, that I'm not a better man."

"I like you just the way you are." Her voice cracked as he handed the bouquet to her. She knew suddenly that she didn't just like him. She loved him. The vulnerability and need in his eyes called to a place inside her, and there was nothing she could do to resist the pull.

He scooped her into his arms and she clung to him as he carried her into the apartment, kicking the door shut. His mouth captured hers with a kiss so possessive, so commanding, it stole her breath. But she met his desire with all the emotions she'd banked up inside. Everything she wanted to tell him but was too afraid to say out loud she tried to show him through their embrace. He seemed to be filled with the same hunger she felt for him. The flowers dropped to the floor as they tore at each other's clothes and he carried her to her bedroom.

Her breasts tingled as he slid his hands over them, over her entire body, trailing kisses in the wake of his skilled fingers. When he moved over her, inside her, she knew that in embracing her freedom she'd also lost her heart to this man. Whether or not he could ever truly be hers didn't matter as they found a perfect rhythm, a connection she knew she'd only ever find in his arms.

He whispered endearments into her ear, coaxing her to the highest peaks of pleasure before finding his own release. He continued to kiss her, lightly and softly. He nuzzled her neck and threaded his fingers through her hair, pulling her close as he sank back against the pillows.

Her head lay on his chest and she could hear his heartbeat, as wild and erratic as she knew hers to be, until it finally settled to its normal pace. She wondered for a moment if anything would ever be normal inside her again.

She knew he wasn't sleeping because he continued to run his fingers lightly over her bare back.

She tipped up her head after a moment. "I've never had make-up sex before."

He grinned wryly. "So I guess now you're going to want to fight all the time."

"Only if you promise to bring me flowers and apologize so enthusiastically."

He shifted her onto her back once again. "Enthusiastic? You haven't seen anything yet."

And for hours more, he proved to be a man of his word.

Scott whistled as he loaded cases of beer into the big refrigerator off the kitchen. It was midmorning and the bar was quiet, his favorite time to get work done.

"Someone's in a great mood today."

He turned to Jon Riley with a grin. "It could be because I just ran the numbers for last month. We're doing better than I ever expected on revenue. I think that has a lot to do with your menu drawing in new customers. I appreciate everything you've done, Jon."

The older man shrugged, looking embarrassed to be singled out. "You've made some great changes here. My father would be happy to see his place thriving again."

Jon made a show of checking supplies in the food pantry. "But I'd guess your attitude has more to do with a certain tiny redhead."

Scott went back to stacking boxes. "We're trying to keep it quiet, you know. She's only here temporarily, but I'm the boss and I don't want it to look..." No matter how he tried, he couldn't stop the smile that played across his lips. "Truth is, I don't care how it looks. She's amazing."

"Everyone can see that you two belong together."

"The hell they do."

Scott's back went stiff as he glanced to where Robert Preston stood in the doorway of the kitchen.

"I assume you're talking about my daughter," Preston said through clenched teeth, "and I'm here to tell you she belongs back home with a man who is worthy of her. Not with some washed-up ex-combat soldier stuck in this town."

"Your daughter gets to make her own decisions now," Scott argued. "You don't own her anymore. You never really did." He stepped toward the man. "You have no business here, Preston."

"I want to check on Lexi. Make sure she's doing okay. I assume she's ready to come back. If you've kept up your end of the bargain in making sure she knows what's best for her."

"She told you she'd make her decision at the end of the month. You agreed to leave her alone until then."

Preston glanced around the kitchen, derision clear in his gaze. "If her choice is the life she left behind or this, I know what she'll choose. I didn't raise her to settle for someone like you. I can offer her safety, security and a guarantee that she'll have a decent future."

Anger coursed through Scott. "Your problem is you underestimate her. Does the name Reid and Thompson mean anything to you?"

"It's a D.C. firm started by one of my old partners. So what?"

"What if I told you Lexi had an interview with them?" She had said she wanted to keep her interviews quiet until she got an offer, but Scott knew she'd get hired and couldn't help but gloat to her father. He enjoyed seeing Preston's face turn blotchy.

"You think you're her only option, but what you forget is Lexi is a hell of an attorney in her own right. There are plenty of places that would be glad to hire someone with her talent. I'm not saying that I'm worthy of her. She's better than either one of us deserves. Maybe now that she's out from under your thumb she'll have enough confidence to believe in herself." He paused, then drove the final nail in the coffin. "Maybe you've already lost her."

Preston stalked toward him, looking as if he was ready for a fight. As much as he'd enjoy pummeling this man who'd caused Lexi so much pain, Scott wasn't that stupid.

"You think you know her so well." Preston spit the words, his face only inches from Scott's. "She needs me. I'm her only family and that means something to Lexi. She'll come to her senses one way or another." His mouth curved into a nasty grin. "And what about you? Hiding out here from your past. This isn't what you want. You need to be where the action is. Do you really think it's all going to work out so easily for you?"

"Maybe this is enough for me." Scott forced his voice to remain even. "You don't know who I am."

"We'll see about that." Preston turned and walked from the room.

Scott stood there, his fists clenched tightly. Robert Preston had hit the heart of Scott's biggest fear. That he was going to mess up this chance he'd gotten at a new life, that the broken part of him would bubble to the surface and cause him to destroy the connections he'd built. That was why he'd chosen to be a loner in life. It was easier to take care of only himself, leaving less chance of collateral damage for the people around him.

He may have been only a boy when his mother died, but he knew he was the one who'd driven her away, even as he'd wanted to save her. When he'd tried to show Sam that his fiancée was no good, Scott had ended up almost ruining his relationship with his brother. And he'd wanted to protect his partner to the point that he'd turned an unintentional blind eye to the drinking that had eventually killed Derek.

He'd opened up to Lexi, let her into his life and heart because he'd believed it was a temporary arrangement. But he knew she wanted more from him, and he desperately wished he could give it to her. She filled the dark corners of his body and soul with her light. She'd become a lifeline back to the world for him, away from the isolation he'd lived with for so long. What would he risk if he fell for her completely? There was a good chance he would eventually hurt her. Scott wasn't sure if he knew another way, despite his best intentions.

Even if he couldn't hold on to her, he knew for damn sure he wasn't going to let her father reclaim her.

"He's intense," Jon said, pulling Scott back to the present.

"He's like a poison to her," he answered. "Toxic."

"Lexi certainly seems happier and more confident than when she first arrived." Jon laughed softly. "She doesn't drop glasses anymore."

Scott felt a smile play at his lips as he thought back to her first bumbling shifts at the bar. "This isn't where she was meant to be, either. It's just a short-term stopping point on her journey."

"What if the path leads to her father again?" Jon asked.

"She can't go back there."

"Maybe you should give her a reason to stay."

Chapter 11

The bead of sweat that trickled between Lexi's shoulder blades had nothing to do with the sun beaming through the clouds. The weather was growing colder, but this morning felt almost perfect. Leaves shimmered on the trees in the park and Freddy played with a pinecone, batting it around with his nose as she sank onto the park bench.

She held her cell phone in her palm, still staring at it, unable to believe the conversation she'd just had. When the Human Resources department from one of the firms where she'd applied had called earlier this morning to tell her she hadn't gotten the position, Lexi had been surprised but not too disappointed. She had several leads on open positions at reputable law firms. But after that first call, her phone had rung almost on cue every fifteen minutes, with all the openings suddenly drying up or the positions going to other applicants.

The final call had come in from the senior partner at Reid and Thompson, her father's former colleague, who'd informed her that they had no room for her at their law firm. When she'd questioned him about the reason, his answer had been cryptic, but he'd eventually suggested her best option might be to head back to Ohio to try to patch things up with her father.

She dialed her dad's private line now, the sinking feeling in her chest expanding as he answered on the first ring.

"Are you ready to come home?" he asked, cutting right to the heart of the matter.

"How did you know I was applying for other jobs? Are you having me followed?" She bit her lip as emotion threatened to overtake her. She wouldn't give him the satisfaction of hearing how upset she was. "Why, Dad? Why sabotage my chance at a fresh start?"

"I want you here with me."

"I have to learn to live on my own."

"You're all I have, Lexi." She heard him draw in a breath, as if he was shocked he'd admitted that much to her.

"I'm your daughter and I love you," she whispered, willing him to accept her right to choose her own life. "Where I live won't change that."

"You don't belong there. Especially not with him."

"Are you talking about Scott?" She adjusted the phone in her hands, realizing her fingers were shaking. "Leave him out of this, Dad. He cares about me."

Her father barked out a bitter laugh. "Always so

naive. That's part of the reason you still need me. The man you think cares about you is the one who told me about your job prospects."

Lexi shivered from the ice that suddenly ran down her spine. "When did you talk to Scott?"

"I paid another visit to Brevia and Riley's Bar. Your boss was very interested in how I could help him return to his real life as a marshal. I still have quite a few contacts in the Justice Department, you know."

"What did you do, Dad?"

"It's time to come home, Lexi. Your little adventure is officially over."

She hung up, stunned to think that Scott would have betrayed her this way. He'd been encouraging her to apply to law firms in the region, bolstering her confidence and making her feel as if she could really contribute if given a chance. He still wouldn't talk about a future with her, insisting she needed to worry about herself before she made any relationship a priority. But Lexi had continued to hold out hope that his feelings for her, or the ones she believed him to have, would be enough to make him realize their relationship was worth taking a chance on.

Now any future they could have had together was ruined, so much collateral damage—just like her heart. She knew he didn't love her; he couldn't with what he'd done. She also knew that as much as she loved him there wasn't a way to repair this kind of betrayal.

Still, she had to know why.

Her hands were shaking as she started walking, Freddy trotting along at her side. She didn't stop until she was in front of Riley's Bar & Grill. Part of her wanted to keep going, to return to the apartment and pack as much as she could fit in her suitcase. She wanted to escape this place and the sad, desperate promise she'd believed it held for her.

She couldn't outrun her past, couldn't pretend it wasn't waiting to swallow her again. She'd gotten what she came for—adventure and a taste of freedom. But now that was done and nothing could change the future she'd tried so hard to avoid.

Scott stood behind the bar, his full attention captured by whatever he was reading. He looked up as she walked through the door, tenderness shining in his eyes. Their light made her heart break even further, creating a wide chasm so painful she clutched a hand to her chest to tamp down some of the pain.

It didn't work. Nothing could lessen the hurt she felt. Nothing but the truth.

"You're not going to believe this," he said, coming around the bar. "The Marshals office has reinstated me. Apparently, their investigation has been satisfied without my review." He reached for her, but she stepped away. Freddy, traitorous canine, wiggled at Scott's feet.

"Was it worth it?" Her throat was so dry the words came out as croak.

"Hell, yes, it was worth it." His smile brightened and he crouched down to pet Freddy. "I didn't have to rat out my partner. I didn't ruin his family. I'm in the clear."

His words were another blow, so much like a punch to the gut that she bent forward with the force of it.

"Lexi, what is it? Come sit down."

"Don't touch me," she said with a painful hiss of breath when he tried to gather her close. "You ruined me. You destroyed us. And you're telling me it was worth it?" She shook her head. "You're no different than my father. I thought—"

"What are you talking about?"

How could he look at her as if he gave a damn? Her pain turned to anger, which gave her the strength she needed to straighten her shoulders. "You told my father about my job applications. He came to see you and you gave him the information he needed to ruin my chances at being hired on at any of the firms where I'd applied."

Scott looked confused for a moment, then shook his head. "No. I mean, yes. He showed up here and I told him that you weren't coming back, that you were going to find your own way in life. It wasn't so that he could interfere."

"But he did," she said, her voice cracking. "I told you he would. I asked you not to say anything until I had everything settled. He's basically blackballed me in the legal community. I guess I could get in my car and drive to California. That sounds like a great option, right?"

"I didn't—"

"And now you've been reinstated. Do you think that's a coincidence, Scott? According to the conversation I just had with my dad, it isn't. He said he offered you a deal—help limit my options and he'd use his contacts at the Justice Department to have your review abandoned. I guess you both got what you wanted." She drew herself up and asked, "So tell me again, was it worth it?"

"It was a mistake, Lexi." Scott ran his hand through his hair, a gesture so familiar to her now it made pain slice through her once more. "You have to believe that."

"Was it?" she countered. "You've told me over and

over how you sabotage your own life. You destroy the connections you have with people."

"Not you—"

"You're a coward." She wanted the words to hurt him. She needed him to feel some of the same pain she did, as if she could hold on to him with any kind of desperate connection.

"Excuse me?" He said the words through clenched teeth.

"I got too close. I think your feelings for me scared the hell out of you and you dealt with them the only way you know how—by pushing me away. Guess what? It worked. I've had a great time, but some things weren't meant to be. I'm not a fighter by nature. I don't want to spend my whole life looking over my shoulder, waiting for the next time my father sticks his nose in my affairs. I'm stronger than I was when I left, and I can go back now, hopefully on my own terms."

She raised her chin, biting down on her lower lip to keep it from trembling. "Tell me I'm wrong." She tried not to let her voice sound as if she was pleading with him. "Tell me there's another way."

For a moment, the pain in his eyes matched her own. He looked as miserable as she felt. She knew that if he reached for her now, told her he loved her and they would figure out another way, she'd believe him. If he could be honest, they might work through this.

But he didn't give her that chance.

He took a step toward her, then stopped. His eyes closed for a second and when he looked at her again, the mask was back in place. The man who cared only about himself had returned. Lexi wondered if he'd ever really left in the first place.

"Don't say I didn't warn you," he told her, his quiet voice a knife across her soul. "I didn't want to hurt you, Lexi, but we both knew it was inevitable. That's the guy I am. It's who I've always been. Maybe you are better back with your father. At least he's an enemy you know."

"And you'll leave Brevia? Leave behind everything you've built here to go back to the Marshals?"

He bit out a harsh laugh. "What have I really done here? I've put a shine on a two-bit bar. Come on, that's no future."

"It's more than that and you know it. It's your family, the friends you've made in this community. Riley's Bar & Grill is a part of the town because of you. You've made a difference. How can you turn your back on that?"

"The town will go on without me. Sam and my dad will do just fine. They were doing fine when I came back into their lives, and it won't take much for things to return to normal."

She wanted to turn and walk away, but something inside her made her keep pushing. "What about you, Scott? What about your pain? Being in Brevia has healed what was broken inside of you. I know that it has."

"When are you going to get it? It's not a piece of me that's damaged. It's the whole thing. I'm broken and there's no fixing it." He paced back and forth in front of her. "I can get on with my life." He stopped, pressed his lips together, then said, "We both can. This was a fun ride while it lasted. You got the adventure you wanted and I had a distraction while I was waiting for things to work out. But it's not real. It never was."

The unexpected rush of sorrow almost brought her to her knees. Wasn't she repeating the same mistakes she'd made with her father? She'd tried to guess what Scott wanted from her. Attempted to meet his expectations without ever knowing what they truly were. She'd hoped their relationship meant something to him, but was too afraid of being rejected to share her feelings. And now when things were difficult, when she wasn't making it easy on him, he shut her out. Just as her dad had done.

She shook her head, not bothering to wipe away the tears that streamed down her face. "It was real for me," she whispered.

Scott's eyes narrowed and she thought he might respond, believed she might have finally found a crack in his armor. But when he said nothing, she finally turned and walked away.

Forever.

The bar was loud and crowded several hours later. It was a Friday night, and in the few short weeks he'd been in Brevia, Riley's Bar had become a favorite hangout for locals and tourists alike. Scott surveyed the room, knowing he should feel pride in what he'd accomplished. All he could see was how he'd ruined things once again.

He poured a round of shots for a group near the front celebrating someone's promotion, then added an extra glass for himself. He hadn't taken a drink of hard liquor since the night he'd moved in with Lexi. The bourbon burned his throat, but nothing could burn away the memory of Lexi's tortured face as he'd watched her heart break in front of him.

It had killed him to see her like that, but he couldn't seem to stop himself from lashing out once she'd accused him of conspiring with her father. Scott was used to people believing the worst about him and meeting their low, low expectations. She'd been different, or so he'd thought. He'd had the crazy idea she'd seen a better side of him, the man he wanted to be. He'd been stupid enough to hope that he could do right by her.

He'd been waiting for her to leave him, but that didn't make it hurt less. When it was clear he'd once again messed up, he made sure the door shut behind her for good. His whole body felt the loss of her.

Now he had to live with the gaping hole that hours ago had held his heart.

He put down the empty shot glass and noticed Sam standing at the edge of the bar.

"Busy here," Scott shouted, indicating the jumble of people in front of him.

"Make time," Sam replied. "Now."

Scott grabbed the arm of the second bartender. "Max, can you handle this for a few minutes?"

The younger man smiled. "More tips for me."

Scott followed Sam down the back hallway and into his office. He swore Lexi's scent lingered in the air, making him catch his breath.

A half-dozen large garbage bags were piled in front of the desk.

"Your stuff from the apartment," Sam said flatly.

Scott's gut tightened. He hadn't planned on going

back there tonight. But to know she'd already packed and shipped him off still got under his skin, even though he knew everything was his fault. As usual. "Is that what you pulled me away for?"

"I know all about making things harder than they need to be," his brother said, instead of answering the question. "I think a Callahan invented the concept. Did you do it on purpose?"

Scott knew Sam was talking about the information he'd given to Lexi's father. "I don't know." He scrubbed his hands across his face. "I was mad and I didn't want to answer the questions he asked. I wanted him gone. I'm not exactly an expert on thinking before I speak. Lexi is better off without me. Maybe this was the only way to show her that."

"You love her," Sam told him, using his best big-brother voice.

"You don't know anything about me," Scott countered. "You never have. I'm not like you, Sam. I'm the black sheep, the one who messes up. I always have been. Why should this be any different?"

"It's different because you love her. You're different."

"You know what happened, I assume. So you know it's over."

"Do you remember when we were little, before Mom died?"

Scott gritted his teeth. He and Sam rarely talked about their mother's death, about life before that. Hell, they'd had a hard enough time getting through their childhood, with their father gone most of the time. They'd dealt with the pain and loss in different ways. Yet it remained a common bond they shared, pushing them apart while at the same time keeping them tethered to each other.

"You were a fighter, the most stubborn kid ever," Sam told him. "When her drinking got bad, I'd make excuses or try to coddle her through the bad nights."

"You also made a lot of ramen-noodle dinners and sack lunches when she wasn't in any shape to do it herself."

"I tried to gloss it over."

"You were making the best of the situation." Scott closed his eyes for a moment. "I couldn't."

"Not you," Sam agreed. "You'd get in her face, dump the liquor bottles, play games, sing and dance, whatever you could do to keep her engaged with her family. You made her step up a lot more than she would have otherwise."

"Look where that got all of us. She went out to replace what'd I'd poured down the sink and died because of it."

"She died because she was driving drunk. That wasn't your fault."

"Well, it sure as hell wasn't yours."

"It wasn't any of ours," Sam told him. "Even after that, you kept fighting. Half the reason you got in trouble was to get Dad's attention, to pull him back into our lives."

"It took twenty years for that to happen, and now he's turned into Dr. Phil. I don't think I had anything to do with that."

"Of course you did," his father said from the doorway.

Scott groaned and rolled his eyes in Sam's direction. "Not him, too."

Joe Callahan stepped into room. "Sammy's right. You were a fighter back then. So what happened, son? What made the fight go out of you?"

"The fight didn't go out of me," Scott said through clenched teeth. "If you both remember, I joined the army, I became a marshal. I've spent my whole damn life fighting." He threw out his hands. "Other than these past few weeks. Maybe that's my problem. I'm going soft." He pointed a finger at Sam, then his father. "Just like the two of you. I let this town make me forget my priorities."

Joe came forward, placing his big hands on Scott's shoulders. "This town and that woman gave you priorities. She made you whole."

"She made me think I could be someone I'm not," Scott said quietly. "Lexi and I both learned our lesson there."

"You need to fight for her," Sam countered.

"She doesn't want me to. It's better for both of us if I let her walk away."

"Are you kidding?" His brother slammed his hand down on the desk. "I saw you with her. I know that look. Hell, I avoided that look in the mirror for ages. But I'm telling you that for the rest of your life you'll regret it if you don't try to make this right."

"It's the truth, son." Joe brought his face close to Scott's. "I'm sorry that your mother drove off that night. I'm sorry I left her with no options and that I didn't do right by the two of you after she was gone. I messed us up real good." He drew in a shaky breath.

"Dad, don't cry." Scott's head began to pound. "I don't need this."

"What you need is to have your butt kicked into next week."

Shrugging out of his father's embrace, Scott turned to Sam. "I suppose you're the guy to do it?" His hands curled into fists. He was angry at himself, but if he could take it out on Sam, that worked, too. He wouldn't pass up the opportunity for a decent release of frustration. "Bring it on."

Sam shook his head. "No, thanks. Hitting me isn't going to make you feel any better."

"I think it might." Scott stepped forward. "Because it sure as hell feels wrong that my brother isn't on my side."

"I'm on your side," Sam answered. "Just like you were on mine when you slept with Jenny."

"That's not the same thing."

"I said I'd never thank you, but I am now. Your method was crazy, but you were right. I would have been miserable married to her. If you hadn't shown me her true colors, I might not have come to Brevia. Julia and Charlie might not be a part of my life. Sometimes bad things that happen are for the best in the end."

"And sometimes they aren't. That's how it works with me." Blood thrummed through Scott's head, making it hard to get the words out. "I pushed Mom until she left that night. I should have found a way to convince you that Jenny was the wrong woman. Instead, I took her to bed, making you look like a fool and guaranteeing that you'd cut me out of your life. I didn't confront my partner when I knew he was drinking too much and too often, and he got killed because of it. Try telling his wife and kids that things will work out in the end for them." Scott drew in a ragged breath. "Now I've given Robert Preston the information he needed to make sure Lexi feels like she has no options but to go back to him."

"You aren't responsible for the fate of everyone around you," Joe said sadly. "When are you going to realize that, Scott? You do the best you can and so does everyone else."

"My best is pretty awful, Dad." He turned. "You might be right, Sam. I hate what happened with Lexi and her dad, but it could work out for the best when she moves on with her life and I'm not a part of it."

"That's not what I mean and you know it."

"I'm sorry," Scott said after a long moment. "I want you both to know that."

"You don't need to apologize," his father told him. "We're your family. We love you no matter what."

Scott glanced at Sam. "I bet Julia wants to kill me."

"She'll get over it. Quicker than you will."

"We'll have to see," Scott answered. "I need to get back to the front now."

Joe pulled him close for another hug. To his surprise, Scott felt some comfort in the gesture, but still he shrugged away. "Go home, you two. There's nothing more to be done here."

He walked into the hall, sagging against the wall for a moment before he continued. He was going soft. That must be the reason all of this was hitting him so hard. Normally he could leave his mistakes behind, keep moving so that things didn't catch him. But now he felt weighed down, as if he'd swallowed a load of boulders and was sinking into a deep pool of misery. In a way he welcomed the darkness. It was familiar, and right now Scott clung to that to keep from totally drowning.

He straightened his shoulders and went back to the bar, jumping on top as he put two fingers to his mouth to whistle for the crowd's attention.

"I got some good news today," he shouted, "and everyone here is going to celebrate tonight. This round's on me!"

A loud cheer went up from his customers and he climbed down to a chorus of congratulations and back slaps. The blackness in him expanded until it blotted out all of the light he'd known this past month. He sucked in a breath and forced his mouth into a smile. This was what he knew, and he was going to relearn to live with faking happiness.

Chapter 12

"You're running away."

"I was running away when I came to Brevia." Lexi folded another shirt and placed it in the suitcase. "Now I'm going home. That's what most people do after they run away."

"You don't want to go back there." Julia plucked the shirt out of the pile and shoved it back in the drawer as Lexi turned away.

"Quit doing that," she said, shaking her head. "I don't know what I want. Not with the options I have left. I came here to find my independence, and instead I traded being dependent on my father with being dependent on Scott. Those jobs I was looking at—their appeal hinged on keeping me close to D.C. so I could be near him. That was stupid."

"That's love. It makes you do stupid things." Julia shrugged. "Trust me, I know."

"I'm going to be smarter now."

"Smarter isn't going home to be your father's puppet."

"I'm going back on my terms."

"You're going back because that's the easy way out."

"Easy? I've been miserable for the past three days. What part of my swollen face and bags under my eyes looks easy to you?" Lexi growled in her throat as Julia put away another sweater. "Stop unpacking me."

"You don't want to leave. Brevia sucks you in until you're a part of the community. I know you like it here."

"Of course I do," Lexi said miserably. "But what am I supposed to do to make a living? I'm not going back to the bar and… I like being an attorney."

"So be one. In Brevia." Julia pointed a finger at her. "You have a half-dozen clients already. Find some cheap office space and hang out your shingle or whatever it is lawyers do."

"I have a handful of people I've helped on a pro bono basis. I can't be paid with free highlights and apple pies."

"Your hair looks a lot better since Nancy got ahold of you."

Lexi couldn't help but roll her eyes. "Not the point."

"The point is you're afraid to try."

"I did try. And I failed. End of story."

"You didn't really. You told everyone that you were having 'an adventure.' That this was just a short vacation from reality. That's not putting yourself out there for real."

"I left my job, my father, everything I knew behind. How is that not real?"

"You didn't leave them. You said 'I'll be back.' You could be someone different because it was a costume you were trying on. Why bother with the guts to make it work? You knew you could go running home to Daddy."

"Running home…!" Lexi said with a sputter. "I was applying for other jobs. I didn't plan to go back."

Julia shook her head. "I don't believe you."

"How dare you—"

"I don't believe you and I don't think you intended to stay with Scott, either."

"You can't be serious. He's the one who betrayed me."

"He did you a favor."

Lexi felt her mouth drop open. "You're crazy. I don't know why I came here in the first place."

"You came here," Julia answered, "because I'm the only person you know who would let you live your own life. But you can't do it. You're not brave enough. I thought you had it in you, but I guess I was wrong."

"Had what in me?"

"The courage to really stand on your own two feet. Not just take 'a break' from life. Your dad interfered with your job applications. So what? Big deal. Stuff happens. Move on. Apply for more jobs, smaller firms. Start your own firm. Right here. What's stopping you?"

"And what would stop him from interfering again?"

"You will. You're the only one who can stop him. But you have to stand up to him once and for all and be willing to deal with the consequences, no matter what they are. You haven't done that yet. You've told him you 'need time.' To him that's an open door. If you really want to live life on your own terms, you have to force him to let you go."

"That's easier said than done."

"Maybe," Julia agreed. "That's why Scott did you a favor. Eventually your father was going to find out you'd applied for jobs. Did you really have any intention of taking one of them, or was it just a ploy to prove to him you were ready to move on?"

"Yes… No… I don't know, when you say it like that." Lexi sat down on the bed, suddenly tired now that the edge was taken off her anger. "I knew he was going to be mad, but I still haven't proved anything to him. I've shown I can live on my own for a few weeks. So what? I wanted to get a job without his help. Everything I've done in my life has been because my dad has been holding the strings. I went to his alma mater. I worked for his firm on the cases he assigned me. I needed a change. I thought a month would show him that there was more to me than he thought. I wanted to prove it to myself, as well."

"And it did, right?"

"I suppose. But you're right, taking a break and making a fresh start for real are two different things. I'm scared of being alone. I'm afraid to be on my own when it's permanent."

"You're not on your own in Brevia," Julia said softly. "You have friends here. You have Scott."

"I don't." Lexi shook her head. "I have friends and I'm grateful for that. Grateful to you. But I don't have Scott. He's going back to the Marshals. He doesn't want anything long-term with me."

"He loves you," Julia told her. "I can see it."

"I don't think he knows how to let himself love someone." Lexi wiped at her damp eyes with the T-shirt in her hands. "We both knew it was temporary. He made sure of that when he told my father about my plans." She shook her head. "I don't think he did me a favor, but either way, we're done. You're right about one thing, Julia."

"I'm usually right about everything," the other woman corrected with a smile.

Lexi mustered a watery grin in return. "I haven't learned to stand on my own two feet," she said softly. "I didn't take control of my future. I only postponed the future my father has planned for me."

"It's not too late." Julia placed a hand on Lexi's shoulder. "Take it from one who knows, it's never too late. Do you know what you want to do with your life?"

Lexi thought for a minute, then nodded.

"Then go do it."

Lexi took a deep, soul-cleansing breath. "You're right. This isn't over until I say it is." She stood up, then smiled as she looked at the empty suitcase on the bed. "Did you unpack everything?"

Julia shrugged. "I basically threw it all into a drawer, so I'm not saying you'll be able to find what you need. But it's here, Lexi. You belong here."

Lexi nodded. As if the clouds had parted after a heavy storm, her path appeared before her, suddenly clear as a blue sky. "I know what I want. And I know just the person to help me get it."

An hour later, Lexi stood on the steps of Frank Davis's office once again. She raised her hand to knock, but Ida Garvey pushed her aside.

"It's a good thing you called me to meet you. After all, I practically paid for this building," the older woman told her, turning the knob and walking right in. "Frank," she called out. "I know you're hiding out in here."

Frank Davis came forward from the main office. "Ida," he said, his voice dripping with Southern hospitality. "To what do I owe the honor of..." He trailed off when he noticed Lexi standing behind Ida. "Why is she here with you?"

"She's my attorney," Ida said simply.

Lexi couldn't help the smile that curved her lips. Listening to Ida ramble on during the short drive downtown, she'd questioned the logic of including the older woman in this confrontation. But she knew she'd get further with Frank Davis if she had his best client in her corner.

"I'm your attorney," he argued now.

"You were for many years," Ida agreed. "And you did a good job. Mainly. Adequate, anyway. Well, except for that time—"

"What's your point, Ida?" The sweetness had dropped from his tone.

"Something's wrong with you, Frank." Ida pointed a fleshy finger at him. "I don't know what, but I smell trouble on you. You're ignoring clients, messing up filings, generally dropping the ball across the board. I want to know why."

"That's not true." Frank's hand shot up in the air. "It's this... Yankee. She's put these notions into your head."

"Yankee?" Lexi asked. "Did you really just call me that?"

"Hush, girl." Ida turned to Frank. "No one puts any notions into my head and you know it. Spill the beans, Frank."

He puffed himself up as if to argue, then let out his breath in a large burst. Frank Davis sank into the chair behind the secretary's desk and ran a hand across his face. "I'm in love," he said with a loud moan.

Ida looked back at Lexi, a question in her eyes. Lexi wasn't sure if the question was *Is this guy crazy?* but that was what she was thinking.

"Well, good for you, Frank," Ida said slowly. "Doris has been gone awhile now and the boys are grown and out of the house. You deserve some happiness."

"Happiness," Frank wailed. "There's nothing happy about loving this woman. She torments me every day. Her expectations, her needs. I'll be sixty-three years old next month. There's only so much this old body can handle, even with them little blue pills."

"TMI," Ida said quickly, then, at his odd look, explained, "Too much information, Frank."

"Maybe this was a mistake," Lexi whispered.

Ida ignored her. "Who is this gal?"

A look of pained adoration crossed Frank's ruddy face. "Miss Lucy St. Louis from down in Atlanta."

"Atlanta, Georgia?" Ida asked. "You've taken up with a woman who lives three hours away? Frank, you're a bigger fool than I thought."

"I love her, Ida." Frank dropped his head into his hands. "She loves me, too. But the distance is part of the problem. She wants to see me every weekend, and I've been driving back and forth. Sometimes in the middle of the week, too, if she wants…"

"A booty call?" Lexi couldn't help but ask.

Frank turned red, but mumbled, "She can't get enough."

"Then move her up here." Ida threw her hands in the air. "This isn't rocket science."

"It's not that easy." Frank leaned back in the chair, hands pressed to his temples. "She's got a little sister in private school down there she takes care of, and she makes good money at her job."

"I don't even want to know what someone named Lucy St. Louis does for a living," Ida muttered.

"Probably not," Frank agreed, then sighed. "I'm sorry, Ida. I haven't been giving my clients my all. I'm distracted and tired and…"

"Then why didn't you take my help?" Lexi asked.

"After what you did last year with Julia's son?" Frank shook his head. "I may be an old fool, but I'm not stupid. I don't trust you and I'm sure as hell not entrusting my clients to you."

"I trust her," Ida said firmly. "Lots of other people around town do, as well. Vera Morgan being one of them."

Frank's bug eyes narrowed in on Lexi. "Is that true?"

"It is." Lexi stepped forward. "I want to do right by the people of Brevia, Mr. Davis. Just like you. I know my introduction to the town was poor at best, but I'm a good attorney."

"Can't deny you there," Frank muttered.

"I'd like to stay in town, but I'm not a waitress."

The lawyer raised his head. "I heard you haven't been breaking as many glasses recently."

Lexi bit out a short laugh. "That's true. But I'm a better attorney than the best waitress I could ever be."

"I could use someone working with me," he admitted, scrubbing his hand across his face again. He looked expectantly at Lexi. "I'm going to be retiring here in a few years. If Lucy doesn't kill me first."

Lexi nodded, her mind such a jumble she could barely form a coherent thought. This was really happening. She was going to stay in Brevia. For good.

"It's settled, then," Ida said.

Frank stood and walked around the desk, grabbing Lexi's hand and shaking it. "Welcome to Davis and Associates." He turned to Ida. "Could you give Lexi and me a few minutes alone to discuss salary and benefits?"

"No way." Ida crossed her arms over her chest. "I'm staying for that part of the conversation."

"You can't leave now."

"It's only for a couple of days." Scott handed Jon Riley a piece of paper. "I've put together a list of deliveries and the schedule for the week with each person's contact information. If you need anything, call my cell phone."

"I'm the cook, not a bar manager," Jon argued, holding the paper tightly.

"You'll do fine." Scott clapped him on the shoulder. "I trust you." *More than I trust myself at this point,* he added silently.

"How can you run away?"

Scott's head began to pound again. "I'm not running away. I have business in D.C."

"Your old job."

He nodded.

"Are you going back to it?"

"I need to discuss some things with them first." Scott rubbed his temples. He wished he was running right now. Away from questions he couldn't answer, away from prying eyes every night at the bar. It had been almost a week since he'd gotten his reinstatement letter, and only three days until the reception for his dad and Sam. Riley's was crowded every night, with many people coming in for dinner and to hang out with friends or family. He'd gotten to know a number of locals, the majority of whom wanted to remind him what a fool he'd been to "fire" Lexi. No matter how many times he explained that she'd quit, the result was the same—everyone telling him how badly he'd messed up.

As if he didn't know that already. He felt the loss of her through every fiber of his being, from the moment he woke up until he dropped to sleep again. His back was killing him from nights on the couch in his office. Sam had offered him a place to stay, and so had his dad, over the objections of both of their wives, he'd guess.

But Scott wasn't going to be a burden to his family, especially not when they were treating him like some fragile doll who'd break in two if not handled the right way. He'd explained over and over that even if he went back to the Marshals, he'd find a good manager for the bar and come back to visit whenever he could. But it didn't seem to be good enough. They wanted him to promise to stay, and he couldn't do that.

He told himself it was because he had too much to lose if he gave up his job, but his heart felt as if he'd already lost everything important when Lexi walked away. Whether he stayed in Brevia or went back to D.C. and the Marshals wasn't really important. All that mattered was that she was gone. His mind might know it was for the best. Hell, he'd almost forced her to leave, but that didn't make it hurt any less. If anything, the ache only intensified, because if he wasn't such a self-destructive fool, he could have prevented it. That part hurt the most.

"You're not leaving, are you?" Misty walked into the kitchen. "Jon says he's going to be in charge now."

Scott rubbed two fingers against his temple. "He isn't in charge. I'm going to D.C. for a few days to wrap up some stuff with my old job."

"Are you coming back?"

He hesitated for the briefest second and she stomped her foot on the floor. "You can't desert us here."

"I'm not deserting anyone," Scott muttered. "I have business to take care of out of town. Jon is going to be running the place for a few days."

"I never agreed to that." Jon slammed the refrigerator door shut.

"The waitresses will never agree to it," Misty repeated. "You'd better make one of them the manager."

Scott wanted to hit something. "Fine. You're in charge."

"I don't want to be the manager," she argued. "Those girls can't get along."

"You two are killing me!"

"We need you, Scott." Misty's voice softened. "I

know you don't want to be needed. I know you've been in a terrible mood since Lexi left, but this bar is yours. Like it or not. Take it or leave it."

He saw the expectation in her face, felt it in her tone of voice. It weighed on him, just as it had with Lexi and his family. Why couldn't anyone see that he wasn't a person to depend on? He'd tried to be honest about what he could and couldn't give. It wasn't that hard to understand.

He'd reached his breaking point. This was how it happened with him. People pushed him further than he could manage, always thinking that he'd step up to the challenge. But he never did. As much as he wanted to, he couldn't make it work.

Now was no different.

He grabbed his duffel bag from the floor next to the desk.

"Leave it," he said quietly and walked out the door.

Chapter 13

Lexi heard the fire truck before she saw it. The big red engine came screaming around the corner of Main Street. She stopped midstride walking out of Julia's salon, riveted by the noise of the siren. Then her heart leaped into her throat as the truck pulled up in front of Riley's Bar & Grill.

Scott wasn't there. Julia had told Lexi he'd left town for D.C. Lexi didn't know why the news had shocked her. Even after he'd told her he wasn't going to stick, some part of her had still held out hope. She told herself it didn't matter. It was enough that she'd found a place to call home. If Scott had to keep looking for his happiness, that was no business of hers.

She hadn't been back to the bar since she'd walked out. But she cared about the people there. She'd had lunch with Misty just yesterday, and Jon had stopped by her new office at the end of the day to bring her a take-out dinner. It was concern for her friends that had her running toward the bar, following two firemen inside.

The scene inside stopped her in her tracks. Water gushed through the doorway to the back half of the building. At least two inches covered the floor of the main room, the legs of chairs and tables standing in it.

"Oh, no," she whispered. Jon waded out from the back, a look of pure panic on his face.

"What happened?" she called to him, not wanting to step farther into the wetness.

"Water line broke, I think." He shook his head. "I got here about twenty minutes ago and this is what I found."

"Why is the fire department here?"

"Dave Johnson, a local plumber, is also a volunteer firefighter. I called him first and he brought the truck. I guess they were worried about an electrical fire or something."

A man dressed in a black T-shirt and yellow overalls came up behind Jon. "We've turned off the water. It's going to be tomorrow morning before I can get the parts here to fix it for real."

"What about tonight?" Lexi asked. Thursday was a popular night out in Brevia.

"Unless your customers have rubber boots," Dave told Jon, "they're not going to want to be in the place."

Lexi took off her shoes and rolled up her jeans, sloshing through the water to get to Jon. "Did you call Scott?"

"At least a dozen times," he answered. "He's not taking my calls." The older man shook his head. "With how he tore out of here, I'm not sure he means to come back."

"Of course he's coming back," Lexi answered with more conviction than she felt. "The reception for Joe and Sam is Saturday night. He's not going to miss that."

"I don't know. He stormed off in quite a huff. Looked to me like he was done with Brevia." Jon shook his head sadly. "Wouldn't surprise me."

A shrill cry had both of them turning toward the door. Misty stood at the entrance. "Did someone forget to turn off a faucet? Why is there a fire engine out front?"

"We have a small situation," Lexi explained. "A water line broke." She turned to Dave Johnson. "What are the options here?"

"Start swimming," he suggested with a smile.

"Not funny."

"Like I said, I'll have the pipe fixed by tomorrow. You're lucky it's fresh water, so that's a plus. Basically, you need to get a team in here to clean things up. I'm guessing it will take a week or so."

Lexi shook her head. "We don't have a week. This place needs to be ready for a party on Saturday night."

"That's right," Dave answered, nodding. "This is the big shindig for Sam Callahan. Sorry, lady, ain't going to happen."

"Who knows what will happen if Scott doesn't get back," Misty called out. "At this point, maybe we should start looking for other work."

"No way," Lexi argued. "We can't leave this place like this. If we don't get this water up quickly, the floor will be ruined. It needs time to dry out. There's got to be something we can do."

"Why do you even care?" Misty asked her. "I thought

you were done with this place. Done with Scott Callahan."

"I am done. But I can't let it end like this. Scott poured his time, energy and money into revitalizing Riley's. I know you all have been making more in tips in the past month than you have in ages."

The waitress nodded slowly.

"We can't just give up on it now."

"What are we supposed to do?" Jon asked.

Lexi turned to Dave. "You said you can get the pipe fixed tomorrow morning?"

"First thing," he promised. "I can make a call to the guys who work on flooded buildings and the like."

"Good." Lexi racked her brain for what to do next. "I'll get ahold of Sam. If anyone can rally the troops around here, it's the police chief."

Jon put a heavy hand on her shoulder. "I'm serious, Lexi. I doubt Scott's coming back. At this point, it might be better to walk away and let him hash things out with the insurance company."

"I don't believe that, Jon." She pointed a finger at him. "He gave you a chance when no one else would, and hired a couple of your buddies for odd jobs around here, right?"

"Yes."

"He's made an investment in Brevia. This place and this town mean something to him. Even if he doesn't realize it yet, he's going to. We have to show him…" Her voice lowered, became shaky. "I have to show him that even if he doesn't believe in himself, I still do. I'm not giving up." She felt her throat tighten with tears. Jon was probably right. For all she knew, Scott wouldn't care what happened here or what she did to make things right. But she had to try. That was what she'd want someone to do for her, and she had to believe her faith would pull him through.

Jon drew her into a tight hug. "You're a good woman, Lexi Preston."

"Let's hope I'm good enough."

Scott thumped his hands on the steering wheel as he drove into town. He'd been calling Jon Riley every fifteen minutes for the past four hours, but Jon hadn't answered his cell. That seemed ominous to Scott, and ominous was the last thing he needed this morning. He'd been delayed an extra night in D.C., wrapping up loose ends. He'd expected to make it to Brevia last evening, but now had only half a day until the reception, and there was so much to do.

If he even had a bar to get back to.

He'd left messages with directions for who to call and how to manage the cleanup. The one time he'd been able to reach Jon, after the man's many messages, their conversation had been cryptic at best. Jon had told him he wouldn't believe what had happened—something about a flood, a miracle, and to return as soon as possible. Then he'd hung up. Scott understood why Jon had been mad. Scott hadn't picked up the phone on Thursday. He'd left his cell in the car while he'd met with his former boss at the U.S. Marshals. That conversation had been bad enough, without having more distractions piled on top.

Now he worried that his carelessness may have put his future in jeopardy once again. It didn't matter, he told himself. He'd get through the reception without letting anyone down. He was going to stick this time. Whatever he found when he got to the bar, he was determined to make it right again.

He came to a screeching halt at the curb and threw his truck into Park. Bolting for the door with his heart in his throat, he rushed through, then stopped, shocked at the scene that awaited him.

The whole bar was decorated in shades of cornflower-blue and lemon-yellow. Linen cloths covered the tables. A mason jar filled with flowers sat in the center of every one. On each corner of the bar was a bouquet of balloons floating into the air. Poster-size photos of his dad and Vera, Sam and Julia, stood on tall easels off to one side. The place looked beautiful and, more importantly, ready for the reception.

"How did this happen?" he whispered, unable to believe how good everything looked. Of all the scenes he could have walked into, this was the last one he'd imagined.

His father was standing inside the front door, surveying the brightly decorated room. "Glad you made it, son." Joe wrapped him in a tight hug. "Did you get everything taken care of in D.C."

Scott nodded numbly. "Where's the water?"

Joe laughed. "You can't very well have a party when people would be getting their feet wet, right?"

"Why didn't anyone pick up when I called?" Scott pulled back from his dad's embrace.

Sam came over and chucked him on the shoulder. "We were kind of busy around here, with your building flooding and all."

"But Lexi had a plan," Misty told him as she finished tying more balloons to the edge of the bar. "She can be quite the mini taskmaster when she sets her mind to it."

"Lexi?" Scott felt his mind go blank.

"She's over at the salon with Julia, Vera and Lainey right now," Sam announced. "Julia insisted that she take a break. Otherwise, she'd still be here working." He threw his hand out in a sweeping gesture. "All of this is her doing."

"She was convinced something had delayed you in D.C.," Joe explained.

"I went to see Derek's wife. I wanted to explain to her what had happened that day. She needed to hear it from me."

Joe nodded.

"We were ready to give up on you," Misty told him candidly. "Not your dad and brother, I guess. They didn't know about the water damage until Lexi called them. But the other waitresses, Max, Jon—we all thought you'd deserted us and we were ready to return the favor."

"I told you—"

"Everyone knows what you said." Jon came out of the kitchen, an apron tied around his waist. "We also know what you did. You left us behind. You don't have a reputation as someone who sticks. Why would we think this time was any different?"

"Maybe because I told you I'd come back."

"Past actions mean more than words." Jon shrugged. "You should know that."

"But Lexi believed in you," Misty told him. "Even when the rest of us didn't have faith, she never actually gave up on you." The waitress clasped him in a quick hug. "Who knew she'd be right?"

"Are you here for the party or to stay?" Sam asked quietly.

Scott hesitated, his mind a whir. For the first time in as long as he could remember, he didn't feel alone. Someone had his back. He'd done his best to push Lexi away, but she'd stayed true. Even though he didn't deserve it.

He was going to change that. If this time had taught him anything, it was that he didn't have to be a prisoner to his own doubts and fear. He could make things right and he had every intention of doing that.

Starting now.

Chapter 14

Her nails drying, Lexi tried to feign interest in the latest magazine gossip. Her eyes drifted shut as she listened to Julia, Lainey and Vera talk, and wondered what it would be like to have grown up with sisters and a mother. The easy camaraderie and obvious closeness was something she'd never experienced. But she'd learned there was no use wishing for things that couldn't be. That might have been the biggest lesson from her grand adventure this past month.

She'd spent her whole life trying to make the people around her happy. Her only goal had been to live up to everyone's perfect image. Each time, the expectations had changed, when she got near enough to believe she might actually accomplish what she'd set out to do.

Now she knew she could only do her best and keep moving forward. She had to be true to herself and what she knew was right. That was what she'd told her father last night on the phone when she'd explained that she wasn't coming back to Ohio. He'd yelled and threatened, and although she'd been shaking with emotion, she'd held steady to her path. Eventually, he'd calmed down, and although he hadn't liked what she was saying, she'd gotten him to agree to stop interfering in her new life. She'd invited him to visit, offered him a chance to get to know her as her own person. He hadn't accepted, but hadn't outright refused, either.

She'd also done all she could for tonight's reception. Part of it was for Julia and Vera. They'd taken her into their circle even though she'd once tried to rip apart their family. They accepted her for who she was now and helped her gain the confidence to believe in herself. No one had given her a second chance like that before.

It taught her a great deal about how to live. Her heart still ached every day for Scott, but her belief in him had been a big part of why she'd stepped up to the plate. She knew that no one had ever given him a second chance when he needed it. That might have been because he'd never stuck around long enough to earn it. But it didn't matter. She believed in him, in who he was deep in his soul. She'd caught glimpses of the tender, honorable man he was inside. Yes, that man was buried under layers of pain and fear, but he was still the essence of who Scott was.

Even if he didn't come back for the reception, she knew he'd eventually talk to Joe or Sam. She wanted Scott to know that he could count on her when it mattered most. Because to her that was what love was, and even if he couldn't return her feelings, that didn't lessen what she felt for him.

A hush fell over the salon and she opened her eyes, wondering what had caught everyone's attention. Scott Callahan stood in the doorway, looking tired, beautiful and directly at her.

Julia strode forward at the same time Lexi rose to her feet, as if something in him pulled her closer.

"You've got a lot of nerve coming here," his sister-in-law told him, her finger wagging. "After—"

"I know," he said, holding up a hand, his eyes never leaving Lexi's. "I'm sorry and you can lay into me later. I need a few minutes to talk to Lexi."

To her surprise, Julia stepped back to let him pass.

Lexi felt her breath begin to come out in short, nervous puffs of air. "I wasn't sure you were coming back."

He nodded. "It may be the first non-idiot move I've made in the past couple of weeks. I'm sorry, Lexi."

He was standing in front of her now, so close she could see that he needed a shave. She could pick out the bright flecks of gold in his blue eyes. She could feel the warmth radiating from him, smell his soap and minty gum. Her whole body tingled, as if telling her how badly it had missed him.

"You hurt me. A lot."

"It won't happen again," he whispered. "I promise."

She glanced around at all the women staring at them and knew that she'd remember this moment, no matter how it ended, for the rest of her life.

"I'm staying in Brevia. I talked to my father and told him he can't run my life anymore."

"I talked to him, too."

Her heart sank. "To thank him for getting your job back?"

"To tell him I wasn't going back to the Marshals. That even if he wanted to make the lies he told true, there was nothing he could offer to make me betray you again."

Lexi's mouth dropped. She didn't know how to answer.

"You're not going back?" she finally asked.

"I want to make my life in Brevia, Lexi." His eyes looked hopeful. "With you, if you'll have me again. I know I pushed you away. I broke your trust and it kills me that I hurt you."

He reached forward and laced his fingers in hers. "I'm nothing without you. You make me the person I was meant to be. I want to spend our whole lives together."

"What about action and adventure? What about adrenaline and the thrill of the chase?"

"Building our life together is all the adventure I need." He raised her fingers to his lips and kissed the tip of each one. "Every time I look at you is a bigger rush than anything else I could imagine. I want to let you into every part of my life. I want to know all there is to know about you. Good and bad. I love you, Lexi. With everything I am and everything I have. Give me a chance to prove it to you."

She heard several women sigh. "If you don't take him back, I'm coming after him," one lady said from underneath a dryer.

A smile broke across Lexi's face. "Oh, I'm taking

him. He's officially off the market," she whispered and threw her arms around his neck.

Scott kissed her deeply, holding her tight against him for several minutes.

Then Julia moved closer. "Do I get to kick your butt now?" she asked him.

Lexi laughed. "Do you still want to?"

Julia hesitated, then smiled. "I guess I'll give you a pass. Since you're family and that was a pretty good speech."

Scott looked at Lexi. "I meant every word of it." He took a step away from her. "But there's one more thing."

Lexi's eyes widened as he dropped to one knee.

"Lexi Preston," he said, pulling a small box from his jacket pocket, "will you marry me? I want to know you're mine forever."

"Yes," she breathed, and he slipped a perfect pear-shaped diamond onto her finger. "Yes, yes, yes."

She looked at him and knew the happiness she saw in his eyes was reflected in her own. He stood, pulling her close once again. Then he looked over his shoulder at Julia and Vera, both of whom were wiping at their eyes.

"Could we expand tonight's celebration to include an engagement?"

"That's a perfect idea," Vera said, and Julia nodded.

Scott turned back to Lexi. "What do you think? Do you mind going public so soon?"

She nodded in turn, happiness filling her completely. "I think all three Callahan men have finally found a place to call home."

Epilogue

"Who wants pie?"

Vera Morgan Callahan came into the dining room with Joe following her, a pie plate in each hand.

"Me do," Charlie shouted from his seat at the end of the table.

Lexi smiled as Julia ruffled his hair. "Are you sure, buddy?" his mom asked. "You practically ate your weight in mashed potatoes."

Charlie grinned at her. "Want more pie and more taters."

Sam laughed. "You get your healthy appetite from your uncle Scott. As a kid, he could put away more food on Thanksgiving than anyone has a right to without puking."

"You eat pie, too." Charlie pointed a chubby finger at Scott.

Scott stretched an arm across the back of Lexi's chair, fingers tickling her shoulder. "You betcha, Charlie. Let's have a couple of pieces and head out back. I want to show you how to throw a football the right way."

"Like I haven't already?" Sam tried to look offended, but his big grin ruined the effect.

Ethan cleared his throat from his seat across the table. "Did you forget you have a real-life former quarterback in the room?"

"You want to prove you've still got your skills in a friendly game?" Scott asked.

Ethan smiled in return. "I've got my hands full here." He glanced down at the baby sleeping in his arms and dropped a kiss on the top of his daughter's head.

Ruby's adoption had been finalized a month ago, and Ethan and Lainey had brought her home. Ruby was a chunky cherub of a baby, sweet and smiley. Lexi knew they'd had a long road to finally have their own baby. It was clear that Ruby completed their family, and everyone in the whole town seemed to dote on her, including Scott.

His eyes softened and he gave Lexi's arm a little squeeze. "That's a good excuse, Daniels." He leaned close to Lexi's ear and whispered, "I can't wait until I have one of my own."

His voice sent a quick shiver down her spine. He kissed the side of her neck and the shivers traveled south. They'd been married only a couple months and weren't even trying for babies yet. Scott was busy with the bar and Lexi was building her practice and taking on more clients as Frank transitioned to more part-time work. But they were certainly practicing, as Scott called it, quite a bit. He joked that he wanted to get it right when they were finally ready. And there was no arguing that he got it very right.

"Lainey, take that baby from your husband." Julia stood and picked up her plate. "I'm either going to suffocate from all the testosterone in the air or lose my tasty turkey watching the newlyweds over here." She waved her hand in the direction of the backyard. "You boys take it outside while we clean up. You can have pie later."

Sam reached for her plate. "You should go sit down, Juls. I'll help with the dishes. In your condition—"

"I'm pregnant. I can still carry plates."

He placed a protective hand on her round belly. "I don't want you to get worn down."

She kissed his cheek. "You didn't seem too worried last night."

Ethan groaned and pushed back from the table. "Enough already." He transferred Ruby to Lainey's arms. "Joe, do you think you can help me whip your sons?"

"Absolutely." Joe turned to Vera. "Mind if we postpone dessert?"

"Go for it." She took the pies from his hands and set them on the table. "Just take it easy on these boys. Even though they're younger, I doubt they have your stamina."

Joe wrapped her in one of his trademark hugs. "Only for you, sweetheart."

Scott made a face. "That's my cue to get out of here."

Lexi giggled as he scrambled from his seat.

Sam helped Charlie climb out of the high chair and the three other men followed them toward the backyard.

"I'm happy to clean up the dishes," Lexi said, collecting plates and glasses. "You three can have a seat."

"Look at you, putting your month as a bar wench to good use," Julia teased.

Vera shook her head. "You don't have to do it by yourself." She waved her hands at her two daughters, clearly shooing them away. "You girls take Ruby to the living room. Lexi and I will take care of this."

A grin broke across Lainey's face. "Do you hear that, Ruby honey? Not only are you the best baby in the whole wide world, but now you've earned me a hall pass from kitchen duty."

"Don't just stand there." Julia scurried around the table. "Let's get out of here before she changes her mind."

As the two sisters disappeared through the doorway, Lexi turned to Vera. "I'm fine to take care of this on my own. It's the least I can do." She felt emotion rise in her throat and swallowed it down. "This is the best Thanksgiving I've ever had."

"I'm a decent cook," Vera agreed, "but not that good."

Lexi shook her head. "The meal was amazing, but it's everything about it. It's having all of you around me, feeling like I'm part of a family. I can't tell you how much I appreciate it."

"I don't mind the cleanup," Vera said as she picked up several plates and led Lexi into the kitchen. "If you haven't noticed, I'm a bit of a control freak." She laughed when Lexi didn't respond and began stacking plates in the dishwasher. "I'm sorry your father couldn't make it down."

Lexi sighed. "Me, too, but he's still having trouble adjusting to me living my own life. I'm glad he came to the wedding, and he promised to fly down for a few days over Christmas." She picked up a casserole pan and dunked it into the sink filled with hot, soapy water. "We're taking small steps, which is more than I ever thought I'd get from him."

"And you're happy still?" Vera asked quietly.

"So happy. I couldn't imagine anyplace feeling more like home than Brevia." She rinsed the pan with clean water and lifted it out of the sink. "I feel lucky to have all of you in my life, especially Scott."

"I'm the lucky one."

Lexi felt Scott's arms wrap around her waist. He took the pan from her hands and stepped to her side. "I'll dry."

"How are the boys doing out there?" Vera asked.

"Charlie's scored two touchdowns. We may have a future football star on our hands."

Vera smiled. "I have to see that. Can you two handle the rest of this mess?"

"Absolutely," Lexi answered. "We're almost finished, anyway." She loaded the last of the glasses into the dishwasher as Vera disappeared into the backyard.

Lexi straightened, to find Scott watching her, his gaze warming her from the inside out. He held out his hand and she stepped into his arms, his familiar scent still making her heart dance as he pulled her close. "I love you," she whispered.

His lips brushed against her forehead. "You are everything to me. You're my home, my heart, my whole life. I love you, Lexi. Everything about you, who you are…who I am when I'm with you. I can't imagine anything better than where we are right now."

His words filled her soul, though Lexi couldn't help but laugh. "In Vera's kitchen?"

"In a kitchen, a dining room. Standing in the middle of the street. It doesn't matter as long as we're together."

"Always." She brought her mouth to his, sealing the promise with a kiss.

* * * * *

IF YOU ENJOYED THIS BOOK
WE THINK YOU WILL ALSO LOVE

HARLEQUIN
SPECIAL
EDITION

Believe in love. Overcome obstacles. Find happiness.

Relate to finding comfort and strength in the
support of loved ones and enjoy the journey
no matter what life throws your way.

6 NEW BOOKS AVAILABLE EVERY MONTH!

HSEXSERIES2020

SPECIAL EXCERPT FROM

⟨H⟩HARLEQUIN
SPECIAL EDITION

*Nina and Douglas Archer are on the verge of divorce.
But they're both determined to keep it together for
one last family vacation, planned by their devious
ten-year-old twins, at the Top Dog Dude Ranch.
Will a once-in-a-lifetime trip show them the way
back to each other?*

*Read on for a sneak peek at
the first book in the brand-new
Top Dog Dude Ranch miniseries,*
Last-Chance Marriage Rescue,
by USA TODAY *bestselling author Catherine Mann!*

Quick beats of the line dance receded. In their stead, a
soulful fiddle was joined by a crooning voice. This was
his moment. He said his goodbye to Jacob and took
surefooted steps toward Nina.

He touched the soft fabric of his elbow. Imagining
already what it'd be like to touch her. To be close to her.
"May I have this dance?"

Her eyes went wide and hesitant. Which made him all
sorts of sad.

"Nina, for the girls. For the vacation." He held out his
arms.

Thank God, she didn't leave him standing there like
a fool. She stepped forward and finally, *finally,* he had

his wife in his arms, her hair flying behind her with each swing, her cheeks flushed and her eyes alive.

In the warm glow of lights strung overhead, her brown eyes glistened, her breath whispering across his skin as a twirl landed her close to his cheek. "I forgot you could dance like this."

"I believe I forgot, as well. But it feels good to see you smile."

"Keep dancing and I'll keep right on smiling, cowboy."

If only it could be that simple.

He felt the electricity hum in the rapidly diminishing space between them. Lips so close as they passed heat and fire in their gazes. Need rose in his chest with each ragged breath.

A fat gray tabby pressed against his legs and hers, seeming to push them closer and closer. Until they were seconds, a mere breath, away. And then she swayed into him, only a hint, but all the encouragement he needed to capture her lips.

Don't miss
Last-Chance Marriage Rescue *by Catherine Mann,*
available September 2021 wherever
Harlequin Special Edition books and ebooks are sold.

Harlequin.com

Copyright © 2021 by Catherine Mann

HSEEXP0821

Love Harlequin romance?

DISCOVER.

Be the first to find out about promotions, news and exclusive content!

f Facebook.com/HarlequinBooks

🐦 Twitter.com/HarlequinBooks

📷 Instagram.com/HarlequinBooks

📌 Pinterest.com/HarlequinBooks

▶ YouTube.com/HarlequinBooks

ReaderService.com

EXPLORE.

Sign up for the Harlequin e-newsletter and download a free book from any series at **TryHarlequin.com**

CONNECT.

Join our Harlequin community to share your thoughts and connect with other romance readers!
Facebook.com/groups/HarlequinConnection

HSOCIAL2021

HARLEQUIN

Heartfelt or thrilling, passionate or uplifting—Harlequin is more than just happily-ever-after.

With twelve different series to choose from and new books available every month, you are sure to find stories that will move you, uplift you, inspire and delight you.

SIGN UP FOR THE HARLEQUIN NEWSLETTER

Be the first to hear about great new reads and exciting offers!

Harlequin.com/newsletters

HNEWS2021